THE
TANZANIA
CONSPIRACY

Max O'Brien Mysteries

The Kashmir Trap
The Roma Plot
The Tanzania Conspiracy

MARIO BOLDUC

THE

TANZANIA CONSPIRACY

A MAX O'BRIEN MYSTERY

TRANSLATED BY JACOB HOMEL

DUNDURN
TORONTO

Published under arrangement with Groupe Librex, Inc., doing business under the name Éditions Libre Expression, Montréal. QC, Canada.

Printer: Webcom

Library and Archives Canada Cataloguing in Publication

Bolduc, Mario, 1953-
[Nuit des albinos. English]
     The Tanzania conspiracy / Mario Bolduc ; translated by Jacob Homel.

(A Max O'Brien mystery)

Translation of: La nuit des albinos.
Issued in print and electronic formats.
ISBN 978-1-4597-3609-2 (softcover).--ISBN 978-1-4597-3610-8
(PDF).--ISBN 978-1-4597-3611-5 (EPUB)

     I. Homel, Jacob, 1987-, translator II. Title. III. Title: Nuit
des albinos. English IV. Series: Bolduc, Mario, 1953- . Max O'Brien mystery

PS8553.O475N8413 2019   C843'.54   C2018-903982-5
                                                 C2018-903983-3

1 2 3 4 5   22 21 20 19 18

We acknowledge the support of the **Canada Council for the Arts**, which last year invested $153 million to bring the arts to Canadians throughout the country, and the **Ontario Arts Council** for our publishing program. We also acknowledge the financial support of the **Government of Ontario**, through the **Ontario Book Publishing Tax Credit** and the **Ontario Media Development Corporation**, and the **Government of Canada**.

Nous remercions le **Conseil des arts du Canada** de son soutien. L'an dernier, le Conseil a investi 153 millions de dollars pour mettre de l'art dans la vie des Canadiennes et des Canadiens de tout le pays.

We acknowledge the financial support of the **Government of Canada** through the National Translation Program for Book Publishing, an initiative of the Roadmap for Canada's Official Languages 2013–2018: Education, Immigration, Communities, for our translation activities.

Printed and bound in Canada.

VISIT US AT

Dundurn
3 Church Street, Suite 500
Toronto, Ontario, Canada
M5E 1M2

AUTHOR'S NOTE

Although based on reality, this novel relates a completely imaginary adventure. Many fictional characters mingle with people who exist or have existed. The chronology of certain events has been changed for the needs of the story.

For Nicole Landry,
with all my affection

And God said, Take now thy son, thine only son Isaac, whom thou lovest, and get thee into the land of Moriah; and offer him there for a burnt offering upon one of the mountains which I will tell thee of.

— Genesis 22:2

PART ONE
The Kandoya Method

PART ONE
The Zanders Method

1

On the small-screen television jammed beneath the instrument panel between a toolbox and a bottle of whisky, Barack Obama's visit to Tanzania was being celebrated with the racket of marching bands and the usual overblown speeches. The flickering, ghosted, washed-out images spoke of a major historical event according to Rashid, the boat's captain, who was manoeuvring his craft with one eye on TVZ and the other on the exit of the Malindi harbour in Zanzibar. It was early April 2009, and the new American president was coming in from Ghana, stopping over in Dar es Salaam, and then touching ground a few days later in Kenya, his father's country. "Obama is Africa in the White House," Rashid had declared as he'd greeted Max

O'Brien on the dock a few minutes earlier, encouraging his passenger to participate in the celebrations.

But Max had other things on his mind. He hated improvisation but had to depend on Jayesh Srinivasan's decisions. Jayesh had told Max more than once over the phone, "Rashid has received and understood my instructions and will obey you blindly."

However, Jayesh hadn't informed Max that this former fisherman who'd become a boat captain was a political junkie, and he had woven a web of talk around Max ever since the two met the evening before. In the smoky little café in Stone Town where they finalized the operation, Rashid prattled on and on about international politics and their consequences — dire, it went without saying — for the African continent.

Once they moved out of the harbour, Rashid pointed out a scruffy-looking dhow at anchor in the middle of the bay where more than a hundred refugees in rags were huddled. A makeshift tarp offered poor shelter from the sun and oppressive heat. Children crying. Babies bawling. Worse, the empty eyes of emaciated people, starving, fresh in from the belly of human misery.

"They escaped from Burgavo," Rashid explained above the rattling of the engine.

Burgavo, in Somalia, near the border with Kenya.

They must have tried to land in Mombasa, farther south, but the authorities would have kept them out of the port, the result, most likely, of the tensions between Kenya and Somalia. They kept on going and entered Tanzanian waters, coming to a halt outside the port, praying for pity.

"They picked the wrong day," Rashid remarked. "The Zanzibar port authority is closed on Saturdays. Sundays, too."

The unfortunate travellers wouldn't see the immigration agents until the offices opened on Monday. More than thirty-six hours of being baked alive in the port with no food and limited water. It was forty degrees Celsius, and the humidity stuck to the skin like a coating of filth.

A hundred metres from the dhow, a glittering floating monster, all whiteness on blue water: Jonathan Harris's yacht, freshly minted at the German shipyards of Blohm & Voss. Heading for the Mediterranean where its home port was — Nice, to be exact — the *Sunflower* was coming from Cape Town and was expecting to stop at Mombasa and Suez after sailing past Djibouti. The Gulf of Aden was infested with pirates. Harris's advisers had tried to dissuade the billionaire from attempting the passage, and even the captain, normally so obsequious, had added his voice to the chorus, but Harris wasn't the type to be frightened off by "primitives with machetes," as he called them. Having done good business in South Africa, he decided to purchase the services of a private militia armed to the teeth that would travel with the crew and passengers. The shock troops would board in Mombasa and remain on duty until Suez.

And with all the security, Harris still had no idea that the Mr. Robert Flanagan who'd offered him his expertise and would be joining him on the yacht today was actually Max O'Brien, a notorious con artist who had Interpol at his heels.

Usually, Max chose his victims carefully; he studied, scrutinized, and plotted. Each scam was carried out according to a modus operandi that was more or less identical. After a long period of observation, after setting out appetizing bait, his accomplices having warmed up the future victim, Max stepped in. The work sometimes took only a few days, or stretched out over several months. Each victim was unique, and adjustments were always necessary. Most of all, total control from beginning to end of the operation was essential.

But when it came to Harris, Max had to trust someone else's plans and preparations, something he despised. Even if the other was Jayesh Srinivasan, his friend he'd worked with in India.

The great age of fraud was over for Max, and he'd sworn those days were past. When he returned from Europe after the business with the Roma, he slowly abandoned his activities and settled in the village of Shela, just outside Lamu, in northern Kenya.

Two weeks ago, Jayesh called Max from Mumbai. Pure gold, according to him. An easy mark, and he'd prepared the perfect trap for the billionaire Jonathan Harris. All Jayesh needed was the master con artist who would put the finishing touches on the operation. Jayesh had thought of Max, since he lived in the region now.

"I'm out of the game, Jayesh. I'm through. I'm not leaving paradise."

Jayesh had insisted, saying he'd give Max a bigger cut — half the take — but Max didn't bite. He wouldn't sacrifice his retirement for all the gold the world had to offer.

‡

Not long after Jayesh's call, Sophie Stroner, Valéria Michieka's daughter, announced she was coming to visit. The news had been a bit of a surprise, though a happy one, indeed. He hadn't heard from Valéria in such a long time, but Max couldn't blame her. Things had ended badly between them. It had taken him months to purge himself of the shape of her next to him, and all that time he could only dream of her calling him out of the blue, or sending him a simple email. Max was a proud man; he wanted her to take the first step toward reconciliation. Perhaps Sophie's visit was a sign.

Max had rented a villa from an Italian industrialist, a dazzling white building looking out over the Indian Ocean. He spent his days strolling along the beach, heading south, into isolation, or north, until he reached Lamu with its handful of hotels, three or four decent restaurants, and the busy life of a small Swahili town with its port and mule trains carrying spices and other goods.

That was where Max went to meet Sophie. Her plane was coming from Bukoba in Tanzania, via Nairobi, and had landed an hour earlier on the other side of the strait where the tiny Lamu airport lay. He spotted her among the tourists, standing in the shuttle, working to keep her balance as the captain brought the boat to a stop at the pier. She was twenty-five and girlish and would probably always look that way, like her mother.

He offered her his hand, and she stepped onto dry land. Slung over her shoulder, her small travel bag showed that she wasn't staying long. To reach Shela, they could go on foot along the beach, the way Max usually did, or they could take a dhow that would drop them off in front of the Peponi Hotel. Sophie was tired, she had set out early from Nairobi, and she was thirsty. Max took her to the bar in the little hotel facing the port, one of the few authorized to sell alcohol, since Lamu was in Muslim territory.

"Happy to see you again," Sophie said, once they were sitting in the dim room.

Max suspected her visit wasn't a simple social call.

"You came back to Africa," she continued.

Max smiled. After his breakup with Valéria, he'd lost his attachment to the continent, yet decided to stay on temporarily. He liked Lamu. It felt as if it belonged to another world, with its sandy streets and sticky humidity.

"How's your mother?"

"Fine. Very good, actually."

A number of years earlier, when she graduated from Makerere University, law degree in hand, Valéria had opened a practice in Bukoba in northwest Tanzania, near the Ugandan border, right on the shores of Lake Victoria. In the Kagera region, to be exact. A place cut off from the rest of Tanzania, closer to Kampala or Nairobi than to Dar es Salaam, the former capital and the country's biggest city. The area inhabited by the Haya people had once been a prosperous kingdom, highly developed economically, but all that had disappeared when the Germans, then the British, colonized the country at the beginning of the twentieth century. Things went slowly downward from then on. The region developed at a painfully slow pace.

Today, as far as roads went, there was only one paved section south of Bukoba, the administrative centre, and the rest of the network was made up of rough dirt tracks, or barely passable trails used by farmers and fishermen from the surrounding villages.

The area around Lake Victoria had witnessed the bloodiest conflicts of recent years, the legacy of the colonization that bled the region dry, thanks to the work of Western predators. Refugees from Rwanda and Burundi to the west found relatively safe haven in Kagera during the 1994 genocide. Two decades earlier, people escaping Idi Amin Dada's regime to the north crossed the Ugandan border in search of something close to peace. Not to mention AIDS, which devoured the survivors and decimated families and whole villages. In the Kagera region at one point, according to Valéria, nearly a quarter of the population was infected, the highest rate in East Africa.

In other words, Bukoba and the surrounding area summed up what was most beautiful and most terrifying about Africa. In that part of Tanzania, history seemed to have revisited the tragedies and cataclysms of past centuries and given them an exotic colouring. Evil, surely, but in a luxuriant environment. Living hell in a magnificent setting designed by a vengeful, cruel, ironic god.

That was where Valéria offered her legal services to a population that couldn't pay for them. In Dar es Salaam, things would have been easier. But she chose Bukoba for one particular reason: the terrible hunting down of albinos, a wound in the social fabric that decimated families and spread destruction.

For genetic reasons, Tanzania counted more albinos — a total of two hundred thousand according to some estimates — than any other African country. And Africa's albino population was already that much higher than in Europe or in the Americas.

Since the beginning of time, people have attributed magical powers to these "white Africans." This superstition pushed gangs of criminals in search of profit to scour the countryside for albinos of any age, kidnapping, killing, and cutting them up, then selling pieces of their bodies to medicine men and healers who flogged them to their customers. An albino would disappear, never to be seen again, the only trace of his or her existence now contained in some trinket or lucky charm.

Trafficking in albinos had changed over time. When Valéria launched her campaign against it in the 1990s, the trade in albinos was a booming business. In past days, people were interested in albinos and their supposed powers in the hope of curing sickness, ending epidemics, eliminating drought. An albino burned during the rainy season guaranteed abundant harvests the following year. Albino limbs attached to fishing nets held out the promise of excellent catches.

But needs were changing. As Tanzania emerged from underdevelopment, a new clientele appeared. Albino internal organs were being sold to ambitious men in search of promotions, employees who dreamed of raises in pay, or as a way to urge Lady Luck to smile after the purchase of lottery tickets.

In her office, Valéria received parents in mourning who had come to seek reparations for the arms or legs that had been amputated from their sons or daughters. She defended these families with limitless energy, and with the support of the Tanzanian government that had decided to declare war on the traffickers. Before Valéria's involvement, such offenders had gotten off with laughable sentences for lack of witnesses. People were too frightened by the climate of terror created by healers and medicine men. The police had little enthusiasm for tracking down go-betweens. Sure, they'd arrest the most colourful bush healers, and some had even ended up in prison, but they were more often quickly released, their sentences never commensurate with their crimes. But now, with the clientele expanding, new sanctions had to be applied to discourage albino hunters. Witnesses were no longer afraid to speak up and denounce the criminals.

Over time, Valéria convinced witnesses to emerge from silence and denounce the guilty parties, eventually leading these courageous men and women to testify in court against the perpetrators so that their campaign of death might be stopped. From her residence in Bukoba, she created The Colour of Respect Foundation to provide support to albinos and their families. She travelled across Africa in search of help and funding and didn't neglect Europe and America, while Sophie, also a lawyer, held the fort back in Bukoba.

How could anyone remain unmoved by the continuing massacre? In 2008 alone, twenty-seven albinos were murdered, bringing back echoes of Africa's troubled past, making people think that, despite all efforts, the continent was as primitive and bloody as ever.

‡

Every leg of the journey had been a trial for Sophie, and she refused to get into one more public conveyance when Max suggested they take the boat after they came out of the bar. He grabbed her travel bag and steered her down the beach path for Shela. Night was falling, but it was still very hot. As they walked, Sophie talked at length about her mother and the practice that was growing ever larger, as concerned with albinos as ever but trying to diversify. Business and real estate law, family law, as well, serving a new sort of client. Valéria was still part of the Women's Legal Aid Centre and had opened a branch in Bukoba. Sometimes she was paid, other times not; as she'd always done, she never refused a client. Sophie now helped her mother at the practice. She'd begun a law degree at McGill University in Montreal before coming home to finish it. Valéria was proud that her daughter had chosen the same profession.

"She talks about you sometimes," Sophie now said.

Max was surprised. He doubted she was sincere. She must be buttering him up.

"She's sorry about what happened."

They walked in silence. Max had no desire to unearth the past. He'd moved on. With Sophie here beside him, it would be too easy to be shrouded in the heartbreak that had paralyzed him for so long — he'd done that much too often as it was. He was still madly in love with Valéria, but things hadn't turned out for the best. Talking about it wouldn't change anything. And neither would Sophie's lies.

"Let's talk about something else, okay?" Max told her.

He settled her on the porch, which he'd transformed into a guest bedroom of sorts. An enormous room covered with bamboo, without glass in the windows, which let the sounds from the main square below filter in. Donkeys braying as they passed, children shouting. In one corner stood a rigged-up shower, cold water only. Warm was unnecessary. The air blazed, even in the early morning. The nights were torrid and barely tolerable.

That evening Max invited Sophie to the Peponi, one of the few places in Shela where alcohol was served. The place was full of tourists, young people for the most part, noisy and demonstrative. Max couldn't wait for dinner to be over. There were uncomfortable gaps in the conversation, as if they'd already started running out of subjects.

On the walk back, as he lit the way for Sophie with his flashlight — the village was completely dark — she took his arm. "Something's happened …" The hazy moonlight was like a veil on her face. "Do you remember Teresa Mwandenga?"

Max had no idea who that was.

"The accountant. You must remember her. Very small, with a gravelly voice."

He recalled having seen the woman with Valéria several times but didn't know she was the accountant. A colleague from the Women's Legal Aid Centre, he'd surmised. People were always visiting Valéria; it was hard to keep track. Every time he came over there were new faces.

"She took off recently, just disappeared into thin air with the foundation's money," Sophie said. "For months she'd been embezzling money and stuffing it in an account we knew nothing about."

A month ago Teresa Mwandenga had asked for time off to visit an aunt in Kigoma but didn't return the following week. Sophie called her cellphone — no answer. The aunt she'd gone to visit didn't exist, and her phone number was fake. Suspecting something, Valéria checked the books, bank accounts, and other documents that were Mwandenga's responsibility. She discovered that not only was the foundation broke, it was in debt in shillings the equivalent of several hundred thousands of dollars. Mwandenga had put off the creditors as a way of amassing still more money, then disappeared like smoke.

"Did you try to find her?" Max asked. "Did you call the police?"

"The police? That wouldn't have helped. I did make a few phone calls. We even thought of hiring a retired detective to track her down, but we gave up on the idea."

When they searched Mwandenga's desk, Sophie and her mother discovered that their accountant had made several calls to Dubai. And purchased an airplane ticket for a flight from Dar es Salaam to the Emirates.

"We're on the brink of closing down The Colour of Respect. I'm here to ask for your help. Valéria didn't send me. She would have never agreed. She doesn't know I'm here. She thinks I'm in Dar negotiating with the bank."

Valéria, always prideful, wouldn't accept such humiliation. Max imagined the picture very well.

"I'll think about it," Max said. Then they started walking toward the house again.

Sleep wouldn't come that night. He paced the porch room while Sophie slept upstairs. Beneath his feet, the cool tiles would quickly turn as hot as coals once the sun came up. Before dawn he left the house and headed for the beach in front of the Peponi. The night was clear. Clouds of humidity rose, and he could see the waves breaking softly along the strand. He'd made up his mind, but he wanted to think it over a little more.

But what was the use?

When he returned home, before Sophie awoke, Max called Jayesh Srinivasan in Mumbai.

2

Rashid brought the boat to a halt at the foot of the ladder that hung down the side of the *Sunflower*, where a man in dress whites, a sailor from a kids' comic book, waited for Max. He climbed the ladder and followed the man onto the bridge. Captain Robson, who looked like a British admiral from another century, an escapee from *Mutiny on the Bounty* perhaps, greeted him with a wide smile and a handshake dripping with humidity.

"Welcome aboard the *Sunflower*, Mr. Flanagan."

Max looked around. The sparkling whiteness blinded him. His head was spinning. Out of the aggressive, pushy light a man appeared, large and tanned, whose grey hair peeked out from under his panama hat, very elegantly placed on his head, as if he were about to pose for the cover of *Yacht Living*. A devouring smile, shining teeth. Wrinkled shirt, but done just right, with the initials *J.H.* on the pocket. In the furnace heat, this dandy looked as fresh as a rose.

He offered his hand to his visitor. "Jonathan Harris. Very happy to meet you."

"Robert Flanagan," replied Max, nodding ever so slightly.

Harris looked him over. *My entrance exam*, Max figured. But happily, the billionaire wasn't wary. A slap on the back, a knowing wink, a convivial smile.

"Poor devils," Harris remarked, pointing to the Somalis.

Harris and his *Sunflower* shared the bay of Zanzibar with other extravagant pleasure craft. That was business as usual, but this rickety dhow out of the jaws of hell belonged to another planet. It was like a cockroach on a wedding cake.

"They've been drifting at sea for a week," Harris continued. "They slipped through the fingers of the Islamic militia, only to fall victim to Tanzanian bureaucracy."

His comment was a little too well rehearsed to be sincere.

Where did his fortune come from? Harris was the president of Sunflower Media in Los Angeles, a company that built electronic devices, handed down to him from his father. The company invested in the development of smartphones when the iPhone and BlackBerry were still on the drawing board. After consumers discovered they couldn't live without this kind of telephone, Harris was ready. His Stellar phone spread across the United States and Europe, but also into the farthest reaches of Africa and the Indian subcontinent. Since then, Harris's company had expanded, diversified its operations, tried its hand with touch screens — with less success, it turned out. The Stellar remained Sunflower Media's milk cow.

Harris pointed toward the dhow again. "I talked to the harbour commissioner myself. I called him at his house, but he doesn't want to lift a finger. That's Africa for you. The bureaucrats think they're the masters of the universe. As soon as they have a little power —"

"You should have offered him a bribe," Max said.

Harris turned and threw him a hard glare. "That's not how I do business, Robert — I can call you Robert? Corruption will get us nowhere. That message should come from us, the West. Do you follow me?"

Max understood he was displaying his principles at a very bad time. "A hundred dollars would have done the trick."

Again, Harris took a long look at his guest. He was probably wondering just who the man before him was. Robert Flanagan, a maritime security specialist? Max knew Harris's underlings would have done the necessary research. Robert Flanagan had his own website, of course, with all the right references. A member of the professional association of security experts and of a tennis club in Dubai. A virtual facade created in under a week, though solid enough to give the impression that Max was an old hand when it came to the region. Jayesh had done his homework. He'd even left scattered hints that behind the name Chris Mason — the maritime reporter who had been writing pieces about piracy in *Aden News*, a digital newsletter popular among skippers — was actually Robert Flanagan.

Despite the tight deadline, his false identity had been carefully assembled.

Harris smiled to put everyone at ease, as if excusing himself for having doubted his guest's honesty. "Why don't we go inside?"

A sliding door opened for Max. The other passengers had chosen to stay inside with the air conditioning. Lawyers, all of them, in cruise wear, the Lacoste and Hilfiger version of it, younger than their boss. They all rose when Max entered the room, a low-ceilinged salon with the obligatory maritime decoration supplied by a reader of Joseph Conrad adventures, with old compasses, antique sea maps, and shiny copper trim.

Behind the group, an enormous television bolted to the wall was showing CNN's coverage of Obama's visit to Tanzania. The choice of country was no accident, people were saying. Like Ghana and Kenya, Tanzania was a democracy, one of the few functional ones in Africa, even if the party in power — the Chama Cha Mapinduzi, the "Party of the Revolution" — had reigned uninterrupted since independence. Tanzania was an example for other nations grappling with bloodthirsty dictators, more or less mentally deranged, who considered their countries their private property, playgrounds for their most outlandish fantasies.

"This heat is something!" Harris exclaimed as he slid the door closed. "On days like this, I envy my son." He turned to one of the passengers. "Barney, you remember Jim? Little Jim?"

A man nodded sleepily.

"Last year he took it into his head to seek enlightenment in a monastery in Nepal in the middle of the Himalayas. He drinks tea and yak's milk, walks around in monk's robes all day, and wears a shaved head. Yoga and meditation, a little levitation now and then, in one of the most spectacular landscapes in the world. He sent me photos. The rocky peaks, snow year-round ..."

Harris smiled, moved by his own words and encouraged by the benevolent glances of his passengers. During this interlude of paternal love, Max observed the group. The *crème de la crème* of the new American society, Obama's version of it. The passengers intended to use their stopover in Mombasa to make a lightning visit to Kendu Bay where the president's father was born. The excursion was sure to be extraordinary, especially for the youngest of the group, a ravishing black woman from Atlanta who radiated unshakable confidence in the future of America.

A door swung open onto a gangway, and a hugely imposing man, a mountain of muscle, stepped out of the cabin and swayed over to the group. Black and dressed in black from head to toe, shaved head, glistening with sweat, wary eyes, a small ring in his ear, and a chain around his neck. A wide scar cut across his face, just missing his nose. His T-shirt, much too tight, stretched across his hypertrophied chest. He bent to avoid hitting his head on the ceiling, which made him look like a starving predator about to leap on the nearest antelope. The central-casting bodyguard that the rich couldn't live without. The kind that shouldn't be provoked — or so he wanted others to think.

But experience had taught Max that these oiled-up, taciturn, steroid-pumped brutes exhibiting their battle scars relied on appearances. Lacking real competition, they sometimes didn't train as hard as they should. When push came to shove, they often revealed themselves to be soft and vulnerable.

"This is Ferguson," Harris introduced him. "My guardian angel, I call him. He thinks I've made a mistake hiring you. He's an intimidating specimen, you have to admit. I'll send him up on the bridge if any pirates show up, and the scarves and turbans will fly!"

The muscle man revealed a timid smile, completely fake. A gold tooth flashed between his lips — of course.

According to Jayesh, he was to be avoided. Extremely dangerous.

Harris told his strongman to serve drinks — iced green tea, lattes, and a few virgin mint cocktails. The era of hard liquor and cigarettes had come and gone. But Max was thirsty: why not play up his role as a mercenary from another time?

"How about some Scotch instead?"

"Then you'll have the privilege of tasting my single malt, Robert. I order it directly from Edinburgh."

Max settled into a comfortable armchair, separated from the group by a low table loaded with contracts and other legal documents, while Ferguson played around with the dishes behind the bar with his ham hands. Harris stood straight, leaning on an old rudder wheel with a patina of years. Out the porthole, off to the right, the Somali refugees baked in the sun. Harris had forgotten all about them.

31

"I looked into a number of protection agencies," Harris said. "Yours seems to be the most solid." He broke into a wide smile and added, "Of course, your prices are steep."

"It's dangerous work."

"You're right to demand what you're worth. I keep telling my colleagues never undersell yourself. That's what Africa has done ... until now. Finally, things are changing."

On the screen, as if to back him up, Obama was reviewing the Tanzanian military guard, accompanied by President Joseph Lugembe. A brilliant economist educated in England, at the head of the country since 2005, Lugembe was slightly older than Obama, but had inspired the same hopes.

The son of a small businessman, he had made his way slowly through the structure of the party in power with the blessing of President Komba, his mentor and former teacher at the University of Dar es Salaam. In 1982 he married Myriam Ikingura, who had two little girls, Faith and Clara. Albino twins, an exceptional phenomenon. Albinos were the fruit of a deficient gene in both parents, who weren't necessarily albinos themselves. The mother had one chance in four of giving birth to an albino, and it was possible, though very rare, to have albino twins. That was Myriam Ikingura's situation. A friend of her husband for years, Lugembe met Myriam at a political meeting. When her husband died, he grew closer to the young woman and ended up marrying her.

The relationship didn't last long. Grappling with overwhelming mental health problems, Myriam was sent to Mirembe Hospital in Dodoma, the only psychiatric facility in Tanzania. She committed suicide in 1986, a few months after her daughter, Faith, was kidnapped and murdered by albino traffickers. In 2002 Clara disappeared in the same circumstances.

Enraged, grief-stricken, Lugembe turned to the police. He promised gifts, bonuses, and other favours to anyone who might bring back his older daughter safe and sound. For a week, fuelled by his desire for vengeance, he appeared on every public forum. His efforts soon produced results. Samuel Musindo, a nurse who worked at a dispensary in Dodoma, had been seen with Clara the evening before she disappeared. An investigation revealed that Musindo had used his job to pass albino children to the region's witch doctors. He'd been caught prowling around the clinic's nursery just before albino newborns disappeared, but until now, no one had been able to link him to the events or incriminate him in any way.

Musindo came from one of Dar es Salaam's wealthy families. His father, Thomas, owned the Bahari Beach golf club, whose members counted some prominent figures in Tanzanian society, only adding to the complexity and the horror of what had occurred. Tanzanians were ready to believe that some half-naked illiterate fresh off the savannah could commit such a crime, but by every account, Musindo was a proper young man. The only dark mark on his record was having abused ephedra for his allergies.

The police intercepted him as he was about to cross the border into Kenya. Interrogated, he finally admitted to having thrown Clara's body into the industrial dump in Dodoma but couldn't remember exactly where. His mind clouded by ephedra, he recalled digging all night long but didn't know where he'd buried the victim. Nor could he explain why he'd hidden the body instead of dismembering it the way traffickers usually did.

For a week the police searched for Clara everywhere, fearing the worst. They finally discovered the girl's swollen corpse at the dump.

While the authorities were interrogating the suspect, a devastated Joseph Lugembe took refuge in his Dodoma residence. Anger gave way to sadness. For days journalists stood guard outside the property, waiting for a statement. It ended up coming from President Komba. To show his sadness and his support for his friend and political heir, he announced the reinstatement of capital punishment for the murder of albinos.

On November 14, 2002, despite the defence attorney Jason Chagula's best efforts, the defendant was found guilty. At the Ukonga Prison in Dar es Salaam, death row was reopened, with Samuel Musindo as its first customer. He was soon joined by other traffickers. The young nurse was executed in July 2003 as President Komba, Lugembe, and Chagula looked on. Musindo's parents hid in a hotel, avoiding journalists wanting to profile the parents of the first man to be executed in Tanzania in years.

3

Jonathan Harris puffed out his chest, his chin tilted upward, face glowing with the self-confidence that had helped him on his way to the position he now held. He had made no false steps; his trajectory was faultless. His flair and intelligence were praised. His emotional capital, one journalist claimed, had developed along with his bank account.

Harris practised alternative capitalism and was ready to shake up the traditional methods. Compassion had become a virtue in an ever more deregulated market, and Harris signalled his by investing as much in charitable ventures as the NASDAQ and other playgrounds of today's lofty entrepreneurial elites. It was no surprise that Africa had pulled on his heartstrings. He had missed the great Asian awakening — it was all over by the time he took over the business — but he wasn't about to overlook the marvellous business opportunities offered by the new middle class that would soon begin emerging from the African cesspool. Even the despots and their bloody kingdoms would soon collapse. And Harris would be there in a front-row seat, poised to profit from the smoking ruins.

He pointed in the direction of the dhow and its cargo of refugees. "That's the Africa of the past, exploited and resigned. Little by little it will disappear, I'm convinced. Thanks to us. Thanks to America. Obama's message about dictators is clear. He doesn't want them to have a seat at the table."

Harris let his words settle, then added, "Our new president's position will have more impact than all of George W. Bush's armies put together. Obama understands that diplomacy and public relations are the best weapons to fight the barbarians weighed down by obsolete customs."

Max caught the expression on the young lady lawyer's face. She was glowing, radiant. She drank in the billionaire's words. America had evolved, and every ounce of her strove to represent that change. Years of chaos and bad decisions, years of international relations that were no more than a farce — now the government was moving in a new direction. America's superiority must be based on a moral contract. Power would be applied through respect and restraint.

"We can't impose justice, democracy, and civil rights on the rest of humanity if we continue to make a mockery of our essential principles," Harris went on.

Ferguson set the drinks before the passengers, then retreated behind the counter where he pretended to polish the copper fixtures.

As Max sampled the Scotch, Harris said, "I admit it. Dominating the world was a responsibility, and we were poorly prepared for it until very recently. That's why there were so many mistakes, bad alliances, and other false starts. We cozied up to every dictator on the planet, and that tarnished our reputation among the very people who needed our help and support."

Silence greeted his words. If Harris expected Max to comment, he made no indication. The Scotch was excellent. Max placed his glass on the table and shot a smile at Harris, who returned it.

Now that the preliminaries were over, it was time to get down to business. Despite the air conditioning, Max was burning up. Was it the Scotch? More than likely nervousness could be blamed. He might appear self-assured, but deep down he knew the stakes were high and the situation might sour at any moment. Too late to turn back now, though.

With amusement in his voice, Harris said, "All these stories about pirates seem exaggerated, Robert. Like you, I've seen the items on TV, but all the same —"

"They're former fishermen pushed out by the boats of other countries that pillage Somalia's territorial waters to their heart's content," Max retorted.

"The poor bastards have no government to protect them."

"They're well armed and bolder by the minute. One day, you'll see, they'll attack ships right outside Mombasa."

"I doubt that. The Kenyans will stop them."

"There's still time for you to turn around."

Harris burst out laughing. "And let those hoodlums decide which way the *Sunflower* will sail? Not on your life."

"As you wish."

"I'm telling you. In my opinion the threat's overblown. Boarding a yacht by force, neutralizing the crew and passengers. Demanding ransom ..." He pointed to the dhow again. "Now those are guys who can't defend themselves."

"And neither can you," replied Max, seizing the opportunity.

"Pardon me?"

"Boarding a yacht. Demanding ransom." Max looked Harris in the eye. "That's exactly what I'm doing."

A moment of silence, then Harris burst out laughing. "That's the best one I've heard all day!"

Max ignored the sarcasm. "Two million dollars."

Harris took a step back. Ferguson stopped polishing his counter. The lawyers on board looked at one another.

"Payable immediately," Max added.

In the *Sunflower*'s salon, a pin dropping could have been heard if the floor hadn't been richly covered in triple-ply shag carpet. The atmosphere had suddenly cooled dramatically, and it wasn't because of the roaring air conditioner.

"So you're not —"

"A maritime security specialist? No." Max paused for effect, then went in for the kill. "I'm a con artist. My specialty is billionaires like you, Harris, self-important, who have too much money for their own good. I've always detested people like you. Your speechifying, your fake generosity, your good intentions absolutely oozing with hypocrisy — it makes me sick. Just be happy making money, Harris, and don't bother preaching your two-bit morals."

For a moment Harris stared at Max in disbelief. He hated to be made fun of, especially in front of his underlings. Hated to be lectured. He was sure Max was making a terrible mistake.

"You're a rat, Flanagan. A bold rat, but not a very smart one." He sighed, finally gathering his wits. Ferguson took a step in Max's direction, but Harris motioned him to stop. "It's obvious you don't know who you're talking to. I don't get kinder when provoked."

Max said nothing. He couldn't wait for this to be over, to be rid of these clowns, starting with Harris.

"Why don't you leave this yacht right now?" Harris offered in the voice of a used car salesman. "I'll forget this even happened and won't call the police. I'm giving you a chance. Your only one. The last one. If I were you, I'd take it." He smiled. "I have a big heart. Too big, some have said."

"Two million dollars."

Harris said nothing. Max kept one eye on Ferguson who, he knew, wanted only one thing: permission to demolish this imbecile who believed he could fleece his boss.

"Come now, Flanagan, be serious. Do you think you can really get away so easily?"

"Yes."

Harris smiled again, munificent. "I made you an offer. Accept it now and get lost. I want you gone from my life."

The silence felt endless.

Max pulled out his Stellar telephone as Harris and Ferguson watched, curious. He pressed a button, as if wanting to demonstrate the phone worked, as if to say that even in the deepest reaches of Africa a man couldn't live without his Stellar.

"What's this all about?" demanded Harris, confused.

Max's call went through. On the screen, mountains appeared, snow and blue sky. He held the phone out to Harris. "Here. It's for you."

Harris frowned at it, puzzled, then recognized the voice scratching through the speaker. "Dad, Dad … are you there?"

He grabbed the phone from Max. His son appeared on the screen, head shaved, wearing the robes of a Buddhist monk.

It was windy in Nepal. From time to time, a length of fabric blew across Little Jim's face, and he pushed aside the cloth impatiently.

The lawyers strained to see. They didn't understand, either, but they did pick up on their boss's distress. Ferguson pushed past them and moved toward Max like an enraged animal, stopping only inches from him.

"Jim, are you okay?" Harris asked, voice trembling.

"Of course," Max answered. "He's in perfect health. For now."

On the screen, a second monk appeared, revolver in hand: Jayesh Srinivasan. He pointed the weapon at Jim's head. With his other hand, he held the Stellar phone, it, too, pointed at the boy.

"Despite what you see, my colleague believes in non-violence," Max explained. "He's been meditating with your son for the past couple of weeks. They've been discussing and interpreting the various sutras that contain the Buddha's teachings. Today the two monks went on an excursion to the mountains. No one has any idea where they are."

A gunshot issued from the phone's small speaker. Harris jumped back.

"My offer is very simple. Either you pay me two million dollars now, or Jayesh puts a bullet in Little Jim's head. After meditation comes reincarnation."

"You're completely out of your minds!" Harris shouted. "This is terrorism!" He had lost his self-confidence, and his billionaire's smile had faded, as well. "If you touch a single hair …"

Another gunshot echoed from the phone speaker. Max took the Stellar from Harris. "If I were you, I wouldn't push my friend too far. He tends to get edgy. Impatient, too. Non-violence does have its limits."

Again, silence. Harris was caught in a trap, and everyone knew it.

A third gunshot rang out.

"I … I don't have that much money on me," Harris stammered.

"That's your problem. In three minutes, if my colleague hasn't had word from you, he'll kill your son."

Ferguson, his muscles bulging, waited for the order to rip off Max's head. Fat drops of sweat stood like beads on his forehead.

"Two million," Max repeated.

Harris turned to the man who did his dirty work, who was waiting for directions.

Max held his breath.

Then Harris glanced back at Max, without speaking to Ferguson. "All right."

Max handed him a scrap of paper with a series of numbers. "Your account in Zurich. And mine in another bank in Europe. A phone call, your password, voice recognition, and the transaction is done."

"They'll refuse. They won't want —"

"It's Saturday," said the lawyer from Atlanta, her voice breaking. "Everything's closed."

"Ask for Alison in the foreign deposit service," Max said. "She's working overtime. And she's a friend."

"You're a bastard, Flanagan," Harris snapped.

"Two million."

Harris took out his smartphone with a trembling hand. Placed a call to Zurich. Asked to speak with Alison, who wasn't immediately available.

Max was concerned, Alison was Jayesh's contact, not his. But she ended up taking the call.

Harris ordered the transfer, choking on the words. A moment later Max received the confirmation on his second phone. The call came from Zurich, as well, from a colleague of Alison's at Deutsche Bank who had been recruited by Jayesh.

It was in the bag.

Max whistled off his drink.

He couldn't resist looking back at Ferguson as he exited the salon. The bodyguard seemed totally bewildered by the situation, his hypertrophied muscles useless all of a sudden. Everyone else, Harris included, wore identical expressions of blank astonishment. Max rarely had the chance to see his victims' faces. Usually, they came to the realization that they'd been bilked long after the fraud artist had disappeared.

On the bridge, the overwhelming heat nearly knocked him down. Rashid was waiting in the boat at the foot of the ladder. His eyes were still glued to the tiny screen where President Obama's visit was being played out.

Captain Robson appeared out of nowhere and came toward Max, surprised to see him leaving so soon, unaware how the visit had ended. Max gave the man's viscous hand a brush-off handshake and put his foot on the first rung of the ladder. Harris and his friends watched from the open sliding door. The sun blinded them.

"You're worse than the pirates, Flanagan," Harris snarled.

"I am the pirates."

"You're going to pay for this."

It wasn't worth answering, or humiliating him further.

Harris cursed but said no more. Max noticed the dhow weighted down with Somali refugees. The boat had drifted and now lay off to starboard. The tarp offered a little shelter to the unfortunate souls who'd been baking in the sun. How many would die before the end of the day?

Max turned to Harris. "Those poor folks are dying of thirst. Invite them on board. A few minutes ago you were so eager to relieve their suffering."

Harris's look changed from anger to incredulity.

"I'm sure your well-stocked bar could be used to good purpose, even if they are Muslims. They're thirsty, they're hungry. You're the only one who can help."

Max took out his Stellar phone again. It had become a weapon as death-dealing as a pistol. It featured a virtual trigger he could pull from far away. Once more, Little Jim's life hung by a thread.

"Come on, Harris. Charity never hurt anyone."

The billionaire hesitated, then nodded to Captain Robson, who didn't react. Harris insisted. Resigned, Robson ordered his crew, who began waving toward the dhow, urging its captain, if it had one, to tie up to the yacht.

Max watched as a kind of frenzy took hold of the refugees. Men began working to start the engine, pushing women and children aside. Shouts and cries came from their craft. Slowly, the dhow moved toward the yacht, which no doubt seemed like an impossible vision to the refugees, as if it were just one more mirage.

Max called out to Harris, who was posted by the sliding door, "Good work! With guys like you, Africa's in good hands."

Harris stalked into the salon as Robson's men sprung into action. The Third World in all its misery was about to invade their space, and measures had to be taken.

Not long after, as Rashid was slowing in preparation for entering the harbour, Max tried to reach Sophie in Bukoba to announce that Valéria's money problems were now a thing of the past. She must have turned off her cellphone, so he left her a succinct message, leaving out the particulars.

Before they docked, Max took a last glance backward. The dhow was securely tied to the yacht and the passengers were moving up the ladder in a steady stream, then spreading across the boat like a column of army ants on a mission. The crew had clearly lost control, though Robson and his men were doing all they could to herd the crowds into one corner. Harris and his guests hadn't returned to the bridge. They must have locked themselves in their cabins as the human wreckage, the other Africa, the Africa of poverty that was supposed to be disappearing, took over their yacht.

The next evening, all around the Serena Inn, Zanzibar was transformed. Decorated. Illuminated. All in honour of Barack Obama, whose face was seen everywhere, on enormous billboards, a combination of rock star adulation and Soviet-style propaganda.

The new president's personality fascinated and charmed the population, and his African origins made him one of them. No one had believed he would be elected, and his victory still felt unreal.

A black man leading the world's most powerful country. No one could wrap their mind around it.

"Now the Americans will have a reason to think about Africa instead of just exploiting it," said the barman from behind his counter.

Max sipped his drink and ignored the attempt at conversation.

"What do you think about it?" the barman wanted to know.

"I don't think anything. I don't know Africa well enough, and the United States, either. A bad combination."

"Finally, Tanzania is turning around."

"I sincerely hope so," Max said in a neutral tone.

At the end of the previous day, Vincent Kalitumba, manager of the Dar es Salaam branch of the Bank of Baroda, confirmed that the money had been transferred to the account Max had opened for Valéria. After his success with Harris, the latter's money had zigzagged across the world, making it harder for an investigator to follow it, if ever one got on the case. Jayesh took his share, and Max did the same, which left a million for Valéria.

"The Europeans are missing the boat!" the barman exclaimed. "Especially the British. Not to mention the Chinese. A new world is about to begin, Mr. Cheskin."

Cheskin — the pseudonym Max had given when he checked into the hotel. He'd been using it since settling in Africa.

"Then that's a good thing," he told the barman.

His cellphone gave him the perfect excuse to escape the babbling barman. It must be Sophie, finally returning his call.

"Robert Cheskin?"

A man's voice. Something was wrong.

"Who are you? Where's Sophie?"

"Inspector Henry Kilonzo, Tanzanian police."

"What's going on?"

"Where are you, Mr. Cheskin?"

He had no reason to lie. "In Zanzibar. I want to talk to Sophie."

The silence was endless.

"Sophie Stroner is dead."

Max felt the earth falling away. "Then I want to speak to Valéria."

"She's dead, too. They were both murdered."

4

Albert Kerensky chose the retirement home because the room on offer had a window on the Walls Unit at Huntsville, the oldest penitentiary in Texas. His entire career had been dedicated to that place, outside of a short stint at the Dallas prison. Stanford Hill wasn't the most modern residence in the area, its equipment outdated, sheets worn thin. Roselyn took it all in the first time she visited.

Money wasn't what motivated his choice. With his generous government pension, he could have treated himself to Woodbridge Manor or even Brighton Lodge on the road to Houston. But Albert insisted on Stanford Hill, and that was that.

Roselyn gave in.

If her husband wanted to end his life in solitude as he contemplated a lugubrious penitentiary all day long, that was his problem. If their daughter, Norah, had been on this earth, she would have convinced him to change his mind. But there was no one left except Roselyn now, and Albert had never listened to her, even when her arguments were worthy and well founded. He wasn't the sort of man to listen. All her life she'd tried to accept his capricious nature as her mother had done with her father. She hadn't had as much success.

After Norah's death from chronic kidney failure several years earlier, Roselyn suddenly saw the extent to which her daughter had been the only thing that had provided a semblance of order and stability in her husband's life. She was the one who provided the motivation for him to get out of bed in the morning. Not Roselyn. After Norah's death, Roselyn thought they might recover some of the companionship they'd had earlier in their marriage, but that wasn't the case. Albert had always been prone to nostalgia, and the tendency worsened as he grew older. He lived entirely in his memories that meant nothing to anyone else except for his pal, Glenn Forrester, with whom he could exchange stories of the good old days.

To her dismay, Roselyn realized she wasn't indispensable to her husband. At age seventy-six she was still alert, strong, even though time had taken its toll. Her back was straight, she was tall and elegant, the way her mother had been. Next to her, Albert was fragile and self-absorbed; over the last year he had lost all appetite and seemed depressed. Even the TV had stopped holding his attention. One evening he announced he was going to leave Houston, where they'd been living since he retired and they had sold their house. He intended to go back to Huntsville and get a room at the Stanford Hill Residence.

By himself.

An entire life together, and suddenly, overnight, he pushed her aside like a piece of old furniture.

After Albert went to bed that night, Roselyn cried as never before, not even after Norah died, when she thought she'd never get over the pain.

The day Albert moved, Roselyn had hoped, naively, that he would change his mind and ask her to come with him. The opposite occurred. Once he was ensconced at Stanford Hill, he ceased all communication with her. She considered moving up there to be closer to him but quickly abandoned the idea.

They had little to do with each other, and when they did, it was Roselyn's doing. Every Sunday morning, like clockwork, she would call Albert, and despite the fact that they had determined the hour ahead of time, she always felt she was bothering him. On some occasions, he'd even step out of his room on Sunday mornings and the phone would ring unanswered.

Although it pained her at the start, Roselyn got used to the treatment. Her husband wanted to live out his days in the solitude of his memories, his eyes glued to the Walls Unit. He preferred being with Glenn Forrester instead of his wife — that was his problem. Roselyn wasn't about to waste the last years of her life trying to convince a grumpy old man to keep her by his side.

Yet she still loved him. She had never stopped loving him, despite the way he behaved. But she didn't know how to act toward this enigmatic, mysterious husband of hers who lived far away, seemingly finding pleasure in cultivating the mystery at her expense.

So Roselyn wasn't wholly surprised when Mrs. Callaghan, the residence director, called her as she was hurrying to an important meeting at the Four Seasons where the annual show of the Wildlife Artists' Association of Texas would take place. Roselyn had always been interested in painting, even before she met Albert. When he moved to Huntsville, she quickly rediscovered the passion of her younger days and joined a group of amateur artists who specialized in animal subjects. She was enthusiastic, dynamic, imaginative. Soon enough, she was elected to the board of directors.

"Sorry to disturb you," Mrs. Callaghan said over the phone. "It's about your husband."

Roselyn pulled over to the side of the road. "Is something wrong?"

"This morning Albert didn't come down to breakfast. Nothing new there. But when the nurse went to his room to bring him his medicine, she found the room empty. The bed hadn't been slept in."

Roselyn stifled her anger. Albert had taken off without telling anyone, despite the residence authorities reassuring her that such an event was impossible. It certainly would have been at Woodbridge Manor or in any other higher-class home. In that slum of a place, the old folks came and went as they liked, security be damned.

"Did you check with Glenn Forrester, his friend?"

"He hasn't heard from him."

If Glenn didn't know what Albert was up to, then there was reason to be concerned.

The director tried to calm her worries. "You know, at least his mind's all there. No problems with his memory, either, not like some of our other residents."

The director's words did nothing for Roselyn. All that meant was that Albert had carefully planned his escape and it would be harder to find him.

"Is this something he's done before — leave without warning?"

"Never."

Albert kept to himself. He always refused everyone's care and wanted people to act as though he wasn't there.

Still, something had to be done. The simplest thing would have been to drive all the way to Huntsville, but Roselyn hated driving at night, which she would have been forced to do on the way back. After making Mrs. Callaghan promise to inform her the moment something happened, she called her son-in-law at the Huntsville Police Department.

Peter Sawyer, the son of a guard from the Wynne Unit, had married Norah right out of the Galveston Police Academy and had immediately been hired by the city. The two of them had met years earlier at Camp Connally in Big Thicket Park, a summer camp for the children of employees of the Texas penitentiary system.

Peter did his best to reassure Roselyn. He would go over to the residence and check in on the situation, as he put it. And he'd have a chat with Mrs. Callaghan.

Roselyn was back home when Peter called her.

"For now, nothing strange outside of his disappearance. I checked with the area hospitals. I asked my men to be on the lookout for an old man on his own."

Thirty-six thousand people in Huntsville, a third of them behind bars. In other words, it was a village. Everyone more or less knew one another. Albert couldn't have wandered with a lost look on his face more than five minutes without someone calling the police. That was what made his disappearance all the more surprising.

"He took his medicine with him," Peter added. "His supply was topped up the day before, so he'll have enough for several days."

Albert was a diabetic, and sometimes his heart acted up, especially since his cardiac incident the year before. The residence's doctor had prescribed him Coumadin.

Meanwhile, Roselyn suffered from hypertension. When they lived together, man and wife would take their pills together. Often Albert would forget his dose; of the two, he was more negligent. Yet he'd had the presence of mind to take his backup supply of medicine when he walked away.

"Along with his umbrella," Peter pointed out.

The next morning, after a sleepless night waiting in vain for another call from Peter, the director of the residence, or even Glenn, Roselyn got in her Mazda and headed for Huntsville. On the way, she called Brian Pallister, the president of her artists' group, and asked him to replace her on the committee that was setting up the show. She was tight-lipped and said only that there had been a family emergency and that she'd keep him posted.

As she drove, she found herself glancing at the side of the road into the bushes in the hope of spotting Albert. Of course, there was no one, not even a hitch-hiker. Who would have picked up a stranger anywhere near Huntsville?

Over the past few months, her visits had become less frequent, but Albert didn't seem to notice. At the beginning she stayed with Peter, which was a way of seeing her grandson, Adrian, and she would walk to Stanford Hill, spending the day with Albert, watching TV, and eating dinner with him.

Most of the residents were former employees of the prison system or their widows. No one seemed to grasp the irony of the situation. Sitting at long tables in a giant room, they differed little from the prisoners they had guarded all their lives. In the Walls Unit and the other penitentiaries of the town, prisoners the same age as these old guards were slurping down the same watery soup in the same lugubrious atmosphere.

Those visits were always painful for Roselyn. She did it for her husband, who was very much aware of her discomfort. But as usual, he stayed inside his own world. No one sought out his company, Roselyn saw, and he seemed like he couldn't care less about that.

After a while, Roselyn put a stop to the painful visits and cut short the time she spent with Peter. She decided to make a visit at Christmas and once during the sum-mer, and that would be that.

The town's strange atmosphere struck her more and more. Her father had been a prison guard in Huntsville — and so as a child, and as she grew into womanhood, she'd become used to this cohabitation with inmates. To those outside the prison town, it seemed strange, but for her and the other children of prison guards, it was ordinary, simply the way the world was. The town landscaping, the maintenance of parks, street cleaning, all these jobs were carried out by inmates judged not to pose an immediate threat by the authorities of the area's seven penitentiaries.

No one questioned the situation that had existed since the middle of the twentieth century. No parents, even the most careful, warned their children about the prisoners in their midst. The townspeople had complete trust in the authorities — and that was still the case. After all, they were family men, they lived in Huntsville, and they wouldn't do anything to endanger their fellow citizens.

As she grew up, Roselyn often crossed paths with prisoners who had just been freed, their debt to society paid, walking toward the bus station, carrying a small standard-issue suitcase. Eleven o'clock in the morning was freedom hour, and nearly every day a recently freed man could be spotted. What would become of them now that they had the chance to start over and build their lives anew? Roselyn had no idea.

She asked her father that question one day. Laconic as always, he answered, "Most of them will be back sooner or later. They've got prison in their blood."

From time to time, there would be an escape. The news travelled fast through the town, and the community circled the wagons. People stayed in their houses and locked their doors. If it happened on a Saturday, Roselyn would order Norah to stay inside. At school the students sat in their classrooms until the chief of police lifted the curfew, the fugitive had been caught, as was usually the case, or it was assumed he was far from Huntsville by then. The escapees were never free for long — a week at most. Sometimes the jailbreak ended violently, with gunfire or the death of the fugitive, but Roselyn never remembered any such tragic denouement in Huntsville itself.

Still, in the 1970s, she took a class in the handling and use of firearms given to the wives of prison employees. A program offered by the city council, it was shuttered soon after she graduated.

To the right of the Walls Unit, at the end of the main street, was a smaller road shaded by oak trees. Farther along was Stanford Hill Residence, where she parked her car. Mrs. Callaghan was waiting by the door, having been alerted to her arrival. A woman in her fifties, smiling, stiff of manner. A former nurse at the Walls Unit, she had poured her savings into this old folks' home after she left the penitentiary.

"No further news, I'm afraid. But a policeman called a while back."

"That would be Peter."

"I told him you were coming. He wants to see you."

Roselyn went down the hallway as the senior citizens nodded in her direction. The place was clean, the residents seemed to be well treated, but she had never cared for the atmosphere.

To get a view of the Walls Unit, Albert had traded in a bit of comfort. The room was smaller than most in the residence, and to Roselyn it seemed loaded down with furniture: a large TV on one side, an enormous La-Z-Boy on the other. A sink on the right, and a small fridge where Albert kept his stock of Canada Dry.

Roselyn opened it. It was empty. Not a can left. He really had planned his escape and left nothing behind.

On the wall was a painting she had given him when he moved in.

"Do you have any idea where he might have gone?" Roselyn asked for the tenth time.

Mrs. Callaghan shrugged. "He's very reserved, you know. He never confided in anybody."

As the director looked on from the doorway, Roselyn went over to the little desk. With the La-Z-Boy and the TV, it was the only thing Albert wanted to bring with him after they sold the house. Back then that was where he kept the phone and electricity bills and the tax returns. She checked the contents of the drawers: nothing but old menus from the dining room that he'd kept for some obscure reason. Roselyn read them over.

"He'd lost his appetite lately," Mrs. Callaghan remarked.

"Did he complain about the food?"

"Never."

"What does Dr. Taylor have to say?"

"He'll be here this afternoon. You can talk to him."

Roselyn glanced at the menus again. Every day Albert had drawn a red circle around his preferred dish. Pork chops, smoked turkey, jambalaya …

Things he had never liked before. Strange.

His eight records were in their usual place, one reassuring detail. Albert's musical choices had never gone beyond American popular tunes with a preference for Johnny Cash, which made sense. Songs about prison pulled on his heartstrings. Albert had no interest in Elvis Presley — a "puppet," he said, "a singer for the ladies." Cash was another story.

The residents of this place found all sorts of hobbies to occupy them between meals. But Albert preferred to stay in his room, sit in front of the window, and stare at the penitentiary. Sometimes he played one of his eight records too loud. Or Glenn Forrester would call, but his visits were very rare.

Little by little, Albert had isolated himself.

Roselyn went to the window. Beyond the trees was the Walls Unit, the Huntsville prison. It had gotten its name from the red-brick wall that surrounded the central courtyard. Why did Albert find pleasure watching this lifeless scene day after day, never growing tired of it?

He'd left the big city of Houston to return to this smaller place, and not just anywhere: directly in front of the prison, with a view of the main building, the walls, and the barbed wire.

A lifetime spent within the penitentiary walls might have affected his mind. "They've got prison in their blood," her father had said of former inmates. Albert's situation was exactly the same. Once he was freed from his job, he was still unable to leave it behind. But neither could he talk about it. He was like a soldier who had seen the horrors of war and fallen into silence once he was back in civilian life. He knew no one could understand what he'd been through.

"Are there any others like him here?" she asked.

"What do you mean?"

"Other executioners."

Mrs. Callaghan hesitated. "He's the only one."

Roselyn gazed at the Walls Unit again. Her husband had applied his craft there on many men over his long career. For twenty-three years, before his retirement, as a member and later head of the tie-down team, as the execution crew was called, Albert Kerensky had given the gift of death to two hundred and thirty-four men.

5

The Bukoba airport was little more than one long strip of beaten red earth, next to which had sprouted a rudimentary hangar like a random growth. Local officials had tried to maintain the facility over the years, but it was so fragile it looked as though a strong wind might blow it into nearby Lake Victoria. The structure served as the waiting room and shelter for passengers during the rainy season in the spring when the landing strip was often unusable. Great streams of muddy water made takeoff impossible and landing risky. A few years ago, the pilot explained, a Tanzanian army plane had hit a tree on its final approach and crashed into a hospital a little farther on.

"How convenient," Max remarked.

At the controls of the Cessna, Roosevelt Okambo evaluated the landing strip, which seemed to drop into the lake. The pilot had been born the day the father of the New Deal died, which explained his name, and he belonged to the lost generation of African aviators. For a time — one not entirely over — travellers had preferred white faces in the cockpits of puddle jumpers across Africa. More often than not, these men were former mercenaries. Okambo had to settled for a career as a bush pilot, mostly in the Kagera region, carrying mail and sometimes passengers. Max had used his services before. He was a reckless flier who liked the sound of his own voice but was a master of his Cessna.

As he began the descent, Okambo pointed to a police vehicle by the landing strip. "Inspector Kilonzo!" he shouted over the racket.

The lead investigator who'd announced the double murder to Max had come two days earlier from Dar es Salaam.

"You know him well?" Max asked.

"Mostly his reputation."

"Good or bad?"

"He's a policeman," Okambo answered darkly.

Henry Kilonzo had travelled to the region once when he was in the army. He had told Okambo as much, but no more. A short, powerfully built man with the rigid bearing of a military man, he seemed to be angry with everyone, as if his bad mood was part of his uniform along with his badge and epaulettes.

Still, Kilonzo's face brightened as Max climbed down from the plane and shook hands with him. "Welcome to Bukoba, Mr. Cheskin. I'm sorry the circumstances couldn't be better."

Max nodded.

"Come, we have to talk."

Kilonzo opened the door to his truck so Max could sit inside. The policeman took the passenger seat. The driver's seat was occupied by his assistant, Lieutenant Bruno Shembazi, a big man who exuded energy, younger than Kilonzo. Max was squeezed into the back with his bag.

Compared to the heat and humidity of the coast, the cool air of this region did Max good. For a time, as Shembazi drove toward Bukoba proper, Kilonzo talked about everything except the murders. Then he got around to explaining that he had been sent by the Directorate of Criminal Investigations in Dar es Salaam to solve the crimes. Normally, an officer from the Kagera Regional Police would have taken care of the file, but Valéria Michieka's reputation and the controversies she'd been in the middle of over the years had moved the government to send someone from the capital.

"Despite the fact that the crime rate in Dar es Salaam keeps us busy enough already. Just goes to show how important the ministry considers this investigation. And that includes the president."

"Lugembe sent you here?"

"It is said he is much affected by the murder of his friend."

His friend?

Max knew they had always been on good terms. The defence of albinos had united Lugembe and Valéria because of his two daughters, Faith and Clara, who had met a tragic end. But friends? Certainly not. Unless the friendship was recent.

From the very beginning of her involvement in the albino issue, Valéria understood that the solution to their problems had to come from the government. At the time Lugembe held a strategic position — he was minister of home affairs — and was President Komba's confidant, so he was an essential ally for Valéria. His support was indispensable. He had shown himself to be sympathetic to the cause, especially since the problem was widening in scope. Over the past twenty years, Tanzania had changed. The country had been setting aside the socialism imposed by Julius Nyerere, the father of independence, whose economic measures had impoverished the country. The new leaders embraced capitalism in all its triumph. The return of the multi-party system, the desire to cut red tape, encouraging tourism in order to compete with neighbouring Kenya ... there was just one dark spot: the traffic in albinos gave Tanzania the image of a backward place mired in bloody, barbarous traditions that people thought had been left behind.

Valéria believed the only way to stop this heinous business was to go after the traffickers, the intermediaries between victims and witch doctors who passed on amulets and other good-luck charms to their clients. The business could be halted only if a clear message was sent to traffickers and everyone else implicated in the racket: the death penalty would be reinstated for anyone, no matter their degree of involvement, even if they had never touched a machete, who was found responsible for the death of an albino.

At first Lugembe thought twice about recommending such extreme measures to his government. Eliminating one barbarous custom and replacing it with a barbarous state response might not be the best solution. The Americans defended the action. But the Komba government didn't want to be discredited in European eyes by reinstating capital punishment. Komba himself had suspended it in 1996 and had pursued the image of a modern, open-minded leader in the tradition of Nyerere, his mentor.

Valéria made several trips to Dodoma and Dar es Salaam to try to convince Lugembe that her arguments were right. Of course, the death penalty was an abhorent form of punishment, but they were facing a horrific problem, and it was pure delusion to think it could be solved with today's milder measures.

Besides, weren't witch doctors and other so-called healers running a veritable dictatorship over superstitious, poor, illiterate peasants? They were a mafia with their hands in everything, including the central government. How many lopped-off fingers, toes, and earlobes, dried and shrivelled, were hidden deep in the desk drawers of bureaucrats?

As minister of home affairs, Lugembe increased the number of policemen and border guards, stiffened fines and prison sentences. The business became riskier, healers had to be more careful, they slipped deeper into clandestine circles, yet their activities continued unabated.

The efforts were well meaning but made little difference. In the Kagera region, albinos lived in perpetual fear. Parents kept their children at home instead of sending them to school, depriving them of an education and sentencing them to a life of poverty. The streets were dangerous, terrifying even, a cutthroat atmosphere. Valéria invited an albino boy to come to the capital with her to tell the story of a childhood marked by terror. When he walked through his village, he felt all eyes upon him, eyes that coveted him. He had dodged death more than once. Even today, whenever he left his house, it was with fear and reticence.

Lugembe was moved. Valéria knew he spent good money protecting his adopted daughter who never went out without a bodyguard, even if albino hunting was essentially a rural phenomenon. Every day Clara was escorted to the University of Dodoma where she studied computer science. She was lucky compared to albinos in the countryside who were defenceless, at the mercy of some madman who was greedier than the rest.

Then everything changed.

In September 2002, despite efforts to protect her, Clara was kidnapped as her twin sister had been seventeen years earlier. President Komba finally gave in to Valéria's arguments.

Arrested and found guilty, Samuel Musindo was sentenced and executed, even if his lawyer, Jason Chagula, used every recourse to lessen the punishment that he considered excessive.

Valéria had two groups of enemies very different from each other. The witch doctors and healers, since her actions interfered with their business. And right-thinking people in the West, believers in the politically correct, who condemned her, a lawyer herself, for her "reactionary" ideas.

As the truck entered the town of Bukoba, honking its way through the gawking passersby, Kilonzo turned to Max. "You tried to reach Sophie Stroner several times. We checked the messages on her cellphone."

Shortly after Kilonzo's call to Zanzibar, Max had left a message with Vincent Kalitumba, manager of the Dar es Salaam branch of the Bank of Baroda. Had Valéria picked up the million dollars that had once belonged to Jonathan Harris, and that he'd deposited in her account? He was still waiting for an answer.

"Well?" Kilonzo asked. "Sophie Stroner?"

Max had no intention of disclosing anything about that subject, nor even Sophie's recent trip to Lamu. Kilonzo didn't mention it, which meant he knew nothing. He was in the dark about why Sophie might have come to see him.

"I wanted to see Valéria again."

"See her again?"

"Personal reasons."

Kilonzo waited.

"She and I had a love affair. It ended badly. That's why I stayed in Africa. I still hoped that —"

"And you wanted Sophie to be the go-between?"

"Yes."

Kilonzo looked away, then returned with a question. "How did you meet Valéria Michieka?"

Max paused. He had to choose among the memories he could tell a policeman and the rest he didn't want to share with anyone. First, he had to hide the way they'd met in October 2006. He was passing through Toronto, where he was plotting a fraud to be carried out against a high-ranking member of the municipal administration. He had set up headquarters in the Sheraton Centre. His stay in the city would be brief. Once the operation began, Max would take the first plane to New York the next morning. As he was paying his hotel bill, he noticed a tall black woman in conversation with the concierge about a problem with the lights or the sound in a meeting room; he couldn't remember which. "It can't happen again, not like the last time," she insisted. The concierge nodded and promised it wouldn't on his mother's grave.

What was it that drew him in? Her beauty, and her determination, too. She was in her forties, slender and elegant. She refused to give in to fashion and straighten her hair — she had something of the political activist Angela Davis about her. Max figured she must work in advertising or marketing with her well-cut clothes and bright colours. That evening she had a presentation for her clients. Her career was hanging in the balance, which justified the dressing-down she gave the hotel concierge.

Despite his attraction, Max saw a possible victim in her. Everything about her, the way she carried herself, the way she spoke to the hotel employee, it all pointed to an ambitious woman who had no doubt trampled on a few people on her road to the top. Max saw that as a weakness, this will to cling to the summit at any price after so many struggles to reach it. He might be able to take advantage, and as a con artist he never missed an opportunity to gather the crumbs that fell from the tables of the rich and the very rich. No doubt about it, this woman belonged to that exclusive club.

In the lobby, as Max was walking toward the elevators, their eyes met. That evening, curious, intrigued, he stopped by the second floor where the meeting rooms were.

He had been wrong about everything.

Valéria Michieka wasn't in advertising. She was a lawyer who ran The Colour of Respect Foundation, an organization dedicated to helping albinos, as the brochure at the entrance to the room indicated. At the time Max knew nothing about the tragedy of these "white Africans" in certain areas of the continent.

He went into the room. Some fifty people were sitting on chairs in front of a long table. Mostly grey-haired, but a few up-and-coming types who seemed to be wasting their time. Has-beens and wannabes sent by their companies, the sign that they had little interest in Michieka's group.

From a spot behind her computer, Valéria addressed the audience. The classic PowerPoint, loaded with statistics and shocking figures, embellished by photos of albino children. Some of them were handicapped. They were missing an arm or a leg. They leaned on crude crutches, their eyes magnified by thick glasses. *A freak show*, Max thought.

Valéria was soliciting funds to create a hospital devoted solely to albinos and their families, which was badly needed, according to her. The government was contributing, but not enough. At least that was what Max understood.

Interrupted by the door closing and the chair Max pulled up to sit on, Valéria glanced at the newcomer, then returned to her presentation. She spoke of her involvement and her mission — her entire life dedicated to the albinos of the Kagera region.

Max watched her discreetly and listened to the music of her voice. She charmed him, it was true. Valéria spoke with great conviction, but without overdoing it, describing the terrible situation of the albinos in plain, hard-hitting language. She didn't weigh her presentation down with metaphors but went right to the point. Valéria needed money, and a lot of it, otherwise these unfortunate people would have no refuge and no place to seek treatment. Their skin diseases quickly became cancerous because their lack of pigment made them vulnerable to the sun's rays, and their sight soon degenerated. Not to mention the abuse they were subject to. They rarely lived past the age of thirty. Those albinos spared by human traffickers fell victim to diseases they couldn't afford to treat.

Slipping out before question period for fear someone would get interested in his presence, Max went up to his room. After a solitary dinner in the cavernous dining room, surrounded by tourists who stormed the buffet as if the end of the world were at hand, he took shelter in the lobby bar for a nightcap.

Leaning on the counter, he felt a female presence close by. He turned around. Valéria was standing there, looking him in the eye. She had probably been in the dining room, too, but he hadn't spotted her.

"I don't know what you're after or who sent you, but I have my suspicions. Let me tell you something. I'm not easily intimidated."

Max held her gaze. There was obviously some mistake. "You have the wrong person."

"I saw you in the meeting room this evening. And in the lobby this afternoon. You're trying to scare me, is that it?"

"I don't know what you're talking about. I was curious, that's all. Your presentation was very good."

"You're not from Amnesty International?"

"Unless someone signed me up without telling me." She relaxed, but only a little.

Max jumped in. "Robert Cheskin. Pleased to meet you."

She seemed embarrassed, caught off guard. "I am sorry ..."

Max invited her for a drink, and she accepted once she'd greeted some colleagues at another table, who were just getting up to leave. Valéria spoke at length about her involvement in the albino cause. About her foundation and the tour she was on in the hope of finding the funding she required. She'd reached out to Canada, the United States, and Europe, too. In magazines and scientific journals, the articles about her and her work had created a buzz.

"Charity has become an institution, Mr. Cheskin. It's no longer just a matter of convincing the rich to contribute. These days they're keen to give, but their generosity needs to be channelled to the right organizations."

"And you're all in competition."

"Even in Africa. Every day is the same battle."

Famines, epidemics, natural disasters — donors were subject to intense pressure.

"And albinos aren't a prestige cause. Not yet."

So she needed to travel the world to stand out from the crowd. To remind charitable souls that her foundation existed and was worthy. The harvest was meagre. Since she'd begun working to instate capital punishment for traffickers in Tanzania, right-thinking people had turned their backs on her cause. The same organization couldn't try to save the lives of those unfortunate beings on one hand, and with the other, put to death criminals who were also human beings. When it came to crime, two wrongs didn't make a right.

More and more often, her presentations were sabotaged by noisy and provocative hecklers, mostly from Amnesty International, which wasn't about to let Michieka, the lawyer, off so easy.

That was her first thought: Max was one of those activists who had harassed her since she'd set foot in America.

Max and Valéria talked for hours, first in the hotel bar, then in one of the intimate salons after closing time.

"I'm sorry. I'm weighing you down with my troubles. You haven't told me anything about yourself."

Max wasn't about to tell her anything. It would have all been lies, in any case. In the elevator, he pulled her close and kissed her. "Let's forget about the victims of human madness," he urged her, "and all the atrocities."

She was in full agreement.

Upstairs in his room, they had sex. Ordered champagne. When morning dawned, Max was in love. He wanted to spend the day, the week, his whole life with her.

When she emerged from the bathroom wearing her professional outfit, she announced, "I have a plane to Montreal to catch in a couple of hours."

She was heading out again to meet more investors and charm more donors. Convince them that her humanitarian work was important and worthy.

Then she would go home to Africa.

"Friday is Sophie's birthday."

Her daughter of twenty-three, who was studying at McGill University.

"When she was born, I made a vow. As long as I live, no matter where I am in this world, I'll be with her on that day to hold her in my arms and wish her happy birthday."

Max was confused. So there was a husband in the picture?

He had a name: Richard Stroner, a Canadian from Winnipeg. Tall, well built, a likeable face, judging from the photos he saw later in Valéria's house. He was an engineer from Alcan sent to determine the value of the bauxite that might be extracted in Tanzania. There were legal problems to settle, permits to obtain, and Valéria was suggested as a resource; she had just opened her practice and was eager to meet potential clients. When he returned to Canada and his wife, Stroner couldn't get her out of his mind. He engineered a quick divorce, it was urgent, and ran back to Tanzania to press his suit. Valéria was in love, too. Never again would they be separated. Ever.

In 1994 the Kagera region became the temporary home for Rwandan refugees who settled in makeshift camps thrown together in chaos. The United Nations gave Richard the responsibility of building the sanitation facilities for a number of these camps in collaboration with the Tanzanian government, which oversaw the work. That summer, as he was going from camp to camp, Richard lost his life in a car crash.

When she got over the initial shock and pain, after she cried herself dry, Valéria considered leaving the region and moving to Dar es Salaam where it would be easier to find work. In the end, she decided to stay put with Sophie, who was born in 1983. The albino cause occupied her full-time now, and Bukoba was the centre for the most zealous witch doctors and self-styled healers.

As time went by, Valéria's reputation spread across the region and beyond, and Max doubted that the people of Bukoba had much use for her. They probably saw her as a fanatic who could have deserted this hole and gone to live comfortably in Dar es Salaam, but who insisted on living among them for the strange, egotistical pleasure of charity.

Max kissed her long, deeply, and passionately.

"Don't ask anything of me," she told him as she pulled away.

He knew very well what she meant. But he wasn't about to obey her. "Can we see each other again?"

"Please, don't ask."

"I mean it."

She looked away and headed for the door.

He thought he had lost her, so soon, but at the last moment she came back and kissed him.

In New York, Max slipped a cheque for one hundred thousand dollars into an envelope he had picked up in the conference room and sent it to the headquarters of The Colour of Respect Foundation, which was also Valéria's house. A week later she called him from her office.

"Are you trying to buy me off, Mr. Cheskin?"

"I did it for the sake of humanity." He already missed her crystal laughter.

"I'll be in New York in December for a conference."

"If you need a chauffeur …"

"That's not exactly what I had in mind."

6

According to Inspector Kilonzo, Valéria and her daughter had been attacked on Saturday evening by a thief. He used a machete to wound Valéria: blows to the shoulder and neck. Sophie tried in vain to defend her. She, too, was killed by a machete. When the police came, they found the two women in a pool of blood. Their deaths were quick, with no excessive violence, or at least that was what the policeman said.

"Any witnesses?" asked Max as the vehicle moved down the road that led to Valéria's lakeside house.

"No. But we're still questioning the neighbours."

"Did you find the weapon?"

"There's a machete in nearly every house. This is the countryside, Mr. Cheskin." Then he put on his bureaucrat's voice. "According to our calculations, the crime occurred around eleven o'clock. Maybe midnight, but no later. This site is deserted. An assailant can slip onto the property without being seen."

Max noted that the inspector seemed to know a whole lot about a crime that had just been committed, and for which not a single witness had yet come forward. An investigator who wasn't from the region and whom everyone seemed to trust, or so he said. Quite astonishing.

Valéria and her daughter had added a wing for the office onto the original house, and that was where they received their clients. A section at the back, larger than the rest, served as a meeting room and storehouse. Stacks of files that the two lawyers had accumulated sat in piles.

The house opened onto a patio where dusty plants grew in disorderly exuberance. According to Kilonzo, the murderer approached the house from the lake, entered through the patio, and came upon the two women in the living room. He must have fled the same way. An accomplice could have been waiting for him along the shore in an outboard.

"Were they alone when it happened?" Max asked.

"The office was closed. The accountant has been away for a few days. With her family, it seems. We're trying to reach her."

Teresa Mwandenga was living it up in the luxury of Dubai. Normally, Max would have told Kilonzo about the embezzlement, but the information would have raised awkward questions.

When he considered the police on duty around the house, he began to doubt Kilonzo's expertise. He had the unpleasant feeling that the inspector and his team were putting on a show for Max's benefit. That was why the policeman had come to the airport to pick him up in his official vehicle: to impress him, plain and simple.

That suspicion was confirmed by the crime site. The living room floor was covered in blood, and now that the blood had dried, it displayed footprints. The scene hadn't been secured. Any number of people, including police-men, had come to see the bodies of the murdered mother and daughter, which had since been taken to the hospi-tal morgue. People had pawed everything in sight, and the bodies had been moved before the so-called experts arrived. That was another of Kilonzo's dubious initiatives.

Watching these Keystone Kops come and go through the house, Max felt the past and the privacy of these two women were being violated. The police were like a crowd of rubberneckers who showed up to rummage through this odd woman's house, a woman about whom many vile things had been said. Defending albinos, all well and good. But how many of these policemen were clients of witch doctors and healers?

"Tell your men to leave the house."

"Pardon me?"

Kilonzo glared at Max as if he'd insulted his mother.

"The bodies have been moved to the morgue. Your men have examined the premises. You have nothing more to do here."

"On the contrary. Clues could be —"

"The hell with your clues. Get out of here!"

Kilonzo gave Max a long look. "Very well then."

He gathered his little group. One after the other they filed out of the house but didn't leave the property. Standing around their vehicles, they chattered like schoolgirls.

Max had no idea if Kilonzo had been chosen for his qualities as an investigator. Probably not. At least he hoped not. One thing was certain: Max could count on no one but himself to find the persons responsible for this double murder.

In the bedroom, the bed was unmade. Valéria had most likely been attacked as she slept. On the way in, he'd noticed the ripped-off hinges of the patio doors. A strange tack for a burglar to take. Instead of slipping in discreetly, without a sound, he must have made a great deal of noise, probably to create panic in the household. If he thought the place was unoccupied, he wouldn't have used such a method.

Max glanced out the window and saw Valéria's Land Cruiser, an indestructible four-wheel-drive vehicle that she hated. Sophie was the one who took the wheel. She was her mother's de facto chauffeur. The Land Cruiser was parked at the same spot, very visible, the night before. The exact same spot. So the murderer had known Valéria was inside.

Right off, that eliminated theft as the motive. Kilonzo maintained that objects and money had been taken, but how could he have known? The intruder had come to attack Valéria and her daughter — Max was sure of it.

He picked up the sheet, then the pillow, and pressed both to his face. Valéria's scent was still present, faint but enough to bring tears to his eyes. He had slept with her and made love with her in this bed. One morning, very early, he'd found her deeply absorbed in a file, at her desk, already at work before the sun rose. Another time they had breakfast on the veranda, then retreated inside when a hard, slanting rain chased them off the porch.

To be here among these familiar objects let him believe that Valéria was still alive, and this was just a bad dream from which he'd soon wake. Everything came back through memory, every move of her body, every word she spoke, her smile, her eyes, but those pictures were only anecdotes. He scolded himself for remembering things that way, in a hodgepodge of important events and insignificant details.

After they met in Toronto, and their incredible week in New York, Max saw Valéria in Europe several times. Then she invited him to visit her in Africa. When he arrived in Bukoba in April 2007, she was his guide and opened the doors to a continent he knew nothing about. He surrendered to the atmosphere, the landscape, the warmth of the people. With wide eyes, he gazed in wonder upon this new world — and mostly at Valéria, more beautiful than any landscape.

Max had never been to Africa. In his mind, he had a series of pictures that were more or less clichés and folklore interrupted by atrocity scenes. He expected to come to a continent full of future and present AIDS sufferers with empty eyes huddled alongside undernourished children with beach-ball bellies. A stink of shit hovering over a world of dust and dried mud. A thick fog full of mosquitoes infected by contaminated blood, where sweating, half-naked humans ran through the savannah, machete in hand, in a sort of morbid frenzy.

The reality was quite different and much less spectacular. Poverty was present on a daily basis, and fatalism seemed to weigh on people's lives, but there was also an extraordinary turbulent energy and raw, unused power, the result of all the great projects that were promised but never happened, often wasted in irrational and gratuitous violence.

Valéria and he decided from the start never to speak of the future and live as intensely as possible in the present, as if the ground beneath their feet might open up at any moment and swallow them.

The past was cut off, too. Max's history was full of false starts and dead ends. Valéria's was surrounded by an air of mystery. At every turn they ran into a new lie. They preferred to avoid painful subjects and live their life together as if it were a gift from the heavens that neither deserved.

The awkward manoeuvrings of two lovers were unimportant now. The memories would fade when there was no one to share them with. Max was immersed in sadness like a rushing tide, and had no more strength to fight. Better to surrender to this universe of pain.... He and Valéria had separated only a few months earlier — but had they really ever been a couple? The sight of all these objects, her things, the small items that made up her daily life, upset him, reminding him that her love was lost forever.

He took her hairbrush, pulled away a strand, and held it between two fingers like a schoolboy in love with his teacher or the neighbour's wife, ridiculous and lost. Until the very end Max had hoped things would get better between them. But Valéria's death ended that dream.

Now he bitterly regretted not taking the initiative, not acting when the time was right. He had played fast and loose with life and destiny, not understanding that when it came to fate, they were all pawns in the game and would never be the masters.

Max stood in contemplation. Any moment now Valéria would burst into view from the next room, her cellphone to her ear, motioning him to wait a minute more as she leafed through a file at top speed. Then it would be Sophie's turn, as wound up as her mother, telling her to relax and make tea, a ritual for the women when the pressure of work became intolerable. They would sit facing each other on the little veranda they had turned into a greenhouse on the south side of the building and drink their tea, calmly commenting on the files at hand. Max had seen them doing that a few times and felt excluded from their world, which he respected, though with some regret.

Strangely, even if Valéria adored her daughter, the usual mother-daughter bond was absent. At times their discussions turned harsh. For an outsider like Max, it wasn't easy to understand that attitude, as if Valéria refused, because Sophie was her daughter, to give the younger woman the smallest break or leeway. Sophie had no margin for error. Stranger still, she seemed to accept her mother's severity.

A few years earlier, when she was a teenager, Sophie found herself involved in some business that could have gone very wrong when she was at boarding school in Dar es Salaam. One evening the phone rang in Bukoba. A policeman on the line informing Valéria that Sophie had been arrested for disturbing the peace, vandalism, and attempted murder.

Valéria immediately flew to the city with the bail money. Sophie spent one night in a cell at police headquarters on Sokoine Drive.

"What happened?" Valéria asked the policeman at reception.

During a fight in front of the Bilicanas, a fashionable bar, Sophie found herself with a bloody knife in her hand and suddenly realized, too late, that she had just crossed over to the wrong side of the law.

"What about the victim?" asked Valéria.

"Superficial wounds. He's already out of the hospital."

"I want to see my daughter."

When the cell door swung open, Sophie threw herself into her mother's arms.

"Mama, I'm so sorry …"

The attempted murder charge was the most serious and could have earned Sophie prison time, even if she was only sixteen. The same was true for her boyfriend.

"What boyfriend?" Valéria demanded, furious and disappointed because she knew nothing about any boyfriend.

Sophie's answer was vague. Her explanations were nebulous. Which is what worried Valéria the most. Slowly, the truth came out. The boyfriend was a man in his twenties, a white man, an American sailor she'd met while out on the town with her friends.

"I'm in love, Mama. I want to go to America with him."

Love had struck Sophie suddenly and would tolerate no compromises.

Valéria sighed and smiled at her daughter. Told her they would talk it over later, but the first priority was to get her out of jail. She promised herself she would give the boarding school authorities a real dressing-down for not keeping on eye on their charges.

"But forget about seeing that sailor again."

"Is he going to prison, too?"

"I'll look after his file if you promise to break it off with him."

Sophie promised, though it killed her to do so. Valéria got in touch with a lawyer in Dar es Salaam who had looked after things for Richard in the past. She gave him carte blanche to get Sophie and her boyfriend out of the mess they'd put themselves in and bribe anyone who needed bribing to spare her daughter prison. After a substantial sum had been paid, the accused were sentenced to one year in prison. The sentence was then suspended, which was very clement treatment under the circumstances. The sailor went back to the States and Sophie returned to class. She was serious this time. In September 2004, she began her first year at McGill.

Why had Valéria and her daughter been attacked? Max had no idea. He continued searching the house. Opening drawers and closets, looking under the beds and the furniture in the futile hope of finding some clue, anything that might guide him. But he had nothing to go on outside of Kilonzo's useless hypotheses.

Who had it in for the two women?

A dissatisfied client, or the victim of that client, frustrated at losing the case he or she had hoped to win and blaming the other party's lawyer for the loss. Max would need to carefully go through the list of Valéria and her daughter's past and present contracts, but he doubted he'd find anything relevant that way. The assailant's violent entry continued to gnaw at him. The racket. The way the door had been destroyed. A regular invasion. Maybe the murderer hadn't been alone. That was possible. Even if Kilonzo, in his infinite wisdom, thought the perpetrator had operated by himself.

A computer sat on the table. Max turned it on: letters, tables, budgets, and the usual documents. Kilonzo had gotten interested in Sophie's cellphone and must have rummaged through its contents but without taking it away for more thorough investigation. The police inquiry was a mess from start to finish. The crime scene contaminated by curious onlookers, meaningless hypotheses, the outside door ripped to shreds ...

If the police had been the murderers, they wouldn't have acted any different. It was clear they wanted the case wrapped up as quickly as possible. Max was getting in the way of their investigation, which is why they'd prepared a show for him.

But the show hadn't convinced him.

That was when he noticed something in a closet. A paper bag holding a toy truck made out of bits of metal and plastic, the kind seen everywhere in Africa. Little masterpieces of imagination and recycling built out of the garbage the consumer society left behind. This truck was particularly well done, and everything was there: the cabin, the open-box bed, even a tiny steering wheel. The windows were fashioned from pieces of mica cut from water bottles. Side-view mirrors smaller still, screw heads for lights in front, wire bumpers ... a magnificent work made with remarkable determination and an enlightened eye.

In Valéria's handwriting, a note was attached to the toy: "For you, darling Daniel, with all my love."

Daniel.

Which Daniel was that?

Who was the child? Who was meant to receive this gift?

7

"Cheskin! Over here!" Surrounded by his phalanx of policemen, Inspector Kilonzo waved him over nervously. Max went over. Squatting down, Shembazi was examining something on the ground. "Move over, Shembazi."

The officer got up awkwardly, unhappy at the way his superior had stolen his thunder.

"Look what we found." The inspector was radiant. He pointed at tire tracks in the soft earth. "He came in a four-by-four."

"I thought his accomplice was waiting along the shore in an outboard," Max said.

"We must investigate all clues. And this one seems more promising than the rest. Isn't that true, Shembazi?"

The officer gave his pro forma agreement.

Max pointed to Valéria's Land Cruiser.

"We checked it," said Kilonzo. "Not the same kind of tire. A newer vehicle. A Mitsubishi maybe. And probably not from the region, maybe even from Uganda. We're checking with the authorities to see if such a vehicle has been stolen recently."

Max sighed. "I want to see Valéria."

The two women's bodies had been brought to Kagondo Hospital, south of Bukoba. Max wanted to go alone, but Kilonzo insisted on accompanying him.

On the way there, Max had the growing conviction that the double murder was linked to the accountant's embezzlement, even if nothing seemed to point in that direction. As soon as Kilonzo stopped trailing him, he would start looking into that possibility. Another theory was that through their work for the albinos, because of their involvement and government support, Valéria and Sophie had riled up a lot of people. They were interfering with an underground business that enriched any number of low-lifes and charlatans. Maybe the women had pushed one of them a little too hard.

When he first visited Bukoba in 2007, the day after he arrived, Valéria took Max down to the port where she rented a boat for the day from a fisherman. Two lovers adrift on Lake Victoria, or so Max had anticipated. Out on open water, she pushed the boat to top speed, steering skillfully. It was clearly not the first time she'd done this.

Valéria cast her eyes on Max. His surprised look made her smile. "My husband taught me."

87

From time to time, they would cross paths with a fisherman. Valéria said a few words to him in Kihaya, then picked up speed again. She avoided rocks and put the engine through its paces. Sitting on the bow, Max watched her with the eyes of a suitor discovering that the woman he loves can jump out of a plane with a parachute or break down a Kalashnikov. He realized how little he knew about her.

Little by little, through their conversations, through hints, words she let slip, incomplete sentences, Max learned she'd come from a very poor rural family. Valéria escaped the usual fate thanks to an Anglican pastor who had opened a school in a nearby village. Reverend Wellington had founded a choir with his wife's help as a way to pull on the heartstrings of charitable souls in Britain. Valéria had joined it as a teenager.

She'd even sung for a record produced by the missionary. Her voice couldn't be heard among all the other girls, but her impact of the record on potential donors must have been remarkable.

After a while, Valéria reduced her speed. This part of the lake wasn't as busy, and the shoreline was different. Instead of huts and wooden piers thrown together, Max saw solid houses, some of them quite luxurious, hidden in the dense vegetation.

"Albinos aren't just hunted by traffickers, but their families, too," Valéria said. "Sometimes even their parents. If you're looking for where this repugnant business began, you have to start with the families." She paused for a moment. "Did you know we set aside part of our budget for the Bukoba cement works?"

"Why cement?"

"To make thick heavy blocks we can give the families of deceased albinos so traffickers won't raid the graves of their relatives. And that includes greedy cousins and brothers-in-law."

Max had no reply.

"The trafficking in albinos reveals Africa's contradictions," she added, as if giving a class or attempting to convince donors.

A barbaric custom, the legacy of a time when witch doctors and medicine men dominated society. Yet it was still alive and well today.

"At the Amsterdam airport, three years ago, customs officers stopped a trafficker. In a secret compartment in his suitcase, they found twelve albino penises. The man was going to London to supply Tanzanian dealers living there. Do you know how much an albino penis is worth in Britain?"

Max had no idea.

"A lot. Way too much."

Valéria went on with her exposé about the origins of the fascination for albinos. These "white Africans" were conceived on full moon nights, or so it was said, either that or they were the cursed offspring of diabolical beings. Yet paradoxically they could bring good luck and let people realize their most outlandish dreams.

"A sort of Aladdin's lamp made of human flesh," Max said.

"And in it we see the paradox of globalization. The specialists who study the continent believe it will let Africa catch up to the rest of the world and offer it the chance to modernize. But the exact opposite has happened. Globalization has helped spread customs and traditions from another age and culture that were once confined to a single region with no contact with the outside and sent them spinning out into the world."

Max felt Valéria's need to speak and free her mind from her disturbing thoughts. She'd taken him out to the middle of this lake to tell him of the struggle she'd been engaged in for years.

"Crimes of honour and arranged marriages — fifty years ago police in Paris or New York never had to deal with that plague. In this case, the families are complicit, just as neighbours and friends are, but witch doctors are at the heart of the trafficking. They're the ones who make the profits and who continue despite the penalties faced by go-betweens."

Valéria became thoughtful all of a sudden. She'd cut the motor and the boat was drifting. "I thought the death penalty would be the only punishment that would truly work. But the bastards multiply like rats. When one dies, others rush in. It never ends."

Max understood that she didn't want him to share his thoughts.

"In Kenya, Uganda, Burundi ... even if they didn't follow Tanzania's example, crimes against albinos have increased. The most extreme measures don't always give the best results."

Max was surprised to hear her question what she'd been advocating for years, her favourite cause that had brought about so much controversy. She had understood that the death penalty wasn't proving much of a deterrent.

90

"Who dies on the gallows? Small-time criminals, cheap traffickers who end up getting caught, who take the fall for the big fish safe in their palaces."

Max nodded. For the albino trade, as with other rackets, it was the same pattern and the same victims on both sides of the equation.

Valéria pointed to a handsome manor on the shore-line. "A witch doctor lived in that house. People came from afar to get his advice. His name is Awadhi Zuberi."

"And the police know that?"

"Yes, but they don't do anything. Zuberi is the brother of the owner of Hotel Hillview. When the politicians and government officials from Dodoma and Dar es Salaam come to the area, that's where they stay, and not at the Walkgard that's much more comfortable. I wouldn't be surprised if he's hiding a few albino fingernails and hair in some secret place in the hotel. To further his career, to make sure every room is rented, or to supply his customers when they ask. Ironic, isn't it?"

Ironic, but more than that — tragic and hopeless.

"The house is empty these days, but Zuberi is still the owner."

Zuberi used to be Samuel Musindo's customer, she explained. Musindo killed Clara Lugembe, the albino daughter of the country's future president, for Zuberi, though his links to the crime were never proved. Musindo was sentenced to death and executed.

"But Zuberi got little more than a slap on the wrist thanks to the prowess of his lawyer, Jason Chagula."

"Who was also Musindo's lawyer?"

"Right. After a few months in prison, he was freed, never to be seen again. Nothing left but an empty house."

"I suppose he had connections with the police and the courts?" asked Max.

"Probably."

Zuberi's popularity began in the 1990s when he started marketing a drug he said cured AIDS. He sold a potion to vulnerable people for a few shillings. When dawn broke, in front of his house, a long line of cars and people who had come to see the healer and buy his miraculous mixture could be seen. Customers had to get it directly from the witch doctor, otherwise the medicine's effect wouldn't work.

"It was a terrible spectacle. AIDS victims who could hardly walk, dragged there by friends and family," Valéria said. "A disgrace."

Zuberi was arrested and his business broken up. An official from the Ministry of Health declared that his famous potion was nothing more than coloured water.

But Zuberi was soon back in business as a healer, this time undercover, but with the authorities' blessing — they looked the other way. After Clara Lugembe was murdered, when the connection between Samuel Musindo and the healer were revealed, and then when Zuberi disappeared, the truth became too obvious to hide. Either Zuberi was involved one way or another with the death of the minister's daughter and had fled, or he had nothing to do with it but understood he'd be the perfect scapegoat. Either way, he decided to melt away into the jungle.

"I swore I'd get that bastard," Valéria had told Max.

Those words still echoed in Max's ears. When he and Kilonzo reached the hospital, he turned to the inspector. "Zuberi, the medicine man. You should see what's up with him. Find out what he was doing the night Valéria was murdered."

Kilonzo didn't seem surprised by the idea. He must have known all about Zuberi. "He's lying low. He has nothing to do with this."

"Do you know where he's hiding?"

"He's not hiding. He's a recluse. It's not the same thing. But I'm telling you — Zuberi isn't responsible for these murders."

"Did you question Jason Chagula?"

"The lawyer? He's left the country."

Kilonzo was strangely eager to declare the medicine man innocent. Every time Max wanted to move the investigation in a new direction, the inspector found a way to justify his inaction.

"It might be a good idea to pay a little visit to the pair," Max said.

"You think Zuberi would risk killing two women with his own hands?"

"Maybe not. But he might be involved in some way. Indirectly. As the one who ordered the hit."

Kilonzo gave Max a long look. "I know Valéria Michieka was very dear to you. But let me do my job. For now, nothing indicates the murders were linked to trafficking in albinos."

"One thing's for sure. It wasn't a burglary."

Max presented his thinking on the subject, which Kilonzo didn't dismiss the way Max thought he would. But still, the policeman told him, politely enough, to mind his own business and stay out of the way. The investigation would take its own course. He would keep Max informed, naturally, but wouldn't be ordered around by him.

"Please believe me, Mr. Cheskin, I'm extremely pre-occupied by this affair. I want to catch the killer as much as you do. But I'll work according to my methods and my priorities."

Max chose to keep the peace.

The hospital was a series of low-ceilinged rooms arranged around a central courtyard, a little like a motel, where the large wards, common rooms, operating theatre, maternity wards, and administration were found. Farther along was a workshop where artificial limbs were made, many of them for albinos who had suffered amputation.

The morgue had its own space apart from the rest.

The two bodies lay side by side on tables, more like counters, really, and next to them were surgical instruments. As if some strange operation was about to begin, an attempt to bring them back to life. The corpses were draped with an oilcloth, part of which was still folded. Once again, haphazard work. It seemed to Max that Kilonzo was putting on a show again, despite what he'd told him in the truck, and its purpose was to demonstrate that the Tanzanian police were as qualified as their counterparts in the West.

The inspector stepped up to the first table and motioned Max to follow. Abruptly, he pulled away the sheet the way a waiter snapped off a tablecloth after a meal. He held it in his hands as Max examined Valéria's body. She was still wearing the clothes she'd had on that night. A nightgown splattered with blood, especially around the shoulder on the right side. Kilonzo had told the truth: she was killed by a machete blow, probably after being thrown to the floor. Her knees and hands were scratched, and bruises were visible on her arms.

Then Kilonzo pulled away the cloth that covered Sophie's body. She was wearing the same clothing, bathed in blood like Valéria's. In death as in life, the two women were alike.

Trying to keep back the emotion that flooded over him, Max turned to Kilonzo. "When is the forensic expert getting here?"

Kilonzo hesitated, rubbed his chin. "You see —"

"Won't there be an autopsy?"

"They wouldn't let him travel. I was just now informed."

"And in Bukoba?"

"There isn't enough staff to take care of the living. The dead, you can imagine …"

Max sighed. If the double murder was a priority for Kilonzo, as he claimed it was, nothing in his attitude proved as much.

"In any case, the cause of death is clear enough. See for yourself. Now we're trying to inform the family, but we haven't found them."

"She cut all ties with them."

"An African woman doing that? Impossible!"

"I knew her, you didn't. Her only family was Sophie. And the albinos."

As he stepped out of the hospital, Max took a call on his phone. It was Vincent Kalitumba from the Bank of Baroda, who was sorry he'd waited so long to answer Max's message. He'd been in a meeting with Chinese investors. Max asked him if Valéria Michieka had picked up the money he'd transferred to her account.

"Just a minute. I'll check."

Max heard Kalitumba's fingers moving across the computer keyboard.

"Yes, it was done."

"Do you have the exact time of the transaction?"

Once more, Kalitumba's fingers went to work. "Sunday morning at two twenty-six a.m."

Max hung up. It made no sense.

The million had been withdrawn shortly after the two women died. The murderer had had access to Valéria's account. He'd disappeared with Jonathan Harris's money after committing his terrible crime.

8

What did Roselyn find most intriguing in the Texas Prison Museum? The electric chair, Old Sparky, as it was called, was the highlight of the visit. Tourists who travelled to Huntsville always asked the curator, Glenn Forrester, for permission to be photographed strapped into the spot where prisoners once died. Glenn always refused. He thought of his museum as a sanctuary, not a theme park. At the Walls Unit, men had suffered and died. Most of them deserved it, but their memory should be respected, whatever their qualities, whatever their faults.

Glenn had placed the electric chair in a setting that recalled the execution room in service until 1964. The rest of the collection was anything but banal:

reproductions of the cells, the warden's office, the prison director's office, the weapons used by the guards or the few inmates who tried to escape. There was artwork created by prisoners out of everyday objects such as toilet paper, cardboard, worn towels, and plastic utensils. As the seven penitentiaries were renovated, Glenn had picked up pieces that spoke of bygone eras.

In 1972, when the U.S. Supreme Court declared capital punishment unconstitutional, the states that still practised it abandoned their electric chairs, and most of them were simply thrown away. Glenn saved the one from the Walls Unit and set it up in his museum but had to give it back to the penitentiary in 1976 when the court overturned its initial decision. Meanwhile, the authorities searched for a way to execute people painlessly. Experiments using lethal injection had been going on for quite a while. In 1982, in the Walls Unit, this method was employed for the first time on Charles Brooks. The good old electric chair could go back to its room in the museum — this time for good.

In Texas all executions were carried out at the old Huntsville penitentiary, though death row was located in the Polunsky Unit.

Albert Kerensky was still a guard when capital punishment was reinstated, and he didn't become an executioner until 1984. Roselyn didn't recall when her husband had been promoted, probably because he'd asked her to avoid the subject in front of their daughter.

One evening, when she was a teenager, Norah asked her father, "What do they say to you, the men who are going to die?"

"Nothing. They talk to their lawyer and have their last meal."

"Are you the last person they see?"

"No. The chaplain and the prison director are there."

Standing by the prisoner, the director gave the execution order to Albert and his tie-down team.

Back then Roselyn, like her daughter, pictured a whole team of executioners working like a firing squad. All were armed with rifles shooting blanks, except for one, who didn't know it. His bullet would kill the condemned man. Later Roselyn understood that the team her husband was directing wasn't designed to dilute the executioner's responsibility but to support him. Each man had a particular responsibility. Albert's job was to inject the famous lethal chemical.

On execution days, he left early for the penitentiary to get there before the witnesses arrived. At first they were the representatives of the state and the condemned man's family. Albert escorted them to a room from which they watched the execution. Later, under pressure from victims' families, they, too, were given the right to be represented at the procedure. The two groups came in through separate doors and never saw each other, for they were confined to different rooms.

By arriving early, Albert hoped to avoid contact with a third group: the demonstrators, a handful of opponents of capital punishment who showed up in Huntsville on execution days. They were always the same people with the same signs, which made the day seem like a well-oiled ceremony, a ritual wherein the participants played their roles without asking themselves too many questions.

Roselyn's husband played his with strict profession-alism. No botched execution took place on his watch as head of the department, the way it happened in other states. On the evening of an execution — they always occurred at 6:00 p.m. — he would come home late and would keep to himself. For the first few years, Roselyn waited for him. She fixed his dinner and watched him eat before going to bed.

One evening, on her way back from visiting a friend at the hospital, she spotted Albert coming home, though he didn't see her. She decided to follow him. He turned left onto a street in the opposite direction from the house. She trailed him, growing more anxious, his foot-steps echoing on the pavement ahead. Albert moved forward without looking around, not suspecting his wife was right behind him. He kept his head down, and it seemed to her that he, too, was walking to the gallows.

A few blocks farther, still without glancing back, Albert entered a church. Strange. He never prayed and had no interest in religion.

Roselyn was too shaken to let him know she was there, and she didn't speak about what she'd seen when he returned.

In the middle of the night, he got up. She followed a few minutes later and found him in the kitchen. "Is something wrong?"

"No."

"What's happening?"

"Nothing. Go back to bed," he told her gruffly.

Albert never wavered. Solid as a rock. But this time Roselyn felt he was about to crack. She didn't know why.

The pressures of his job perhaps. That evening was the third straight execution in as many days. But then her husband quickly pulled himself together. He never had another moment of weakness.

Glenn Forrester hadn't spoken to his old friend for a week. He and Albert didn't spend as much time together now that they no longer hunted together. Albert was distancing himself from Glenn, too, Roselyn realized. She had assumed he was growing estranged with her, his wife, but he was doing the same with everyone. Roselyn was wrong to think she held a special place in his life.

"It's good to see you," Glenn said. "A shame the circumstances aren't ..."

"Maybe nothing's happened."

"You're right. With Albert there's no sense worrying."

Although Albert was taciturn, Glenn was a fountain of words. At the museum he took personal charge of every visitor, wanting every visit to be special. When he wasn't answering the phone, he was busy making urgent calls, but that was only a facade. Albert had chosen to live out his old age in contemplation, whereas Glenn needed action. He would die in this room, Roselyn thought, busy doing his accounts, dusting off his hunting trophies, bawling out a supplier over the phone, as he was doing when she arrived.

"It's not the first time," Roselyn told him.

"The first time for what?"

"You said it — no sense worrying."

Glenn sighed. "I never told you, but at the beginning, when Albert was chosen to join the tie-down team, I didn't think he'd be up to it."

The two men had been guards at the Walls Unit and had met when their careers were young. Albert alone answered the warden's call.

"He came to see me at home the evening before he was supposed to start," Glenn continued. "He told me he'd never be able to do the job. That he'd never be able to go through with an execution."

Glenn had poured him a double bourbon to stiffen his resolve.

"And yet he managed to do it?"

"Yes."

The team Albert had been part of, the same one he'd eventually lead, numbered a dozen members. His first execution had been Lewis Autry. Guilty of having shot a grocery store cashier and a witness in the head after a disagreement over the price of a six-pack. Autry had been the beginning of a long list. Initially, Albert was too nervous to sleep, but then slowly things got easier.

His new responsibilities changed him little by little, and a greater transformation occurred once he took over leadership of the execution team. He'd always been reserved and discreet; now he became secretive, even with the other guards and with Glenn. The latter figured that, after Albert retired, he'd once again become the man his old friend had known. But that never happened.

"His job marked him the way it marks all of us," Glenn now said. "It was just deeper for him."

According to Glenn, Albert could have asked for a transfer out. No doubt the administration would have moved him to another unit. Yet he refused every chance for a promotion.

Roselyn was more than surprised. At home, even if he never showed his anger, Albert sometimes criticized the prison authorities. He claimed they knew nothing about how difficult his job was, especially since the workload had increased dramatically after the year 2000. For a time, the Walls Unit chalked up forty executions a year.

Yet Albert never took the opportunity to change his working life. When retirement age dawned, he was still the head of the tie-down team, though several of his predecessors had climbed the ladder of the hierarchy when the chance came. Grimly, he stuck to his position.

"He called me last week or the week before," Glenn said. "I don't remember exactly. He wanted me to go with him to visit Norah's grave."

In honour of her birthday, Roselyn thought.

Glenn smiled sadly. "He needed my car now that he'd gotten rid of his. He didn't want to be driven around by those happy-go-lucky volunteers at the residence."

Roselyn had always hated the old Dodge her husband had driven into the ground, a rolling ruin he refused to let go of. It had taken weeks of negotiation for Roselyn to convince him to send the wreck to the scrapyard.

The two men went together to North Side Cemetery. Glenn walked Albert to Norah's grave, stopping several times along the way to let him catch his breath. Albert stood silently in concentration in front of the stone, and Glenn moved off, not wanting to disturb his meditations.

Then, according to Glenn, a strange thing happened. He heard Albert whisper, "I'll do it for you, Norah. Just for you."

Roselyn didn't follow. "You're sure he said that?"

"In any case, that's what I understood."

"What was he talking about?"

"No idea. And I didn't ask him, either."

After the cemetery, Albert became indifferent to everything. To shake him out of his lethargy, Glenn invited him to Los Pericos, the restaurant they used to go to when they were guards. Sitting in front of their enchiladas, all the two men could muster was small talk. Glenn might as well have been talking to himself. Albert's eyes roamed the restaurant, settling on nothing.

"I drove him back to Stanford Hill. We promised to get together again soon. And that was that. I'm his best friend, or at least I was for years. I can't imagine how he acts with other people. And with people he doesn't like."

"He just ignores them."

"That's right. But he isn't violent."

"An executioner who wouldn't hurt a fly."

"But maybe a few deer now and then."

Glenn burst into hearty laughter that transformed him into a younger man for a moment. He was still a handsome fellow. Then he turned serious. "I hope nothing happened to him."

"Me, too."

I'll do it for you, Norah. Just for you.

Now what did that mean?

Instead of going to see Peter, her son-in-law, who had offered his hospitality as always, Roselyn went past Stanford Hill Residence and kept going, ending up at

North Side Cemetery. It had once been out in the country, but little by little the suburbs had swallowed it up, surrounding it with bungalows, two-car garages, and swimming pools shaped like swordfish.

Roselyn felt some vague guilt at not visiting her daughter's grave more often. As she'd listened to Glenn's tale, she'd realized she'd hardly ever gone here with Albert. She'd thought he hadn't been to the grave since his return to Huntsville, but now knew from Glenn that her husband had visited regularly and never asked her to come along, as he did with Glenn — another surprise, almost an insult, really, that complicated the picture.

It had taken her years to understand she wasn't the woman he needed. Norah was all that kept them together. When their daughter died, nothing and no one united them.

Roselyn walked to the grave, hemmed in by two enormous elms. What was she looking for? Did she think she might come upon Albert, as if he were living in the cemetery now?

There was nobody, of course.

Roselyn stood in silence in front of the stone, trying not to think of the final moments of Norah's life, her endless hospitalization. For weeks, every day, Albert and Peter had held a hand that grew bonier, thinner, more fleshless, life seeping out of it. Doing the best she could to retain her tears, Roselyn stayed away, looking after her grandson, unable to watch her daughter waste away. Her death was liberation, as much for Norah as for her family after weeks of suffering attenuated only by morphine that slowly lost its effectiveness. Adrian was as shaken as Albert, and Peter had to use all his wisdom and care to keep his child on an even keel.

Albert had visited the cemetery on Norah's birthday. It had rained that day, Roselyn remembered. Glenn had said as much: *It was raining and I helped Albert get back into the car and I kept him dry with my umbrella.*

Why had Albert picked that stormy day to meditate upon his daughter's grave? It was her birthday, that was true, but why this absolute need to go on that particular day?

And to speak those enigmatic words?

He was intending to do something, Roselyn realized. A long journey, perhaps he had planned it, perhaps it had something to do with Norah's death.

9

It happened during Max's third or fourth visit to Bukoba, a few months after he met Valéria. Early one morning, before dawn, the two of them were awakened by banging on the bedroom door. Sophie was in a nervous state, close to a breakdown. She had just gotten off the phone with an officer from the Kagera Regional Police. A shallow grave had been discovered in Minziro near the Ugandan border. It was all that remained of what would later be known as the "Zeru Night." Over the past few weeks, an ever-growing number of parents had come asking for Valéria's help. It was clear the traffickers were back on the hunt again, but no one could find them or their victims. The massacre had taken place at nightfall, away from prying eyes, turning defenceless little beings into ghosts. In Swahili, albinos were called *zerus* — spirits or spectres.

Sophie didn't have the strength to travel to the site, but Valéria couldn't escape her duty. A number of her clients' children were surely among the victims. Max decided to go with her, despite her warnings. What they would look upon would be horrible, and would haunt Max for years to come.

There was almost no traffic until Kyaka, so the first part of the journey was easy. But once they crossed the Kagera River, the road turned into a wide track used by the local villagers during daylight, coming and going from the markets with heavy burdens on their heads, or on bicycles they pushed in front of them through the lengthening shadows.

Two hours later Minziro came into view: a hamlet of no consequence in a forest preserve that extended onto the other side of the border with Uganda. The officer had informed Sophie that he and his men were gathered north of the village in a clearing that could be reached after several kilometres on a muddy trail used mostly by poachers.

After a while, a police vehicle with a Tanzanian flag blocked the way. A sleepy policeman with puffy eyes let them through without bothering to check Valéria's papers, or those of her passenger.

She turned to Max a minute later. "There's still time to go back. I'll catch up to you afterward."

"No, I'll be all right."

Some distance on, they saw a four-by-four, and next to it, Sergeant Masanja. He was the one who had called

Sophie. Max and Valéria followed him along an over-grown path that seemed to lead to another clearing a little farther on. They encountered more policemen who were clearly disturbed by what they'd witnessed.

Max had readied himself for the worst, but *worst* couldn't describe what came into view. Blood every-where. A swamp of blood soaked the sandy ground. Masanja's men waded through this marsh, picking up pieces of clothing bare-handed. Another group was busy piling them up in separate heaps, an improvised mausoleum of bloody cloth, all that remained of the vic-tims' short time on the earth.

"Farmers tipped us off," Masanja explained. "The killing happened here two nights ago. They were in a hurry. They didn't have time to burn the clothes." He turned to Valéria, who was clearly shaken. "They took every part of these poor people. We won't find a single fingernail or an eyelash."

The traffickers had stolen them from their families, in their very houses, grabbing them as they'd slept, small white heads in the heart of the deepest darkness.

According to Masanja, the guilty parties were long gone. From where they stood, they could see the bor-der with Uganda. The albinos had probably been killed the night they were kidnapped. At dawn their bodies had been piled in a truck heading for Uganda. A smug-gler had gotten the vehicle across to the next country. Medicine men and witch doctors were already inquiring about how to buy the limbs of the victims, which they would dry and cut into ever smaller pieces, selling them off one by one.

"How much do they get?" Max asked.

"For an albino? As high as seventy-five thousand dollars, sometimes more."

The traffickers had to have the means to back up their ambitions: bribes to pay, relations to maintain …

"Do the Ugandan police know about this?" Valéria asked.

"We informed them the first day," answered Masanja. "But they're as powerless as we are. We'll be finding albino body parts for weeks, as far as Kampala and Nairobi. And on the stock exchange, too."

He was referring to a recently arrested stockbroker who was using an albino thumb as a good-luck charm to help him pick the right stocks. And the travelling salesman whose suitcase was opened by Congolese police during a routine search. Inside was a shrunken albino head.

Masanja had interviewed all the *mchawis* — the witch doctors — in the region. Some of them had been arrested in the past for dealing in stolen albino limbs, but his questioning led to nothing concrete.

Valéria looked at Masanja. "What about Awadhi Zuberi?"

He'd been under surveillance since he left prison. If he was involved in something, they would soon know, Masanja said. But neither Max nor Valéria was reassured.

"Do you think Zuberi could be behind this carnage?" Max asked her, once they were out of Masanja's earshot.

She shrugged. "Maybe."

A tarp had been spread under an acacia tree at the edge of the clearing. A group of men were gathered there:

the chief of police, investigators, and various specialists whom Masanja had managed to bring together.

Max caught up to Valéria. She was devastated by the scene. Coming closer, he saw she was crying bitterly. She fell into his arms, sobbing uncontrollably. "I want to go home."

In the night, Max awoke with a start. Valéria was gone. He found her in her office in a state of collapse, eyes red but dry. He held her close but didn't speak. She hardly knew he was there, as if he'd ceased to exist for her. Clothing picked up by the police had been checked and identified. Some of it belonged to children whose parents had come to see Valéria. Tomorrow she would have to tell them that their sons or daughters hadn't been found, that their bodies hadn't been located, either. Only what the traffickers couldn't sell. A pile of bloody clothes like worthless envelopes, the only thing their parents could have and hold.

The inhabitant of a strange, closed, and forbidden world, Valéria looked straight ahead and paid no attention to Max. She was shaken by what she'd seen, but he felt her pain had more distant sources, a time and place he couldn't reach. Excluded from her past, all he could do was hold her in his arms, rock her the way he might a child, whispering comforting words.

He thought she'd fallen asleep, but suddenly she lifted her head. "I think of him every day."

Max didn't understand. He waited.

"Evans. My big brother."

In her warm voice, with infinite sadness, Valéria told Max the story.

Evans and Valéria worked on the railway with Dickson, their father. Evans was the oldest of his eight sons, and the one he loved the most, or so Valéria said. One day, as they were coming back from work, she noticed Evans was in pain. He and Dickson were walking side by side on the little track that led to the village after the other workers had branched off toward Lulando beyond the hills. As they climbed Dew Hill, as the old folks called it, Evans felt a sharp pain in his left knee. At first Valéria thought he'd hurt himself during the day, since the Chinese had put him on cleaning detail, which meant he spent long hours bent over. He had probably leaned too much on one knee, which had now started to complain. But the pain didn't let up. Evans sat on a rock at the edge of the road, put down his pack, and began massaging his knee.

Valéria and her father turned and looked at him.

"Are you all right?" Dickson asked.

"Go ahead. I'll catch up."

Evans managed to make it back the village eventually. Valéria lived with her family in a modest house that over the years her father had expanded. The next day Evans's leg still hurt. Dickson bent down and took his son's face in his hands as if it were a precious jewel. He gazed at him, eyes brimming over with love, which embarrassed Evans.

Dickson's wife, Maria, sent for the doctor in Kibau. He was a humourless man with thick glasses. "Show me your knee!" he ordered.

Evans gazed past the doctor at his family. Maria was posted by the door, arms crossed, next to Dickson. Valéria stood behind them. Evans raised his leg, an action that seemed to demand much effort and pain.

"Come here, child," the doctor told Valéria.

She stepped forward and held on to her brother as the doctor palpated his leg and examined the knee. A minute later he took off his glasses, his face serious. *The face he wears when he hands out bad news*, Valéria thought.

The doctor turned to the parents. "You must get him to Iringa, to the hospital."

"You think I'm a rich city man who doesn't know what to do with his money?"

"I'm serious, Dickson." And then, in his gravest voice, he added, "I can't be one hundred percent certain. Further examinations are necessary. And I don't have the equipment in Kibau."

"Is he very sick, Doctor?" Maria had come to her son's side.

"As I said, I can't be certain … he needs treatment."

They stood there and studied Evans as if he were a wounded animal. The boy looked away. Valéria understood that he was humiliated by his weakness. She was angry with her mother for having invited the doctor, a stranger, into the house. She placed her hand on her brother's face, and he covered her hand with his.

When the doctor left, her parents broke down. They were discouraged, devastated, at the end of their rope. Later that evening her father came and spoke to Valéria. "The other day, the worker from Mlimba came with his niece. I saw you talking with her under the acacia."

Valéria stared at him. She didn't understand.

"A *zeru*," he added.

"Mlimba is a long way."

"Your brother's going to die."

They walked for hours, stopping only to drink and rest their legs. They hadn't thought of how they would separate the albino girl from her family. They didn't talk about it, as if avoiding the details of what they were preparing to do. Faith and superstition guided them, a sort of mystical madness, Valéria later said, the belief that obstacles would disappear by themselves without them having to confront them. In fact, all their thoughts were on Evans. On the terrible loss his death would bring.

When they neared Mlimba, Dickson seemed to lose his confidence. He walked more slowly, dragged his feet, had trouble breathing. He was looking for a way to change his mind. Away from Evans, his eldest boy's sickness seemed less serious, less urgent.

Valéria answered his unspoken question. "She'll come with me. She won't be afraid of me."

The little girl lived in a hut at the edge of the village. Her family raised chickens. They had no trouble finding the place. Dickson wanted to wait until nightfall but that wasn't practical. The girl would be sleeping with her parents and harder to separate from the others. It would be easier during the day.

On the hill overlooking the village, Valéria and her father waited for the sun to set. They had nothing to say to each other, as if the gravity of what they were about to do had left them speechless.

Valéria felt her father's will waver once again. "Think about Evans lying on his straw mat, wracked with pain," she told her father, "and your courage and determination will return."

He handed her his leather drinking gourd that he carried to work every day. His hand trembled. She looked away, embarrassed by his weakness. At that moment, she said later, she hated him. His son was going to die, and he was still hesitating over whether to save him. At eleven years old she was the strongest and most determined of the two.

From their spot on the hill, Valéria and Dickson saw the little girl return to the village with her father and a few other people. Children ran up to the girl and touched her head as if she were a good-luck charm. Valéria had seen that before on the work site. The girl's father shooed away the children and guided his daughter toward their hut.

A few minutes later they were home. The albino girl came out to feed the chickens. It was now or never. Valéria and her father moved down the hillside without a sound and slipped behind the house.

Her feedbag in her hand, the little girl was surprised when Valéria appeared.

"Come here," Valéria said. "I have something to show you."

The girl hesitated.

"Don't be afraid."

The albino girl moved closer, still fearful, but reassured by Valéria's smile. Then everything happened very fast. Dickson appeared out of nowhere, grabbed the girl by the arm, and began running, his hand over her mouth to keep her from crying out.

Into the forest, far from the village.

The albino girl fainted. She lay before Valéria and her father. They gazed upon her as they would a sacred image, a statue, an idol. Respect, yes, but also an incredible feeling of power. The little girl reminded Valéria of an insect caught in a trap, a fly stuck in a spider's web. Her skin was pale with pink blotches because of the sun. Her hair stood straight up, a sickly white, unreal. During the kidnapping, she'd lost her little white shoes, and now her bare feet were in a patch of mud.

"She's going to wake up," Valéria said.

Dickson pulled out his machete.

He grabbed the girl's leg by the ankle.

And aimed just below the knee.

The child's screams and whimpering pursued them for hours, when finally Valéria and her father made it back to their village, wild-eyed, exhausted, having spelled each other off to carry the tiny pale leg, white but stained with blood, their trophy, the talisman, the miracle cure that would save Evans from certain death. They'd left the little girl writhing in a bloody puddle of mud, paying no heed to her cries, fleeing in panic, their arms streaked with red, unable to speak or look at each other, accomplices in a crime that was bigger than they were, and from which they would never be free.

What had they really planned to do? To cure Evans — yes, but how? They would have to rub the leg on his knee in order to transfer the healing energy it contained. Either that, or something else. The superstition didn't come with a user's manual. They would have to improvise, or turn to a witch doctor. Time would tell.

When they reached the village, Maria was waiting for them in front of their shack. Evans had died. Valéria and her father were too late. Dickson collapsed on the ground, beating his forehead against the earth, cursing God and the entire world, offering his life to get Evans back, while Valéria, at a loss, not knowing what to do, ran through the brush, following the river, holding that ghostly white leg by the ankle. It had been of no use except to cast her farther into a hopeless night that would be her life from then on.

Squatting near the river, she closed her eyes. Along her leg she felt a thin stream of blood, her first menstruation. As if her blood could replace the dried blood and dead leg of the little albino girl. Disgusted, she threw the leg into the river, a grotesque trophy, a sullied fetish that disappeared with the current.

It was late. Sophie was asleep in the next room. Valéria fell silent, still haunted by the story she'd told. The story she'd lived with for all these years. Max put down his glass of Scotch — his third in the past hour — and held her close. She was crying silently.

10

At the Hotel Hillview, where Max had been staying since arriving in Bukoba, the staff dragged its feet with energy, as if trying to punish the floor for some ancestral insult. An indescribable and unpleasant odour arose from the kitchen hidden behind a filthy curtain. The only living beings that took their work seriously were the cockroaches, discreet yet fearsome as they did battle with customers and staff and emerged triumphant every time.

Max chose this palace to be as far as possible from Henry Kilonzo, who had his headquarters along with his sidekick, Shembazi, at the Walkgard, the region's best hotel, even if the Hillview was the favourite haunt of state employees, at least according to Valéria. Swimming pool, breathtaking view, excellent dining, and other delicacies — the two police officers must have partaken liberally of those things at their accommodations.

For greater freedom of movement, Max had cut back on comfort. At first sight the Hillview seemed to aim for a Ugandan clientele. Did Zuberi the witch doctor's brother slip his guests fragments of albino bodies as part of the welcome package? The place was a rest stop on the road to Mwanza that bordered Lake Victoria to the south, and bus passengers from Kampala took a break there. After changing buses in Mutukula, travellers were tortured by the bad road that led to Bukoba, often flooded in the rainy season. In the lobby, beat-up burlap or cardboard suitcases stood in a heap. Many women were among the guests who killed time in the lobby, resigned and in good humour, sucking on Coca-Colas. The men were dressed like Jehovah's Witnesses: black-framed glasses and shiny suits, fashion, African-style.

At the front desk Max interrupted the clerk's conversation to show her the toy truck he'd picked up at Valéria's. He asked the clerk if he could find one like it in Bukoba. The question must have been common, since she told him right away where the supplier's workshop was — at the edge of town.

"Do you want a taxi?"

"No thanks. I'll find my way."

Relieved, the woman went back to her phone.

A gasping elevator deposited Max in front of the door to his room. Inside, the light flooded in through large windows stained with bird droppings. A view straight down to the swimming pool two floors below. With it came a strong odour of chlorine.

Max placed the toy truck on the desk and opened the mini-bar. He needed something strong to help get his thoughts in order. Sipping the tepid whisky, he considered Valéria and her tragic destiny. Pain and sadness gave way to questions; to keep from surrendering to melancholy, he had to keep his mind occupied. Max wracked his brain. To find out who had committed the double murder, he'd need to sift through Valéria's past and find the little thread that hung down, and when he pulled on it, make the entire garment unravel.

First, the albinos.

This lifelong cause she'd been fighting for stemmed from the crime she'd committed with her father. She'd confessed to Max, hoping to lighten her burden, but to no avail. Why had she chosen him to tell her story to? Her helping the albinos was a way of lessening the evil and undoing the horrible act she'd taken part in that day. She'd devoted herself entirely to the cause, giving unstintingly to it and pulling Sophie in with her. No wonder they neglected what was happening behind their backs at the foundation and hadn't discovered the dishonest accountant's plot.

Valéria and Sophie did their best to hide the theft and save the foundation. Max understood why they acted carefully and discreetly. They didn't panic, which was remarkable in itself. If the donors learned that the foundation had been victimized by an embezzler and that its finances had been overseen by a criminal for a number of years, they would have suspended their contributions and demanded a reckoning from Valéria. She'd always treated them with care, knowing that without the donors' participation her work with the albinos would fail. Her campaign for capital punishment had cooled some of them — most notably the members of certain church groups — and Valéria had to work hard to reassure them all. She couldn't afford a financial scandal that would imperil her organization.

The disappearance of Jonathan Harris's million got Max thinking. The murderer was behind it, or so it seemed. The two women had been forced to provide the banking details needed to access the funds, just as Max had done with Harris. But the transaction had taken place more than two hours after the murders, according to Kilonzo's evaluation. Normally, the killer should have waited to get his hands on the money before liquidating the two women. But what if the money had been cashed in by someone else, like Teresa Mwandenga, the accountant, now in Dubai? That might be. The murderer could have been her accomplice — that was a possibility, too.

At the Women's Legal Aid Centre, where Max went after he returned from Kagondo, Désirée Lubadsa, a small, energetic woman with sparkling eyes, described Valéria's deep involvement in the causes of Tanzanian women and the way she did everything in her power to help resolve the many problems they faced. Rapes, divorces, custody of children …

"Valéria might have angered a husband or a family member," Max suggested.

Lubadsa shook her head. "Not very likely. To my knowledge, no one ever threatened her."

"Do you have a list of the women she helped recently?"

"No. Everything was done informally. Every week, on Wednesdays, Valéria used one of these offices to talk with the women who would come to see her. That was all."

"She didn't use her volunteer work to recruit new clients?"

Lubadsa was scandalized by the insinuation. Valéria didn't need any more work. On the contrary, she and her daughter had their hands full. Yet Sophie had told him in Lamu that her mother wanted to branch out and find new customers.

Max hadn't picked up on that at the time.

"Valéria was the very definition of honesty," Lubadsa said decisively. "She never took advantage of anyone. It was the other way around, really. In Bukoba, everyone abused her generosity to the point that Dr. Scofield had to talk some sense into her."

At the start, when she first became interested in the albino cause, Valéria had set up a London office presided over by Dr. Harold Scofield, a retired ophthalmologist. Max had found several emails addressed to him on Valéria's computer. Each time Max visited, she had long conversations with the doctor.

From his room at the Hillview, Max called Scofield in Greenwich. He identified himself as an investigator from the Canadian police mandated by the High Commission to shed light on the double murder. Thanks to her marriage to Richard Stroner, Valéria and her daughter had Canadian citizenship.

"I'd be glad to help. What do you want to know, Mr. …?"

"Cheskin. Robert Cheskin."

"We spoke to each other on a regular basis, but we haven't seen each other for at least two years."

"What exactly is your role?"

"Concerning the foundation?"

"Yes."

"Essentially, I reassure donors."

"Do they send the money to you?"

"At first they did, but not anymore. Valéria and her daughter administered the foundation directly from Bukoba. My job is to promote their work within my own circle which, to be honest, isn't that wide."

A year earlier, for example, at Valéria's request, he'd helped finance the construction of a school on the eastern side of Ukerewe Island. A significant community of albinos had found safe haven there.

The population of the island had no use for the superstitions attached to albinos and didn't hunt them down as happened elsewhere. Over the years, the place had become an oasis for them and had taken on the name Albino Island. It had the largest albino population in Tanzania.

"That's why there's such a great demand for schools and health services," Scofield explained.

"And was this school actually built?"

"Yes. With foundation money."

"Were the sums you raised sent directly to Valéria?"

"To her accountant."

"Teresa Mwandenga?"

"Yes."

"Did you go to the school? Did you see it with your own eyes?"

"Why are you asking?"

"Are you certain it was built?"

"I saw the photos. What are you insinuating, Mr. Cheskin?"

"Nothing. Valéria and her daughter were murdered, and I'm trying to find out why. For now, their work with albinos seems to be the strongest angle."

"Don't overestimate the traffickers' power and organizational abilities. They're low-life types with no scruples, but they live hand to mouth with little idea of what they're doing."

In Scofield's opinion, this wasn't a structured business with a hierarchy like the drug or arms trade. On the contrary, it was the work of small, opportunistic operators.

Yet on the evening he travelled to Minziro, Max felt he was witnessing the work of an efficient organization. No one could kidnap a dozen albinos from different villages, kill them, dismember them, and ship their body parts across East Africa without some level of organization and a clear hierarchy with contacts in police forces throughout the region.

Max decided not to follow that line of inquiry just yet. Instead, he asked the doctor, "So you don't think the traffickers are responsible for the death of the two women?"

"I have no idea. From my point of view, it's difficult imagining them attacking Valéria and her daughter. What would they have to gain? Nothing."

Scofield was right. Valéria's actions in the political arena had made waves, but the traffickers' schemes wouldn't be made easier if she disappeared. The death penalty would remain, and so would the initiatives adopted by the Tanzanian government. And with the death of the two women, pressure might just mount on traffickers and their clients, the medicine men. The murder of Valéria and her daughter wouldn't benefit the albino hunters.

Max would have to look elsewhere.

"Who sent you the photos of Ukerewe? Valéria?"

"The school principal, Naomi Mulunga."

"When was your last conversation with Valéria?"

"Last week."

"Did she seem preoccupied?"

"As always."

"Did she ever talk to you about a boy named Daniel?"

"Who's that?"

"I don't know. I thought you might."

"She never mentioned that name," Scofield told Max.

After a shower and a quick lunch, Max tried to reach Jason Chagula, the lawyer who had defended Awadhi Zuberi and done the same for Samuel Musindo. Max had learned in the meantime from Kilonzo that Chagula was working in Rwanda now, in Kigali, as a consultant for the Kagame government. Max left him a detailed message and asked him to call back as soon as possible but didn't mention his relation with Valéria.

In the afternoon, Max headed for the address the desk clerk had given him. As he left Bukoba behind, he came upon a street bordered by stalls and restaurants, full of merchants, mostly Indian, their ears glued to their cellphones. They were businessmen chased out

of Uganda by Idi Amin and his ethnic cleansing program in the 1970s. They'd stayed on in Tanzania after
the dictator had been toppled thanks to Julius Nyerere's
intervention.

In his madness, Idi Amin took it into his head to
invade Tanzania and aimed his aggression at the Bukoba
region and the western shores of Lake Victoria. This
followed years of provocation by the Ugandan dictator
whose hatred for Nyerere was legendary.

The two men couldn't have been more different. Idi
Amin was a bloodthirsty brute who could scarcely read
and write and whose cruelty was his trademark — he had
even been accused of practising cannibalism. Nyerere
was educated at the University of Edinburgh, a former
teacher, an intellectual who happened to stray into the
political arena. Yet in the recordings made public after
his death, Idi Amin admitted to loving Nyerere with a
passion as strong as the kind a woman has for a man.

Was Nyerere Idi Amin's fantasy?

Whatever the case, the dictator's fascination didn't
soften Nyerere. As soon as Ugandan troops bombed
Bukoba and invaded northern Tanzania, he sent his
army, equipped and funded by the Chinese, to fight
Idi Amin's troops, themselves equipped and funded by
Libya's Colonel Gaddafi. The Tanzanians chased their
rivals back to Kampala, forcing the dictator to flee to
Libya where he found refuge. Later, in 2003, he died in
exile in Saudi Arabia.

It was a spectacular operation, but it cast a shadow
on Nyerere's more important and daring policies. In
the 1960s, as well as imposing his African version of

socialism called *ujamaa*, he put forward a program to mix populations. The goal was to end social divisions based on tribal criteria and pursue his Marxist-Leninist ideal of equality of all people and the struggle against ethnic nationalism. Criticized at first, the policy produced a more mixed Tanzania, preventing outbreaks and epidemics of tribalism that had tarnished the independence of several African countries. No racial or religious conflict in Tanzania. No ethnic cleansing like elsewhere around Lake Victoria. The annexation of the island of Zanzibar, independent until 1964, was carried out calmly, a first for any African state.

Julius Nyerere went even further in his experiment. He made Swahili, one of the country's minority languages spoken by no more than five percent of the population, the official language of Tanzania. It was all the more surprising since it wasn't even his native tongue. The founder of the republic made that decision to prevent one of the more common languages — Sukuma, for example, in the Lake Victoria region — from becoming the dominant one, which would have left the impression that Tanzania was being governed by one particular ethnic group.

That decision encouraged the flowering of Swahili, a language from then on spoken along the eastern coast from the borders of Somalia to south of Zanzibar.

When Max showed a peasant the toy truck, the latter pointed out a dirt track that angled off toward the north. A workshop came into view a few minutes later, with a yard filled with objects of all kinds surrounding an old shed. He parked the Jeep and walked over to a man shovelling garbage into a bucket. The man straightened. An Indian with a round belly whose forehead dripped with sweat. He beckoned Max into the workshop. It was filled with toys of all kinds, all made of cast-off objects. Max showed him the little truck.

The man took out his glasses and inspected it. "It's very well made," he said, as if commenting on a Makonde sculpture.

"Does it come from your shop?"

"I doubt it. This kind of truck, a dump truck, I rarely see."

"Did you know Valéria Michieka?"

"The lawyer who was killed? I know who she is, but I never met her. What happened is terrible."

"Did Valéria come and buy this toy?"

"No."

"Outside of you, who could she have gotten it from?"

"Everyone."

These sorts of recycled toys had become all the rage for poverty tourists visiting the continent. These days they were found in every gift shop next to African sculptures, real and fake.

"This one probably comes from Mwanza or somewhere near. Look at this part."

Max came closer and squinted.

"Right here, you see?" The man pointed out one of the sides of the dump truck. "It's the logo of the Mwanza Brewery. A popular beer east of Lake Victoria. If you ask me, that's where your artist lives."

11

Roselyn had always liked her son-in-law, Peter Sawyer. Solid, honest, though a little too plain for her. After Norah died, she figured he would leave and pursue his career as a policeman elsewhere. But for whatever reason, he chose to stay in Huntsville and never remarried.

Peter looked up from the file he was reading when Roselyn came into his office at police headquarters. In his official voice, the same one he used to introduce her to his colleagues, he spoke. "To one degree or another, as leader or member of the tie-down team, your husband was involved in two hundred and thirty-four executions during his career."

"I know that."

He handed her a sheet of paper that she merely glanced at. Names that meant nothing to her, dates going back to 1984 when Albert received his promotion. As well, in a column to the right, the list of crimes of which these unknown men were guilty. For the first time, she understood how extensive her husband's work was.

More executions were carried out in Texas than anywhere else in the United States, the only country in the Western world still enforcing capital punishment. And Albert Kerensky had been the greatest legal killer in the Western world during those years.

The idea made Roselyn's head spin. She set the paper on the desk in front of her. "What are you trying to tell me?"

Peter cleared his throat. "Even if I don't think we'll get anywhere with this, I have to examine every possibility."

The day before, Peter's superior had entrusted the file to Kenneth Brownstein, one of his colleagues. After questioning Roselyn, Brownstein went to Stanford Hill with her to meet Mrs. Callaghan. Roselyn felt a little guilty when she realized the woman knew Albert's habits better than she did. The policeman seemed not to notice.

Glenn Forrester, with whom Brownstein had already spoken, hadn't mentioned the visit to the cemetery, or at least that was what Roselyn concluded. She decided to keep mum, as well. Glenn must have had his reasons for staying tight-lipped. She didn't want to make trouble for him, and besides, nothing had actually happened apart from Albert's one short sentence.

That evening Peter had promised Roselyn he would check out certain things, but without saying what they were.

And now this list.

"Do you think Albert's disappearance is related to one of these men?" Roselyn asked.

"I have no idea. I hope not. But I can't ignore that possibility."

Roselyn said nothing. She could have reminded Peter that Albert had left on his own, of his own free will. He had planned his departure, as his preparations showed.

"I asked Kenneth's assistant, Nancy, to pay particular attention to the last thirteen years," Peter said.

"Why?"

"Starting in 1996, the families of the guilty and the victim were allowed to attend the execution. People witnessed Albert at work, if I can put it that way. Until then the executioner was just a cog in the penitentiary machine. No one knew who he was. Things changed in 1996. People could put a name and a face to the man who administered the lethal injection."

Observers didn't see the tie-down team at work, but the head of the team accompanied the families of the condemned man into the room to watch. For years that person was Albert Kerensky.

And now Peter seemed to be saying that a family member or friend of someone Albert had executed could have returned, looking for revenge.

Roselyn closed her eyes. Maybe Peter's theory was the fantasy of an overzealous policeman, but the logic did hold up. If what he said was true, the conclusion could be terrible. She imagined her husband in a sordid basement where he would be made to pay for one of his executions.

"Are you all right?"

Roselyn opened her eyes. "Yes. I'm sorry. All that's just so …"

"Again, I'm getting ahead of myself, ahead of the facts. Any moment now the phone might ring and we'll find out that Albert's been found safe and sound, and we'll forget about all this. Life will go back to normal."

But the phone didn't ring.

Peter cleared his throat again. "I printed out the list of people who attended executions while Albert was the head of the tie-down team, and I sent it to the Texas Department of Criminal Justice, as well as the National Name Check Program of the FBI in Washington. This morning the list came back to me with some troubling results. Criminals did attend several of Albert's executions. I was able to check the files of the ones who seemed to present the greatest danger. My conclusion is that we need to look into four of them."

Peter set out what he'd learned. First, the two younger brothers of Franklin Crispel, executed in March 2002 for the rape and murder of a young woman kidnapped in front of a cash machine in the San Antonio suburbs, were later found guilty of several counts of armed robbery, as if the execution of their brother had pushed them into crime. Six months ago Carl and Kenneth Crispel were released from a Pennsylvania penitentiary. They currently lived in Austin.

Duane Berkley broke into a house in Dallas, not knowing that the owners, a couple in their sixties, were inside. He killed them both after torturing them, wrongly believing they'd hidden a large sum of money somewhere in the house. Berkley's wife, Colleen, was in the room when he was executed in 2004. A year later to the day, Colleen was stopped by the Huntsville police for going through a red light. In the trunk of her car was a pump action Mossberg 500 rifle.

And then there was the Keith Busby case. Busby was found guilty of murdering his girlfriend, who'd recently left him for another man — and Busby killed him, too. To the very end, Busby claimed he was innocent. Among the family members who attended the execution, there was the condemned man's father, Cleve, who had contacts with the criminal element in Miami. He left the room that morning, shouting that the people who killed his son would pay, and pay dearly. The guards had to escort him out of the Walls Unit.

Roselyn had stopped listening. All those ruined lives made her sick. For years her husband had shrouded his job in silence, and now the true nature, the horror of his work, had become clear to her. The men Albert executed were all guilty, of that she had no doubt, no matter what they claimed. But the wounded souls they left behind continued to suffer, and not only the victims' families. The crimes had contaminated the lives of everyone associated with them, even at a distance, the guilty party and the victims united by the same event. Roselyn now understood why Albert had wanted to distance his wife and daughter from this reality. It was his way of protecting his loved ones so they might live a normal life like any other American family. Roselyn had considered him cold and distant, but that was his way of defending himself and her.

"Again, we shouldn't be too quick to draw conclusions," Peter reminded her. "At any moment the phone —"

"I know."

By the time she left the police station, Roselyn was badly in need of normality, to get her bearings back on solid ground. She was dizzy and swallowed an Aspirin in the car, then waited for it to take effect. On her way to Peter's house, where she was staying, her phone buzzed. It was Brian Pallister from the Wildlife Artists' Association.

"Has Albert come back?" he asked.

"No. But the police are optimistic."

A little white lie, but what else could she say?

Still, Roselyn felt reassured. One of her friends cared about her husband. Brian was a retired architect, and time weighed on him, so he turned his interest toward amateur painting. She made a note to thank him when she returned to Houston.

"How is it going at the Four Seasons?"

"They've followed our recommendations. Everything's ready for the show."

"You know I won't be there."

"I understand. If ever you need anything ..."

"That's nice of you. I'll be in touch."

She ended the conversation just as she was turning into Peter's driveway on his tree-lined Huntsville street.

Adrian was stretched out in front of the TV as usual. Since turning thirteen, he'd fallen into the sullen, secretive silence of teenagers. Roselyn asked him how his day had been.

"Did you find Grandpa?"

"Not yet."

Adrian didn't seem concerned. Roselyn envied him as she fixed him a plate of milk and cookies.

"Your friend, Brian, called the station," Peter told her when he came in at the end of the afternoon.

"I know. I talked to him."

"What's up?"

"Nothing. I don't want him to worry."

"Of course."

At first when she came to stay here, the concern, care, and warmth were welcome, but now all that attention weighed on her. Roselyn wanted to be alone with her distress, but she was forever being called on to talk, explain, and give an account of her feelings. She was exhausted.

She made dinner for Peter and Adrian, and they ate in front of the TV, but she didn't touch her plate. She went out onto the porch that overlooked the garden that Norah once tended but that Peter had transferred to a neighbour, a secretary from the Ellis Unit who'd come here to live with her family. Sitting comfortably in a wicker chair, Roselyn tried to make sense of things. In any renovation project involving architecture, Brian had said to her one day, there always came a time when, caught between the city's demands, budgetary constraints, and the contractors' hidden agenda, the parties seemed to lose control of the project. When that happened, he sought out his own counsel, with no external influences, and trusted his judgment untainted by the interests of other parties. Roselyn felt like that now.

What exactly did she know about her husband's disappearance? His departure was voluntary, or at least it appeared that way. No one had shown up at Stanford Hill Residence, a sawed-off shotgun in hand, no one had thrown Albert into a car blindfolded. He could have been the victim of someone's call to lure him away from Huntsville. In that case, the trap would have had to be set long ago, since Albert had waited for his prescriptions to be filled before heading for the hills.

And how could anyone communicate with Albert? Through the Internet, like teenage girls seduced by cyber-predators? Albert didn't know what the Internet was, he didn't own a computer, and Roselyn had never seen him in the basement common room with the others, where Mrs. Callaghan had set up a small computer centre. She would have to check with her. Albert could have gone digital without informing her. Anything was possible.

And then there was that surprising visit to the cemetery with Glenn Forrester. What Albert had said to Norah, the promise he'd made her. His silence and indifference afterward that was so hard to fathom.

The more Roselyn thought about it, the more she was sure Albert had left of his own volition, but for reasons she knew nothing about. Her husband didn't have an impulsive mind; he planned everything ahead of time, sometimes months in advance. Perhaps his decision to separate from her and live on his own at Stanford Hill was part of his scheme, the first step. He told her nothing to protect her, once again.

Protect her from what?

Roselyn had no idea. After Albert's promise at the cemetery, it made sense that his disappearance might have something to do with their daughter. Had something happened to Norah in the past that had led her husband to set things straight now? But their daughter's short life contained no drama, no major upset until the sickness that had laid her low.

There had to be something else that Norah had hidden from her. Roselyn was saddened when she considered that her husband and daughter could have shared a secret and kept her out of it. Norah would have never concealed something from her own mother. Sooner or later she would have broken down, let something slip, and burst into tears, making her confession.

Roselyn closed her eyes. She feared Albert's disappearance would lead her to discover terrible things, things best hidden in the shroud of time, things that would tarnish her memories of their lives together, the three of them, a happiness she never suspected had been so fragile.

12

Nyamukazi, south of Bukoba, was a combination port and public market where merchants from the area came to buy fish directly from fishermen. A canning plant stood higher on a hill, and it was common to see refrigerated trucks from the company waiting as boats came in at the end of the day with their cargoes of Nile perch. Once their catch had been divvied up by the wholesalers, the fishermen inspected their nets and repaired them before going out again early the next morning. In the meantime, they sat on the pier in a semicircle or alone, patiently darning the mesh, commenting on the day's events.

Max liked observing the action. It was a mix of laughter and hard work, weighing and selling fish to middlemen, the fishermen yelling jokes or insults at one another, or both at once, it was hard to tell.

But today they were all on their best behaviour. Three police vehicles were parked on the beach.

Inspector Kilonzo had set a meeting with Max near the wharf where several policemen encircled a fisherman. His fellow workers kept a healthy distance from him as if they, too, were afraid of being questioned and pushed into self-incriminating answers.

Kilonzo spotted Max and walked over to him. "We might have something."

He escorted Max toward the group and pushed aside his officers. A man in work clothes was sitting on the edge of a boat, back bent, eyes averted. At his feet lay a net that he'd probably been repairing when the police had shown up.

"Tell him what you saw," Kilonzo ordered, pointing at Max.

Because of engine trouble that day, not far past Bukoba, the fisherman had to quit work before anyone else. After paddling for a good hour, he came to rest on the shore south of the town.

He barely spoke English, and the little he knew he'd probably learned from the rare tourists who ventured to this side of Lake Victoria.

"What day was that?" Kilonzo asked, giving the man a cigarette that he slipped into the pocket of his coveralls.

"The day before the murder."

This was clearly not the first time he'd told his story, and he seemed to have grown fond of it, as if he'd rehearsed his presentation in preparation for Max's arrival.

"Go ahead, talk," Kilonzo urged.

The fisherman had dragged his boat onto the beach and started working on his engine, trying to find the problem. That was when he noticed the four-by-four higher up, near the road. Beside it was a man with binoculars. The guy noticed the fisherman but wasn't surprised or alarmed. A minute later he went back to his observations. In the fisherman's opinion, he had his eye on Valéria Michieka's house.

"Are you sure?" Kilonzo asked. "He wasn't a tourist?"

The fisherman shrugged. "Not him."

From the point, he went on, you could see Valéria's place.

Once he'd fixed his engine, the fisherman headed back onto the lake without giving the event a second thought. Later, after he heard what had happened to Valéria and her daughter, despite his friends' warnings not to, he decided to call the police.

When he was finished talking, the fisherman snapped up his net and rolled it into a ball.

Max was suddenly reminded of the men in Zanzibar who attached albino fingers to their trawl lines for a better catch. "Do you know where the four-by-four came from?"

The fisherman had no idea. But he was surprised to see the Codan satellite radio communication system that the vehicle was equipped with. That kind of equipment was rarely seen in the area, except in national parks and hunting grounds. Two years earlier the fisherman worked in Rubondo Island Park cleaning vehicles used on safaris. There, he'd been around high-end Land Rovers and

Mitsubishis that were almost never seen on the Kagera roads. When he spotted the four-by-four higher up on the beach, he recognized the type right away.

"Then what happened?" Kilonzo asked.

"Nothing. The guy with the binoculars got into the vehicle and left."

Max glanced at Kilonzo, who was delighted at this new information.

"The tire tracks outside Valéria's house," the inspector said. "I bet they come from that four-by-four."

Max thought Kilonzo was a little too eager, as if, once again, his investigation had only one goal: to impress him. A scene-setting that was done for his benefit. He needed convincing. The truth came second.

Three national parks lay several hours' distance from Bukoba. Rubondo Island, where the fisherman had worked, wasn't easy to get to. The occasional ferry and a few private boats made the trip. Most visitors preferred to arrive by plane from Mwanza or Arusha, Kilonzo explained. They were tourists or photographers looking for less frequented safaris than the usual ones in the Serengeti. The two other parks, Biharamulo and Burigi, catered to a different clientele: hunters. From Bukoba the parks could be reached by the road that met up with the Dar es Salaam highway farther south.

The witness returned to work, and Kilonzo led Max to his own vehicle. Without asking permission, the policeman sat next to him, trailed by Shembazi.

"I'll guide you," the inspector said.

Kilonzo motioned his men to follow, and the caravan got under way. *A hell of a way to run an investigation,*

Max thought. But this was no time to show that he wasn't fooled by the policeman's antics.

A few kilometres past Nyamukazi, Max spotted a group of Chinese men wearing black suits and ties, appearing very studious, guided by a young woman showing them around a construction site. The infatuation for the Chinese had spread across the continent. They were the new saviours who would break Africa out of its doldrums.

"President Komba got on the train too late," Kilonzo remarked. "He still thought America would save him."

"You forget the railway between Dar es Salaam and Zambia."

The Chinese had carried out that colossal project in the 1970s, and Valéria's family had worked on it. That was where her big brother, Evans, first felt the pains of the disease that killed him.

"Those were the days of Julius Nyerere," Kilonzo replied. "He broke with the West Germans and the British for ideological reasons. He opened his arms wide to Chinese aid."

As a socialist, Nyerere preferred to do without West German help than stop doing business with the East. And he slammed the door on the British when they refused to boycott the racist regime in what was then called Rhodesia.

"That's ancient history," Kilonzo said. "Forgotten quarrels."

"But the Chinese are still here," Max pointed out.

"We've always been able to count on them."

The inspector was right. When Nyerere decided to answer Idi Amin's attacks and liberate the people of

Uganda from his reign of terror, neither the Germans nor the British supported him, but the Chinese did.

The Chinese appetite for raw materials increased their interest in Tanzania. And the Komba government answered by opening the doors wide.

"Joseph Lugembe continued Komba's work when he took over the presidency," the policeman told Max.

Lugembe owed his meteoric rise to power to Komba, as Kilonzo explained. After Nyerere stepped down, Komba found himself head of state. He set out to modernize the country and dust off its civil service. In 1991 the fall of the Soviet empire, once a model but a model that had run out of steam, marked the beginning of a formidable decade of economic progress for Tanzania.

Komba surrounded himself with modern, educated men with their eyes on the future, who could discuss with the West as equals. Joseph Lugembe was that kind of man. It wasn't surprising that when he sensed the time was right to retire and to begin searching for an heir apparent to continue his work, Komba turned to Lugembe. For the international community, Lugembe seemed to be a credible leader, one of the hopes for a new Africa, far from tyrants like Mobutu Sese Seko, Laurent Gbagbo, or Robert Mugabe, who pillaged the wealth of their countries and got rich off their citizens' poverty.

"Perfectionists accuse Lugembe of being a despot in disguise and playing at democracy," Kilonzo said. "Maybe that's true. But he was able to preserve Nyerere's legacy and set us on the path to the future. Barack Obama was the first to see that."

Obama again. Were Africans so discouraged by their leaders that they had to transfer their hopes to the president of a foreign nation?

After an hour and a half of driving, the town of Biharamulo came into view. Followed by Shembazi and his men, Kilonzo led Max to the park's administrative headquarters. Inside was a counter where permits were issued and checked, a small office where an employee worked, who was astonished and impressed by the police deployment. On the wall, the usual photos of big game brought low by hunters in paramilitary getup, rifles in hand, an impala or a leopard lying at their feet in imitation of Ernest Hemingway.

In 1994 the prey changed. The Tutsis, who were being hunted down, flooded into the reserve, since Biharamulo and Burigi weren't far from the Rwandan border.

"When that country went crazy," Kilonzo remembered, "Komba's government had to send in the army to keep the peace and make sure the Hutu militias didn't invade."

At the worst points in the civil war, and continuing afterward, Burigi was host to one of the largest refugee camps in the region. Coming back from a visit to one of those camps, Richard Stroner, Valéria's husband and Sophie's father, met his death in a road accident.

The guard on duty was from Bukoba. While Kilonzo kept Max busy outside, his men went through the list of employees. They had already undergone a security check before being hired to make sure they weren't mixed up in criminal activities, especially those involving poaching.

The list was examined and produced nothing. Kilonzo questioned the guard personally and made no further progress.

"If you ask me," said the guard, "you'll find the same thing at the other reserves and parks. Key positions aren't given to just anyone."

Max looked on, bemused.

"Could it have been a freelance guide?" asked Kilonzo.

Many safari companies used such guides, and it was impossible to determine their character. And some of those companies had Land Rovers and Mitsubishis equipped with Codan communications.

"But those vehicles normally display the company's logo on the door," Kilonzo told Max.

The guard nodded his agreement. The fisherman hadn't mentioned seeing any logo. But it wouldn't be hard work to hide, or simpler still, borrow a private vehicle that belonged to someone else.

"You need a permit to use satellite communications," Kilonzo retorted. "I'll order the list of permits for the Kagera region and eliminate commercial companies like the travel agencies that offer safaris and the like."

The guard nodded again.

Shembazi got in touch with the Ministry of National Parks. A few minutes later Kilonzo had a list of five names, all linked to churches or missions around Bukoba. The information would need to be verified, though with subtler methods than the one used with the guard at the reserve. The missions were never happy to have the police show up, especially if they were there to check on employees.

Max nodded. Kilonzo was playing his role perfectly. He seemed determined, professional. Max had no doubt that a guilty person would be found sooner or later, though he thought it unlikely it would be the man responsible for killing Valéria and her daughter.

Shembazi checked the online archives to see if one of the five names had been investigated, or if a complaint had been filed. Four of the five missions boasted clean slates, but the fifth, All Saints Church, an Anglican mission, had registered a formal complaint against the witch doctor Zuberi, Samuel Musindo's alleged accomplice. The church owned an all-terrain vehicle with the Codan satellite communication system.

The coincidence was promising, at least at first sight. "Remember," Kilonzo pointed out, "All Saints Church specializes in rehabilitating former prisoners and giving them a second chance. One of them, dazzled by the thought of a rich lawyer living nearby, a potentially defenceless woman, to boot, might have carried out the operation. The anonymous four-by-four, impossible to track down, would never have been noticed if not for the fisherman making repairs on his engine."

Kilonzo had staged the scene flawlessly. Nothing was left to chance. Max couldn't help but admire how the inspector was playing the game.

The mission was located in the back country, on the way to Rwanda. A series of smaller buildings were set around a solid red-brick structure that reminded Max of Lancashire cottages. The place seemed surprisingly calm but that hadn't always been the case. In 1994, Kilonzo told Max, Pastor Summers had opened the church's grounds to Rwandan refugees. For weeks the area had been a regular anthill, teeming with refugees and soldiers from the Tanzanian army sent to the border by President Komba.

As they drove up to the mission, Max looked for a four-wheel drive in the lot, but there was only a beat-up Toyota. A tall bald man stepped out of one of the smaller buildings and came out to meet them. He was British, in his sixties, and had spent the past forty years in this country, surviving one tragedy after another without losing hope in human nature. Nothing could faze the good man.

In his office lined with photos of Dover, where he was from, he explained to Kilonzo and Max that he'd stopped hiring former prisoners several years ago. He'd had too many bad experiences. He trusted people, opened the doors of his mission to them, and too often had been the victim of his own generosity.

"You own an all-terrain vehicle according to our records," Kilonzo said.

"A Mitsubishi. It was stolen ten days ago."

"Right before Valéria's death," Kilonzo pointed out.

Max was bored. *Let's just get to the end of this bad melodrama*, he thought.

"I informed the police when I learned of the theft."

Kilonzo shook his head and frowned as he glanced at Max. No one in Bukoba had bothered sharing that information with him. When all this was settled, he would have to clean house. Find out who had betrayed him and make him pay.

"Do you suspect anyone?" the inspector asked. "One of your former employees?"

"I lent the vehicle to everyone who asked. My mistake."

"Do you have a list of who used it?"

The pastor handed Kilonzo a sheet of paper. He passed it over to Shembazi. A minute later, as they were preparing to leave, Shembazi returned with an answer. One of the ex-prisoners lived in the area.

"Would you like to come with us, Cheskin, and see how an arrest is made?"

"I'm sure you'll do fine. The poor criminal doesn't stand a chance."

Two hours later, as Max was entering Bukoba, a voice he recognized came on the radio. It was Kilonzo, announcing a major new development in the murders of Valéria Michieka and Sophie Stroner. A suspect had been identified, to all intents and purposes the guilty party. A small-time criminal from Dar es Salaam who was well known to police.

Disgusted, Max switched off the radio.

His cellphone rang. It was Jason Chagula, agreeing to meet him at his office tomorrow at noon.

13

From the airport to downtown Kigali, heavy trucks loaded with goods blocked the road. Or perhaps it was the city employees, sending traffic down side streets to avoid roadworks, only to find those, too, were under construction.

For the past hour, the driver had been muttering and swearing, furious and impatient, shaking his fist and leaning on the horn. The *matutus* tried to make their way among the bicycles, motorcycles, and pedestrians, stoic, moving through the crowd nonchalantly, carrying all kinds of products. Land Rovers from humanitarian aid organizations tried to avoid the traffic jam, but they were bogged down along with the Audis and Mercedes-Benzes that belonged to the beautiful people of the new Rwandan economic boom.

There was no way out. No matter what the vehicle, the roads were a mess and forward motion was impos-sible. Max thought he was travelling to a sleepy capital city. Instead he got a forest of cranes and building sites.

"That's the Kigali City Tower!" the driver shouted.

Since Paul Kagame had taken power, Rwanda had been on the road to economic development. At the airport Roosevelt Okambo's Cessna had flown over enormous billboards praising the country's economic stability. The customs official smiled at the tourists like a carpet seller. The airport was clean and functional, more like an exhibition hall than a place to take a plane. An hour away, the Nairobi airport, a dusty, disorderly place, seemed to belong to another time. At first sight the 1994 genocide was far in the distant past, a painful memory that everyone tried to forget by working frenetically.

Max had hired Okambo for the day, hoping to return to Bukoba before nightfall. Jason Chagula, the lawyer, had answered the call of the Kagame government to help reduce and then eliminate corruption to make the country more attractive to foreign investment. Chagula had built up a certain amount of experience in the field, having worked for the Tanzanian government in its fight against corruption, once he put aside his career as a criminal lawyer. Still more proof that Kagame wanted to align himself with English-speaking Africa. After all, he spoke very little French himself, having spent many years in exile in Uganda. A few months earlier he'd made English the language of government and education.

Chagula waved him over the minute Max stepped onto the terrace that bordered the swimming pool at the Hôtel des Mille Collines. Even if he worked for the government, he admitted to Max, he kept a few private clients and liked to receive them here under a parasol with a glass of lemonade, his files on the table and his cellphone close at hand. During his career in Dar es Salaam, he'd cultivated an image as a dandy who never lifted a finger, though his track record said different. Very casually, before setting up shop in Kigali, he'd managed to achieve acquittals or reduce the sentences of the accused he'd defended over the past twenty years.

The lawyer had failed with Musindo but succeeded in freeing Zuberi the witch doctor, whom the authorities had suspected of inciting the former to kidnap and murder the minister of home affairs' daughter.

Chagula had heard about Valéria's tragic death. They'd been law students together at Makerere University in Uganda. Back then they'd shared the same ideas when it came to shutting down the trafficking in albinos but had gone their separate ways when Valéria demanded the return of the death penalty.

"I didn't agree. And I told her more than once. But she wouldn't listen to me."

"Did she criticize you for defending Musindo and Zuberi?"

"Yes, probably. But we'd broken off contact well before the trials."

"Tell me about Zuberi."

"Not much of a talker. Shy despite his threatening air. I saw that immediately. He'd always wanted to be a pastor, but the Presbyterians rejected him. So he turned to magic — potions, creams, and other accessories."

"Including albino body parts."

"Maybe. Like all the others."

"And you defended him, anyway?"

"Whatever you might think of Zuberi, the evidence against him was slim. Vague threats against Lugembe. Indirect, as well. When Zuberi was in jail, a few months before the minister's daughter was killed, Lugembe supposedly received a message that his daughter would be harmed if Zuberi wasn't freed … and fast. Those were just rumours. Nothing concrete was ever presented."

"Musindo and Zuberi knew each other, right?"

"The dispensary where Musindo worked is close to the village where Zuberi was born. At the time he had a practice there. Patients move back and forth between science and superstition. They didn't want to risk offending either, or missing out on some benefit. I would've done the same. You, too, most likely. That's human nature. Before the trial, when I first visited him in his cell, I tried to make him understand that his closed, hardened face would play against him. I put him in front of a mirror. I told him, look, that's the guy who's going to face the jury. Would you give him the benefit of the doubt? These aren't your patients, your customers, your victims. These are educated people who aren't going to believe in your miracle cures and visions."

Chagula laughed at his own joke. But his next question was serious. "Do you think he could be involved in the murder of Valéria Michieka and her daughter?" Chagula was obviously trying to tease out what Max knew.

"What do you think?" Max asked.

"I can't imagine him killing anybody."

"That's been said of many killers."

"You're right, but Zuberi isn't the type. A strange man with a twisted manner — that's true. But not a killer."

"He could've hired someone to do it."

Chagula sighed, as if bored with the subject. "You need to understand the role of healers in Tanzanian society."

More magician than mafioso, Chagula explained, they invented potions, elixirs, and other concoctions that they tried out on the poor and defenceless, the desperate. The authorities didn't trust them, but they played a role in the Tanzanian health care system nonetheless: where the government didn't have the resources to go, witch doctors took its place. Valéria attacked the lot of them, and Zuberi in particular, without provoking any reprisals, at least according to Chagula. No matter what she might have said, their business wasn't affected.

"Except for Zuberi," Max pointed out. "He did time in jail, had to leave the region."

"Yes, but he was already a millionaire — in dollars, not shillings. He used the unpleasantness to disappear. It's as simple as that."

"Has he contacted you since he was freed?"

"No."

"Do you know where he is? Where he lives?"

"Last I heard he was hiding somewhere in northern Tanzania. I don't know any more than that."

"His house is empty. But he's still the owner, according to what people say."

Chagula smiled. "I try not to maintain contact with my former clients unless they need my services a second time." The lawyer bent close to Max and lowered his voice, as if afraid someone was eavesdropping. "I don't know who's behind the murders, but I'd start with the murder of Clara Lugembe. There's a lot more hiding behind that story ... hard to separate truth from fiction."

Max waited for what was coming next.

"Did you know that Valéria Michieka met Samuel Musindo? They knew each other. There were pictures showing the two of them standing in front of the dispensary where he worked. Then all of a sudden the photos disappeared, and it's impossible to find them anywhere. I wanted to use them for the trial, but I couldn't."

Max was more than surprised. No one had ever told him that Valéria knew the man who murdered Clara Lugembe. And that included Valéria herself.

That set up a trio: Zuberi knew Musindo, who knew Valéria.

Chagula smiled again. "There are other disturbing facts. The living ghost of Zuberi the witch doctor has the authorities afraid. But it also hides many things and keeps people busy at certain key times. Do you want proof? You came here, didn't you?"

Max had to admit the man was right.

"What is the expression — a kangaroo court? Musindo's trial was stained with irregularities. And not just regarding Zuberi."

"Are you trying to say Musindo was innocent?"

"There's no doubt he was guilty. He admitted to the crime. All I was hoping was to commute his sentence to life in prison. But the authorities decided to make an example of him."

According to Chagula, more attention needed to be paid to the benefits Valéria Michieka and Joseph Lugembe derived from the trial. Michieka saw capital punishment reinstated for the murder of albinos. And Lugembe became a martyr, which earned him points in the race to replace President Komba.

"During the 1992 presidential campaign in the U.S., do you remember how Bill Clinton decided to attend the execution of Ricky Ray Rector, the man found guilty of killing an Arkansas policeman?"

"Vaguely," Max said. "I must have read about it in the papers."

"The man tried to kill himself when he was arrested, and all he managed to do was cause himself brain damage. Despite his diminished mental capacity, Rector was sentenced to death. Clinton's decision, not only to support the sentence but to attend the execution, gave him increased credibility among conservative voters. And that helped him win the presidency."

According to Chagula, the trial of Samuel Musindo, which was on the front page of every newspaper, helped Lugembe strengthen his position within his party and among Tanzanian citizens in general and build his reputation as a solid, trustworthy, rigorous man of state who wouldn't hesitate to apply the law if he became president. The tragic death of his adopted daughter made him into a larger-than-life character.

"Do you think he might have been responsible for the crime?" Max asked. "Or that he could have ordered the murder?"

"I wouldn't go that far. But from the political point

of view, the trial was very beneficial to him. He became president — to some degree he owes that to Clara's death."

At the airport Okambo was deep in conversation with a man in a wrinkled suit, a doctor the pilot was taking back to Bukoba. He sat in the back of the plane, his nose in the *New Times*. Max exchanged a few words with him and discovered that he shuttled between the two cities on a regular basis. There was a shortage of doctors in Kigali, what with the influx of people from the countryside streaming into the city searching for a better life. Whatever infrastructure the old regime had built wasn't up to the task. A new hospital was being planned, though no one knew where the staff would come from. When he found out Okambo was flying back to Bukoba, he asked if he could come along for the ride.

As he stared down at the hills of this magnificent country, Max had the clear feeling that his lightning visit had been useless and that his investigation was going nowhere. The only thing he'd learned was that Valéria and Clara Lugembe likely knew their murderer.

The Cessna began its descent toward the Bukoba airport. Max turned around; the doctor was tapping him on the shoulder.

The man spoke into his ear but loudly enough to be heard over the engine noise. "I knew Valéria Michieka very well."

He owned several houses just outside Bukoba and rented them to people working on contracts in the area.

Over the years, some of his tenants caused him problems, and he had used Valéria's services. For that, and other issues he didn't expand on.

"I don't share the conclusions of the police."

"You mean about Valéria's death?" Max asked, surprised.

"They're trying to cover something up. That's obvious." He paused. "I'm the one who wrote the death certificates, you know."

Max looked him in the eye. The doctor held his gaze. This plane ride might not be an accident, after all. "When did you sign the certificates?"

"A few hours after their deaths."

Kilonzo hadn't breathed a word about that.

"I was called immediately after the police found the victims."

"Kilonzo called you?"

"He hadn't shown up yet. When he found out I'd examined the bodies, he ordered me not to say anything to anyone."

"Why would that be?"

"My conclusions were very different from the song and dance he made up for the media."

When Kilonzo read the doctor's report, he chose — no doubt with the approval of his superiors — not to make it public. A way of avoiding embarrassing questions most likely. But which ones?

"What was in your report?"

"Besides the wounds made by the machete, there was damage to the muscles of the thorax caused by an extreme and prolonged stretching of the victims' arms.

Probably they'd been tied behind their backs, which would have damaged their neuromuscular function."

"They were tortured?"

"For several hours, the evidence shows. It's called *kandoya*."

According to the doctor, Valéria died quite some time after her daughter, as if the assailant had first attacked Sophie and forced her mother to watch to break her will and make her talk. The degree of rigor mortis wasn't the same for the two victims.

Max had to close his eyes. The image was just too vivid, too painful: Valéria and her daughter, tortured. Seeing her own daughter suffer before her eyes, knowing it would end in death, and choosing not to shorten Sophie's pain even if it was the best choice given the circumstances. Valéria had accepted that both she and her daughter would be martyred, but why?

"*Kandoya* is the unmistakable signature of the elite corps of the Ugandan army," the doctor added. After Idi Amin took over in 1971, a number of men who'd opposed him crossed the southern border to safety, most of them around Kyaka. They formed a unit of fighters who were the avant-garde of the Tanzanian army when Nyerere ordered the invasion of Uganda.

They were a rebel faction of former soldiers whose patriotic fervour covered less honourable ambitions. In reality they were a ragtag party of thugs who engaged in pillaging and violence the minute they crossed back into their country. They were so out of control the Tanzanian army had to rein them in hard to keep them from running amok. They practised torture, using the same methods Idi Amin favoured. Among them, the *kandoya*.

During the war, mobilized by the Tanzanian army, the doctor had treated several such cases inflicted by the rebels against their own countrymen suspected of being allied with Idi Amin's regime.

"I wouldn't be surprised if the man who killed them was part of that rebel group or knew its methods," the doctor said.

"And the machete wounds?"

"To finish off the victims, no doubt."

Max said nothing. The doctor's revelations moved him deeply. Why such cruelty? A wave of anger rose within him, more intense than the nausea he felt. He would find and punish whoever was responsible for this horrible act. He had never killed a man, had always been able to master the violent impulses that had returned to haunt him throughout his life. But right then he wouldn't have resisted the urge. He would kill the bastard who'd done this and without the slightest hesitation or remorse.

The plane touched down.

While the propellers were still turning, the doctor added, "Valéria and her daughter were doing admirable work, but they got on the wrong side of a lot of people. And the people who resented them weren't necessarily the ones she challenged and denounced publicly."

"What does that mean?"

"After Samuel Musindo's execution, the rumours started flying. What a strange coincidence — the death of the albino girl occurred just as The Colour of Respect

Foundation was urging the government to reinstate capital punishment. Convenient, isn't it?"

"Valéria engineering the kidnapping and murder of the girl? That's insane!"

"I agree, but the rumours won't go away."

"What does Lugembe think about that?"

The doctor had no idea. "But imagine if someone was able to prove that the minister had been manipulated in the death penalty affair," he added. "What would be his reaction if Valéria or someone else in the foundation had sacrificed one albino to ensure the safety of all the others?"

And what if he discovered, as Chagula had insinuated, that Valéria and Musindo knew each other, and that with Zuberi's complicity, she'd used Musindo to kidnap and kill the minister of home affairs' daughter?

14

Every autumn it was the same ceremony. Albert Kerensky and his friend Glenn Forrester took a week off to go hunting at Lake Amistad along the Rio Grande on the border with Mexico. And during the summer, from time to time, they loaded up for feral hogs in the Bosque River area. This was their unchangeable ritual, and Roselyn had to live with it. Other than Glenn, Albert had no human contact. What he liked was to sit and watch television, a beer in hand, underneath the great set of antlers that had belonged to a moose he shot in 2003 in the Glass Mountains. Fixing up the house, gardening — no thanks. He didn't care for baseball, either, a sport Roselyn loved.

There was always Frank Cosgrove, a little younger than her husband and a member of the tie-down team for a number of years. He was from Dallas and had been transferred out of Houston at the beginning of his career. They weren't best friends, but Cosgrove had come over for dinner a few times.

Shortly after she arrived in Huntsville, Roselyn decided to pay him a visit. She remembered him as a big man, overweight, with a strong, resounding voice. Whenever he walked into a room, Cosgrove was the centre of attention, unlike Albert, whom nobody noticed.

All these years later Cosgrove had lost nothing of his charisma. A few months from retirement, he looked after administrative duties at the Walls Unit.

"I heard about what happened," Cosgrove answered when Roselyn explained why she'd come. "I hope you'll find Albert, and especially that nothing bad has happened to him."

She summed up what the police had done so far, and revealed Peter's suspicions about the families of men Albert had executed.

Cosgrove shrugged. He didn't have much use for that trail. He'd never heard of a case of revenge against an executioner and his team, not in any of the American states where the death penalty was in force.

Cosgrove walked ahead of Roselyn down the narrow corridor whose windows, very high up, let light filter in but gave no view of the outside world. Strange, but in all these years she'd never been inside the penitentiary, never seen the place where Albert had plied his trade.

"What was Albert's attitude at work?"

Cosgrove stared at her as if he didn't understand her question.

"Did he like what he did?"

"It's not the kind of job where you go home after the day is done and tell your wife, 'Honey, I had a good day at the office.'"

She couldn't help but smile.

"Some executions are harder than others."

A number of the men slated for execution were drug addicts, hooked on heroin, and their arms were covered with tracks, their veins sclerotic from abuse. Sometimes it was complicated finding the vein needed to carry out the execution. In those cases, the needle was inserted into the leg. An inexperienced worker could miss his mark and inflict intolerable pain. That happened at times but never with Albert. At least as far as Cosgrove knew.

Once again, it was confirmed: her husband was very good at his job. He was conscientious. Maybe a little too much.

They came to a room filled with filing cabinets and violently lit by fluorescent tubes.

"The department still hasn't finished computerizing its records," Cosgrove explained.

He walked over to a young woman sitting behind a desk. Her name was Margaret. She'd never met Albert — she'd been hired at the Walls Unit after he retired. Handing over Albert's file, she found them a spot in an empty office next door.

Each executioner had a personal logbook, a record of the technical details of how each execution was performed, and he passed it on to the warden afterward. Cosgrove paged through his old colleague's book.

"Nothing out of the ordinary," he declared. "Albert was a professional in every sense of the term."

And a conscientious worker who had once interrupted his vacation to return to Huntsville and carry out an execution. Roselyn remembered the time that happened. They had gone to the Baja Peninsula in Mexico with Norah. It wasn't their first time. In the early years of their marriage, Albert rented an RV, crossed the border at El Paso, and drove all the way down to Cabo San Lucas, a resort spot where Californians liked to go.

That year he was true to his habit. Then a call came from the director of the Walls Unit. The head of the tie-down team had gotten sick, everyone was on vacation, and there was no one to turn to. Albert agreed to cut short their time away, which touched off a spirited argument with Roselyn. He had never compromised a hunting trip with Glenn Forrester, but he didn't mind sacrificing a family vacation to execute some bum who'd been wasting away in prison for years. The atmosphere was heavy for weeks afterward, but the lesson had been learned. The following year, when the same situation arose again, Albert turned down the warden.

Cosgrove paged through the record book. "Now that's strange. Did you know Albert was treated for burns to his hand?"

Roselyn had no idea. "When was that?"

"November 2006."

A few weeks after Norah's death. And a few months before he retired.

"In the report, it says the injury was caused by a firearm. That's what Albert declared to the insurance company."

"His Winchester?"

"No. A handgun, according to the doctor."

Roselyn didn't remember her husband having a revolver, except for the service pistol when he was a guard, an eternity ago. "Was he treated here in Huntsville?"

"No. Galveston."

He was sent to the University of Texas medical school where the sick and wounded prisoners from the Huntsville penitentiaries were treated.

Roselyn didn't have to ask. Cosgrove picked up the phone and punched the number in Albert's file. After being transferred a number of times, he reached Dr. Maxwell, who had looked after Albert. Cosgrove described the wound and gave the doctor the file number. Maxwell remembered the incident involving the executioner.

The mishandling of a firearm was to blame for the injury. That sort of thing happened frequently among neophytes. Albert must have acquired the weapon recently and didn't know how to use it correctly. He must have bought it for a particular reason: to defend himself. He felt threatened, had been attacked. He used the gun, but in his panic, mishandled the weapon and suffered a burned hand. The wound wasn't serious, but enough to involve a doctor.

Roselyn wondered how it was that she hadn't noticed anything. As far as she could remember, Albert had never been hospitalized anywhere, let alone Galveston. He could have gone to the Memorial Hospital in Huntsville. Why hadn't he said anything about the revolver and his burned hand?

"What was the date?" she asked Cosgrove.

"November seventeenth."

Where was she that day? And why did he hide the incident from her? Where was the gun now? What had Albert done with it? When he left, did he carry it with him, and why?

Those questions tormented Roselyn. She was thoughtful and perplexed when she exited the Walls Unit after thanking Frank Cosgrove for his help. Over these past few days, her husband's portrait, once so clear and transparent, had begun to blur. His attitude had been strange and disconcerting, to say the least. The purchase of a revolver and the injury he'd treated in another city troubled her. If he hadn't disappeared, she would have never discovered those things about him.

In the car, she called Brian Pallister, her friend from the Wildlife Artists' Association. "I have a big favour to ask you."

After the sale of the house, a few bulky items had been placed in storage in a Houston warehouse. Roselyn asked Brian to look for a particular box that sat on an old chest of drawers, if her memory served.

"What do I do with it?"

"Bring it home with you and call me right away."

Back at Peter's house, Roselyn asked him if he knew about the events that were recorded in Albert's logbook. Peter was as surprised as she'd been.

"I didn't notice a thing," she admitted. "It's incredible."

Peter kept all his old datebooks. He consulted the one that corresponded to November 2006.

"On November seventeenth, you weren't here. You were in Biloxi with Adrian and me."

A vacation for three in Mississippi. Roselyn had been feeling a sense of loss then, and like Peter, she couldn't seem to get back into the stream of life. She needed a break, a cutting off from the past, a change of pace. Peter volunteered to accompany Adrian's school group on its trip to the Mississippi coast. On an impulse, Roselyn offered to go along and help out. The teacher in charge of the excursion was overjoyed; it was difficult to convince parents to get involved in field trips. Before they left, she made Peter promise not to talk about Norah. He agreed. He needed to move on, as well.

So Albert stayed behind in Huntsville and managed to wound himself in the hand with a firearm. He'd gone to Galveston for treatment. But why so far?

She hadn't even noticed the burn. Wait ... she'd picked up on something. She remembered now. When she returned from Biloxi, Albert told her he'd hurt himself fixing the car. If it was the same injury, he'd hidden the real reason why.

Once Adrian was tucked away in bed, and Peter had his eyes glued to a basketball game, Roselyn announced she was going out for a walk and that she needed to think. Peter grunted a noncommittal reply. She walked all the way to Stanford Hill Residence. At that late hour a number of residents were asleep, but a few hard-core cases were in one of the common rooms by the entrance, locked into a game of poker. Mrs. Callaghan had gone home, leaving a young woman in charge at reception.

"I'd like to see my husband's room," Roselyn said in her most convincing voice.

The young woman knew about Albert's disappearance. She gave in to Roselyn's request even if, according to the rules, she should have told her to come back tomorrow, after a discussion with Mrs. Callaghan. At the higher-class establishments like Woodbridge Manor and Brighton Lodge, Roselyn wouldn't have been able to waltz into her husband's room.

The young woman moved away, and Roselyn closed the door behind her. Leaning against the doorknob, she took in the room with a treasure-hunter's eye. Where was the revolver? It was essential, though she couldn't say why, or justify the need, but she absolutely had to get her hands on the gun. Albert used it three years ago. Maybe he'd gotten rid of it. Maybe not. Roselyn counted on Albert's innate tendency to keep everything, even useless stuff.

Methodically, she searched all the places a firearm might be concealed: the drawers, closets, under the sink, even in the tank over the toilet, just the way she'd seen characters do on TV. Behind the curtains, under the bed, between the mattress and the box spring. Inside the shade of a floor lamp that opened like a flower. Underneath the coat rack where a loose floorboard might lie. Behind the mirror to the left of the door. And behind the painting she'd given him as a present.

Nothing.

In the closet, she searched his clothes, starting with the jacket he used for hunting, that he'd insisted on keeping after he moved to the residence, even if his deteriorating health kept him away from his sporting habit. He'd had to sell his beloved Winchester 94 to Glenn Forrester. It had been like the end of the world for him.

An hour later she was running with sweat and had to face the facts: she was getting nowhere. Albert had either disposed of the revolver or taken it with him.

That was when she caught sight of the bulletin board by the door. Management pinned the menus for the week and other such relevant information there. The head of maintenance added a note about replacing some tiles because of a recent leak. "If you have suffered damage," the note read, "please report it to the front desk."

A leak? Tiles?

Roselyn lifted her head. The ceiling was made of acoustic tiles, actually a false ceiling, behind which was hidden the electrical wiring and plumbing. If Albert had kept the revolver, Roselyn was sure that was where he would have hidden it.

Standing on a chair, she began to remove one of the tiles. It took considerable effort. Not that they were heavy, but to grasp one adequately, she had to add a telephone book and an inverted garbage can to the chair. Balancing on the improvised scaffolding, she managed to push a tile into the area above the false ceiling and look inside. She made out a space filled with wires and pipes, with a good helping of dust. There was no gun. She peered farther inside. An object caught her eye, just above where the desk stood. A small suitcase, an attaché case. She couldn't reach it from her position. She pulled her head out of the ceiling cavity, replaced the tile, and went to Albert's desk. Why hadn't she thought of that before? To reach the ceiling, Albert used the desk. She set her chair on top of it, climbed up again, and pushed aside the tile just above her head. It was easy to grab the case by the handle and pull it down.

Once she was on solid ground, Roselyn examined the little briefcase. It was dusty and hadn't been opened in quite some time. The case was locked. After searching unsuccessfully through the drawers for a key, she picked it using her nail file. Inside was a photo album. No firearm, no revolver, just a cheap drugstore folder for displaying photos.

Now what did that mean?

Roselyn opened the album, which was literally falling apart. It didn't contain photos, but locks of hair. They were displayed in orderly fashion, six samples per page over some forty pages, complete with name and date. She understood immediately. These locks of hair belonged to men who'd been sentenced to death, whose executions Albert had participated in, either as a member or the leader of the tie-down team. Moving through the pages, she recognized certain names: Franklin Crispel, Duane Berkley, and Keith Busby, with the dates they were executed. And the first of Albert's career, Lewis Autry.

For all these years, he'd kept a souvenir of his ... clients, you might say. A macabre memory that her husband had hidden from her since he was first appointed to the execution room in 1984.

The man was obsessed with death, no doubt about it.

A plastic packet slipped out of the album and landed at Roselyn's feet. She picked it up. Inside were two more locks of hair held together by a rubber band. These had no identification. She paged through the album again but found nothing to tell her whom they might have belonged to.

Roselyn felt sick. Shaken, and suddenly frightened. As if she realized, years later, too late, that she'd shared her life with a serial killer with his little fetishes, his double life, his obsessions. A killer who had operated with full impunity under cover of the law, who was paid for the crimes he committed, and who now enjoyed the comforts of a full pension.

PART TWO
The Arrest

15

Outside city hall, by the entrance, men in suits conferred in low voices, cigarettes glued to their lower lips. Others paced as they talked into their phones, gesticulating for invisible listeners. A small group sitting on the steps seemed ill at ease: these were the men charged with carrying the caskets containing Valéria and Sophie to the cemetery once the ceremony was over. The remains were purely symbolic, since the bodies had been cremated. Now that the guilty party was behind bars, there was no need to keep them. *One more masquerade*, Max thought.

He wasn't sure he wanted to pay his respects to the women. The goal of the ceremony was to honour their public memory, and all he knew of them was their private lives — the part they'd chosen to share with him. Exposed to all and sundry, Valéria's death seemed meaningless to him. Secret, intimate, his pain was all the greater. He couldn't share his sadness with anyone.

He looked for Inspector Kilonzo in the crowd. The policeman stood to one side along with Shembazi. The two men were wearing their ceremonial uniforms, loaded down with medals and ribbons bearing the colours of the republic.

Max didn't know what attitude to take. It was clear that Kilonzo was plotting in the shadows — that had been clear since he'd come to Bukoba. But he wasn't sure for what purpose. Was he acting on his own or for someone else pulling strings behind the scenes? Should he confront him head-on or try to find out more through subterfuge?

Both options had their advantages.

He chose confrontation.

"Hello, Inspector."

Kilonzo turned around. A smile crafted for the circumstances. A manly handshake. "The ceremony will begin in a few minutes. Madame Michieka and her daughter had many friends. They were much appreciated for their work."

Kilonzo was radiant. For the policeman, Max thought, this public funeral marked the end of the affair. Despite the nature of the event, he was wearing a triumphant smile.

"I don't see Valéria's friend," Max said.

"Her friend?"

"President Lugembe."

Kilonzo shot Max a penetrating look, wondering where he was leading him.

"You said so yourself when I first came here. Don't you remember? The president was deeply affected by Valéria's death. She was his friend."

The tension left Kilonzo. "I spoke to him. He was relieved to learn we'd found the guilty party."

"What happened to him? Did he confess?"

"Not yet. But he will. I have full confidence in my interrogation team."

Max couldn't help thinking of the *kandoya* method.

Last night at the hotel he'd researched the rebel Ugandan forces at the end of the 1970s. He discovered that the Uganda National Liberation Army of the time was made up of disparate groups, including the Kikosi Maalum — "Special Force" in Swahili — the Front for National Salvation, and the Save Uganda Movement. It was a fragile coalition composed of units that often had divergent interests. Hardly surprising that once Idi Amin was toppled, his former opponents began fighting within the new government. It had taken years before Uganda achieved stability and could turn its back on the memory of Idi Amin and his reign of atrocity.

It was possible, as the doctor in Okambo's Cessna had suggested, that one of those rebels was responsible for the torture and murder of Valéria and her daughter.

That hypothesis didn't explain the killer's motive. But at least Max had something to go on. And Kilonzo had tried to conceal the information, which showed it was important. Paradoxically, hiding elements had a way of bringing them forward.

After a few minutes of idle chat, Max led Kilonzo away from the others. He went straight to the point. "Why didn't you say that Valéria and her daughter were tortured?"

Kilonzo took a step back. "Who told you that?"

"At the morgue you hid that from me. And you knew about it, I'm sure."

"What difference does it make?"

"All the difference. A thief wouldn't have done that."

"He must have been a sadist."

"A veteran of the war in Uganda, maybe?"

Kilonzo said nothing. Max could see the inspector studying him, wondering if this was just a fishing expedition. He was sure he'd hooked the right fish, though. "Your suspect wasn't even born at the time."

"I don't see what Uganda has to do with this."

Max told him about the *kandoya*, which Kilonzo might have practised himself. As he described the torture and how it worked, Max wondered if the policeman would interrupt him to correct and add some missing detail.

"None of that proves anything."

"Why won't you do your job, Kilonzo? For some reason, you're ignoring Zuberi the witch doctor. Then you try to fob off a fake suspect on your president. Why don't you look at the veterans of the campaign against Idi Amin?"

"That was for a just cause," Kilonzo declared right on cue. "It liberated Uganda from a cruel and backward despot."

"Did you fight in that war?"

His silence spoke volumes. Once again, he must have been wondering what Max really knew.

"How old were you in 1979? Twenty-four, twenty-five? You served in the army, from what I understand. The dates work out. That winter I'm sure you weren't confined to barracks and made to shine boots. The entire division was sent to conquer Kampala."

One hundred thousand soldiers. As well as regular troops, Nyerere mobilized policemen, prison guards, and various militias. A khaki-coloured tidal wave had overwhelmed Idi Amin's forces.

"What are you trying to insinuate, Cheskin?"

"That you probably had contacts with the Uganda National Liberation Army. Their members worked with the Tanzanian army."

"Are you accusing me of being responsible for the death of these two women? You're out of your mind."

"You were involved with the rebels in exile. They showed you how to convince recalcitrant prisoners. You wanted to hide the doctor's conclusions because they associated the rebels with Valéria's murder."

"This is madness!"

"By refusing to reveal the contents of his report, you're protecting someone. Maybe even yourself …"

"Be careful, Cheskin! Or I'll have you arrested for contempt for a high-ranking police officer."

"If I ever find out you were involved with Valéria's death in one way or another, you'll regret it for the rest of your life. Your threats and your tin medals don't frighten me. Neither does your fake outrage."

Max walked into the building, leaving Kilonzo visibly shaken.

‡

The large salon had been cleared of its heavy teak tables, replaced by straight-backed chairs set here and there. Empty chairs, as if the decor was simply decorative, a little too prim, too formal, too orderly to satisfy this unruly crowd, in mourning but not too much, noisy with perpetual whispering. In front of a starched curtain, at the foot of a low stage where the municipal authorities usually held court, sat a table covered with a navy blue cloth; on it two coffins were displayed. Funeral wreaths of various dimensions, placed against the table, some as big as tractor tires. A few bouquets of flowers, fading already, were placed here and there at random, filling out the decoration. A large photo of Valéria and her daughter in the garden, unposed, that Max had noticed in the living room of the house, completed the setup and replaced the portrait of the mayor in his best Stalinist pose, temporarily taken down and stacked in a corner behind the stage.

The room was filled with Valéria and Sophie's friends and acquaintances, along with a number of clients. Among them, standing under the artificial breeze of a fan, several albinos with their moon-pale features. Max had no idea how rich Valéria's social life was. He had the impression Sophie and her mother lived in isolation, supporting each other without outside help. The women spent their lives on the margins of Tanzanian society, and they distrusted it. Their involvement with albinos was a living accusation of their countrymen, a negative judgment of Bukoba's passive attitude, its complicity.

Did Sophie have a lover? On Max's first visit to Bukoba, once when Valéria was with a client in her office, he walked into the guest room where he'd left his suitcase and stumbled upon Sophie kissing a boy her age. She hadn't been back from Montreal for long, and had already resolved not to return, but hadn't announced the bad news to her mother yet. Sophie had thought she would come back and have her mother to herself, and now a stranger — Max — was hanging around the house.

At first relations were tense. Valéria made an effort to bring her daughter into their activities, but after three days, she dropped the attempt. They ate each in turn, as in a cafeteria, with Sophie doing her best to avoid Max.

One morning he came across the girl on the veranda. He wanted to break down her cold resistance, since it bothered Valéria and made Max unhappy.

"I love your mother, Sophie. And I believe she loves me, too."

"You hardly know each other."

"That makes no difference."

"She'll never leave Bukoba. You're wasting your time."

So that was what was bothering her. Not being separated from Valéria, but that her mother might abandon her obligations in Bukoba. Sophie saw herself as the guardian of Valéria's social conscience.

Max was relieved. "There's no reason to worry."

"Don't you want to take her to Europe?"

"Who told you that?"

Little by little, things improved between them. Sophie accepted that Max was part of Valéria's life, perhaps because he didn't try to absorb all her attention and wasn't out to turn her away from her work and her darling daughter. The time they spent together was furtive, quick, unpredictable, stolen from their daily lives. When she needed stability and fresh air — to recharge, as she called it — Valéria could count on the world of Bukoba, and on Sophie, who waited for her the way a wife waited for a husband after a long business trip. By then the girl had moved on to something else: law school in Dar es Salaam. Her studies were her way of staying close to her mother. Max suspected the girl was interested in becoming a lawyer as a way of remaining near Valéria and her entourage, instead of striking out in the world and starting a family the way most young people did.

Suddenly, it was very hot, the atmosphere heavy in the crowded room. Max moved to the corner in search of better air. Valéria's support for the death penalty for albino traffickers and her constant conflicts with Amnesty International attracted a handful of journalists, bored in the roomful of guests. Cameras slung over their shoulders, they looked as though they were sorry they'd made the trip. What were they hoping for? Noisy demonstrations for or against Valéria's decision to call for capital punishment for traffickers? The debate belonged to ancient history. The murder of the two women was garnering little interest in the media.

Max stepped up to the twin coffins. More photos of Valéria and her daughter were placed on the table for the guests to look at. He picked up one of the portraits. In it Valéria wore her hair short, her tight curls relaxed. The photo dated back to the years before they met, perhaps before Sophie was born, her university years, after she left her village for good.

She'd told Max how that happened, once. The Anglican pastor who taught her English, the choir leader, had encouraged her to apply for a scholarship, which meant she could move to Dar es Salaam and attend business school. She was an outstanding student, industrious and concentrated, with iron discipline — or so she claimed for Max's benefit.

Valéria had pulled herself out of the back country and had no intention of returning there. She studied with desperate energy, afraid she might miss her rendez-vous with the modern world. Her parents were illiterate, her brothers and sisters had never set foot in a school, she was the first of the family and among the few in the village to do so, and she would show the way for the others. A pioneer who, to everyone's surprise, went to live in Bukoba once she earned her diploma at Makerere University. What happened to the prediction that she would launch her career in the capital, or elsewhere in East Africa, or even Europe? Instead, she settled into this nowhere town to sort out quarrels between neighbours and unmask cattle rustlers. And, most of all, devote her life to albinos.

Pastor Randy Cousins presided over the cere-mony. He was a jovial man with a faint resemblance to Desmond Tutu, and he'd consulted Valéria in the past. In his warm, welcoming voice, he described her with true emotion, speaking of her ability to listen to others with empathy and compassion. She could enter into her clients' situation, so said Cousins, as one with the fears and worries that had moved them to take their savings in hand and come in search of her help.

As if waiting for his cue, an albino took the pastor's place at the microphone. He spoke of how he'd met Valéria. And with her, Sophie. And of all the things the two had done for him.

Other tributes followed, all charged with emotion. Flanked by her colleagues from the Women's Legal Aid Centre, Désirée Lubadsa described the remarkable work Valéria had done for the women of the Kagera region.

Then voices rose in common prayer, a melody of infinite slow sadness, sung by the crowd shaken with emotion.

The heat was stifling, its intensity intolerable for Max despite the revolving fans. He could scarcely listen; he was thinking of everything he'd learned during the ceremony, and the new possibilities that made the picture more complicated. He wondered what the link was between Valéria's involvement with the albino cause and the forgotten war against Idi Amin.

What was the dictator's attitude toward albinos during those terrible years when he held power? Max had no idea.

Kilonzo seemed sincerely surprised when Max had insinuated that he was somehow involved in the two women's murders. That, too, had been a shot in the dark.

The ceremony went on forever. Max was just about to head for the exit when Cousins's voice rose above the murmur. "And now we'll hear from Teresa Mwandenga."

Max stopped and glanced toward the front of the room. Teresa Mwandenga, the accountant who'd run off with The Colour of Respect Foundation's funds.

Pastor Cousins went on. "Teresa knew Valéria and her daughter very well. She worked at their side for a number of years."

Teresa was a woman in her forties, her hair pulled back and securely fastened with a barrette. She strode up to the microphone as the pastor made way for her.

Max turned and moved toward the front of the room.

16

Pushing his way through the crowd, Max followed Teresa Mwandenga outside and around the back, into an empty lot used for parking, a playground, and an all-purpose space. Teresa walked toward an elegant man standing by a Mercedes, smoking a cigarette. Max recognized him. He'd seen his photo on a calling card attached to a wreath next to the two coffins. The flowers were a gift of the Kagera Farmers Co-operative Bank.

The banker was a tall man with glasses. He wore a serious look, and it seemed to Max that he represented the new Africa that Jonathan Harris had told him about on board his yacht. A modern, enterprising, educated, motivated Africa, ready to lift the continent out of its immobility. For the past few years, men like the banker, rare birds when Max had first come to Bukoba, had sprouted up everywhere, ready to leap into action and shake up the old habits that kept the merchants and local entrepreneurs in their rut.

Had he helped Teresa with her embezzlement? Had he been her accomplice in cooking the foundation's books?

Mwandenga returning to Bukoba to pay her respects to Valéria and her daughter might be surprising, but her absence would have set people thinking, and the police might have gotten interested in the accountant. She must have known that the two women had said nothing, afraid of damaging the foundation's finances.

"Madame Mwandenga?"

The two of them turned in unison to look at Max, the banker sizing him up from his great height, above the fray.

"Robert Cheskin," he said to Teresa. "I was a friend of Valéria and her daughter."

"Two extraordinary women," the banker replied. "Everyone in Bukoba loved them. I don't understand what could have happened."

"An ex-con, according to the police. He thought Valéria was keeping a lot of money."

"From Dar es Salaam," the man added, as if spitting. "No one from here would have lifted a hand against her."

Except for the albino traffickers, Max thought bitterly. Then he turned to Teresa. "May I have a word with you?"

Teresa glanced at the banker, who threw his cigarette onto the ground, walked toward the hall, and went through the door, bending his head in the process. "What can I do for you?" she asked.

"I thought you were in the Emirates spending the foundation's money."

Teresa stared at him. "Who are you? What do you want?"

"You were sure Valéria wouldn't say anything about the embezzlement. That's why you came back. But you made a mistake."

"What are you talking about? What embezzlement?"

"You disappeared with the cash. Maybe even with the help of your banker friend."

"I have no idea what you're talking about."

As briefly as possible, Max told her about Sophie's visit to Lamu shortly before she was murdered, though he kept quiet about how he'd swindled Jonathan Harris.

Teresa listened with rapt attention, seemingly astonished at first, then perhaps with more sadness than anger, not knowing how and why Sophie had invented a story like that. "I didn't steal anything. I left Bukoba to visit my mother in Arusha, who's sick. Ask anyone."

"What about the suppliers who weren't paid? And the debts that kept piling up?"

"The foundation isn't rich, but we don't owe anyone anything except for the usual current expenses."

Suddenly, it dawned on Max: he'd been conned by Sophie. It was painful and humiliating to have been tricked like a rank beginner. He pictured Sophie in Lamu with her resigned smile, playing the go-between for an innocent fool who saw and heard nothing besides the purring of his own self-assurance. He imagined Sophie contacting Valéria the night she arrived, informing her that, of course, the idiot fell right into the trap, headfirst, without realizing that the ground had disappeared from under his feet. A naive, harmless fellow, so easy to manipulate. A shame they hadn't thought of this before.

Had Valéria been in on the scam?

Max couldn't imagine Sophie coordinating an operation like that without her mother's approval. It would have been so simple for him to call Valéria and check her daughter's information. But he hadn't had the presence of mind to do a little investigating on his own.

A perfect amateur.

And a complete disaster that might have turned against the two women and led to their deaths.

Teresa was telling the truth, and that truth was devastating for Max. Until now he'd cherished the illusion that Sophie's visit and her appeal for help might have been Max's first step toward reconciliation with Valéria. But the opposite was true. The two women had conspired to swindle him with cold determination that now left him speechless, disoriented, lost.

Valéria's revenge, he realized. She'd never forgiven him for not revealing the true nature of his "work" from the start, his "business" as a con man, his "vocation" as a professional fraudster. He remembered the sudden end of their relationship that day in Paris in a modest hotel off the Champs-Élysées where Valéria had offered to meet him. She was standing in the lobby in the midst of the students and retired people, packs on their backs, jet lag on their faces, waiting for a noisy room smelling of French cigarettes. In the narrow elevator, inches apart, she avoided his eyes as if he were a stranger she was forced to associate with.

In the room, Valéria relaxed a little, loosened her hair, offered him a drink. Max could feel the change, though he didn't know why. She asked him how his trip had gone and didn't wait for his answer. Her forced smile lacked the warmth of their previous encounters. Max understood that something had been broken, but he was in no hurry to discover what. Valéria couldn't meet his eye, and just looking in his direction seemed to be hard work. Max wasn't going to offer her a way out.

She opened the window and stood there at length, her back turned, hesitating.

"What's going on, Valéria?" he finally asked.

"You're not Robert Cheskin."

Back in Bukoba, in her house, he might have left a chequebook or a passport or a letter lying around. Valéria looked at him with cruelty in her eyes, horrified but filled with an unhealthy curiosity she could hold back no longer. "Just who are you, really?"

Max revealed his identity, the true one, the one he always kept hidden. He told her about his life as a con man, described the scams he'd mounted alone or with others, here and there around the world, following rich people's money like those small fish that attached themselves to the hulls of ships on the high seas, feeding off the garbage jettisoned by the crew.

A tense silence followed.

And then, furious, Valéria spoke of the foundation, the importance of her work, her mission. And her obligation to maintain an exemplary attitude at all times. If she made a misstep, she wouldn't be the only one to pay; all the albinos who depended on her initiatives would suffer, too. How could he have been so cruel, exposing her to such risk? What had he been thinking?

Max stepped closer to her. "I love you, Valéria. If you want me to stop doing this, if you —"

She wheeled around and slapped him as hard as she could. He drew back, surprised by her strength — she was as surprised as he was, as if her hand had taken on a life of its own beyond her control.

Before he could say or do anything, she threw open the door and dashed down the stairway, pushing through the grey-hairs and the backpackers as she went.

Max ran after her.

On the sidewalk, he searched for her. He was gasping for breath as if he'd almost drowned. Quickly, he ran to the Champs-Élysées and spotted Valéria among the crowds of pedestrians at the corner of the next street.

When he caught up to her, she turned and spoke. "If you really loved me, you wouldn't have lied to me all these months."

"Please try to understand."

His love for her was the most precious thing in the world, he pleaded, his words tumbling one over the other in his haste to convince her. He lied to protect her. But now that things were out in the open, he realized his arguments were worthless. Could anyone trust a liar and a con man? His love for her could be no more than another fraud, a bait-and-switch, a mirage.

"Go away. Disappear. I don't want to see you again, ever."

In tears, Valéria disappeared into a crowd of onlookers, showing him what it meant to desert someone.

When he boarded the plane to New York later that day, Max was good and drunk.

At JFK Airport, in a sodden, nauseated state, he came across a special issue of the *Wall Street Journal* featuring a battery of statistics about the "new Africa" that everyone was so eager to believe in. Instead of AIDS, famines, and dictators, another Africa was emerging, and the media were only just realizing it, an Africa of initiative and bold enterprise, the best-kept secret of the twenty-first century.

The usual media crap.

Max collapsed into the first taxi he found and was delivered to his apartment on Sixth Avenue. He had three different ones in Manhattan under three different names, a way of covering his tracks in case Interpol started catching up to him and his activities.

For days he stayed inside, a prisoner of himself. The blinds drawn, alone in the darkness but for a bottle of Johnny Walker, he tried and failed to get Valéria out of his mind. She slipped into every thought, loomed in his dreams, turning night and day into an endless nightmare he thought he'd never escape. Valéria … he still loved her, though he'd made her a victim of his lowdown conduct, his half-truths, his unbelievable inventions. He was the great con man, but she saw through him with amazing ease, and now he was shrinking into nothing, alone, in an anonymous room without a past, without a future.

Max brought his Jeep to a stop in front of a small house by the lake, outside the city. The water was choppy that day, and the waves broke against the barrier at the edge of the property. Teresa Mwandenga was standing at the front door. Max had requested a meeting with her after the funeral. She ushered him into her house. If she'd been guilty of embezzlement, she hadn't found a way to spend the funds yet. The little house was clean and well kept and seemed on the new side, but it was no castle. In the kitchen where Max stood, the appliances were modest and showed no sign of being the lavish property of an ambitious schemer. Compared to most people in Bukoba, Teresa was doing well, but this wasn't opulence by any means.

A man appeared in the doorway that led to the living room.

"This is Matthew, my husband," she said.

Max tried to reassure him. He simply wanted to continue the conversation they'd begun after the funeral. Clear up a few things. And understand why Sophie had cooked up this incredible lie. What was the point, and was Valéria in on it?

"They arrested the guy who did it," Matthew announced.

"Yes, they did."

It was too soon to challenge Inspector Kilonzo's competence.

Matthew sighed, then stepped aside as if giving Max permission to be alone with his wife and ask her questions. "Let's just get it over with" seemed to be his attitude.

Loaded down with work during the day, Valéria often had to wait until evening before tending to the foundation's administrative tasks. There was always a form to fill out, an official document to complete, a pressing demand from some self-important ministry, or from Harold Scofield in London, who always had priority.

Valéria had become increasingly involved in the foundation over the past few years, explained Teresa. The administrative part of her job was heavier than ever, forcing her to take more time away from her regular clients. Luckily, she could count on Sophie, who helped lighten the load. Before leaving the office in the evening, Teresa tried to wrap up as many files as possible with Valéria.

"On the day she was killed," Max asked, "did you work with her as usual?"

"Yes."

"How did she seem?"

At first Teresa kept silent. Then she glanced over at Matthew, who was pretending to read a newspaper by the window. "Anxious," she admitted to Max, "as if she had a premonition. I told Kilonzo."

So the policeman had questioned her, something he'd forgot to inform Max about. He must have caught up to Teresa at her mother's house in Arusha.

"What did he say?"

"Nothing."

"Had Valéria received any threats recently?"

"I don't know. But she was worried. Since her trip to Ukerewe, she was absent-minded, didn't seem to listen, spent her time daydreaming instead of concentrating on her work. When she heard a noise outside, she jumped. I'd never seen her so agitated."

"Ukerewe? The Albino Island? What was she doing there?"

She went to discuss expanding the recently built school, the one Harold Scofield had mentioned. It was a last-minute trip, and she was gone only three days. Max asked Teresa if she remembered the exact date.

"Yes, it was at the beginning of the month."

"How did she travel? By plane?"

"No."

"With a driver, or with Sophie?"

"Alone. She took the Land Cruiser."

Strange. Valéria didn't like driving, and in Tanzania she was never alone at the wheel. It didn't make sense, her insisting on making such a long trip without a driver. Teresa felt the same, which was why she'd been surprised.

"What did Sophie think about all that?"

"She never mentioned it."

"Did you overhear any conversations? Was there tension between them?"

"No."

Max had no idea why Valéria would have travelled to Ukerewe, but she went on her own and returned upset. It seemed unplanned and out of character, and Teresa was in the dark about it.

The trip must have been difficult, Max thought. More than four hundred kilometres on rough roads to Mwanza, then the ferry to Ukerewe. Valéria could have taken a plane, which she usually did when she went to Dodoma or Dar es Salaam to defend her cause in front of some bureaucrat. Yet she chose the Land Cruiser despite the long distance and the miserable road system. A person would really need a very good reason to make the trip that way.

"Wasn't Sophie surprised that her mother decided to leave like that, on her own?" Max asked.

"If Sophie was worried, she didn't tell me."

Sophie had to know the reason for the trip. Otherwise she would have shared her concern with Teresa. And there was something else, too: Valéria's quick trip took place just as Sophie was arriving in Lamu to make her appeal to Max.

Before he thanked Teresa, he asked her, "Did she ever talk to you about Daniel?"

"Daniel?"

"A little boy. She might have mentioned him to Sophie."

"I've never heard of anyone by that name."

17

Peter Sawyer sat behind his desk, holding the small plastic bag containing the two locks of hair — one brown, one blond — which Roselyn had found in her husband's album. Peter studied them, as if he could, by some still-hidden property, discover their significance simply by fiddling with the bag. Roselyn had finished sharing the story of her discovery, and the worry that had grown in her since.

The first lock was tightly curled. More frizzy than curly, really, perhaps a black person's hair. Short — likely a man's. The other lock a long, fine strand. A woman's?

"Did you know about the album?" Roselyn asked.

"No. Neither did Norah, I don't think. She never mentioned it, at least."

"Albert's little secret."

"A strange obsession, isn't it?"

Roselyn frowned. "That's what scares me. An obsession."

He'd chosen to live out his days in a room with a view of the penitentiary where he'd plied his trade as an executioner. Another sign of his obsession, one that Roselyn had missed, too focused on the separation he'd insisted on. She'd been turned in on herself, licking her wounds, and hadn't noticed the deterioration of Albert's faculties.

"And what about the victim's parents?" she asked. "Anything new on their end?"

Peter shrugged. His theory wasn't looking good these days. After having shared the relevant information with the police, he'd run out of steam. All his suspects had rock-solid alibis, or they'd become exemplary citizens. That had been a hard blow to Peter, though Roselyn had seemed relieved. It meant her husband hadn't fallen prey to some madman out for vengeance.

"Let's not celebrate too soon. It's still possible — and you better believe I hope it isn't the case — that whoever's responsible for Albert's disappearance is linked, one way or another, to these executions." Peter kept fiddling with the plastic bag. "I could ask for a DNA analysis of the hair. At this point ..."

Roselyn smiled. A few moments ago she'd asked Peter to conduct a DNA analysis. He'd given her a hard no. It was such an unusual procedure and was sure to raise a few questions. And it meant they'd have to hand over these "new" clues to Kenneth Brownstein, the officer in charge of the file. He wouldn't be happy to see Roselyn conducting her own investigation, or that she'd kept relevant information from him.

Roselyn had told Peter that his colleague was unlikely to be deploying much effort to find Albert. In his eyes, this whole affair could be summarized by a confused, diminished old man out for a stroll, gone AWOL from his retirement home. Should the authorities really be giving this much importance to such a case when there were so many more urgent matters cluttering his desk?

Of course, for Roselyn, the only thing that mattered was finding her husband. Peter couldn't give up on her now, especially with all these new leads, new avenues, opening up before her.

The results of a DNA test wouldn't be available for a few days, anyway, Peter explained. He'd send the samples to the Harris County Institute of Forensic Sciences in Houston. They'd compare the result with the FBI's database.

"There's something else," Roselyn flatly stated. "Albert owns a gun."

The night before, Brian Pallister had called her back. He was standing in front of the box she'd asked him to pick up at the warehouse. Roselyn told him to open it. Inside, targets, ear and eye protection. Anything else? No. Nothing.

So the handgun that should have been there had disappeared. Likely taken by Albert. Unbeknownst to Roselyn.

A Beretta. Purchased by Roselyn in 1976 when the wives of Huntsville penitentiary COs had been offered weapons classes.

Peter sighed. "Do you remember the gun's serial number?"

That night Roselyn went out to grab a bite in town, despite Peter's invitation to share a meal with him and Adrian. She needed to clear her head. Alone.

She slipped on a flattering dress, tamed her hair, and put on some makeup. Then she stepped out to prowl the streets on her own, as she used to do when she was sixteen. A fantastic feeling that, too. Nostalgia had been her closest companion since her return to Huntsville. That night, for the first time, she had no desire to push it away, to ignore it. No, instead, she let herself fall prey to it entirely, not denying herself the pleasure of enjoying the city where she'd once been happy. Time had moved on, endlessly on. She missed her youth, that blessed period when her life still held all the promises that adulthood would take away.

She hadn't truly fulfilled those promises, had she? Norah's passing had been a terrible shock. And yet Roselyn didn't think her daughter's death had truly modified the way she evaluated her own life.

Her only real failure had been Albert. She had never been able to change him as she had so desired when they first met. She was the one who had compromised, shaped herself to his cracks and bumps and mounds. Made herself his negative.

Despite all that, she'd loved him. And still loved him. Despite everything she knew, or thought she knew, about him. Another woman might judge him harshly. But she wasn't another woman; she was Roselyn Kerensky, who would have given anything to see Albert appear suddenly around a corner and force him to answer a few questions about some stray locks of hair.

A trophy, she thought.

So he'd found pleasure in killing. That was the reason he'd refused promotions: to continue to kill in utmost impunity, to add a few more locks of hair to his collection.

Roselyn was sure she'd end up running into prison guards, maybe some of her husband's old colleagues, no matter which restaurant she chose. But tonight it didn't matter. She ended up at Fenian's Pub, a place that hadn't existed when she lived in the city. A sort of Irish coffee bar that tried a bit too hard to look modern — at least what passed for modern five years ago in Houston. Young waitresses in black tights, younger customers, some young enough to be her grandchildren! One day, not too far away, Adrian would come here with his girlfriend.

She sat at the bar and soon enough was chatting away with the barman — he was Norah's age — and then with a few customers who came near to chat her up. *I'll feel guilty tomorrow*, she told herself as she danced with one of them, twirling around like a teenager. Roselyn hadn't danced in a century, at least! The first time she went to the Christmas party of a theatre troupe she'd participated in, some computer technician drunk as a skunk had chased her all night. She'd sworn off such activities since.

But here, now, it was different. After a few glasses of wine, she began to feel light, free, unburdened as she spoke with one customer after another, as if every person she talked with could offer a life-changing experience, though surely they'd fade into a haze as soon as the night was over. She was carefree, a tantalizing and surprising feeling all at once.

Roselyn burst out of the bar at two in the morning, closing time. The barman locked the door behind her. He offered to drive her back to Peter's place, but Roselyn declined the invitation. She could just imagine herself arriving at her son-in-law's place with the barman on her arm — an old woman with a young man. She was just imagining things, of course; the barman's intentions were surely sincere. At her age you couldn't expect anything else from men.

She found herself suddenly alone in the middle of the night surrounded by thousands of inmates, and smiled at the notion. Exactly the same as when she was a young woman, though she hadn't thought about it at the time. These days she couldn't help but turn her mind to that reality. *Irony*, she told herself, *sharpens with age when we begin to sense the absurdity of the world surrounding us.*

Naturally, her feet guided her to her old house. How many times had Roselyn pretended to be sleeping deeply when Norah came home late at night, some new boyfriend in tow. Or returning with Peter, her best friend, the one who'd become her lover and would ask for her hand. Why hadn't he ever remarried? Too kind perhaps. And a little beige, you had to admit. Roselyn could easily imagine the long, boring nights with a policeman who couldn't help but yammer away about his work. At least Albert had always spared her the details of his.

The place hadn't changed much. The trees had grown. The new owners — two professors at Sam Houston University — had repainted the front door and changed the garage door, but everything else seemed as it used to be. It was strange to be there in the middle of the night without being able to tiptoe up the stairs and slip into bed. To find Albert there, still covered in prison stink. But she was no longer that Roselyn; she'd been chased out of his life without regard.

One night, it was in August she remembered, a few years after their wedding, while Norah was spending the summer at Camp Connally, Roselyn had awoken to a cold, empty bed. Worried, she'd found Albert sitting on the porch, lost in thought. She'd approached him without a sound, thinking he was sleeping, but he turned and looked up at her. Sorrow was painted on his face. There had been an execution earlier that day.

She crouched next to her husband without a word. He draped his arm tenderly around her shoulder. Just as her father had done when she was a child, when they curled up together after dinner. With Albert at her side, she felt that same sensation of contentment, of peace that no one and nothing could destroy. The State of Texas's hangman wouldn't have allowed it.

"You can't sleep because a man is dead?"

"No. Because Norah's not here."

Roselyn had been surprised by the answer. Each summer Norah left for Big Thicket with a gaggle of other kids her age. She spent the summer at Camp Connally — she eventually met Peter there. Adrian also went to the camp, though his father wasn't a penitentiary employee.

"She'll be back in three weeks."

"I'm scared she'll hurt herself, or worse ..."

"You're exaggerating. Nothing's ever happened there. It's a safe place."

"I'm afraid, anyway."

That year, when Norah returned from camp, Albert had taken her in his arms and held her tight, tighter than usual.

Norah.

Poor Norah.

She always seemed so tired. Slept late on weekends and during the week it was practically impossible to get her out of bed and send her on her way to McCarthy Aeronautics, where she worked in human resources. Worried, Peter had insisted she see a doctor. Tests soon showed she suffered from chronic kidney failure. The constant trips to Houston to the Texas Kidney Institute began. Dialysis and other treatment followed.

One night, when Peter returned home with Adrian in tow, he found her in bed, her face bloodless. Paramedics transported her to Houston. She received dialysis once, twice. Her kidney doctor informed Peter she only had a few weeks left to live. She wouldn't be returning home.

Albert was utterly devastated. He spent his days at the hospital, at his daughter's bedside, with Peter. Stood vigil. Refused to eat. Anyone who stumbled into the room by accident would have taken a moment to figure out who was dying. All through Norah's last days, Albert weakened, withered, as if in solidarity with his daughter. In the final few days, Norah fell into a coma, but Albert stayed there, seated in a straight-backed chair, holding his daughter's fingers tightly in his hand.

When Norah passed away, Albert was still sitting beside her. Roselyn was there, too, of course, as was Peter. Adrian, distraught by the repeated, demoralizing visits to the hospital, didn't have the strength to accompany his family, so Peter left him with a neighbour.

Over that period, Roselyn had kept busy, taking care of everything, since both Albert and Peter had been unable to function. She immersed herself in details to keep sadness at bay. It was only after Norah died that her anguish bubbled to the surface. It was as if she hadn't wanted to show her powerlessness to her devastated husband and son-in-law.

Peter and Roselyn had agreed to meet in a restaurant in the northern suburbs on the road to Dallas after work. He opened a file folder on the table as she pulled out a pill.

"Would you like some water, Roselyn?"

"Thanks."

Once she'd taken her medication, he said, "The first lock. Blond hair. Nothing in the FBI database on it. The brown hair, though, they got a hit."

In 1993 American justice had begun accepting DNA evidence as irrefutable. And so, in 1997, officers at every level started collecting DNA samples from every arrested person and compiling them in an FBI database. This so-called "administrative" procedure had made police work far easier.

Every criminal arrested since 1997 had a DNA sample in the FBI's database.

"The frizzy hair is from Angel Clements. Born in Georgia, arrested in 1998 for grand theft auto. Resale of stolen electronics, too. Pimping. The classic route for a thug coming out of black ghettoes, like the one in Savannah."

He'd been abandoned, careened from one foster home to another, running away often, hanging out with the wrong crowd. A few misdemeanors in childhood, and once he'd turned eighteen, the pattern continued until he found himself in prison. Three years in jail …

"Here in Huntsville?" Roselyn asked.

"No, in Georgia."

Roselyn couldn't understand the link to her husband. "Was a member of his family executed by Albert?" she suggested, trying to get Peter back on track.

"Never any official connection with Albert or the Texas penitentiary system."

"But how …"

"Angel Clements was shot and killed on November 16, 2006."

Roselyn felt nauseated. The next day Albert visited a hospital in Galveston for treatment of a burned hand.

Peter had come to the same conclusion. "The Savannah Police Department never found the killer. Or the weapon. Ballistic tests showed it was a Beretta."

The investigation had concluded it was a drug-related killing. With Clements's criminal past and the fact that the police hadn't been contacted by family members clamouring for answers, no one had worked too hard to find the killer. Soon it was case closed and down the memory hole.

Three years later, a few strands of hair, another trophy in the former executioner's scrapbook.

It was altogether possible that Albert had been the killer. Perhaps even likely.

But why?

Albert had gotten the Beretta from Roselyn and learned how to use it. Had he practised shooting old tin cans somewhere out in the woods? Roselyn had no idea. But it seemed clear that once he thought he knew the gun well enough Albert had travelled to Savannah, found Angel Clements, and shot him in the back of the head. In cold blood.

But he'd injured himself with the Beretta. Back in Texas, the former executioner had stopped at the University of Texas medical school, which was why he hadn't been treated in Huntsville.

"It just doesn't sound like Albert," she said. "I mean, the whole thing feels out of character."

"I agree with you."

"Something extraordinary must have happened for him to resort to violence."

Roselyn's husband was a civil servant. He'd never lifted a hand against anyone. Wouldn't have ever turned a gun on someone.

In his eyes, the death he meted out to the condemned man wasn't an act of violence but simply the continuation of a decision made by a judge and jury, by an appellate court and the governor. In short, by the entire justice system.

But in the case of Clements, if Roselyn's suspicions turned out to be true, Albert had taken the unusual decision of acting outside the law without the protection it offered him.

"Perhaps to punish him for a crime," she told Peter.

"I'm sorry?"

"Angel Clements might have committed a murder and never been punished for it. So Albert would have felt the need to inflict the death sentence."

Peter nodded. "Maybe. But Clements doesn't fit the bill. He was never charged for a violent crime. On the other hand, he might have been responsible for some action against Albert himself. The fact that he retrieved the gun without telling you, the whole series of events seems to me like he went to Savannah looking to take the law into his own hands."

In Peter's eyes, Albert had some unfinished business with this stranger. The only way to get back at the man? In utmost secrecy, shooting him dead, knowing no one would look too hard for the killer.

"What should we do?" Roselyn asked.

"We need to give everything we've found to Kenneth Brownstein."

18

Roosevelt Okambo's Cessna took off early from Bukoba. The night before, after his conversation with Teresa Mwandenga, Max had contracted his services to take him to Ukerewe Island. The accountant had given him the foundation's financial data, and Max had called the account manager at the local branch of the National Bank of Commerce. The man had confirmed the organization's solvency. Max had also contacted a few customers and suppliers. Mwandenga hadn't lied to him: The Colour of Respect Foundation was in good financial health.

What was more, the money Max had gotten off Jonathan Harris was nowhere to be found in the foundation's books or in the personal accounts of the two lawyers. Max's hunch had been right: the money had disappeared, cashed in by some stranger — perhaps the same person who'd killed both women.

In the plane, Max scanned the brochure he'd gotten from the receptionist at his hotel. Hilly Ukerewe, Lake Victoria's largest island, a paradise for birdwatchers. Namely eagles and black-crowned cranes. "Fishing is one of Ukerewe's most enjoyable activities," the document claimed. Bicycle tourism also seemed like a popular option. Bikes were available for rent, and a network of paths criss-crossed the island.

Nothing, however, on the albinos who'd found refuge on Ukerewe, fleeing human traffickers. No one seemed to know when this exodus had begun. But the elders remembered albino children, abandoned on the island's beaches by their parents who had sailed across from one of Lake Victoria's numerous lakeside villages. Fishermen would pick them up and bring them to local families, who adopted the children, allowing them to live a normal life. Well, almost normal.

Most of them couldn't read or write. Hence the importance of Sandy Hill School, founded with the help, among others, of European donors recruited by Dr. Scofield in London.

Max knew that Valéria was fully committed to the initiative. Sandy Hill was her pet project, as Teresa Mwandenga had confirmed.

Why had the lawyer visited a few days before her death? Max could have simply called Naomi Mulunga and questioned her over the phone, but he was convinced it would be more effective to surprise her. Not that he believed she was responsible for anything. Instead, since he'd landed in Bukoba, he had the impression he was operating in the full light of day, observed by everyone, beginning with Inspector Kilonzo. The Tanzanian police officer wasn't aware of this trip, unless Okambo had warned him, which Max thought might be possible.

The island appeared suddenly, followed by Nansio's airport — even more rudimentary than Bukoba's. The pilot had communicated with a taxi company. A small van waited for Max at the end of the airstrip made of hard, deep red earth.

"Sandy Hill School, please," he asked the teenage driver.

Max was expecting a bumpy ride and wasn't disappointed. The young man played chicken with every curve, yanking the steering wheel at the last possible moment in a cloud of red dust. His leaden foot on the accelerator, his car rattling its last breath, the teenager seemed to be auditioning for a stuntman's role. Asking him to slow down would have been useless. They reached the school in one piece, and Max got out on shaky legs. In the shady schoolyard, fifty or so children were in the midst of a physical education class. A number of them were albinos. Their teacher walked toward the fence that marked the limits of the property. "Can I help you?"

Max asked for Naomi Mulunga, not mentioning the reason for his visit, though adding he was there following an invitation from Dr. Scofield. A white lie which, he thought, would reassure the school's principal and motivate her to meet him quickly.

The tactic didn't work. Thirty minutes later Max was still standing in the schoolyard, left to hope that

Mulunga wasn't trying to reach the ophthalmologist to check on his claims.

A burst of children's laughter attracted Max's attention. Curious, he walked toward an open door and peered in. There was a large space in the middle of a room left by a table moved to the far wall. Small albino children were playing with toys similar to the truck found in Valéria's office. Max asked one of the children to show him his toy. It, too, was made from materials discarded by the Mwanza Brewery. Farther off, in a sort of net, were other identical toys. It was clear now; Valéria had gotten the small truck from this place when she came through to visit. A gift for Daniel. Who was he? And what role had he played in Valéria's death?

"Mr. Cheskin?"

Max turned around. A teacher stood in the doorway. He led him toward a short corridor that began on the other side of the schoolyard. A few moments later he opened the door to a room shrouded in darkness, its shutters closed tight. Seated behind a desk, Naomi Mulunga lifted her eyes as Max entered.

She was a woman in her forties, an albino, something the ophthalmologist had failed to mention.

Max apologized for dropping in unannounced. He was investigating Valéria and her daughter's deaths. He gave her the same story as he'd given Scofield.

She waved a hand toward a chair, apologizing for the half-light. "I'm very sensitive to the sun."

The room was cooler because of it. Max wasn't about to complain.

"And what do you want to know exactly, Mr. Cheskin?"

"Valéria came to see you a few days before she died. During that trip she bought a small toy truck she wanted to give to a child named Daniel."

"Daniel?"

The woman seemed surprised. In the dim light, Max couldn't tell whether she was play-acting or sincere. In any case, the tone of her voice made it sound as if she was truly surprised.

"I haven't seen Valéria in months. Last year, actually."

"She didn't visit to check on how the work on the school was going?"

"No."

"Perhaps she visited without you learning about it."

"Why would she do that?"

"Without casting doubts on your honesty, the foundation has put a lot of money into your establishment. Perhaps Valéria wanted to discreetly make sure the funds were being well spent."

The principal was quiet. Max regretted having spoken so crudely. He was half expecting her to kick him out of his office and be done with him. Instead, she asked, "What do you know of Valéria Michieka, Mr. Cheskin?"

Max wondered what she meant.

"You weren't sent by Dr. Scofield," she added.

He had no intention of telling her the truth, but clearly his earlier lie wasn't getting him anywhere. He told her he was investigating the killings of Valéria and her daughter as a private matter, since he wasn't much impressed by the competence of the police, who he thought were dragging their feet. He wanted to find the guilty parties and bring them to justice.

A small, sad smile appeared on the principal's face. "Justice? What a strange idea."

"The person or persons who did this must be punished."

"In that case, it has nothing to do with justice, not in this country at least."

"Why?"

"I have never believed in it."

"In justice?"

"Yes."

"Unlike Valéria. It's why the death penalty was reinstated in Tanzania."

"But the trafficking in albinos hasn't stopped."

"Valéria would have agreed with you."

Mulunga looked away.

"And you, what do you think about it?" Max asked.

The principal avoided the question by talking about Valéria and her lost causes, how the lawyer put her energy only into projects that were bound to fail, as if she feared people would think her lazy if she aimed for something that was actually possible.

"Well, she had a lost cause with albinos, all right," Max said.

The principal nodded, adding, "Do you know what motivated her in her heart of hearts?"

"I think so, yes."

The woman seemed surprised. "So you knew her well?"

"Well enough for her to tell me her story."

"So she spoke of me."

Max shook his head. "No, sorry."

"Yes, yes, I'm sure she did." The principal suddenly got up, and Max realized that her right leg stopped below the knee. Cut off.

He reeled for a moment, gathered himself, and looked at the woman again.

"Come with me," she said.

A large, floppy hat on her head, Mulunga, leaning on her crutches, walked almost unimpeded by her handicap. She told Max she'd never been able to get used to the artificial limb the foundation offered young crippled children. When Valéria found her, years after she was mutilated, Mulunga had already learned to move around on her homemade crutches. After what she'd been through, each step she took, no matter how uncomfortable or difficult, reminded her she was still alive.

Valéria and her father had abandoned her in the forest to bleed to death. Villagers, worried by her absence, quickly found her and carried her to a nearby clinic. Thanks to the doctor's quick work, Mulunga was saved.

"How did you get in touch with Valéria?"

"She got in touch with me, actually. Years later in the village. I didn't even recognize her. She was a city woman, now, a lawyer from what she told me. She was surprised to see me alive. She'd learned of my existence and came to see me right away."

"You must have been so angry, so —"

"No. But I understood that she felt guilty. That she wanted to atone for her mistake. Or at least unburden herself."

Valéria had offered her money, a house, anything. She was ready to give every penny she had to ease her conscience.

"I didn't know what to say. She reappeared in my life so suddenly, and her simply being there brought back so many dark memories."

Valéria insisted, and so Mulunga had blurted out, "I want to learn to read and write." ·

To combat illiteracy, the Nyerere government had ordered that at least one child, any child, from every household would be forced to go to school. It was always a boy, of course. Mulunga hadn't had the opportunity to see the inside of a classroom.

Valéria found her a teacher, a young man from the area who came several times a week to teach her the basics. Later, Mulunga was able to enter a boarding school for young girls in Dar es Salaam, paid for by Valéria. The albino was far older than the other children, but her determination was clear. After a few years, supported by Valéria, she accomplished her goal.

"My amputation opened the doors of knowledge," she said with a laugh.

After finishing her studies, she naturally transitioned into a role working with Valéria. That was how she'd come to run the school on Ukerewe, though it was only the latest stop in a series of responsibilities for The Colour of Respect Foundation.

Max wondered why Valéria had never mentioned Mulunga, despite having told him of the crime she'd committed with her father. And why had she made up this false visit to Ukerewe?

"I have no idea. We weren't very close, despite the unique circumstance that bound us. I was part of this small part of her life, one she locked in some corner of her mind ..."

"So she visited the school last year?"

"Or the year before. I can check if you want."

"And she brought back this little gift."

"It's possible."

"Who could have hated her so much to the point of torturing both her and her daughter and killing them both? Do you have any idea?"

"Valéria had enough enemies for ten lifetimes, but she was never directly threatened. At least not to my knowledge. Even when we began recruitment in clinics."

"Recruitment?"

Traffickers tended to buy children straight from their parents and hand them over to healers. Over the years, Valéria realized that maternity wards were hot spots for this sort of traffic. A large number of albinos disappeared straight out of the nursery.

Valéria had built a network of informants who warned the foundation when new albino babies were born, as well as putting them in touch with families and inviting them to move to Ukerewe or give away their children for adoption.

"How did she choose these informants?" Max asked.

"Nurses and clinic workers first and foremost, who cared about putting an end to the trafficking."

A thought tugged at Max. And suddenly, disparate information became clear: Samuel Musindo, Clara Lugembe's killer, had been a nurse in a village near

Dodoma. Chagula, the lawyer, had pointed him out in a picture, one that showed Valéria and Musindo in front of the clinic where the young man worked.

"Samuel Musindo was one of those contacts, wasn't he?" Max asked.

The woman hesitated for a moment, confirming his intuition. "At first, yes."

"And that's why Valéria attempted to purge any record of her association with him. She wanted to avoid being compromised during his trial." Max told her about the pictures.

"Musindo used the foundation," Mulunga told him. "He led us to believe that he cared about our project by giving us information about newborns and putting us in touch with their families. However, half the time he handed the babies over to the witch doctor Zuberi. Valéria discovered it all when he was arrested for Clara Lugembe's murder. She hadn't a clue before then."

"Strange that he never mentioned his contact with Valéria during his trial."

"That wouldn't have had an impact. What the foundation was doing in maternity wards across the country was well known by then."

Valéria might have wanted Musindo to incriminate Zuberi, which could have helped his case. But the nurse had refused, for a reason the principal didn't know. Even after being sentenced to death, waiting for his execution, he hadn't said a word.

"And who photographed Musindo with Valéria?" Max asked.

"I have no idea. Minister Lugembe knew about the foundation's work and tolerated it. He might have destroyed the pictures so as not to compromise the case against his daughter's murderer."

Perhaps. Max was getting a clearer picture of Valéria's anger, and her desire for revenge against Musindo. She had trusted the nurse, who ended up betraying them. Yes, traffickers were responsible for the worst atrocities, but Musindo was a reminder that the problem was deeper than that. The poison had spread to the roots of society, including hospitals and clinics where albinos should have been able to find respite and protection. Worst still, Musindo had chosen to carry his truth to the grave, a truth that would have put an end to Zuberi's dirty business — the man Valéria had been gunning for from the start.

A bell rang, shaking them out of their recollections, and a troop of children went scampering out of class-rooms into the schoolyard. Max and the principal were soon surrounded by overexcited children, shouting, roughhousing, full of energy. It was easy to identify the albinos, their heads covered, dark shades over their eyes, long sleeves down to their hands. A few of them already showed signs of skin cancer. Others had an arm ampu-tated, or a hand. Here was where the pictures had been taken for The Colour of Respect Foundation's pamphlet that Max had seen at the Sheraton Centre in Toronto when he'd met Valéria.

It seemed clear that Mulunga had brought him to this place to see the end of classes and look upon this group of children who only moments earlier had been listening to their teachers with a mixture of respect and fear.

Every time Max was in contact with African school-children, he'd always been struck by their concentration and solemnity. As if school, even the most modest school, was a gift they were grateful for. Children aware that they alone among their cousins, brothers, sisters, and friends could gain knowledge. They knew how lucky they were.

The principal turned to Max. "Valéria worked her whole life to repair the harm she did, even though she wasn't as guilty of it as she herself thought. We both came from an old world, one that clings to modernity's underbelly. We were both victims of ignorance and superstition. Valéria's initiatives weren't always well understood and she sometimes made mistakes. But she always aimed to help the poorest, the least privileged, those who had no one else to turn to."

Max, lost in thought, watched the children play their games with boundless enthusiasm.

She added, "Mr. Cheskin, nothing, no one, will bring Valéria and Sophie back to us. Let them rest in peace, please."

"You don't want the killers to be arrested and punished?"

"I told you — the legal system isn't the right tool for the job. You'll never get what you want."

"You have a better solution?"

"Too many have died already. Too much pain. Aren't you sick of it?" She gestured toward the children. In a solemn voice, she added, "We need to live now. To enjoy the light. Not the one that burns the skin, no, of course, but the light that guides us."

19

Back in Bukoba, Max couldn't stop thinking about his conversation with Naomi Mulunga. Jason Chagula, the lawyer, had counselled him to look into Clara Lugembe's case, and now Sandy Hill's principal was inviting him to do the same, though only implicitly. Her speech on how he must abandon his quest to preserve the memory of the two women hadn't convinced him. What was more, Max had no idea why the woman would have said such a thing. For him, the only way to free yourself from the past was to confront it, not sweep it under the rug, deny it, or attempt to minimize it.

Max had hoped the small toy truck and Daniel's name would hold the key to Valéria's secrets. So far his search hadn't given him any answers. The mystery had only deepened. He felt farther from the truth than when he'd landed in Bukoba, despite the fact that Samuel Musindo's name was back in the conversation.

The next day, without taking time to have breakfast, Max returned to Valéria's house. He found Teresa Mwandenga there, putting some semblance of order into the foundation's papers. Piles and piles of paperwork were laid out in front of her on the large desk: documents, letters and dossiers, all tied to Valéria's work as a lawyer.

"You're trying to figure out her papers?" Max asked.

"For what it's worth."

"Can I take a look?"

"Of course."

The accountant had been clear: Valéria worked for the foundation, but only once she'd finished her day job. In the evenings, she'd write an article for a magazine, reply to a blog, or simply correspond with sponsors and fundraisers in London or elsewhere. Hence her numerous exchanges with Scofield.

Albino hunting, a horror economy, found its sources in the dark side of African beliefs, a sort of perverted animism that most people thought long dead and buried but which was never far beneath the polished surface of the new man that Nyerere, Komba, Lugembe, and other Tanzanian leaders were trying to bring into existence.

Examining Valéria's papers, Max once again took stock of the sheer scale of her involvement. She lived for the cause, putting aside all her desires, as if wishing for a happy, uncomplicated life would have been a betrayal of the mission she'd taken on years earlier after the crime she committed with her father. Max had thought she felt for him close to what he felt for her, that he'd finally found someone with whom he could share a life of passion and love, someone to give meaning to his existence. He was wrong. Their separation had been painful, but more for himself than for Valéria. He was beginning to see that clearly now.

While the accountant was making coffee, Max rifled through a large metal file cabinet. Nothing of interest there. He then made his way to Sophie's room, which he hadn't searched the last time he'd been there. Contrary to the disorder of the rest of Valéria's house, this room was impeccable. Clearly, of the two women, she was the organized one.

Another desk, between the bed and a chest of drawers. More papers, files. One file contained old press clippings taken from Tanzanian papers — all about the Musindo trial. Sophie seemed to have collected everything ever said and written about the murder, the trial, and its aftermath, including the reinstatement of capital punishment. Valéria had always refused to explain the contradiction of her support for the death penalty, and this file might help Max understand. In it statistics indicated a net decrease of the traffic of albinos since capital punishment had been reinstated. Max didn't think the decrease was significant enough to justify its use. Valéria had told him as much the night she'd brought him to see Zuberi's home.

"What do you know about the relationship between Valéria and Minister Lugembe?" Max asked Mwandenga when she brought the coffee over.

She looked up at him, surprised.

"I heard they were very close," Max added.

"He protected her. Discreetly. Especially during the Musindo trial. And even before that."

When Valéria began her crusade to convince Minister Lugembe, the foundation's situation had become more complicated, Mwandenga explained. Valéria soon received warnings from funders and other NGOs uncomfortable with her fight for the reinstatement of the death penalty. In their eyes, you had to be virtuous through and through if you were to lead a battle against injustice. Valéria rejected this notion. The organizations that supported her mission were willing to demand more severe sentences for traffickers but not to the extent of demanding capital punishment.

During Samuel Musindo's trial, Mwandenga recalled, battle lines were drawn between Valéria and her traditional allies. Amnesty International and others accused her of eating out of Lugembe's hand, using the tragic death of his daughter to reach her goals. Valéria did nothing to calm the storm, nor justify the position she'd taken, believing she'd made her point of view clear more than once over the past months. The fact Lugembe's daughter was involved this time made no difference to her at all. She was only glad he'd finally seen the light.

Valéria made her way past the cameras and into the Dodoma courthouse every day to attend the nurse's trial. According to witnesses, Musindo was a drug addict, taking large doses of ephedra, a drug also known as herbal ecstasy. A banned substance in Tanzania. His motivation for the crime? Money, plain and simple. He made a profit every time he stole an albino child from the maternity ward. But not enough, never enough. According to his statement to the police, which he'd given freely before Chagula's arrival, he'd met his victim at the clinic where he worked. Clara Lugembe wanted to flee the region, fearing for her life, despite the bodyguards and the militia that protected her. Musindo claimed he could help, though he had other plans: to hand her over to the witch doctor Zuberi, who'd promised him a high price — that much was impossible to prove, however. And that fact alone explained why Zuberi spent so little time in detention, once Musindo refused to incriminate him.

When the young woman figured out the nurse's true intentions, she tried to get away from him. Musindo gave her a slap to get her to obey. Slapped her a bit too hard. She fell, smashed her head on the floor. "I don't know what came over me," the nurse said during the trial. Zuberi refused the body once he learned the identity of the victim. So Musindo tried to dispose of it in Dodoma's industrial dump. An anonymous phone call warned the authorities of his plan — the call had likely come from Zuberi himself, trying to demonstrate his innocence.

The trial took place over the course of a few weeks. Chagula attempted to show that Clara Lugembe's murder was not linked to the trafficking in albinos. A particularly clumsy approach, clearly improvised, that revealed how panicked the lawyer actually was. Seeing the jury unmoved by this argument, Chagula changed direction. He spoke of Musindo's health problems, his chronic allergies that required constant medication. Temporary psychosis was invoked — it was a potential side effect of ephedra. The nurse had been a victim of the illicit substance he'd ingested. The drug had made him feel invulnerable, he'd lost control. In other words, the accused needed medical care, not a prison term.

That approach wasn't too convincing, either.

Chagula's last try was to paint Musindo as a sympathetic character, getting local farmers to testify about the exceptional health services he'd dispensed. Among the clinic's employees, he was the most devoted, especially to his poorest patients.

But it was too little too late.

Of course, media speculation in Tanzania and elsewhere only complicated the case. Fuelled by rumours and secrets spilled by anonymous informants, the press in Dar es Salaam didn't hesitate to publish the wildest accusations. It sold papers — what else needed to be said? A hopped-up nurse had killed the minister of home affairs' daughter and now faced the ultimate punishment. Thanks to Valéria's lobbying, among others'.

As the defence tried to spin its yarn, Valéria realized that Musindo's cause was lost, which meant a golden opportunity to reinstate the death sentence.

The trial followed its course without political interference — at least not publicly. In private the state was preparing to kill a man. If the young man was found guilty, which everyone expected, the sentence would have to be quickly applied. He couldn't be kept behind bars for years. His punishment had to be exemplary, his crime used as a symbol.

The execution was set for December 2002, one month after the verdict was announced, in accordance with the new Tanzanian law the National Assembly had adopted at top speed. Chagula appealed, delaying the process by a few months. But the lawyer had nothing new to bring to the court's attention, so the initial verdict was upheld.

Musindo's family tried everything to save his life. In vain. They even contacted Joseph Lugembe personally, demanding mercy, clemency. The final decision was up to President Komba.

And Komba refused to budge.

On July 23, 2003, in a room specially set up at the Ukonga Prison, Musindo was rolled in on a gurney. He wouldn't be hanged, but executed by lethal injection. The nurse's family had visited the night before. They'd barricaded themselves in a hotel room soon afterward and were now awaiting the bad news.

Musindo, meanwhile, seemed resigned to his fate. He didn't fight. His eyes were glassy, dull, as if his soul had already left his body.

At six o'clock the first injections were administered, and the condemned man's face convulsed as if a nightmare had overtaken him. Then, after a last injection, Musindo's face became a mask forever frozen.

Clara Lugembe's killer was dead.

Valéria left the room, emotionless, under the machine-gun flash of reporters' cameras. She wasn't happy, no. She was sad instead, Mwandenga recalled. She hoped that the punishment, publicized as it had been, would put an end to the traffickers' horrible trade and those who profited from it: bush healers and witch doctors first and foremost, but also their clients in Tanzania and elsewhere in Africa.

Max's visit to Ukerewe hadn't helped him with the other facets of his investigation. He had been the victim of Valéria's scam, and he wondered why she'd needed the money and where it had ended up. And there was the matter of her secret trip just before her death. Valéria had told the accountant she'd visited Ukerewe, but according to the school's principal, she hadn't set foot in the school in years.

Where had Valéria gone … and why?

She had made an effort to keep everyone out of the loop, including her own accountant and the principal of Sandy Hill School. Wanting to keep her destination a secret, she'd travelled by road. A commercial flight would have left a paper trail. She could have asked Roosevelt Okambo for his air taxi, but it seemed she didn't want any witnesses. The Land Cruiser gave her the freedom to come and go as she pleased, with no one the wiser. She'd mentioned Ukerewe, a plausible destination, but only to avoid questions. But she'd gone somewhere else.

The Land Cruiser was still in the backyard. No one had moved it.

"Do you have the keys?" Max asked.

Mwandenga opened a small drawer, took out a set of keys from a metal box, and handed one to Max.

According to the accountant, one of the village's mechanics checked the vehicle once in a while to make sure it was in working order. Max thought he should visit the man in case Valéria had brought him the Land Cruiser before her long trip, but he doubted she would have revealed anything of interest to the man.

He unlocked the door, got into the driver's seat, and quickly rifled through the glove compartment, looking under the seats and then in the back. The vehicle was spotless, contrary to Valéria's habits. Sophie, sure, but not Valéria. She'd taken the precaution of cleaning everything once she returned. Valéria had suspected someone might check.

So she'd had her guard up.

Max examined the inside of the car. Nothing. He stepped out of the vehicle and peered at the frame: it was beat-up, covered in the telltale battle scars of potholed roads, though no recent major damage. He crouched and gazed at the bumper: stray splotches of red, chalky mud — laterite, which gave him no indication of Valéria's destination. Vast regions of Tanzania were covered with the clay-like soil, inlcluding many streets in Dar es Salaam.

Particles of laterite in the tires, as well. Scrutinizing them closely, Max noticed a tiny object stuck in the dried mud. He pulled it out, wiped it clean, and inspected it. Made of yellowish wood. Curious, Max wondered how this small piece of wood came to be lodged there.

Suddenly, he understood. It was a piece of golf tee, broken in half lengthwise. Cleaning it further, Max noticed a half-erased letter *B*, traced on the tee's head. While he might not know where Valéria had gone before her death, he now knew she'd driven on a golf course or at least near one.

B for Bahari Beach Golf Course, perhaps.

Whose owner was Thomas Musindo, the father of the man who'd murdered Clara Lugembe.

20

Roselyn stayed in the restaurant after her son-in-law left. Alone at the table, she tried to wrap her head around what had happened, and especially, what had sent her husband on this murderous rampage. According to Peter, Albert had strayed from his role as executioner: he'd become judge and jury. She could only conclude that he'd been motivated by some injustice or violence done to him or a member of his family. Norah or Adrian perhaps, or Roselyn herself. Since she had no memory of any deep wrong done to her, or Albert, for that matter, she cast her suspicions on something Angel Clements might have done to Norah or Adrian, or both.

Norah, most likely.

Roselyn recalled what Glenn Forrester had heard Albert murmur at the cemetery: *I'll do it for you, Norah. Just for you.*

Clements had done something to their daughter, caused her some harm, and Albert had decided to mete out his own brand of justice by killing the man. Roselyn could very well imagine that the person with the blond hair had suffered the same fate. If only Roselyn could figure out what these men had done to her daughter, she might better understand her husband's secret life. And perhaps, if these events were connected to his disappearance, she might uncover the clues that would help her find him.

That evening Roselyn forced Peter into a long conversation about Norah. Usually, Peter avoided the topic: his wife's illness and death were taboo to him, casting him too easily back to his darkest moments. Roselyn had mourned and managed to continue on her way, though not easily or lightly. For Peter it was the complete opposite. Each time Norah's name was mentioned, Roselyn saw him well up, and she changed the subject quickly, fearing she might start to cry herself.

But now she needed to know what had happened. How were Clements and Norah connected?

Peter furrowed his brow. "Why don't you let the police do their job?"

Roselyn knew he'd handed over everything they'd discovered to Kenneth Brownstein, including Albert's strange hair collection. She'd expected that Peter's colleague would be intrigued by the information and investigate the case with newfound vigour, but Brownstein's reaction had unsettled her. She had the impression that he saw her as a crazy old lady who bothered the police every time the wind blew the lid off her trash cans.

"You really think your colleague is criss-crossing the malls and bus stations, searching for a lost old man? He probably just opened a case and filed the basic paperwork."

"He's a conscientious officer."

"I don't doubt it. All I'm saying is that we need to take care of the matter ourselves. That we shouldn't wait for Kenneth, or anyone else."

"You think Albert's disappearance might be linked to Norah?"

"I don't know. I'm looking, thinking, exploring."

Peter sighed. "Norah was a wonderful woman. She would never have had anything to do with a scumbag like Clements."

"Sure, but Clements might have approached Norah."

"She would have mentioned it."

"Maybe not. Not if she was ashamed …"

"Ashamed?"

"Imagine this. Clements makes her believe he's got some medical miracle if only she has the money to spend. She loses a fortune on his treatments and feels like a fool for being had. She talks about it to Albert, who decides to act."

"Clements was killed months after Norah's death."

"True."

"She was always on her guard and would never have fallen for a scam like that."

"I was only trying to give you an example, Peter."

Roselyn understood that she wouldn't be able to get any information from her son-in-law except for a fairy-tale version of Norah and Albert. No matter which tack she tried to take, Peter kept avoiding the crux of the issue, visibly pained by her insistence.

"Try to remember," she urged him. "Something must have happened. I don't know what exactly, but Norah must have come into contact with Clements."

"To my knowledge, she never went to Georgia. Maybe before we met, but we never took a trip to Georgia or to anywhere else."

They hadn't even had a honeymoon, Roselyn recalled. Peter was walking the beat the day after their wedding.

And every other trip they'd planned remained just that — a project. They'd only travelled together, at the end, to Houston and back.

"What about the hospital?"

Peter shook his head. "How could Norah have met this criminal there?"

"A patient? Or maybe even a staff member?"

He shook his head again. "It's possible, but we'd have to go through a list of every staff member and every patient."

"What about Adrian? Maybe Clements went after him."

Peter stared right through Roselyn, preoccupied all of a sudden, then turned white as a sheet.

"Are you okay, Peter?"

He glanced away, got up, leaned against the window.

"What's going on?"

"Adrian might have met Clements."

Roselyn jumped to her feet.

Peter turned toward her. "At Camp Connally."

"What?"

Peter massaged his temples. The conversation was taking a painful turn. In a few words, Peter told her what had happened to Adrian in the summer of 2003 when he went to camp. He was seven and would be away from his family for the very first time. Norah and Peter had driven him to the camp one Saturday morning. At first everything seemed to go well, but one day Peter received a call from the director: Adrian had gotten lost in the woods during a treasure hunt. Immediately, Peter and Norah rushed to the camp. Everyone was looking for him ... in vain. The other children and the staff were in a state of shock. Rangers from Big Thicket were searching the area. They feared the worst.

"Why didn't you ever tell me?" Roselyn exclaimed. "Did Albert know at least?"

"We didn't want to worry you. What would've been the point? How could you have helped?"

"Where was Albert?"

"Off hunting with Glenn Forrester near Bosque River."

Roselyn sighed. "So the Rangers found Adrian?"

"We searched for two nights. A helicopter was being called in to assist from Houston when a farmer contacted the police. He'd found a child lost in his fields."

Adrian hadn't remembered a thing. He'd fallen while in the woods, and his first memory was of the kind farmer who'd taken him in.

Roselyn was furious. How could her son-in-law have kept this from her? "A pedophile?" she whispered. "Clements took Adrian? Abused him for days while he was unconscious?"

"A doctor examined Adrian. There were no traces of rape or assault. Not a single mark or injury."

A strange, incomprehensible situation. But her grandson was safe and sound, in good health, and hadn't been mistreated, or so it seemed. The doctor claimed he could have suffered a concussion that left him unconscious for hours.

"The police opened a case," Peter said. "Nothing came of it."

The happy denouement convinced Norah and Peter to simply stay quiet about the incident. Soon Adrian's misadventure was behind them, and they forgot all about it. The rest of the summer passed without a hitch. The following year Adrian didn't return to Camp Connally.

Roselyn and Peter were silent for a long time, looking out the window.

"I'd like to know where Clements spent that summer," Roselyn finally said.

Peter hurried to his office to read through the ex-con's file. "After coming out of prison, he was assigned to a halfway house, which means we should have details on his movements." He shuffled through the files and cleared his throat. "Still in Savannah. He never left Georgia, at least that's what's written here."

"You're sure?"

"It was a condition of his release. He was closely followed. The authorities knew he was no saint."

Another dead end. Dejection filled Roselyn.

"Wait a minute," Peter muttered. "It's written here that he asked his parole officer for permission to leave Savannah to do a job interview."

"Where?"

"In a garage in New Orleans. He took an auto repair class while behind bars."

Roselyn jumped. "When?"

There were no specific dates. Sometime during the summer of 2003.

"New Orleans is pretty far from here," Peter said.

"From here, sure. But Camp Connally is just north of Beaumont. That's thirty miles from the state line."

"You're saying Clements used this pretext to come to Texas, take Adrian, drug him in some way, then free him after a few days before disappearing altogether?"

Peter wasn't wrong. It did seem beyond belief.

However, for a reason they still didn't understand, Albert somehow came to learn of Clements's actions. What had happened in November 2006, months after Norah's death, to convince Albert to take out Roselyn's old Beretta, learn how to shoot on the sly, then drive to Savannah and put a bullet in Clements's head?

The next morning Roselyn was on the road to Louisiana. She'd written down the name and address of the garage where Clements had interviewed for a job as a car mechanic. Since he'd returned to Georgia, that meant he hadn't gotten the position. It wasn't much of a lead, but it was the only one she had. As she drove to New

Orleans, she thought that perhaps she'd shed light on the strange ties between Albert and Clements and that Adrian might be the key to the mystery.

Roselyn had taken her grandson aside before he left for school. She'd asked him a few questions, but he'd given no more answers than he had after his disappearance.

She'd been driving east for a while when her cell-phone rang. It was Peter. He asked her if everything was going well so far. He hadn't been very enthusiastic about her going off on the trip, and Roselyn knew why. He wanted to come along, wanted to be invited. It wasn't a good idea, according to her. Anyway, he had to stay in Huntsville to take care of Adrian. Over the past few days, she realized, Peter felt he had to play the role of protector toward her.

"You promise you won't take any risks?" he now asked.

What risks could she take? Angel Clements was long dead. It was ancient history, the lot of it.

"Just be careful, that's all."

Roselyn promised.

Two hours later the silhouette of New Orleans sky-scrapers stood in the distance.

The Whitney Hotel was the sort of old building Roselyn loved. Clean, anonymous, well managed, without frills, but with charm to spare. She felt calm as she walked through the crowd in the lobby toward the elevator, then went up to a spacious, sun-filled room. Roselyn had feared the noise from the hordes of tourists in the streets, but the windows were soundproofed. She took a shower, discovered a comfortable bathrobe behind the bathroom door, slipped it on, and lay on the bed, exhausted by so much travel in a few short days. Albert would have fitted well in this room, this hotel, this city. Why hadn't they ever come here? Why had he chosen to remain behind the walls of his memories of the penitentiary? She imagined him waking up in the middle of the night to rifle through his album full of locks of hair, while she slept soundly upstairs. They could have travelled together, like most couples their age. Maybe go back to Mexico, even spend a romantic weekend in this city. Roselyn had to admit that her husband hadn't been in love with her for a long time, perhaps as far back as Norah's death. As if their daughter had taken to the grave every ounce of love Albert had been capable of.

Late in the afternoon Roselyn left her car in the hotel parking lot and grabbed a cab up Esplanade Avenue, getting out on North Broad Street. Several houses and buildings had boarded-up windows, giving this poor, entirely black neighbourhood a doleful air. She was a bit worried as she headed toward Pontchartrain Auto Repair, a garage surrounded by a high metal fence, and hesitated at the entrance. All around, cars were in various states of dismemberment.

Roselyn was about to turn around when a corpulent man in overalls came out of the office, asking her what she wanted.

"I'm looking for my husband."

That was the first thing that had come to her.

Why? The words had popped out of her without her thinking about it.

The man looked her over. "He came here?"

"Maybe. Can we talk? Do you have five minutes?"

She followed the mechanic to the far end of the garage, trying to avoid dirtying her shoes. There was a small office there, covered in faded pin-ups. She wondered how many of the assembled mechanics there, all indifferent to her, were ex-cons like Angel Clements. Men trying to rebuild their lives. To leave the errors of their past behind them once and for all.

"I'm Gene Saltzman, by the way," he said, offering a surprisingly clean hand. "This is my garage. What can I do for you?"

"My husband disappeared a few days ago," she said, not volunteering too much information. She avoided mentioning Huntsville. She would have been forced to tell him that Albert worked for the prison system. It didn't seem like the time or the place for that sort of information. "He never came here, that much I'm sure of, but a friend of his, a man I'm trying to get hold of, who might know where my husband is, once applied for a job here. He even came for an interview but was not hired."

"Name?"

"Angel Clements. Back in the summer of 2003."

Nothing in Saltzman's face indicated he'd ever heard of him. "Before I got here. I bought the garage in 2005." He turned toward the workshop. "Hurley!"

A few moments later an older black man, muffler in hand, appeared. He leaned heavily against the door frame.

"Angel Clements, that name mean anything to you? He applied for a job here in 2003 as a mechanic."

Saltzman turned to Roselyn. "He was from New Orleans?"

"Savannah, Georgia."

The man with the muffler scratched his head, thinking hard, but soon gave up. No idea. He turned around and went back to the shop.

Roselyn looked at Saltzman. "Clements spent some time in jail. He was on parole when he came to New Orleans. Maybe he'd seen an ad in the paper?"

"That's not how mechanics are recruited. Not here at least."

"Clements came all the way from Georgia …"

"Did you visit any of the other garages? He might have given a fake address or made a mistake."

"Maybe."

"I don't know what to tell you. All my employees come from Delgado College. Back in the day it was easier to recruit mechanics, that's for sure. You just took a young kid with a good attitude and partnered him with someone who'd been in the shop for a while. Today cars are stuffed with electronics, you know …" He smiled, and Roselyn nodded. "Give me your number, anyway. If I hear something …"

Roselyn told him.

"You're from Georgia, too?"

"From Texas," she said without giving details.

As she left the office, Roselyn could feel the mechanics looking at her this time. She was convinced that someone here knew Clements and that they were feigning indifference to avoid uncomfortable questions.

Back at the hotel, as she quickly ate a tasteless sandwich she'd gotten out of a vending machine in the lobby, Roselyn faced the facts. If she didn't change her methods, she'd get nowhere.

As night fell, without a specific place in mind — the map given by the hotel turned out to be completely useless — she meandered about the French Quarter, ignoring the soulful jazz pouring out of every door. Tourists, young people mostly, were drinking crouched on the sidewalk, their bottles hidden in paper bags. Drunks crossed the street shouting after licence plates. A man pissed against a lamppost, another had passed out in a store entrance. While the old town was attractive during the day, at night it became simply repulsive. The whole area smelled like bad pizza and vomit. Roselyn suddenly missed Huntsville. All things considered, she told herself Albert would have hated this place.

21

It was a habit they'd inherited from British clubs, according to the president of the Tanzania Golf Association whom Max reached over the phone. Free publicity, of sorts. A small letter traced or engraved on the tee, given to players when they joined. Haki Suleiman, an outdoor sports store owner, had joined the organization — which he now headed — to promote golf among a new generation of Tanzanian business-men. The association distributed prizes and trophies in an annual ceremony.

"It's the ideal sport for professionals, that's what I always say. On the links, you can meet customers, nego-tiate contracts, and develop new partnerships."

"Fascinating," Max said.

Suleiman added, "Did you know Barack Obama plays golf regularly?"

Max sighed. "So this letter *B*, it's for the Bahari Beach Golf Course?"

"Correct you are."

"Still owned by Thomas Musindo?"

"Should be."

A few days before her house was invaded, before she and her daughter were tortured to death, Valéria had visited the father of Clara Lugembe's killer. What would have been the reason for this meeting? One thing was sure: her trip had begun in a panic, Valéria hitting the road suddenly in utmost secrecy. On her return, someone had broken into her home to kill her — and it wasn't the nobody hoodlum Kilonzo had dragged before the cameras.

The Bahari Beach Golf Course was forty kilometres from Dar es Salaam, off the road to Bagamoyo. After speaking with Suleiman, Max tried to reach Thomas Musindo at the golf course, but no dice.

Max got on his computer, looking for information about the man. After his son's arrest, a few articles testified to the despair and distress of the nurse's parents. Pictures on the *Citizen*'s website showed Musindo, a tall, powerful-looking individual. Another photo showed him in front of the clubhouse, trapped by journalists, forced to answer their questions. In another picture, also taken on the sly, he was seen jumping into a car beside the courthouse in the early days of the trial. In the background, a woman, her face half hidden by a policeman's extended arm. His wife, already ill, who would die from a heart attack the following year, according to another article.

In the *Daily News* and the *Express*, the same sort of pictures and articles.

And nothing else.

Max pulled a bottle of Scotch from his suitcase and collapsed onto the couch, glass in hand. He should be sleeping. Recuperating. But his mind rattled in every direction, trying in vain to find the link between leads that seemed to point in different directions.

His cellphone rang, waking him up, his glass still in his hand. A man's voice.

"So you're looking into me, I hear."

Max shook his head, clearing the cobwebs. He sat up, wide awake all of a sudden. "Who's this?"

"Awadhi Zuberi."

Jason Chagula, the lawyer, had lied to him. Not only had he stayed in contact with his former clients but he'd called Zuberi right after their meeting.

"I'd like to talk," Max replied.

"I've got nothing to do with Valéria Michieka's death," Zuberi said.

"I'm sure you know something that might help me find whoever's responsible."

"I know nothing. I haven't spoken to her in years."

"But you might be able to talk to me about Samuel Musindo."

A long silence.

"I'm not the police," Max continued. "And I've got no intention of repeating what you tell me. I'm looking into her murder for a single reason — I want to find who did it. That's it."

Silence again.

Zuberi's voice faded back in, weak, distorted by static, as if he was calling from some faraway place. "Do you know where I live?"

"Yes ... but the house is empty."

"I'll be there tonight. Midnight."

An hour later Max was driving alongside Lake Victoria. He wasn't happy about the idea of meeting the witch doctor, a criminal, in the middle of the night, a man who might be partly responsible for Valéria's death. But Zuberi was his only lead. He couldn't ignore it.

Outside Bukoba the darkness was complete. Opaque. As if some great tanker had foundered at the horizon, spilling its oil across the land. Max drove slowly, afraid he might hit an animal, or worse, a peasant walking along the road.

But the lakeside was deserted.

Chagula had described Zuberi as inoffensive. Fine and good, but that didn't exonerate him, which was why Max was nervous.

But this meeting with the so-called healer was his first break since he'd started investigating the affair.

Around a bend, right before Kemondo Bay, a police roadblock. Why would they be watching this stretch of road in the middle of the night?

Max brought his Jeep to a stop.

A man sauntered out of a small van, higher up on the road. Inspector Henry Kilonzo, looking as fresh as a daisy. Max felt a sinking feeling: was this entire road-block just for him?

"Mr. Cheskin ..." The inspector smiled.

"What are you doing here, Kilonzo? Going after chicken thieves now that your murderer is behind bars?"

"Please exit the vehicle. Leave the keys where they are."

Max sighed and opened his door.

Kilonzo led him aside while two police officers directed by Lieutenant Bruno Shembazi tore through the Jeep.

Another car appeared, drove right through the roadblock, and continued on its way.

So it is all just for me, Max realized.

"I thought I'd been clear," Kilonzo said. "The police are taking care of the investigation, and we very kindly informed you of all developments."

"You should think of a new career. You're the funniest officer this side of Lake Victoria."

Kilonzo wasn't in a laughing mood. "You went to Kigali."

"So?"

"And what were you looking for exactly?"

"Truth."

"The truth is here before you. We've got our suspect. He'll be confessing soon."

"Confessing to what? And in any case, I don't believe your suspect is the killer. And I don't believe you do, either."

"Why did you go to Rwanda?"

"To see a friend."

"And you came back the very same day?"

"We got into a fight."

A long silence. Kilonzo's animosity was palpable. Max should have been a bit more careful around the inspector. But enough was enough. He was about to tell him to go bother someone else when Kilonzo spoke.

"I've had my eye on you since you've gotten here. I don't trust you, Cheskin."

"If we're being honest, I feel the same way about you."

Kilonzo sighed. "I'll try again. What are you looking for exactly?"

"Valéria and Sophie's killer."

"I know. But what else?"

"I have no ill will toward you, Inspector, if that's what you fear. I don't care about your boss, or you career. I won't shout from the rooftops that you're an incompetent officer, more than likely corrupt, who's done everything in his power to impede this investigation."

Kilonzo remained silent, doing a poor job of hiding his anger.

"When I find who killed Valéria and her daughter," Max continued, "I promise I'll leave the country and won't bother anyone anymore. Now let me go on my way."

Kilonzo was about to give him a piece of his mind when a shout came from behind. It was Shembazi. "Sir, we found it!"

The two men turned in his direction. In the officer's hand was a plastic bag with a gun in it.

Max was sitting in the back of the van, flanked by two goons. Shembazi drove. Kilonzo, in the passenger seat, turned around occasionally to glance at his prisoner. Looking through the window, Max tried to understand where he was being driven to. He was lost. They might not even be near the lake anymore. From the darkness, suddenly, people emerged. Obedient roadside ghosts that moved out of the way of the passing van.

Inside, total silence.

Zuberi had phoned him out of nowhere. Kilonzo knew all about his trip to Kigali. A police checkpoint on the road to the witch doctor's house, its only target Max. And now this little trip in the middle of the night with Kilonzo and friends.

Max sighed. This wouldn't end well.

Soon, the van began moving down a poorly maintained gravel path.

Max couldn't help himself any longer. "Where are we going?"

Kilonzo gazed at him, impassive. What was the point of this masquerade?

"Oh, by the way, the revolver — not the most original trick. It doesn't intimidate me, Kilonzo. Where did you get it?"

The man held his silence.

Max tried again. "I'm sure you know all sorts of things I don't. And I might be able to tell you a few things. We could work together, you and I."

"You! Tell me something I don't know? What are you talking about?"

Max burst out laughing. "Not here, not like this. Bring me back to my Jeep, take your gun, and let me go to my meeting."

"What meeting?"

"Free me and I'll tell you everything."

‡

The van stopped in front of a warehouse, a sort of hangar, where a number of other police cars were parked. The constant to and fro of uniforms stopped when Shembazi got out of the van with his prisoner. Max recognized a few faces from the initial investigation of Valéria's death, men he'd seen at her house in Bukoba.

Shembazi dragged Max toward the warehouse door. Kilonzo led them in, making an entrance. He walked quickly, determined, overbearing. In a strange, solemn, theatrical atmosphere, Max felt he was playing the role of the protagonist, the tragic hero expected for far too long and now finally coming onto the scene to the audience's great relief.

"If you're trying to scare me, Kilonzo, you've done it."

Not turning around, the inspector barked, "Shut up."

"If you'd just listen to me for five minutes ..."

Without answering, Kilonzo opened the door, with Max preceding him inside. The place seemed like storage space for farm equipment. He noticed spotlights farther off, policemen crouched or leaning over the ground, absorbed by their work. Serious-looking men in lab coats.

A crime scene.

The men moved aside in silence.

Kilonzo pushed his prisoner in front of him. On the ground, a body, covered in plastic sheeting that bore the symbol of the area's regional police. Kilonzo gestured with his head for an agent to pull back the tarp.

Max peered at the man. Dried blood covered his chest, hiding the fatal gunshot wound.

Kilonzo approached the body, gave it a little nudge with his boot. "Awadhi Zuberi. A pioneer of AIDS treatment. Benefactor to the poor and maligned. But you know him, don't you? You're the one who killed him. With the gun we found in your Jeep."

Kilonzo turned to face Max. Stared at him in silence, knowing his colleagues were watching the show. Clearly, the inspector was enjoying every second of this charade.

"That's why you went to Kigali, right? To meet his lawyer so he'd introduce the two of you. I have no idea what you offered him. Money, most likely. Or perhaps you threatened him. With what? It doesn't matter. Chagula gave you the healer's location, just as you wished."

"You're crazy, Kilonzo."

"Zuberi said the same thing when I warned him. I told him that one of Valéria Michieka's former lovers had landed in the country and was convinced he was guilty of her death, as well as her daughter's. I told him to keep his head down, to leave the country even. But, no, he wouldn't listen. Curiosity overcame reason. He called you at your hotel to meet you."

"Enough! This is ridiculous."

"He wanted money, too, didn't he? You refused to give him a penny. Or maybe you got into an argument over something else. It doesn't matter, either. You felt threatened, you killed him."

"Are you done?"

"I'm just getting started, Cheskin. Over the past few days, I've been hearing about a con man who scammed

Jonathan Harris, Sunflower's CEO. You've heard about them, I'm sure? They're in the mobile phone business. Harris is an old buddy of Joseph Lugembe. The president is furious that someone went after one of his friends, and on Tanzanian soil, no less! He promised Harris he'd do everything in his power to find the man responsible."

Max was blinded by a flash of light. Next to Kilonzo, an officer held a camera in his hand.

The inspector smiled. "I'm sure Harris will have no trouble identifying you. When I discovered that you matched Robert Flanagan's description, I felt confidence in the future. This arrogant foreigner who treated Tanzania's police like the most awful amateurs, giving lessons to everyone, was, in reality, nothing more than a vulgar criminal."

He walked toward Max, leaned close to him, and whispered, "I'm going to get a promotion thanks to you, Cheskin. The president called me already to congratulate me. He claims I bring honour to the Tanzanian police, says I'm bound for a bright future." He smiled again. "All we need now is to find Harris's money and we'll close two cases at once. How efficient can one man be?"

Shembazi handed the plastic bag with the gun to Kilonzo.

"Ah, I almost forgot. We haven't checked yet, but I'm sure the investigation will prove that the bullet that killed Zuberi came from the gun you were hiding in the Jeep." The inspector grinned triumphantly. "All's well that ends well, Cheskin."

Max felt exhausted. What Kilonzo was telling him was a complete fable, but it would be viewed as true.

Max was the perfect patsy. He fitted the bill for this crime, or any other, real or imagined, they might want to pin on him.

He'd been trapped.

Kilonzo bent nearer to Max again, forcing him to look the inspector in the eye. "You're alone. The High Commission won't intervene. They don't even know you exist. You've got too many identities. You're mine, Cheskin, or Flanagan, or whoever you are. I can do whatever I want to you. No one will ever know. Welcome to hell, Cheskin."

22

The headquarters of the Kagera Regional Police was an old elementary school, recycled though not transformed. There were still school desks here and there, reminders of what the place had once been. Each office had a blackboard, though now covered in obscenities. At the back of the building a new section had been built housing a handful of cells. It still smelled of fresh paint and plaster. A few moments earlier Inspector Kilonzo had paraded Max in front of the intake counter, handcuffs around his wrists, before being forced to sit in a greasy waiting room on a plastic chair. The walls sweated with humidity. He was forced to empty his pockets in front of a surprised-looking young officer. Kilonzo accompanied his ward to the new cells, all deserted, curiously enough. As if Max was an honoured guest.

"Only the best for you," Kilonzo crowed.

The inspector pushed him into a cell and closed the door. Max heard him walk away. Then, not a sound, the intolerable silence of lifeless places.

His cell was tiny, poorly lit during the day, only a thin streak of light finding its way in. But at night it blazed like a carnival, harsh fluorescents bursting forth from behind metal mesh on the ceiling as soon as the sun went down.

Max spent his first night in that surreal atmosphere, going slightly mad from a liminal state both awake and asleep. Dream and reality mixing together in an awful soup that made him nauseous.

As the sun rose, he felt someone yanking at his hair. He fell off the cot onto the concrete. Standing two steps back, Kilonzo watched him. The goon who'd woken him placed his combat boot on Max's head. A child stamping on an overripe melon just to see it burst.

"Walter was part of the Uganda National Liberation Army, the one you've so much affection for," Kilonzo said. "That's where we met, he and I. Since then I've kept him close. Whenever I need to make an impression on a prisoner, I call upon his services. He enjoys it so much, you know."

Walter smiled.

"You were right to ask me questions about my service during the war against Uganda. We couldn't have beat Idi Amin if it hadn't been for men like Walter. They literally led the way to Kampala."

Max tried to move, but the goon applied a bit more pressure with his boot.

Walter laughed.

"A war that liberated the world of a bloodthirsty tyrant," Kilonzo continued. "And how did the international community thank Tanzania? We had to pay for every penny of the conflict. It took us twenty years to get back to our feet. Twenty years of paying debts for this war that we didn't even declare." Kilonzo put his hand on Walter's shoulder. "He could kill you. Easily. But it'd be a shame to get rid of you so quickly."

"Like you did with Valéria and her daughter?"

Kilonzo approached. "What did you say?"

"Don't take me for an idiot," Max said. "They busted down the door. The two women tortured. The *kandoya*. Your bulldog came off his leash, didn't he?"

"And you dare claim I'm responsible for their deaths?"

Max didn't respond. He tensed up for a blow he was sure Walter would deliver. But it didn't come.

Kilonzo crouched. "You can disagree with my methods all you want, Cheskin. But don't you dare call me a murderer."

"Prove me wrong."

The inspector smiled and turned to Walter. "He wants proof of my innocence! Can you believe it? From the very beginning this thief treated me like I was some dumb black without an ounce of sense. When he spits on me, he spits on you, too, Walter."

Walter grunted.

"Think of your mother," Kilonzo continued. "Your mother raped by Idi Amin's white mercenaries paid for by Gaddafi. You never got your revenge. Well, here's your chance. Make him pay for what they did. Hurt him, Walter. Hurt him bad."

Walter grabbed Max by the hair and pulled him to his feet. A first blow across his face, throwing him to his knees. Then more blows, slow, regular, a drumbeat, as if Walter wanted to enjoy himself. As soon as Max was about to lose consciousness, he'd stop. Max would crumple breathless for a while and then Walter would begin again. Kilonzo, bored, left the cell after a few minutes. But the blows kept coming. Eventually, Max fell into unconsciousness.

He woke, his head heavy, filled with strange noises, strange thoughts. On the floor stood a bowl of fetid water that hadn't been changed since he first got to the cell. He was dirty, exhausted, his brain unable to make connections between his exhaustion, the filth around him, the bowl of water, and his cot. How long had he been unconscious?

Walter returned to the cell shortly after and resumed his work. Max fell into darkness.

And the rhythm continued for what seemed like an eternity. Max tried to keep a sense of time by the change in lighting, artificial or natural. But soon enough he lost count — too much pain, too much confusion.

His life became a formless substance in which his mind wandered, always oscillating between conscious and not, incapable of latching on to anything.

Then one day the door to his cell opened.

Max put his arms around his head, thinking Walter was back. Footsteps. He kept his chin on his chest, unable to move, trying to protect himself, waiting for the blows that were sure to come.

A hand grabbed his head and pulled hard, forcing Max to look up: Inspector Kilonzo. He was wearing his dress uniform, the same he'd worn for Valéria and Sophie's funeral. The policeman released Max. His head, heavy and bruised, fell down again against his chest.

"Don't say I never did anything for you. I managed to save you from a lengthy, costly trial, at the end of which you'd be convicted of what we know you did — you murdered Awadhi Zuberi. Turns out that was a good thing, anyway. He was a charlatan. He exploited the poor and the sick. Why waste public funds to punish a man who rendered a service to the nation?" Kilonzo gauged the effect his words had on Max. Finally, he ordered, "Get up!" Then the inspector and his men dragged Max to a van behind the penitentiary where there was a group of onlookers.

"A few hours ago on the radio," Kilonzo continued, "I announced that Zuberi's killer will be transferred to a tribunal in Mwanza where he'll face a judge who will determine whether he's fit to stand trial."

Max said nothing.

"Unfortunately, the trial will never take place. Because — and this is sad news indeed — you will try to escape and we'll have to open fire. We can't let a killer loose on the population. So, you see, you'll be punished for your crime, but the taxpayers won't pay a penny for a drawn-out, pointless trial ..."

Before pushing Max into the van, Kilonzo took him by his collar and forced him to look at the small crowd. Young people mostly, but older men and women, as well. A few peasants, but also some who were visibly better off.

"I want them to see the face of the man who killed their favourite witch doctor," Kilonzo whispered in his ear.

Onlookers stared at Max with fascination mixed with disgust. There was fear, too, as if the monster before them could free himself from the police and send them to the grave as he had Zuberi.

Kilonzo pushed Max into the van, and they drove off. Other onlookers were posted along the road. The officers were clearly having great difficulty controlling this angry, grieving mob, thirsty for revenge. The inspector was offering them Max on a silver platter.

"Turn right," Kilonzo ordered the driver.

But that escape path was blocked, too. The driver turned and reached the main road on a barely passable dirt track. A police car was parked on the shoulder.

Kilonzo told the driver, "Go straight now."

"There are people everywhere."

"Just go," Kilonzo repeated.

From his position in the back of the van, Max couldn't see what was happening, but he could guess it was quite a scene based on the shouts, jeers, and honking. A roiling mass of people, their anger growing, looking for a scapegoat.

The van advanced slowly, despite the police escort. Kilonzo's nervousness was rubbing off on Max. The vehicle finally picked up speed, and the passengers breathed easier, including Max. But as they exited a village, an abandoned scooter blocked the road. The driver tried to avoid the obstacle, as did the patrol car that opened the way, but a crowd materialized, obstructing the van. Men pressed themselves against the vehicle, rocking it, trying to flip it over. Inside, Max and his guards, shunted about, had to yell to make themselves heard over the thump of fists pounding the van.

Kilonzo was barking orders to the driver when the driver's side window exploded in a shower of glass and dozens of grasping hands pulled him out of the car. A few moments later the truck flipped onto its side. Max protected his head as best he could, pulled on his handcuffs, and threw off the guard, who went flying, smashing his skull against the metal interior. Chaos ensued, with the crowd trying to get into the van through the passenger seat. Max, whom everyone seemed to be ignoring, went through the unconscious guard's pockets for the keys to the handcuffs. He found them and quickly unlocked his shackles.

Freed at last, he flung himself at Kilonzo, slamming the inspector's head against the side of the van and grabbing his gun just as the mob broke open the back door. Threatening them with the gun, Max ordered them to get out of the way. The crowd deflated with an almost audible gasp. It was easier to lynch someone when the victim was defenceless.

Max didn't leave them any time to recover their courage. He hurled himself out of the van, shouting, brandishing his weapon like a madman. The mob backed off. The murderer was free and had a weapon, too, a bloodthirsty killer on the loose.

Where to?

Max needed to find a place to flee before the crowd reassembled. He climbed along the embankment, hearing the panicked cries of his recent assailants. A man tried to start his motorbike. Max ran up to the fellow, pushed him down, jumped onto the bike, and raced off at full speed. Onlookers leaped out of the way as he revved the engine. Max saw the patrol car make a U-turn, rushing to save the other policemen trapped in the van.

He accelerated and, driving north, found himself on a deserted road lined with huts. Their occupants stared at Max roaring by, knowing nothing of the events.

Speeding straight ahead, he thought only of salvation and hoped he had a full tank of gas. Soon he was completely lost. Paths forked every which way. He had to choose one of them, get off the main roads, but where would they take him? He didn't know the countryside. He was easy prey, too easy. He needed a place to lie low, and fast.

Suddenly, around a small hill, Lake Victoria reappeared, as wide as a sea. A poorly maintained road followed the shore. Max headed straight to it, rounded another bank, and joined the path, picking up velocity again.

With a bit of luck, he told himself, he might make it. If he could reach the border with Uganda and find a way out of Tanzania. A chance in a million, but he didn't have a choice. In Uganda he'd try to make it to Kampala. He could reach out to Jayesh Srinivasan in Mumbai. What would he do then? Go back to Tanzania? That would be suicide, but he'd figure it out later. For now, all that counted was getting away from Kilonzo and his men.

After driving for a long time, making sure no one was following him, he sped through the small village of Rubafu, then on to Kanyiragwa. Along the dirt road were a few huts lost in the middle of fields.

With the peasants ignoring him, Max pushed the bike to the limit for the last kilometres. He hid it in some bushes, then walked to the shore, certain he could pay a fisherman to get him across to Uganda. But how? With what money? He had no idea.

Then he heard the rumble of a familiar engine. He raised his eyes. Roosevelt Okambo's Cessna was circling above.

He waved. Okambo tilted his wings. The plane was landing a bit farther off on the savannah.

Max ran.

23

Roselyn believed in capital punishment despite the statistics that demonstrated it was ineffective when it came to discouraging murder and other criminal activity. States that had abolished capital punishment weren't more violent than others, like Texas, which continued to kill at a sustained rate. Criminals didn't choose the time or place for their crimes based on the severity of the sentence. Yet she believed in the death penalty for moral reasons. It was just punishment as long as it stayed far from vengeance. It was unacceptable to kill innocent people. It was also needlessly cruel to let men rot on death row for fifteen years or more. Why give hope that a phone call from the governor might spare them the ultimate punishment?

In Texas clemency was never handed down. During his mandate as governor, George W. Bush hadn't reversed a single decision made by a jury for the one hundred and fifty-two executions he presided over, including the death of Terry Washington, a man with a cognitive disability who had the IQ of a seven-year-old. Cases like those outraged Roselyn, just as judicial errors did, but not enough to get her to disavow capital punishment and demand its repeal, as the demonstrators did who gathered in front of the Walls Unit on execution days.

To them, Albert Kerensky and the tie-down team weren't worth a dime more than the killers they executed. In Roselyn's eyes, her husband was no more than the executor of a policy put into place by democratically elected representatives. Albert knew nothing about the condemned person's previous life, his crimes or attitude in prison. Perhaps his ignorance was willed to protect himself. He had supervised the execution of Terry Washington in 1997. Had he known that the man he'd injected with a lethal cocktail had a disability? Newspapers had written about it so much that it was hard to imagine he hadn't heard about it. And what about Karla Tucker the following year? The first woman executed in Texas since 1863. And Frances Newton in 2005, guilty of having killed her husband and children. How had he reacted afterward? Had he discreetly gone to church as he always did?

Roselyn had no idea. She was in the dark when it came to whether there had come a point when Albert had had enough, where he'd wanted to give up. Pass the syringe on to someone else, hand the management of his team to one of his staff. He'd never done it, continuing month after month, that infernal rhythm, handing out death with all the regularity of a metronome. Roselyn could still recall those difficult weeks when he was finally forced to retire. Albert was irascible, impatient, anxious at having to leave his job for good.

His life, his real life, was at the Walls Unit. In that doleful execution room, decorated like a hospital. It surely wasn't at home with his wife and daughter. His retirement had been a sentence for him. An abrupt end. His own death row.

Albert kept a memento of each of his executions, a trophy of each of his victims. In her heart of hearts, Roselyn now knew that Albert had found deep pleasure in killing, or at least, great satisfaction. Perhaps it had been a profound need and his life had lost meaning when he couldn't kill anymore. She had always seen him as the detached executor of justice but, in fact, each of his killings had been a complex tapestry of emotion. He enjoyed the act but regretted having to do it so regularly, and that perhaps explained his trips to church. He couldn't help himself. He needed to kill but hated himself for not being able to control his impulses.

In short, if her husband was a serial killer, as she now believed, he was the most fearsome of them all, because his murders were permitted and justified by the law. His obsession, his madness, encouraged by the state.

Over breakfast, the day following her visit to Pontchartrain Auto Repair, Roselyn was absorbed by watching parents with their children in the hotel dining room, and barely felt the vibration of her phone. She thought it was Peter calling her, but it turned out to be Gene Saltzman.

"I might have something on Angel Clements."

On second thought, the old man had remembered Angel was a friend of Mitch Arceneaux. Mitch had worked at the garage back in the day. Anyway, Roselyn mentioning Clements's criminal past had shaken something loose for the old fellow. Arceneaux had heaped praise on his pal to the garage's former owner, so the latter had organized a meeting for them to perhaps offer him a job.

"Mitch said he was an incredible mechanic, a guy who worked quickly and efficiently."

"And why wasn't he hired?"

"He didn't mention his time in prison. If he admitted the fact, without being asked, he might have had a chance. The owner didn't mind he was a criminal that much, but he wanted an honest man."

"Where can I find Mitch?"

"He hasn't worked here in years. I still have his mother's address, though. When he left, he gave it to us in case we needed to reach him. But I don't know where he lives now."

After thanking Saltzman, Roselyn left her barely touched breakfast, jumped into her car, and headed for Fordoche, northwest of Baton Rouge.

As she drove on Highway 10, Roselyn tried to sort through what she'd just learned. The interview had been a front for Clements, who needed to trick his parole officer. He'd come all the way to New Orleans on this pretext solely to kidnap Adrian at Camp Connally. Why? And why had Norah told Albert what had happened but hadn't said anything to her?

It was a painful line of thinking for Roselyn. Only now learning a fact her husband, daughter, and son-in-law had been all aware of. She was in the dark about Adrian's kidnapping while everyone else knew. She hated her train of thought, hated blaming her daughter who, surely, had a good reason for acting as she did.

Once she passed Metairie, the highway seemed suspended above Lake Pontchartrain, weaving over the bayous. In Baton Rouge she crossed the Mississippi and continued west on 190 through a rural landscape. Modest homes along the road, a few farm buildings on a verdant plain.

The oil boom of the 1970s ensured the prosperity of Fordoche, at least at first glance. Located on a small street, the Arceneaux family home was clearly from another time. Two storeys of wooden shingles in the New England style. A house that had been extended and repaired over the years with diminishing success. These homes had once been the outward-facing symbols of the wealth of the families who lived inside. Not anymore. Clearly, whoever lived there now hadn't seen a penny of oil money.

Roselyn parked on the street in front of the house. The place seemed abandoned. No car in the driveway, no signs of life. A rusted mailbox that obviously wasn't in use anymore.

Peter had warned her to be careful, and so far she hadn't heeded his advice. But now she wasn't feeling too confident. Yet she couldn't stay here, sitting in a parked car.

She got out and walked toward the house. The blinds were drawn, no light peeking out from inside. She rang the doorbell, convinced there was no one inside, or at least no one who'd want to answer the door.

A few moments later a woman cracked the door open just as Roselyn was getting ready to walk back to her car. Apron, grey hair in a bun, slippers on her feet. A woman around Roselyn's own age, but who looked older. A German shepherd barked behind her. The living room was bathed in grey, faded, dirty light. The woman lived alone, that much was clear. She was afraid of everything, which explained the large unfriendly dog.

"I'm looking for Mitch," Roselyn said. "I'm not with the government or the police. He doesn't owe me money. I just want to talk."

Through the half-open door, the woman looked her over, not with hostility but curiosity. Unannounced visitors were probably a rare sight for her.

"Only a few moments of his time, no more," Roselyn continued when the woman didn't react. "My name is Roselyn Kerensky. I live in Houston, Texas. I've come all this way to speak with your son."

Silence.

"If he's not here, would you be so kind as to tell me where I could find Mitch? I have no quarrel with him, I swear. I'm ready to offer money to get him to speak with me."

Finally, the woman opened the door, turned around, and walked into the house. Roselyn considered that an invitation to follow. Carefully, scanning the environment, she followed the woman.

The living room hadn't been used in a century. More of a parlour, really, from another time. Entry forbidden to all, to be used as window dressing, actually, a showroom for visitors. Rare visitors, no doubt. Yet the woman in the apron kept up a semblance of normality. The only guest she was expecting now, Roselyn was sure, was death.

"You're Mitch's mother, right?" Roselyn called to the woman's back. She added a bit louder, "Do you understand what I'm saying? I'd like to speak to your son."

Hesitant, almost faltering, the woman walked to a chest of drawers and turned on a lamp. A single ray of light pierced the grey. It didn't light the room so much as highlight the gloom. The woman invited Roselyn to come nearer. On the dresser, in front of a mirror, a collection of small frames, all showing the same young man. A few mortuary pictures among the lot … Mitch had died. He was thirty years old in the pictures. A rangy, devastating smile. Eyes full of laughter.

And hair as blond as autumn wheat.

On the drive back, Roselyn mulled over what she'd discovered. First, Mitch Arceneaux was a friend of Angel Clements — there was no doubt about that. It was also possible, though it remained to be proven beyond a doubt, that the lock of blond hair in Albert's collection was his.

Talking with Mitch's mother, Roselyn learned that her son had died in an accident. It happened in Clear Creek in Jackson Parish. He'd gone up there to hunt deer. One day he fell out of a blind he'd built in a tree. A group of hunters found his body the next day.

Without checking Albert's schedule, Roselyn was sure he hadn't been home that day, that he'd been on the road for Clear Creek. He'd figured out the mechanic's schedule and put an end to him in the forest. Just as he had with Clements: murder in cold blood. Planned and executed. Punishment for those who'd harmed his grandson.

But there were questions unanswered. What had happened during those long hours when Adrian had been kidnapped? How had the perpetrators committed their crime? Where had Adrian been held? And what had they done to him? Roselyn could only imagine the worst but, seemingly, the worst hadn't happened. Adrian had come out safe and sound from his adventure without a single injury. Yet Albert had taken extraordinary measures to kill the two men.

Roselyn didn't have the answer. And nothing she could think of could explain her husband's behaviour. But she felt deep in her bones that the murders and his disappearance were connected.

How had Albert found the kidnappers? His search had been fruitful, extraordinarily so. One might have expected him to bog down in an endless quest for the two men, eventually becoming discouraged. But Albert had found them quickly and acted without hesitation. A true professional.

What am I thinking? Roselyn asked herself. *He's a professional.*

A killer with two hundred and thirty-four executions under his belt. And that was before Clements and Arceneaux.

Roselyn felt closer to the truth than ever; it was right around the corner but still just out of reach. Yet she could feel the shape of it.

As she approached the Texas state line, her phone vibrated: Peter calling from Huntsville. "They've got a lead on Albert. He's in Chicago."

Roselyn stopped the car on the shoulder as a concert of honking came from behind her.

"Roselyn, are you there?"

"Yes."

A cleaning lady at a Holiday Inn had called the police. One of the hotel's customers fitted the description for Albert Kerensky. He'd rented a room under a false name a few days before. By the time the police got there, Albert was gone. They confirmed his identity after going through his belongings.

"Where is he now?" Roselyn asked.

"No one knows."

"Why was he in Chicago?"

"I haven't a clue. And there were no answers in anything he left behind."

The Chicago PD had found his phone number and called the residence. Mrs. Callaghan had passed the message along to Peter a few minutes earlier.

"He hasn't returned to the room?" Roselyn asked.

"No."

Cars were flying by on the highway. A buzzing, a vibration that only accentuated her distress.

Albert, in Chicago … Albert, gone again.

"Roselyn?"

"Yes."

"Where are you now?"

She told him she was near Beaumont. Peter offered to come to her place in Houston that very night. The next day they could get on the first flight to Chicago. Her reply: she needed to be alone and take stock.

"I understand."

Peter gave her the phone number of the policeman in charge of the case. He had explained the situation to the officer and told him who Albert Kerensky was.

"Roselyn, if you need anything at all, I'm here for you."

She hung up, inhaled, and burst into tears. The dam broke all of a sudden. Roselyn cried for a long time, all self-control gone, hundreds of cars passing her, completely oblivious to her suffering. She could have stayed there for hours, but a police car soon pulled up behind her. An officer got out and stepped up to her window. Seeing her face ravaged by pain, he asked if she needed help.

She told the man that her husband had disappeared and that she'd almost found him, but he was gone again.

The man nodded, as if understanding, though he gave a quick look in the rear seat before turning back to Roselyn. "You can't stay here. It's dangerous."

The officer waited for Roselyn to drive off onto the highway before starting up his own car and merging into the stream of traffic.

24

Two hours earlier Roosevelt Okambo's plane landed on a strip at Kisarawe's private airport, forty kilometres from Dar es Salaam. In flight the pilot reached his cousin, Godfrey, "the best cab driver this side of the Sahara," who was waiting for Max as he deplaned.

In Godfrey's Mercedes, with a brand-new phone in hand, Max reserved a room at the Kilimanjaro, the local Hyatt Regency. Having left Zanzibar after learning of Valéria and her daughter's murders, Max had planned to retreat to Dar es Salaam in case things went south, which was definitely the case now. He had left a fresh passport at the hotel, with a matching credit card, an American driver's licence, and ten thousand dollars.

Despite being home to the busiest port in East Africa, the Heidelberg cement plant, and a sprouting of modern buildings — though modest in size compared to its rival city Nairobi — Dar es Salaam retained something of its past as a simple fishing village. A metropolis now, flanks open to the sea, greenery among its minarets, steeples, and satellite dishes, it still retained some of its old charm.

The Germans founded the place, though they were booted out of it at the end of the First World War. The British took over and helped develop it when the country was called Tanganyika, and the city naturally became the capital of the new state created in 1961 by Julius Nyerere. The government's seat had been transferred to Dodoma since but that hadn't convinced members of Parliament or civil servants to move there, except for Joseph Lugembe, who owned a home in Dodoma. When Parliament was out of session, everyone returned to Dar es Salaam. Ministries and embassies were still located there.

"Welcome to the Kilimanjaro, Mr. Coppersmith. Your luggage will be following you at a later time, I imagine?" the employee at the reception asked him, seeing Max arrive empty-handed.

"Took a left turn in Nairobi, or so that's what they told me."

"Our shops are open and at your disposal, sir. Our spa, as well, if you need any relaxation."

"Let me tell you, that was the most exhausting safari I've ever been on."

"Ah! But you'll always have the memories, won't you, sir?"

"That's true. I'll need a car, as well."

"We'll get right on it, Mr. Coppersmith."

Max sought shelter in his room. Beyond the palm trees, on the water, a parade of sailboats reminded him of the gathering of fishermen in Shela on Kenya's Lamu Island. Every amateur yachtsman in the city seemed to be present. A hundred, a thousand delicate handkerchiefs placed on the water, stirring with the breeze. But Max wasn't here to enjoy the view. He called the Bahari Beach Golf Course. No answer, no answering machine. He let the phone ring a long time, out of principle, before giving up.

In a little more than two hours, it would be full dark. It was too late now to go hunting for Thomas Musindo. He ordered room service instead and told himself he'd go to bed early.

The next morning, at the helm of an Audi provided by the hotel, Max took the Bagamoyo Road, heading north. He breezed through the outskirts of Dar es Salaam without a worry.

After Kunduchi, Bahari Beach appeared.

With a little trouble, Max found the golf course right behind a large hotel near a complex with tennis courts, a playground, a banquet hall, and other installations. The golf course was set farther back, as if hidden from motorists. A modest course, probably just nine holes. Max took the path to the clubhouse, flanked by long greens scattered with acacia trees. The place was deserted. A single vehicle in the parking lot, a Toyota pickup. He could have been hundreds of kilometres from Dar es Salaam and half a century earlier, too, in a private club the old British colonists so loved.

The main building was a long, squat rectangle, a sort of rustic bungalow. The front door was locked. A small poster indicated that the place was closed for renovations.

Max looked around.

Rather discreet renovations, it seemed to him.

At the hotel, when he was given directions for the golf course, no one had mentioned this temporary closure.

Carefully, Max circled the clubhouse. The windows at the back of the building were boarded up. Old golf carts parked haphazardly. On the ground, a small box of yellow tees. Max took one in his hand. It was identical to the tee he'd found caught in the Land Cruiser's tread. The engraved *B* was clearly visible.

But no trace of Thomas Musindo.

Max was about to return to his vehicle when he heard a distinct sound. Weak and far away, but there was no doubt — an engine. He scanned the golf course. There, in the distance, someone was mowing the greens.

After a moment's hesitation, Max walked toward the sound, using a path marked for golfers. The first green was in much better shape than the clubhouse. The grass had recently been cut, and with care.

Max saw the tractor near the second green. He hurried in that direction. The vehicle's engine was running, though Max couldn't see anyone. He came closer to the tractor when he heard a voice behind him say, "Can I help you?"

A man, fifty years old or so, emerged from a grove of trees, zipping up his fly. Clearly, Max had caught him at the perfect time.

"Are you Thomas Musindo?" he asked, knowing the answer. According to the pictures, Musindo was a stocky, well-built man, and looked a little like a farmer. This man standing in front of him was tall and lanky, more the city type.

"Gone. I'm the new owner."

"Do you know where I might find him?"

"What do you want with Musindo?"

His rudeness didn't suit him well. He seemed like an uncomfortable teenager trying to flex his muscles.

Ignoring the question, Max approached the man, who was getting back on his tractor. "You just bought the place, right?"

"Why do you want to know?"

"I'd like to talk to you. Just five minutes."

"I'm working. I'm busy."

"Five minutes."

The man sighed loudly before turning off his engine.

Jacob Buyogera had been pestering Thomas Musindo for years. The latter remained inflexible. The golf course barely made enough to cover its costs, attracting only lost or misinformed tourists who never came back for a second round. Yet Musindo refused to sell.

"Until recently," Buyogera told Max.

Buyogera was surprised to get a call from the man. He was now ready to get rid of it, and at a pretty good price as long as the transaction was rapidly closed.

"When did he make you the offer?"

"Earlier this month."

A few days before Valéria's death, and not too long after her visit to Musindo. She'd come here to warn him of something, which made him decide to get out of Dodge, and quickly. A hurried and definitive exit, forcing him to sell his beloved golf course on the cheap.

Again, Max couldn't figure out what the link between Valéria and Clara Lugembe's killer was. And where did the threat come from? What was its nature?

Max questioned the new owner without much to show for it. His description of Musindo corresponded more or less to the image Max had in his mind after reading up on the man. A fellow not inclined to give up, even when the deck seemed stacked. Except, for some reason, a few weeks earlier when Valéria had come to warn him and advise him to flee. Something she herself hadn't had the time to do.

Max mentioned Valéria Michieka's name to Buyogera, asking him if he'd seen her visit Musindo either recently or in the past. The new owner had a vague memory of hearing the name but hadn't seen Musindo in the company of any woman since his wife had passed.

"Do you know where I might reach Musindo?"

"At his place."

As he drove back to Dar es Salaam, Max tried to figure out Valéria's relationship with the killer's father. Little by little, he began piecing together an explanation that made sense: he had to return to the lawyer's childhood when she accompanied her father to a far-off village to find an albino to heal Evans, her big brother. When

Valéria told Max about her terrifying journey to the edge of horror, the secret that had upended her life, Max concluded that Valéria's existence was centred around this crime, fed by an insatiable desire for redemption. Max's recent encounter with the principal of the school on Ukerewe had confirmed what he felt back then. Valéria had handicapped an albino child, a crime she worked to atone for the rest of her life, first by tracking down the young victim and offering her an education, and later through her involvement in the defence of albinos. Max still didn't know how, but surely there was a link between the mission she'd dedicated herself to and her interest in the man who'd murdered Lugembe's daughter.

Thomas Musindo lived in a grand home surrounded by jacarandas near the Kivukoni Fish Market. Max rang the doorbell. No answer. Same result with the number Buyogera had given him, which he'd called a dozen times.

Max stood in the middle of the road, more like a large gravel path, pitted with holes the size of meteorite strikes. You could barely drive on it. He looked around. This whole neighbourhood appeared to be made of similar houses hidden from passersby.

Making sure he wasn't observed, Max slipped into an opening between the shrubbery and found himself in front of the home with its adjoining garage. He circled the place and reached a garden in the back, left fallow. He noticed that the back door had been forced. The lock broken, handle hanging loose. A recent break-in, or so it seemed: wood chips still littered the ground. Clearly, he wasn't the first to come looking for Musindo.

Carefully, he pushed the door open.

He was expecting the usual disorder of a rushed departure, but the inside of the home, the kitchen especially, didn't give the impression that someone had fled. A recent newspaper on the counter, a garbage can topped with fresh apple cores eaten that very morning perhaps. In the living room, a bit more disorder, but nothing that would indicate panic. Evidently, Musindo lived like a bachelor. Clothes left hanging from every chair, a bottle of beer abandoned on a low table. And a lamp left on, the only incongruous sign in this sunbathed room.

On a desk, photos of his son, Samuel. Many of them taken on the golf course: a young boy goofing off on the greens, or hiding behind a cart. Another picture, more recent, showed him at the Bugando School of Nursing, diploma in hand, a wide smile on his face.

Max pushed open the door to the bedroom. The bed was undone. He was about to continue his exploration when he noticed, on the floor, a drop of blood. Fresh blood. Max wheeled around: a body curled up on itself. Two arms tied by the elbows behind its back by a belt that circled its rib cage.

The *kandoya*.

He felt nauseous. Surely, that was how they had found Valéria and her daughter. They, too, had been tortured, like Musindo. But here, no machete. The man's suffering had come to an end with a bullet through his heart.

Max approached the body. Musindo's death was recent. The killer had gotten to him only minutes earlier; he might still be in the house. Max straightened, listened carefully. Total silence. Nobody in the other rooms.

Musindo had been tortured. Someone wanted information out of him. *A slow, painful death, the work of a professional*, thought Max. The killer had taken his time. He started on the parts of Musindo's body he could maim without causing the victim to die or black out. He'd worked him over, trying to get something out of Musindo. Just as he'd done to Valéria. She hadn't said a thing, clearly, since Musindo had suffered the same fate.

The Ugandan rebel group of which the doctor had spoken in Okambo's plane on the return from Kigali? No. He didn't think Kilonzo and his team were responsible this time, even if the policeman and his friend, Walter, were undoubtedly killers. Someone else's work then. He'd beaten Valéria and Sophie to death, gone after Zuberi next, and now Samuel Musindo's father.

A single connection between the killings: Clara Lugembe's murder by the young nurse. The four victims were tied to it one way or another.

Max decided to go through the house, even if the murderer hadn't thought it useful to ransack the place. What the killer wanted was in Musindo's head, not any information he could find in the home. He recalled the hypothesis of the doctor he'd met in the Cessna: what if Clara Lugembe's murder had been only a pretense, a conspiracy to force Komba's hand and re-establish the death penalty?

Max had no doubts about the nurse's guilt but was now beginning to have his suspicions about Valéria's innocence. Blinded by her activism for albinos, believing decision-makers were giving up on the fight, she might have orchestrated the kidnapping and murder of the daughter of the minister of home affairs, or perhaps, had manoeuvred to throw this first-class albino into the arms of Samuel Musindo. Once this death march had been put into motion by Valéria, it had grown out of control — in the media, among the president's closest aides — and it simply couldn't be stopped. Thomas Musindo's son had been led to the slaughter in the interest of Valéria's philanthropic ambitions.

What if, after his son's death, the father, having learned of Valéria's role, had threatened to alert the authorities? To buy his silence she needed money, a lot of money. The cash Max had extracted from the pockets of Jonathan Harris, Sunflower's CEO.

Who had killed all of them? And what role did the victims play in this story?

The phone rang, tearing through the quiet of the place. Max hesitated. On the fourth ring, he answered.

"Mr. Musindo?" a feminine voice asked. She sounded professional, hurried, and a little impatient, as if she was accusing Max of having taken his sweet time to answer the phone on purpose.

"This is him."

"South African Airways. We've had a problem with our web server. That's why the two tickets you purchased haven't been emailed to you yet. They'll be available at the South African Airways counter at the airport."

Two *tickets*, thought Max.

"Mr. Musindo?" the woman insisted.

"I'm sorry. Yes, I … I'm listening … do you think …"

"Yes?"

"Can the person I'm travelling with get the tickets for me?"

"Of course. I'll put a note in your file that Ms. Katala will pick them up, right?"

"Yes, that's it."

"They'll be available at one p.m. Thank you, Mr. Musindo. Have a good day."

On the drive back to the hotel, Max called the customer service number for South African Airways and explained the delicate situation he found himself in: there had been an error with his wife's first name. They couldn't well take the plane with that mistake now, could they? Might it be possible to have it fixed?

"I'm Thomas Musindo, by the way. My flight leaves tomorrow afternoon."

"So Janeth isn't the correct first name for Ms. Katala?"

"It's actually Janice," Max improvised.

"Okay, same for the passport and visa?"

"Visa? I didn't know we needed a visa!"

"For South Africa? Absolutely."

"You're right, of course. I have it right here. Sorry."

"So I've made the changes. Anything else I can help you with, Mr. Musindo?"

"That'll be it for now. Thanks."

Thomas Musindo was murdered as he was getting ready to leave for South Africa with a woman named Janeth Katala. The name meant nothing to him. Back at his room at the Kilimanjaro, Max went through the phone book and searched the Internet. Nothing, not a trace of Janeth Katala. Musindo had rushed through the sale of his golf course after a surprise visit by Valéria before purchasing two tickets for South Africa. He'd been getting ready to flee but had been one step behind. Why hadn't he disappeared immediately after the death of the lawyer and her daughter? Perhaps Musindo was waiting for someone. Janeth Katala, for example.

On the news that night, no mention of Thomas Musindo's murder, or Zuberi's, for that matter. Two killings, neither of which attracted media attention. Max looked at the schedule for South African Airways' flights to South Africa. There was only one, early the next morning. Destination: Johannesburg.

25

Roosevelt Okambo's cousin had a way into Julius Nyerere International Airport. Among the warehouses, behind the major installations, an employees-only entrance. The place was monitored like the rest of the airport, but with less zeal, according to the cousin. Security guards there didn't want to take the chance of asking the wrong questions to a minister or a high-ranking civil servant trying to get from point A to point B with some discretion. So they did little more than routine checks, and with not much enthusiasm.

Max managed to get into the departures hall through the back entrance and made his way to the South African Airways counter without being bothered by security or police. If his description had been passed around, no one seemed to have paid it any attention. Despite the early hour, the place was busy already. Max saw that the office to the far right seemed quieter. A woman behind a pane of glass, frenetically typing away at a keyboard, ignoring the bustle of the airport. In the window, her name: Linda Henning.

From the souvenir shop facing her office, Max called the South African Airways general number and asked the employee to use the public-address system to call Janeth Katala's name, his travel companion. She was at the airport, but he couldn't find her. He was afraid she might miss their flight to Johannesburg. He was waiting for her with their tickets in front of Ms. Henning's office.

"And you are?"

"Thomas Musindo."

Soon Janeth Katala's name rang out over the sound system. No one appeared. Max was worried Musindo's assassin might have gotten to Katala. But after ten minutes or so, a young woman arrived at Linda Henning's office and popped her head inside. The employee seemed confused. The woman pointed to the ceiling, indicating the public-address system. Anxious, she scanned her whereabouts. She had a wheeled bag beside her.

Max left the souvenir shop and approached the young woman. "Ms. Katala? I'm the one who called you. Sorry for the bother."

"What do you want?"

She seems more worried than scared, Max thought. "Robert Coppersmith, South African border services. For a visa verification. If you would follow me ..."

Katala looked around for Thomas Musindo. Max knew nothing of the nature of their relationship. This was not the time to ask.

He offered his widest smile to Henning, his involuntary ally, then bent down to take Katala's travel bag. He led her toward a coffee shop where Godfrey was waiting for him with a handful of other cab drivers.

As they walked, she rifled through her handbag searching for her passport and visa. Max stopped and turned to her. "Thomas Musindo won't be joining you this morning."

She glanced up at Max. "What's going on here? Who are you?"

"A friend."

"Where's Thomas?"

Max sighed. "He was killed. And your life is in danger, too."

Fear flashed in her eyes. She scanned the terminal again, hunting for someone perhaps. Fear had won over worry. Then her eyes returned to Max. "And what do you want from me?"

"First and foremost, to bring you somewhere you'll be safe."

"I'm not leaving the airport."

Around Max, an oblivious crowd of hurried travellers. The last thing he wanted was to attract attention. "I was a very good friend of Valéria Michieka. She was killed with her daughter, just like Musindo." Katala didn't seem surprised. Max reassured her. "You've got nothing to fear from me. Let's just not stay here."

Godfrey approached and picked up Katala's bag. She

followed him outside the terminal. When they reached the taxi, she hesitated, but ended up slipping into the back of the cab next to Max.

He waited for the car to leave the airport before continuing his conversation with the young woman. He kept glancing behind and around him, fearing Musindo's killer might be trailing them.

Once they were on the main road, convinced they weren't being followed, Max started to relax. "We'll be okay now."

"Where are we going?"

"To a hotel. Outside the city. I've reserved a room for you under a false name." Then he added, "Do you have family in Dar es Salaam? People who could be in danger?"

"No. My mother lives in Mwanza."

"Did you tell her about your trip?"

"I was going to call her and tell her once I was in Johannesburg."

"A wise decision."

"What happened to Thomas?"

"While I was investigating Valéria Michieka's murder, I discovered that Valéria had visited Thomas Musindo a few days before her death."

"Who killed him?"

"The same person who murdered Valéria, her daughter, Sophie, and the witch doctor Zuberi. Though I don't have conclusive proof yet."

A specialist in the finer points of torture Ugandan-style.

Max summarized how he'd discovered her name, and why he'd decided to reach out to her. Clearly, Thomas

Musindo hadn't revealed Katala's existence. That had saved her life.

"And what's your role in this story?" he asked.

"I have no role at all."

"Did you know Valéria?"

"Only by reputation."

"How did you hear of her? Was it the foundation, her work with albinos?"

"Through my brother, Lewis."

"Your brother?"

"He died last year."

"And why would anyone want to harm you?"

"Because I know things. Things Lewis told me."

Max waited for the rest.

"My brother is the man who executed Samuel Musindo at Ukonga Prison."

Max couldn't believe his ears.

Valéria Michieka and her daughter, Awadhi Zuberi, Thomas Musindo, and now Lewis Katala, all linked one way or another to the nurse's death.

The Oyster Bay Hotel on Coco Beach deserved its reputation. A lush garden, a magnificent view of the Indian Ocean, an excellent kitchen. The business people who frequented the Kilimanjaro were nowhere to be seen. Instead, it was all rich tourists, plump pink skin floating in the pool. Or wandering along the beach among the locals. Max had chosen the place because it was far from downtown, and most important, far from the Kilimanjaro Hotel. He had to be careful not to fall into a trap set by Musindo's killer. Janeth Katala had to be kept safe.

In the room, Max offered her a drink, which she declined.

"Tell me about your brother."

A graduate of the Tanzania Military Academy in Monduli, Lewis had hoped to become an officer one day, Janeth told him. For a reason she didn't know — perhaps he lost interest in the prospect of a military career — he eventually applied for a job with the Tanzania Prisons Service, which was looking for new guards for Ukonga. He got the job but first had to follow a six-month training program with other recruits. At the end of his training period, as he was about to begin working in earnest, he was approached by the higher-ups. They offered him a better-paying job, one that many guards had refused: executioner and death row guard at Ukonga.

All this took place during Samuel Musindo's trial for the murder of Clara Lugembe. The issue of trafficking in albinos was making front-page news, and some media outlets were actively hunting for witch doctors and self-styled healers. Zuberi, in particular, who had been arrested at the same time as Musindo.

When the guilty verdict came down, and the death sentence was being considered, Katala prepared himself for his first execution. There would be others ... later. Each harder than the last as he gained experience.

From time to time, Lewis returned to Mwanza to visit his mother. She'd hidden her son's true occupation from the neighbours, even though he hadn't asked her to. She didn't like what he did, but he was paid well and was generous with his family.

What was more, Ukonga's executioners — Katala had two colleagues — held a certain status in the prison and rather exceptional work conditions.

"And then one day it just became too much for him," Janeth continued. "He could barely sleep anymore, and when he finally managed to fall asleep, nightmares tormented him. He went to see a doctor and received exemption papers. He was able to return to Mwanza with a small pension."

Katala's life and career hadn't been out of the ordinary, quite the opposite. Predictable, really. Lewis had withdrawn into himself after his time at the penitentiary. He'd always been a jovial guy, ready to laugh. Now he was taciturn, preoccupied, unable to leave his old life as executioner behind.

Janeth had corresponded with him for his first few months at Ukonga. Far from home, he missed his family, and sometimes expressed doubts as to whether he'd made a mistake by accepting the post. But he was trapped by a contract that paid generously and allowed him to offer a better life for his family. As well, he wasn't allowed to communicate with the outside world, so he suffered alone. At Musindo's trial, when the death sentence was handed down, and after Chagula's appeals had been rejected, he'd begun writing more and more to his sister. A sort of diary wherein the executioner described the preparations, and especially, his contact with the prisoner.

Lewis told her about the daily routine on death row, surprisingly workaday. The increasingly frequent visits from Thomas, Samuel's father, as well as his mother, a discreet woman, always crying, who couldn't speak three full sentences without sobbing. Thomas would take over then, as distraught but not as brittle. What did they speak about? Everything and nothing, especially nothing. As if talking about the weather might make them forget the true reason of their visit, and why they were in this place.

"Lewis witnessed these conversations?"

"No. Samuel talked with him once his parents left."

They must have made strange bedfellows indeed: the death row inmate and his executioner. And while Musindo might not have spoken to the media, or gone into much detail with his family, he'd been far more loquacious with Katala. In this singular environment, the two men formed not a friendship but a kind of complicity based on shared solitude.

Max could visualize those long conversations. He imagined Samuel defensive at first and then slowly warming up to his nervous and sheepish executioner.

They had found mutual comfort in isolation behind bars. In Mwanza, Lewis sometimes summarized parts of their conversation to Janeth. He described a Musindo who was a far cry from the bloodthirsty killer portrayed in the media. Lewis spoke of another Musindo, one without animosity for anyone. What the nurse had done was vile, and he regretted it with all his heart, but he couldn't erase the wrong he'd done to Clara Lugembe and her family. He believed he deserved the death sentence.

Max tried to understand the motive behind this last-minute confession to someone who couldn't help him. Plainly, Musindo had accepted his fate. His life was over, and Lewis Katala allowed him to take stock one last time. Did he know about his guard's correspondence with his sister? According to Janeth, he didn't.

Two letters in particular had shaken her to her core.

One, dated July 15, 2003, a few days before the nurse's execution. A missive longer than most, written in the urgent moments before the end.

"What he told me in that letter … it's hard to think back to it. He thought he was losing his mind with all the pressure he was being put under. And then the day after the execution, July twenty-fourth, he repeated the same thing: that if the truth came out, he would lose his job."

"What truth?"

"Samuel Musindo wasn't executed."

Max stared at Janeth Katala, unable to understand.

She quickly added, "I had the same reaction. I didn't believe it."

"The execution didn't take place?"

"Yes, yes, it did. Musindo was executed, but he didn't die. He feigned death for a reason Lewis didn't know."

"Didn't your brother give him the injection?"

"Yes, but it wasn't the lethal cocktail it should have been. It was some harmless liquid."

Max was confused. Musindo's execution had been a well-orchestrated piece of theatre? Someone had given him a second chance, and it hadn't been Lewis, at least according to Janeth. The execution had been public. Max knew that government representatives had witnessed the procedure, including Minister Lugembe and President Komba, in addition to Valéria Michieka. With such a

MARIO BOLDUC

select audience, no one would ever doubt the execution
had, in fact, taken place. And this had been the first death
by lethal injection — in the past, Tanzania's inmates had
been hanged.

Musindo had been allowed to pretend to die. Since
no one had ever seen such a method of execution before,
no one could tell whether it had taken place as it should.
But how could such a thing happen? High-level contacts
with the penitentiary authorities would be needed, perhaps even as far up as the Ministry of Home Affairs.

Max closed his eyes, shaken by the repercussions of
what the woman had told him. "Why hide this information all these years?" he finally asked.

"I didn't want to cause trouble for my brother. He'd
left his job, sure, but I was afraid it might come back
to haunt him." She paused, then added, "A few weeks
ago I got a letter from the United States. The letter was
addressed to Lewis, but since my mother died last year,
and with him gone ... the letter ended up in my hands."

A long missive, written in a tone that seemed sometimes a hair's breadth from madness. An American
executioner writing to an African colleague. The letter
was all about how it was necessary to close the loop, to
end what had been started, to not let debts remain outstanding ...

Reading and rereading this strange letter, Janeth
had understood that the American was looking for
Samuel Musindo, hunting him, really, to kill the man
who'd walked free years ago.

"I was afraid. I called Samuel's father and told him
everything."

"And who was this American?"

"Albert Kerensky. A man they brought over from the United States to support Lewis."

"Another executioner?"

"Yes. It was my brother's first execution. He was unsure about the technical details. He didn't want to make a mistake. The authorities brought this Kerensky fellow here to supervise his work. An expert in lethal injection. It was all done in secret, of course."

Janeth didn't know any more than that. In his letters, Lewis often spoke of Kerensky, sometimes recounting their conversations, but never in much detail. Musindo hadn't developed the same relationship with Kerensky as he had with the younger executioner. Janeth knew the American had returned to the United States right after the execution.

Clearly, the decision not to execute Samuel hadn't come from Lewis Katala. Had it come from this American? Or was Kerensky following somebody else's orders, someone complicit in the crime?

Max knew he absolutely had to find the American to learn more about Janeth Katala's surprising revelation.

"Did you keep the letters?"

"I burned everything. I was afraid someone might find them."

26

The decision of the Republican governor of Illinois to suspend executions in 2000 surprised pundits and citizens alike. Then, on the very last days of his mandate in 2003, George Ryan cleared death row, sending waves through the political establishment. One hundred and sixty-seven inmates saw their sentences commuted to life in prison. And Ryan was no angel, quite the opposite, in fact. Accused of racketeering, corruption, and fraud, the governor was clearly attempting to put part of public opinion on his side, perhaps trying to avoid too severe a prison sentence. Hence, this last-minute spectacular measure, which did not end up helping him, in the end. George Ryan was sent to jail, anyway. He paid his debt to society in an Indiana prison.

Phil Stanway, the inspector in charge of Albert Kerensky's disappearance, guided Roselyn through the corridors of the Chicago Police Department, telling her about the former governor's stunt. She would have preferred he speak of something else. Or not speak at all.

"Today," Stanway rambled on, "with DNA testing, handing out a death penalty is a total crapshoot. I don't know how you do it in Texas. You just keep going full speed ahead like that."

Roselyn had taken for granted that her husband had done his job diligently over the years, without questioning the role of capital punishment in society. She might have been wrong. Some of the men he'd executed might have been victims of a miscarriage of justice. Roselyn couldn't remember if her husband had ever been confronted years after an execution with new evidence about someone's innocence. However, she did remember when one of the death row inmates had received a retrial sometime between 1972 and 1976. His sentence had been commuted to life in prison.

Albert had been irritable and nervous then, like all his colleagues most likely. A few years ago he'd even gone off on a rant — a rare occurrence for him — about DNA tests that were increasingly showing up in courtrooms as irrefutable proof. Albert was worried that old cases might be reopened and that the stories of men who'd been executed years or even decades earlier would end up being discussed in courtrooms across the state. Lawyers sticking their noses in every which way, trying to prove the innocence of long-dead men through DNA testing.

Thankfully, Texas authorities had resisted these requests. After all, there were currently too many prisoners on death row to think about criminals from a long time ago. The men were dead already, and nothing — except more pain — could come of reopening their files.

All the same ... did Albert go to sleep at night picturing the poor souls he'd put to death, trying to figure out which of them was innocent? He wasn't responsible for the trial, for the sentence, but he was the man who put the needle in their arms. He caused their deaths directly. He saw each man have his muscles contract, face contort, then fall silent. He pulled the needle out of their arms once death had been confirmed by the doctor.

The abolitionist waves of the 1990s hadn't seemed to bother Albert. Maybe he didn't have an opinion on the question, and Roselyn had refrained from discussing it with him.

Perhaps she should have. Today there were so many subjects she regretted never having talked about with her husband.

Phil Stanway led her into a room where the objects they'd found in Albert's Holiday Inn room were displayed. On the table, she recognized his clothes, razor, toothbrush, an old copy of the *Chicago Tribune*, an unopened bottle of Tylenol, a can of Canada Dry. Out of a small leather case, Stanway pulled out a cellphone. Years earlier, after months of Roselyn's nagging, Albert had gotten a phone. But it wasn't this one.

Stanway read her thoughts. "We checked. No messages, no calls."

Roselyn asked him whether he had any idea where her husband was, or why Albert had come to Chicago. According to Stanway, her husband had registered under a false name and paid cash, as if attempting to avoid someone's attention.

"It's the most plausible hypothesis," he said. "However, we also discovered that your husband made a passport request with a private company that specializes in the speedy procurement of travel documents."

That surprised Roselyn.

"He received his passport three days ago."

"He was trying to leave the States?"

"Looks like it."

He'd gotten the room as he waited for the passport. Roselyn renewed hers out of habit, even if she hadn't had the opportunity to leave the United States in a while and had given up on travelling to Mexico.

"We've sent his name and description to border agencies and airports. No one has seen him so far."

"Why Chicago? You can get a passport anywhere. He could have gotten it back home in Texas. Why come so far?"

Stanway didn't have a clue.

"And how did he come here?"

"Most likely by bus. I've had his picture sent out to the terminal. We'll see."

An employee walked into the room and handed Stanway a regulation cardboard box, which he filled with Albert's personal effects. Roselyn signed a document the young woman gave her, took the box, and followed Stanway through the corridors again.

"If we hear anything, you'll be the first to know. Do you have a place to stay in Chicago? Or would you like —"

"I'm fine. I have friends in the area. Old friends." Roselyn hadn't prepared herself. If only she'd accepted Peter's offer. He would have helped her keep a cool head, make sure she was organized. She was completely lost.

Roselyn felt Stanway could see right through her, knew she didn't have friends here, and was cross with herself for acting this way. Why had she refused his help?

Stanway handed her his card, telling her to call if she needed anything, at any time — he even added his private number — but Roselyn understood it was a form of politeness. Surely, he wouldn't be happy if she bothered him at home.

"Can I call you a cab?"

"Yes, please."

Roselyn just wanted to get away from him and be alone. To puzzle through everything that had happened in light of what she'd discovered in Louisiana, as well as what Stanway had told her. Of course, she hadn't told the officer she suspected her husband of having murdered Clements and Arceneaux. That would only complicate things. And she didn't feel like having to explain Albert's behaviour.

Roselyn had gone straight to the police station from the airport. Now she needed to find a hotel room. The Westin seemed both luxurious and anonymous. Why not? The taxi driver dropped her off at the entrance while a bellhop grabbed her luggage.

By the time she got into her room, her back ached and she had but one objective in mind: get some sleep. Despite her exhaustion, she called room service and ordered something to eat. She then got in touch with Stanway to tell him where she was staying and thank him for his efforts. Roselyn even had time to take a shower before the food arrived; she placed the tray on a small table next to her bag.

Her phone vibrated: Peter trying to reach her again.

"How are you? Did you see Inspector Stanway?"

"He's in charge of the investigation. He seems like a sharp fellow."

"Good, good. You told him about Clements and Arceneaux?"

"No."

"Why?"

She sighed. "I just can't see Albert as a killer. And I don't want the police looking for him as if he were a murderer at large. I want them looking for an old man who's gotten lost."

"I understand."

"How's Adrian?"

"Fine. He misses you."

"Tell him I miss him, too."

Roselyn hadn't yet opened the cardboard box she'd received from the police. As she ate, she examined its contents. In addition to familiar objects, a flyer caught her attention. An ad for an organization called The Colour of Respect Foundation, showing African albino children. The last sheet of the pamphlet was an envelope in which donors could send their contributions. Headquarters were located somewhere in Africa. In Tanzania.

The pamphlet was a strange thing to find in Albert's belongings. What was more, Valéria Michieka's name was familiar. Roselyn had encountered it in a police report. When Mitch Arceneaux died at Clear Creek, the police concluded it had been an accidental fall, though they had investigated his criminal past. Mitch had been arrested for fighting in Tanzania and was charged with assault and battery. Valéria Michieka, a lawyer, worked his case. Thanks to her, Arceneaux had been able to return to America. Later, still according to the report, he'd kept up a relationship with the Tanzanian woman, though no further details had been given.

Roselyn furrowed her brow. Angel Clements, Mitch Arceneaux, and Valéria Michieka. All three linked to Albert one way or another.

Valéria Michieka.

Roselyn turned the name over in her mind. Where had Albert gotten the pamphlet? Here in Chicago? Why would her husband come to a city he knew nothing about and rent a hotel room for a few days? Why had he left in such a hurry without packing his bags or taking his papers with him, all information that could easily identify him? Unless, of course, this precipitous departure was involuntary. Perhaps he'd been lured to Chicago, someone making him believe he could find something he was looking for. A trap. Albert was somewhere, in a bad spot, in the hands of individuals who wanted to harm him.

She pushed that hypothesis out of her mind. Her husband was armed, definitely, and the weapon wasn't part of his personal effects. Neither was his new passport. Reality was far simpler, she was sure: the hotel management was worried about this customer and had contacted the police. Albert had noticed the commotion and decided to disappear discreetly.

With a passport and a gun.

A bad combination if there ever was one.

After her meal, Roselyn thought about calling Stanway at home but decided against it.

The next morning she went into the lobby where the Westin concierge apologized for the renovations to the business centre. Wi-Fi was still available in every room and the lobby. Since Roselyn didn't have a computer, she was directed to the Harold Washington Library, Chicago's main branch, a few blocks away.

Roselyn walked to it and found herself among a horde of schoolchildren on a field trip. Behind the counter, a young librarian greeted her with a smile. "May I have your ID? It's mandatory for computer use."

Roselyn handed it over.

"Kerensky! What a famous name! Shared by the man who replaced the tsar as the head of the short-lived provisional democratic government in revolutionary Russia. Driven out of power by Lenin."

Roselyn recalled having seen the name somewhere during her studies a long time ago. She couldn't remember the context anymore.

"Do you know what happened to Kerensky?" the librarian asked.

Roselyn had no idea.

"He died in New York City in 1970. Can you imagine? He outlived the instigators of the Bolshevik Revolution, many of whom were victims of Stalin's atrocities, and ended up in New York. Amazing, isn't it?"

There were three computers in a tiny room behind the children's section. The librarian showed Roselyn how to operate them. Once the librarian had returned to her counter, Roselyn googled The Colour of Respect Foundation and found the organization's website. The front page was dominated by a text written by the foundation's director, Valéria Michieka.

There was a picture of an elegant woman smiling at the camera. A short presentation gave information about her activism for the albino cause. The lawyer, according to the site, had dedicated her career to defending these poor souls. Roselyn discovered, as she read, the horrors these children and even adults were subjected to. Pictures of young women, mutilated, forced her to close her eyes. How could men be so cruel? Why this pathological obsession with hurting one another?

On the right of the screen, a button offered a recording of a portion of a speech. Roselyn opened a new window: a warm, rich voice came out of the speakers after a musical number. A traditional Tanzanian song. Roselyn had been expecting an exotic, strangely arrhythmic beat — one evening, Norah had brought her to an Indian music showcase at the university, and Roselyn had been bored half to death.

The song kept playing, its tempo regular, strong, a song you could almost dance to, making you want to jump out of your seat, clap your hands, and holler along with the beat. *A world away from Johnny Cash and his doleful airs*, Roselyn thought.

On the screen, over the song, Michieka spoke of her work, her foundation. A younger woman, looking just like her, stood next to her. Her daughter, Sophie. The mother seemed proud of her. Roselyn saw Norah in her mind's eye, her heart tearing anew. She quickly banished the thought. She was already making herself sick with Albert's disappearance. Norah would have to wait.

Curious, Roselyn found the Wikipedia entry for Valéria Michieka. Some of the information was the same, though the article gave more details on her private life and that of her daughter.

All interesting stuff, but Roselyn couldn't understand why Albert had looked into Michieka and her foundation.

Then a paragraph attracted her attention. Valéria and her daughter had recently been killed. Roselyn was filled with unexpected sadness. She knew nothing of the two women, but simply seeing them together in that short video, so happy standing next to each other, made her feel as if she'd just lost a friend. She clicked on a link and followed the story on the *Daily News* website. Reading through it, Roselyn discovered with disbelief that Valéria had been an advocate for the reinstatement of capital punishment in order to punish those who trafficked in albinos. Her cause had triumphed thanks to the trial that resulted from Clara Lugembe's killing, the albino daughter of the minister of home affairs at the time. Samuel Musindo had been executed on July 23, 2003.

Roselyn leaned back against her chair. Returning to the hotel, she called Peter in Huntsville. "Tell me again. When did Adrian disappear from Camp Connally?"

Peter put the phone down to get an old calendar. When he returned a minute later, he flipped through it. "The week of July twentieth, 2003. From Tuesday to Thursday."

Just as Samuel Musindo was being executed in Tanzania.

Roselyn thanked Peter, hung up, and called Glenn Forrester to ask whether he'd actually gone hunting with Albert in July 2003. It was years ago, and Glenn's memory wasn't what it had been. He promised he'd look through his old records for the answer.

An hour later he called Roselyn, after communicating with a student who occasionally helped him at the museum. The student confirmed that Glenn had gone hunting, but according to the young man, Glenn had camped out that week.

"Albert hated sleeping in a tent. When we went together, we always rented one of the cabins the park has. If I was camping that week, it means Albert wasn't with me."

That was just too much of a coincidence. What if Albert had led everyone, including his wife, to believe he'd spent the week with Glenn while in reality he was on the other side of the world to execute a man?

In utmost secrecy.

27

On the ground floor of the Westin, a travel agency was flanked by a salon and a car rental counter. Back from the library, Roselyn asked the young woman at the agency for information on flights between Chicago and Tanzania. The woman shot Roselyn a curious look as if to say, "You don't look the type to be going on that sort of trip. Why not Rome or Madrid?"

"It's an anniversary present for my husband. He's always been a hunting enthusiast."

That was what people did in Africa, right? Hunt exotic animals?

The travel agent tapped on her keyboard, then smiled and glanced up. "British Airways has daily flights from Chicago, with a layover in London. It's really your best choice. Or else you need to go through Cairo or Addis Ababa."

Albert had travelled all the way here with a clear idea in mind, Roselyn thought — travel to Africa. Though she didn't have the proof just yet.

"Is it easy to book a flight?"

"I'm at your service."

Albert, in Africa. He'd gone once. Today, trying to return.

"I hope my husband didn't make the mistake of buying the ticket himself. Did he?"

The agent smiled. "It's rare for me to sell trips to Africa. For Rome or Madrid, however …"

Roselyn didn't feel like returning to her room just yet. She stopped in one of the hotel's coffee shops and ordered a cappuccino that she drank facing the window, seated at a small round table. The place was swarming with noisy tourists, exhausted after a day of exploration. Roselyn envied that feeling of happy weariness, their laughter, their carefreeness.

What should she do now? Where could she find the next clue? And where was he, where was Albert? Already headed for Tanzania with a Beretta in his luggage? Could he actually even do that? And why? Did he intend to kill someone, as he had Clements and Arceneaux?

And what if he'd killed other people? Valéria Michieka and her daughter perhaps. No, that wasn't possible. They had been murdered days before while Albert was still in Chicago.

Maybe the passport was for travel to another country. But where?

"Is this seat taken?"

Roselyn hadn't heard the man approach her, double espresso in hand.

"Sure, sure," she answered distractedly, taking her bag off the chair on the other side of the table.

The stranger sat down, back against the window. Roselyn returned to her contemplations. Albert hadn't taken the plane, she was sure, because he wouldn't have been able to take the Beretta with him. He was travelling some other way. He was on the Greyhound, Stanway had said as much. But he'd gotten a passport, so he must have been intending to leave the country.

"I'm looking for him, too."

Surprised, Roselyn looked up. "What did you say?"

The man sitting back against the window was gazing right over her head. "I'm looking for your husband." The stranger seemed to be scanning the room. "Albert Kerensky. You're Roselyn, his wife?"

"Who are you?" she asked, worried.

"Max O'Brien."

A tall, elegant, proud-looking Southern woman. Preoccupied. Her eyes touching people and objects without really seeing them. Since she'd arrived in Chicago that very morning, Max had crossed paths with her a few times in the Westin lobby without her noticing him. Before speaking with her, he'd decided to get to know her a little.

From Dar es Salaam, Max had communicated with Texas correctional services, where he'd been transferred to Stanford Hill Residence. A woman named Callaghan, dry and hurried, had told him that all questions concerning Albert Kerensky had to be referred to Peter Sawyer, his son-in-law, or Roselyn, his wife. Max understood that the old man had left the residence without warning and his family had been looking for him for days.

When Mrs. Callaghan informed him that Sawyer was a police officer — "You're a journalist, did you say?" — Max had asked for Roselyn's number. She'd left for Chicago, the residence director said, so you're better off reaching out to Peter Sawyer. A few calls to Chicago's main hotels were all it took for Max to locate Kerensky's wife at the Westin.

While Janeth Katala flew to Johannesburg on a South African Airways flight, Max took a Lufthansa plane that landed at O'Hare eighteen hours later, after layovers in Addis Ababa and Frankfurt.

Despite being a little hazy with jet lag, Max had gone straight after Roselyn. He overheard her asking for directions to the public library. Max had taken that opportunity to go through her room and had come to the conclusion that Albert Kerensky's wife had no idea where her husband was. The man's belongings had been tipped out of a Chicago PD cardboard box and spread over the bed. A single thing left in the box: Inspector Phil Stanway's business card. A notebook lay nearby, names and numbers written and later crossed off. All of it testi-fied to a search for something, or in this case, someone.

At the coffee shop Max approached her with deter-mination. Roselyn could have run, could have tried to contact the police about this importuning stranger. But she hadn't. Out of curiosity, it seemed, she agreed to follow him to the room he'd rented on the eighteenth floor. It wasn't a room, actually, nor was it a suite. It was a fully equipped apartment, tall windows offering a view on the forest of skyscrapers. A luxurious, if artificial, living room. Drab colours on the wall, sober furniture, boring art hung here and there that fitted with the rest of the apartment. A flashy chandelier hung from the ceiling. Heavy velour curtains.

Max was dying to hear Albert Kerensky's story and discover where it intersected with his own, this long bloodletting that had begun in Africa and led him here to this unlikely place to hear the secrets of the wife of the former executioner for the State of Texas.

"What business do you have with him?" she asked Max when they sat down in the living room. "Why are you looking for him?"

He'd prepared tea, which sat cooling between them. She sounded more curious than aggressive.

Max answered that Kerensky had put into motion an infernal machine in Africa that had already caused the deaths of Valéria Michieka and her daughter, as well as Awadhi Zuberi and Thomas Musindo. A machine that destroyed everything it came into contact with.

He summarized what he'd learned so far in his investigation. Kerensky had been mandated by the State of Texas to help a young executioner in Tanzania, which Roselyn already knew. The country had reinstated capital punishment, suspended a few years earlier. But for the first time, the prison would be using lethal injection to execute an inmate, as was the case in the United States, including Texas.

"The job was done in utmost secrecy," Roselyn added. "I'm sure the American government didn't want to be accused of interfering in the proper dispensing of justice in Tanzania."

"The Dar es Salaam prison authorities likely made the request in secret," Max said. "I'm guessing the Tanzanian chief justice, who answers to the president, made the deal."

"And Albert was chosen because of his perfect record," Roselyn interjected.

"I have no idea how it happened and why he was chosen, but your husband came to Tanzania where he supervised the work of Lewis Katala. The man they executed was Samuel Musindo, a nurse found guilty of the murder of a young albino, Clara Lugembe, the daughter of the minister of home affairs, who today is the president of Tanzania."

Later, the situation got more complicated, Max went on. Musindo hadn't actually been executed, for reasons that were still nebulous. But Kerensky had to have known about it.

"I can't see my husband messing up an execution by mistake. Someone forced his hand."

"Are you sure?"

"Absolutely."

Max looked at her, surprised.

"In July 2003, when Albert was in Tanzania for the execution, our grandson, Adrian, was kidnapped from a summer camp in southern Texas. Two men were responsible — Angel Clements and Mitch Arceneaux. I met Arceneaux's mother. She told me everything. Her son had been a mechanic in the Merchant Marine.

In the late 1990s, he got into a fight in Dar es Salaam during a refuelling stop. Valéria Michieka helped him out of trouble."

That man was the sailor Sophie had fallen in love with when she was still in boarding school. Valéria kept in touch with the young man and called him during Musindo's trial when it became clear that the death sentence would be applied to him.

"Arceneaux owed her a favour," Roselyn said. "Thanks to Michieka, he managed to avoid a Tanzanian jail, which is probably no vacation."

"Why the kidnapping? To pressure your husband?"

"Exactly. If Samuel Musindo was executed, he'd never see Adrian again."

"And your husband gave in to the threat?"

"I know Albert. He almost never leaves the United States. The only times were during our vacations together in Mexico. And always at the same spot. He never went to Europe or Asia. And certainly not Africa. The only exception is that whirlwind trip. I have no trouble at all imagining him lost and confused in a strange world, unable to trust or confide in anyone, especially the police. He couldn't even call me and ask for advice, since I didn't know about any of it."

Her eyes were filled with tears. "If all this had taken place here in the United States, the situation would have been different. He could've gone to the police or the warden. But he was on the other side of the world in a country he knew nothing about, where potential threats lay around every corner. A place he was travelling to in absolute secrecy."

"So he obeyed …"

"Adrian had been kidnapped. Albert had to give his answer quickly. I told you that already. He was torn between his duty and the life of his grandson. He couldn't have gone on living if he caused Adrian's death. So he gave in."

"How did he do it?"

"Sabotage the execution? I've got no idea."

But there was no doubt in her mind that Albert knew the content and dosage of the various drugs used in lethal injections perfectly. He'd executed two hundred and thirty-four people since the beginning of his career … and not one mistake.

"He was the best at what he did."

An expert, a champion.

Over there, at the penitentiary in Ukonga, no one knew how to execute a man by lethal injection except for Lewis Katala, of course. According to his sister, he'd been informed by the American of his intentions.

"That man was his tie-down team," Roselyn added. "Albert had to tell Katala, had to convince him to be part of the plan."

"And what about Musindo? Do you believe he knew what was going on?"

"I don't know. He might have had the most beautiful surprise of his life waking up after what he thought would be eternal slumber."

According to Janeth Katala, Kerensky himself confirmed Musindo's death, even though, not being a doctor, he shouldn't have gotten involved in the process. Once again, it was a first for Tanzania, so they'd trusted Kerensky.

Musindo's body had been transported to an empty morgue to be prepared for cremation. At least that was the plan. In reality he was given time to come to his senses. A set of false papers was ready for him.

The two executioners remained silent about it. Kerensky couldn't very well go home and say he'd been forced to botch an execution. And Katala was just starting his career. For the first time, his mother and sister were secure. Admitting his role in the plot would have meant he would never hold a job in the government again.

Adrian had been freed, unharmed.

It was better to simply forget the whole story that had been without consequences for both Kerensky and Katala. And better than that for Musindo …

The two men kept their secret for years. Then, out of the blue, Kerensky had opened up.

"My husband was obsessed with every single execution of his career," Roselyn explained. "He kept … relics of all the people he put to death, something I learned just recently. When he retired, after Norah's death, he fell into a bloodthirsty rage."

Making his own investigation, Kerensky first found Clements, then Arceneaux, and murdered both as punishment for kidnapping his grandson. Yet his anger remained raw. He took it in his head to finish the execution he'd started years earlier. And this time on his own terms. Kerensky wanted to retire with a perfect record.

"Which explains his letter to Lewis Katala," Max said. "He didn't know that Ukonga's former executioner had died. He wanted to enroll him in his deadly mission. He asked for his co-operation — one colleague to another."

What role had Valéria played in all this? For months she pushed for the death penalty, demanding Samuel Musindo's head. She'd pushed so hard, some began to believe she'd kidnapped the minister's daughter herself to force President Komba's hand in reinstating capital punishment for the murder of albinos.

Max had learned that Valéria knew Thomas and Samuel Musindo and had been seen in their company. She had approached Samuel in the context of her efforts to send albino children for adoption to Ukerewe Island. Before learning that Musindo had another objective entirely.

Once Thomas Musindo had learned of Kerensky's plan through Katala's sister, he'd contacted Valéria, who'd secretly made her way to Dar es Salaam to help Thomas Musindo and Janeth Katala flee the country before beginning her own preparations with Sophie. All of this likely financed by the money Max had scammed off Jonathan Harris.

"All four of them were afraid of Albert?" Roselyn asked.

"Someone else. More threatening still."

But Max didn't know who that person was.

He had first thought that Inspector Kilonzo was trying to sabotage the investigation to hide his own involvement in the crime. The policeman was both ambitious and incompetent but hadn't been involved in the murders of Valéria, Sophie, and Thomas Musindo, even though, just like the real killer, he had the profile for the job: a veteran of the war between Uganda and Tanzania, linked to members of rebel groups in exile, an expert when it came to violence to serve the "cause."

Though that cause was his own personal advancement, of course. No, not Kilonzo. Someone else was acting, hidden in the shadows, likely carrying out some bloody vendetta. A man more dangerous than Kerensky.

The real killer, who'd taken out the witch doctor Zuberi, erroneously believing he knew where Samuel Musindo had hidden.

More questions, always more questions.

"What I don't understand is why Valéria played this double game. Why did she demand Musindo's death while, behind the scenes, she purchased fake papers, orchestrated a fake execution and the kidnapping of a child, and found a place for the nurse to live secretly all these years? Why did she make such an effort for this man?" Max was thinking out loud.

Roselyn watched him for a moment. "I thought you knew. Samuel Musindo is Valéria Michieka's son."

PART THREE
The Execution

28

Max stared at Roselyn Kerensky in a state of shock. Samuel Musindo, Valéria's son? That explained why she'd made such an effort to save him and guarantee his safety. "Where did you learn that?"

"Mitch Arceneaux's mother. After I came across Valéria Michieka's name in a police report, I asked Mitch's mother about her."

The elderly woman had told Roselyn all about her son's misadventure in Zanzibar and the role played by the lawyer. She also mentioned a call Mitch had gotten from Africa in June 2003. The son of this African woman was going to die. She'd asked Mitch to save his life. To help her, as she'd done years earlier for him. Without explaining what that meant exactly.

"To me it was clear," Roselyn continued. "Samuel Musindo was Valéria's son, despite the fact that he didn't bear her name. Later, when I learned how hard she'd advocated for the death penalty in her country, it became obvious why she needed Arceneaux's help."

Trying to save her son's life at all costs, Valéria had called on every contact she had.

Max paced the living room, unable to stop. He now understood why Sophie had come to visit him in Lamu. Kerensky had thrown a grenade into the room, and Valéria was worried for Samuel's safety. She needed money, a lot of money, to procure a new identity for her son, a new hiding place, getting him to disappear deeper and farther than before. To run from the man who had begun his hunt. Valéria leaned on Max, without his knowledge, to further cover her tracks.

Sophie and Valéria had split the task in two: while Sophie travelled to Lamu, Valéria prepared Samuel, getting her hands on a new identity. No matter where he might hide in this world, his departure had to seem justified.

That also explained Naomi Mulunga's attitude in Sandy Hill on Ukerewe. "Let them rest in peace," she'd said about Valéria and Sophie. She must have known all about Samuel's story and feared that Max might uncover the truth in the course of his investigation. Her only objective had been to protect Valéria's son. But her attitude, far from calming Max, had only made him dig deeper. It made him feel as if he was the only one who wanted to know the truth, the only one who wanted to discover and punish the real killer.

How had Valéria and Thomas Musindo come to know each other? Samuel was older than Sophie, which meant Valéria was with him before her marriage to Richard Stroner. An unplanned pregnancy likely. She'd left the baby with his biological father, who later married another woman. Or perhaps she'd left him with this man in Dar es Salaam whose wife was barren. Whatever the case, Valéria had made a terrible sacrifice and chosen to put her son up for adoption. Later she reconnected with Samuel. Before Clara Lugembe's murder, there had been meetings with him and his father, Thomas.

Max couldn't believe Valéria had hidden all this from him, this foundational fact about her life. It made him furious. Roselyn could only agree. After all, she'd been deceived by Albert, who had hidden such a large part of his life at the penitentiary. That was what had brought them together: lies and omissions by people they'd loved, who had jealously guarded their most intimate secrets.

"We're not worth much in the lives of others," Roselyn said. "We're sure the people we love care about us and then it turns out it's nothing more than an illusion, a projection, a self-created fantasy. And we believe them because we want to think we're indispensable."

Cruel words, a cruel judgment of both of them. But Max had no counter-argument in good faith. As his investigation revealed new information, Valéria seemed to move farther from him. Instead of letting herself be known, she became a furtive silhouette, harder and harder to distinguish. What he was discovering about her was changing his memory and modifying the image she'd left him. An image she'd partially manufactured.

How could Valéria have tolerated her son's participation in the trafficking of albinos? On Ukerewe, Naomi Mulunga had told Max that the lawyer hadn't known about Samuel's involvement at first. She'd learned the truth only after Samuel had been arrested, discovering with horror that the young man used his position as a nurse to funnel albino children to traffickers, and in particular to the witch doctor Zuberi.

Her reaction? Astonishment. A terrible, horrible mess. He'd broken her trust. She'd solicited his help to save these children from horrible deaths by sending them to Ukerewe, as she herself had saved Samuel's life by entrusting him to Thomas Musindo. He'd then turned around and taken advantage of the situation to make some money — betraying everything Valéria stood for in the process.

Then, during the trial, her maternal instinct had taken over. Yes, he was a killer, but he was her son, and despite his horrendous crime, she couldn't just let him die. Max could imagine Valéria's dilemma. She couldn't look away and wait for the state to kill him. She had to act, yet without harming her cause.

Still, questions remained in Max's head. How had the person who'd killed Valéria, Sophie, Thomas Musindo, and Zuberi learned of Samuel's faked execution? Perhaps a rumour had been started in Janeth's circles, or even Valéria's, when Thomas Musindo had shared the news? Whatever the case, someone knew about it, and that was what had begun this terrible wave of murder and violence, this long trail of blood, with Valéria and her daughter the first victims.

Had the perpetrator been a former Ugandan rebel? A Tanzanian soldier using the methods he'd learned from Idi Amin's opponents? It hadn't been Kilonzo, no. Then who? Walter? The man who'd tortured Max in the prison he'd briefly been incarcerated in? It was unlikely.

And where was Samuel Musindo hiding?

"What should we do now?" Roselyn asked.

Max looked up. He'd practically forgotten about the woman. He shrugged. No matter the reasons that motivated Kerensky and the other killer, Valéria's son was still a target. He had to do everything in his power to prevent another murder. But how? Only one option made sense to Max: to reveal it all, to set the cat among the pigeons, to tell everyone what had happened years ago. Force Musindo to come out of hiding to finally face justice.

Roselyn frowned. "You want him to be executed a second time?"

"Sooner or later his secret will be revealed and he'll have to flee again."

"Which he's done already, I'm sure."

"Or he hasn't moved at all. He's lying low in whatever lair he's found, knowing that any movement might attract attention."

"Possible."

"We're dealing with an animal that's being tracked, fearing for its life, in survival mode."

"Where do you think he might have gone after the execution?" Roselyn asked. "He could have stayed in Africa."

Now that the news of his faked execution had come out, Samuel wouldn't be able to live in peace, no matter where he was hiding. Sooner or later Kerensky or someone else would find him. Samuel would disappear without a trace, since he was already dead in the eyes of the legal system. They had to find him before Kerensky and the other killer.

For Max, Valéria might just be the key to the whole affair. If she was at the origin of the subterfuge, as he believed she was, she needed accomplices. Mitch Arceneaux had been responsible for one facet of the operation, and Sophie had lent a hand, as well as Thomas Musindo. But at least one key person was missing: the man or woman who had prepared fake papers and sent Samuel into hiding.

But, more than anything, the question Max had to ask was this: Where was Samuel?

Max, a connoisseur of fake identities, knew how difficult it was to disappear and reappear elsewhere under another name, perhaps with modified physical features. If Samuel had feigned his death with Valéria's help, if he was the artisan of the hoax with his mother, they likely needed the help of a few experts, including a counterfeiter.

Another element preoccupied Max: either Samuel hadn't been informed of Valéria's death, or he had and had decided not to show his face.

How could they go about finding him?

Or send him a message?

"Do you have children, Mr. O'Brien?"

Max shook his head. Roselyn was looking at him intently.

"Norah was adorable," she continued. "An intelligent girl who became an incredible young woman.

Albert and I were both absolutely amazed we'd brought this person into the world."

Roselyn glanced away, her eyes unfocused, staring out at Lake Michigan. "I haven't stopped thinking about her since she passed. Sometimes I have dreams where I die, just so we can be together again. I join her in a place known to just the two of us, where we can pretend death is only a bad dream, or a practical joke on life, on our friends, on our neighbours, on all of us."

Max fully understood what she was saying.

"If I were Valéria, if I had a chance to see my son for real … I'm certain she visited him regularly. If I were her, I couldn't have stayed away for very long. Did she ever travel outside Africa?"

"Only for fundraising. She never really took a vacation." Max grabbed his phone. What time was it in Bukoba? Who cared? He woke Teresa Mwandenga, asked her to tell him everything about Valéria's travel plans since July 2003, after Samuel's execution. The accountant didn't have that information on hand but promised she'd get in touch with him as soon as possible.

Two hours later, as Max and Roselyn were eating together, Mwandenga called back. Valéria had travelled to London a few times, as well as elsewhere in Europe and to the United States. But her most canvassed donors were located in Vancouver.

"Do you have the dates of those trips?" Max asked.

"Every year in February. Since 2004, she didn't miss a trip."

Around February 8, probably. Samuel Musindo's birthday. Even after her son's execution, Valéria hadn't broken her promise of spending every birthday with him. The same promise she'd made to Sophie. Max recalled what she'd told him that first time they'd met in Toronto: "When she was born, I made a vow. As long as I live, no matter where I am in this world, I'll be with her on that day to hold her in my arms and wish her happy birthday." A promise she'd kept with Samuel, too.

Vancouver, Canada.

"Put yourself in Valéria's shoes," Max said to Roselyn. "She wanted to keep Samuel safe. They wouldn't take the chance of sending him to a country with an extradition treaty with Tanzania. It would put Samuel in too much danger."

That explained Canada as a destination of choice. Its government hadn't signed such a treaty with Tanzania.

They weren't the only ones who had come to the same conclusion. Roselyn told Max about what she'd deduced from her husband's movements. He carried a Beretta and could cross borders only by bus or car, hiding his weapon. According to her, if Samuel was in Canada, Albert knew it. Which is why he'd renewed his passport. Kerensky's only objective was to find Musindo and finish what he'd started. Repair the one mistake of his career.

Max and Roselyn had to locate her husband and neutralize him before he could follow through.

29

From O'Hare Airport, Max and Roselyn grabbed an American Airlines flight for Seattle. In the plane, unable to sleep, Max tried to gather his thoughts. Since Valéria and her daughter had been killed, it seemed time had accelerated. Revelations came one after the other, some answers had been revealed, while many truths still remained shrouded. Although the events that had transpired were now clearer, their meaning still escaped Max.

For years Samuel had lived under an assumed identity, leaving Africa — and Clara Lugembe's murder in particular — behind him. He'd spoken to no one from his old life except for his mother. Which put her at risk, of course. She could be made to talk …

At least once a year Valéria had visited her son. Her fundraising trips were her alibi, allowing her to justify frequent trips to Vancouver, one city among many. No one had ever noticed that these trips weren't as lucrative as others in her fundraising ventures — even Teresa Mwandenga hadn't noticed.

Albert's madness had made a mess of her plans.

The plane landed in Seattle four hours later. Another Westin, and a car rental agency where Max picked up a Lincoln Town Car while Roselyn rested in her room adjacent to his. He woke her very early the next morning, and they hit the road, heading for the Canadian border. After Bellingham, Max turned off on the 539. This early in the morning they were almost alone at the Lynden-Aldergrove border crossing, sharing the lanes with a few tourists eager to beat rush hour. The size and luxury of Max's car piqued the interest of the customs officer, though not his suspicions. The elderly woman in the passenger seat seemed to lower his guard.

Soon Max was gaining speed, reaching the Trans-Canada Highway before heading for Vancouver. Once they were settled into a suite at the Wedgewood on Hornby Street, Max and Roselyn took a moment to breathe.

"So what do you suggest now?" Roselyn asked after emerging from a long shower.

Max had neither plan nor strategy. On the drive from Seattle, he'd tried to put himself in the killer's shoes. After avoiding his own execution, Samuel had travelled under a fake name, a fake passport — probably a Canadian one — before landing in Vancouver. Had someone been waiting for him? No way to know. But if

Valéria had managed to organize Adrian's kidnapping from Bukoba, she'd certainly taken care to properly organize her son's exile. It would have been Musindo's first time in Vancouver, and with fake papers. Surely, he had needed some help.

"Airport cameras?" Roselyn suggested.

Even if the tapes from six years back were kept, which Max doubted, it was unlikely he'd get access to them. What was more, if by some miracle he could locate them, there would still be hundreds of hours of tape to go through, and Max didn't know how long after his non-execution Musindo had actually reached Canada.

"He might have come through Europe," Max said. "Spent a few weeks in Paris, for example, to confuse anyone tracking him."

Not to mention his appearance. To change his life so radically, Samuel likely had a new face. Facial surgery. Likely high-quality work.

Roselyn sighed. "Does this trip serve any purpose? Will looking for Musindo really lead us to Albert and stop him from committing yet another murder? And let's say I manage to reason with him and divert him from the bloody quest he's begun. Then what? Albert will be arrested and extradited to the United States, where he'll have to answer for the murders of Angel Clements and Mitch Arceneaux, each one of which could get him the needle. Those murders were committed in Louisiana, a state that's not shy about handing out the death penalty."

Max could see that Roselyn had grasped the tragic irony of what could happen for the first time. She'd agreed to follow him, knowing she was setting off a series of events that could only end in her husband's death.

Roselyn and Max didn't have much to go on in their search for Musindo. They knew he was in Vancouver, but even that could be wrong. Max could try to reach out to him by publishing an ad in a newspaper or on the Internet, something that might make the man curious enough to contact him. But that was counting on Musindo's willingness and desire to show his face. Max doubted Musindo would emerge from his lair. What was more, through such a message, they'd be signalling to Kerensky and the other killer that more hunters had joined the fray. They would keep a low profile, even if that didn't guarantee their safety.

"He's a black African," Roselyn said. "Perhaps he joined a community group for immigrants."

"Why would he do that?"

"Nostalgia? Homesickness?"

"Any other immigrant and I'd say you were right. But not Samuel Musindo. It would be too risky to bump into someone who might know his identity. A Tanzanian who'd followed the trial closely, as well as his execution. A small risk, sure, but a real one."

In short, there wasn't much to go on. Almost nothing.

"What about Valéria Michieka?" Roselyn suggested. "We could try to retrace her movements, figure out when and where she visited her son."

"Good idea."

The following day Max began his search. Valéria likely hadn't stayed at a hotel, since she would want as much time as possible with her son. There wouldn't be much point going to the major hotels with her picture. Max tried to follow the money but couldn't figure out where her fundraising sessions took place. In the file given to him by the accountant, there were no receipts for room rentals or audiovisual equipment, supporting the hypothesis that Valéria travelled to Vancouver only to visit her son, not to raise funds.

Had they celebrated Samuel's birthday in a restaurant?

Roselyn combed through the Yellow Pages and questioned the hotel concierge to figure out the perfect place to hold such an event. But the calls she made to various restaurants yielded no results. On February 8 of this year or the previous year, Samuel and his mother hadn't been seen dining at any establishment, at least not under their real names.

It was time to change tack. Since looking for Valéria wasn't generating any leads, Max and Roselyn thought they should reach out to allergy specialists. Musindo might have needed to continue his treatments.

"Discreetly, you know," Max said. "As soon as he got to Vancouver, perhaps he found a clinic where he wouldn't be known. Never misses an appointment, doesn't make waves, he'd just be one patient among others."

Roselyn doubted that would generate any leads, but it didn't hurt to try.

On the phone with Susan McGillivery, a representative for a local association of allergy specialists, Max discovered a new passion: the integration of recent immigrants into British Columbia's health care system, especially those suffering from allergies. On the Internet, he'd found the name of an obscure magazine catering to the newcomers and was now calling under the guise of writing a piece for the periodical.

McGillivery agreed to meet with him, and later that day, she welcomed him to her messy office on Davies Street. An energetic woman who didn't have a minute to spare, she thought Max's mission was a little on the pointless side but had agreed to help, anyway.

"Our patients aren't indexed by race or colour," McGillivery stated as soon as they shook hands.

Max couldn't help but smile. "Of course, of course. What I'm more interested in is their origins. Anglophone Africa, for example. Allergies that are unique to Kenya and Tanzania are of particular interest to me."

"That's confidential information."

Meaning the information existed, Max understood.

"I'd be interested in statistics, in a way of describing the phenomenon, you understand?"

"I'm sorry I can't help."

Max tried to convince McGillivery how useful his article would be, how he'd be able to demonstrate how hard the government was working to ensure that recently arrived immigrants received top-flight care for their allergies. McGillivery was unmoved.

He then contacted an association working for the integration of recent immigrants, but again, the information he required was confidential. Perhaps it was time to think outside the box and search different avenues.

Perhaps in a less official manner, off the beaten path. But where and how?

Back at the hotel, Max couldn't hide his discouragement from Roselyn. As they ate, his thoughts were elsewhere. He was worried. Preoccupied. Roselyn looked the part, as well, as if Max's pessimism was contagious.

She rummaged through her bag and took her hypertension medication out. When she raised her eyes, Max was staring at her curiously.

"What is it?"

To fight his allergies, Samuel Musindo frequently used ephedra. An illegal drug, though easy to obtain. During the trial, it was established that Musindo got his supply from Chinese workers trying to make a few yuan in Tanzania. The plant grew in China and was used as a stimulant there when mixed with tea.

Max and Roselyn made their way to the nearest pharmacy. There, they learned some good news: products containing ephedra were heavily regulated by Health Canada. Only tiny quantities could be sold over the counter, just as in the United States. If Musindo had continued using ephedra as regularly as in Tanzania, he must have found a source outside the law.

That meant the black market.

It was a bit of stretch as far as clues went, and it might lead nowhere at all, since it was based on three hypotheses they couldn't confirm: that outside Africa Musindo still had strong allergic reactions and needed to use ephedra to manage his symptoms, that he'd been forced to find large quantities of the drug outside the law, and — the shakiest hypothesis among the three — that he had chosen to contact the same sorts of people here as he had in Tanzania to get his fix — Chinese workers.

Max and Roselyn went off to explore Chinatown. Long a rundown part of town, this neighbourhood near

Vancouver's core had been slowly revitalized thanks to massive investment from Asia. In the 1990s, fear of the imminent annexation of Hong Kong by China had incited millionaires to move their fortunes to the other side of the Pacific, especially after the repression in Tiananmen Square. To these Chinese fortunes was added the money spent by Japanese tourists. Often Vancouver was their first port of call in Canada.

Max tried to put himself in Samuel's shoes. He wasn't looking for coke or heroin, but a once-legal medication that would help him control his allergies.

Where would he start?

Max and Roselyn wandered across Chinatown. Around a corner, the Sun Yat-Sen Hotel, a baroque construction halfway between a rice cake and a fortune cookie. The concierge was taking care of a customer's car. Before Roselyn could stop him, Max asked the man where he could find ephedra in large quantities. The man had no idea. But clearly ephedra wasn't unknown to him.

"It's for my mother," Max said, gesturing toward Roselyn.

The concierge peered at him.

"She can't sleep at night," Max added.

The man suggested a souvenir shop on Pender Street that also imported natural products. While Roselyn returned to the Wedgewood Hotel, Max walked deeper into Chinatown. The shop on Pender looked like any other, a red-and-gold-striped storefront filled with knick-knacks. Multicoloured plaster Buddhas stood guard over the shop, casting greedy looks at passersby.

Customers could walk into the shop and get lost in a shamble of various Chinese-looking objects: waving cats, fans, music boxes, incense, and plastic flowers. Here and there, glass cases filled with DVDs, likely pirated, featuring stars of Chinese cinema. Traditional garb and a pile of straw sandals completed the decor. It wasn't like being in China as much as being in a cheap souvenir shop at the Shanghai airport. A mix of garbage-in-waiting and shady business.

The owner had the body for the job. A square-shouldered Chinese man, not very tall but strong. He wore Gucci glasses with all the indifference of a triad boss.

Max didn't think a subtle approach was called for with that sort of man. He went straight to the point. "I'm looking for ephedra."

"Never heard of it."

The man didn't have time to turn his back. Max grabbed him by the collar and threw him against a glass counter. The glass shattered, and as the man collapsed against it, the entire counter fell apart.

Max crouched over his victim, ripped his glasses off, and threw them across the shop. "Actually, I'm looking for a man who buys ephedra for his personal use. Large quantities. An African."

The man was breathing heavily, blinking. Without his glasses, he suddenly lost all his cool.

"An African. From Tanzania."

The man said nothing.

Max stretched out a hand and pushed a faux Ming vase that shattered on the floor. "I've got all the time in the world. And all this stuff to break."

Suddenly, the alarm went off. Max glanced up. In the street, passersby had stopped to gawk. Max ran out of the store, cursing his impulsiveness.

Back at the hotel, Roselyn was waiting for him with a message from Teresa Mwandenga. The accountant had gone through Sophie's papers and discovered that Valéria's daughter had travelled to Vancouver, as well, in August 2003. A few weeks after Samuel's faked execution.

So she'd accompanied him in his escape. Since she had nothing to hide, Sophie had been able to travel with her own passport and name, unlike Samuel.

Pretending to be an employee of Revenue Canada, Max contacted a number of hotels near the Vancouver airport, looking for information concerning Sophie Stroner.

His intuition was right. On the fifth call, a receptionist at the Fairmont informed him that the young woman had spent a night there in August 2003. The hotel had a deal with a car rental company, and Sophie's name was in its records. The day after she landed in Vancouver, she rented a Toyota, which she left a few days later at another location eight hundred kilometres away in Prince George.

30

The next morning Max and Roselyn hit the road. If Valéria's son had wanted to fade into a crowd, he was doing it rather strangely, choosing a sparsely populated area in northern British Columbia with almost no black residents. Sooner or later someone would notice him, or at least ask questions about how he'd ended up in that part of the world.

"Do you think Albert knows where he's hiding?" Roselyn asked.

Max had no idea. The night before they left Chicago he'd called the five companies that had scheduled flights between Chicago and Vancouver, pretending to be Kerensky and claiming he'd lost his ticket. No one had a record of Albert's name.

Roselyn was right. If her husband had come to Canada, he'd driven, just as they had.

"What about the other killer?" Roselyn asked, worried.

Max had no idea about that, either.

On the other side of Cache Creek, RVs became rarer; most of them had taken the road for Banff or Jasper in Alberta. The highway was now mostly occupied by eighteen-wheelers. Campgrounds had been replaced by truck stops. Restaurants with large parking lots with big rigs, their owners sleeping in their cabs, or inside having a quick burger before returning to the road.

Max and Roselyn stopped at one such place a few kilometres outside Quesnel. After their meal, while Roselyn was finishing her coffee, Max went outside to gas up. That was when he noticed the Subaru with the tinted windows he'd first spotted outside Cache Creek three hundred kilometres to the south. The vehicle had stayed a fair distance behind his Lincoln, though always keeping Max in sight. When they'd reached Williams Lake, construction had forced Max to take a dirt road heading west. He'd gotten lost and been forced to make a U-turn and return to the beginning of the detour. The Subaru had been waiting for him on the shoulder.

He wasn't surprised to see the vehicle choose the same gas station. The Subaru drove off a little, then stopped near the exit ramp, ready to follow Max and Roselyn when they returned to the highway.

After paying for the gas, Max motioned Roselyn to join him.

"Is everything all right?" she asked.

"We've got a tail."

The Subaru drove off toward the highway, preceding the Lincoln. Max started the car, pretending he was heading for the highway, as well, then at the last minute made a sudden U-turn just before leaving the parking area. The Subaru had gone too far on the ramp and couldn't reverse. Max saw the vehicle accelerate, likely in order to reach the next exit and turn around as quickly as possible.

Max had a few minutes to execute his plan. He abandoned the Lincoln in the parking lot, taking care first to disconnect the battery, then called the car rental agency to say the car wouldn't start. The agent answered that a tow truck was on its way from Prince George, but it would take a while, at least two hours. Max told the man he didn't have that kind of time.

"I'll leave the keys with the gas station attendant."

Which he did, as Roselyn looked on, astonished. She didn't understand what Max was trying to accomplish but could tell it wasn't the right moment to ask.

"Let's go," he told her.

"What about our bags?"

"We'll get them later. Now let's go."

Max led Roselyn among the parked trucks. He saw one of the truckers leave the restaurant, baseball cap on his head, plodding toward his vehicle.

Max approached him. "My car broke down and I don't have time to wait for the tow truck. Could you take us to Prince George? Her doctor is waiting for her at the hospital."

"Sorry, man, I can't, company rules …"

Max pulled out three one hundred dollar bills.

"You know how difficult it is to get an appointment."

The trucker looked Roselyn over — maybe she reminded him of his own mother — then scanned the lot. No one was watching them. "Come on then," he answered, sticking the money in his coat pocket.

The truck left the station, Roselyn seated between the driver and Max. Just as they exited the parking lot, Max noticed the Subaru coming their way, searching for the Lincoln. The driver seemed relieved to see the Lincoln still there, bags in the back seat. He parked his car farther off.

"So where are you coming from?" the driver asked.

"Kamloops," Roselyn lied.

The driver whistled through his teeth, as if to say it was quite a way to go to see a doctor.

"An excellent rheumatologist," Roselyn added quickly. "The best, really, though he chose to settle in Prince George."

Max glanced at her, and Roselyn smiled.

Clearly, this woman had a few tricks up her sleeve.

Prince George wasn't a tiny trading post anymore. There was a time when it, along with Fort St. James, had been the main meeting point with Indigenous people who came to sell their furs to representatives of the North West Company. The small city had changed vocation with the development of the railway and the pulp-and-paper industry, with train and factory workers replacing trappers and fur traders. Prince George and its surrounding region had built itself on the backs of Indigenous workers. First serving adventurers — offering canoes, guides, and staff — then later forest workers. At this time of year the place was filled with tourists from Vancouver who were being picked up in small planes like Roosevelt Okambo's. The local airport was the busiest in the region.

Max asked the truck driver to drop them off at the Prince George Regional Hospital.

Once the man had gone on his way toward Dawson Creek, Roselyn turned to Max. "Now what do we do?"

"Follow me."

Max led Roselyn through the parking lot, then offered her his arm to help her cross the street. In Hudson's Bay, they filled two sports bags with new clothes. After their purchases, they took a cab to the Ramada downtown. Several cars and recreational vehicles were parked in front. A busy place.

Under a fake name, Max rented two rooms he paid for in cash, then asked the receptionist about flights out of the Prince George airport later that day. One to Edmonton, another to Calgary, Seattle later in the evening.

Roselyn stared at him, confused. "What's this all about?"

Max motioned her to say nothing.

In the elevator, he called the car rental company and told them he was at the airport and would be taking a flight out soon, without giving his destination. All the fees incurred by the tow truck could be charged to his credit card. The agent apologized for the inconvenience, and Max told him not to worry. He would have fond memories of Prince George.

"Do you prefer the room with the view of the parking lot?" he asked Roselyn in the corridor.

"I don't care. All I want is for you to tell me what's going on."

"It would be best if we ate here tonight."

Roselyn's room was larger, and calmer, too. Max ordered two hot meals and grabbed a beer from the mini-bar. Roselyn preferred mineral water. The Subaru's mystery driver had likely questioned the agent at the car rental place. By now he was probably patrolling the airport waiting room, hunting for them.

"Do you think it was Albert?" Roselyn asked.

"I'd say someone else."

Having been followed all the way from Vancouver worried Max a little, but it also reassured him. It meant that someone thought they were on the right track. Which meant that whoever was following them was ignoring where Musindo was. The man in the Subaru must have thought Max knew something.

He'd been tempted to stay at the gas station to get a good look at the man, but it had been safer to just disappear.

All that meant that Musindo hadn't been unmasked.

But Kerensky might have gotten further than them. Clements and Arceneaux, the two men he'd killed, might have spilled the beans. Though it was unlikely they'd have known anything about Musindo's location. His fake death had occurred in Tanzania, and the two kidnappers had simply executed a minor mission.

Max couldn't help but think that Valéria had had some help, besides Mitch Arceneaux. That person was lying low since his life was likely now in danger.

The fact they were being followed forced Max to

change his approach. This mystery man wouldn't just give up so easily. He would not believe that Max had taken a flight for Edmonton, Calgary, or even Seattle. He'd stay in Prince George, looking for them and Musindo. Max and Roselyn would need to be discreet if they wanted to stay under the radar. They couldn't simply criss-cross the city with a picture of Musindo in hand, hoping to bump into someone who might know him. Too dangerous.

Since they'd reached Prince George, Max had noticed the Indigenous people in the city, easily recognizable. They occupied low-level jobs, like their fathers and grandfathers before them. Taxi drivers, sales assistants at Hudson's Bay, their hotel's maintenance staff. They'd come from surrounding villages looking for work. Many seemed to cause trouble with the local authorities. In the middle of the night, Max was woken by shouts and the sound of fighting from under his window. In the morning, he was told that a bar around the corner was frequented by "Natives." At closing time things sometimes heated up.

Max turned his thoughts to Samuel Musindo.

Though a nurse, the young man wouldn't have taken the risk of working in a hospital. But he might have offered to help organizations that provided services to the poor and needy. In Prince George, those establishments catered mostly to Indigenous people.

A thin lead, but somewhere to start. Max and Roselyn grabbed a cab that dropped them off just outside town in front of a mission. The basement of a Presbyterian church that had been transformed into a dormitory and a resource centre by the pastor. With the help of other volunteers, he welcomed drug addicts and drunks without asking questions, offering them a roof and some food but also hand-me-down clothes given by Prince George do-gooders.

His name was Brendon Wilson. He welcomed Max and Roselyn into his office behind the small kitchen. Max showed him a picture.

"A nurse, you say? Who worked with Indigenous people?"

"Possibly."

Wilson scanned the picture. Shook his head. Hadn't seen the guy.

"If he's a nurse, he might be at the hospital," Wilson suggested.

"I doubt it."

Max told him a vague story about a family member searching for his son. Wilson was skeptical, though he tried to hide it. And Roselyn's incongruous presence made him wary.

"Why don't you go to the police?"

Yes, why not?

That evening, after wishing Roselyn good night, Max found himself leaning against the Ramada bar, breaking his own security rules. This search was going nowhere.

He was about to return to his room when he felt the eyes of the Indigenous busboy on him. The kid had been hovering around him all night. When Max left the place, he followed him outside.

"The man you're talking about. I've seen him."

Max stopped in his tracks. Checked the busboy over. "Do you know where he might be?"

"Why are you looking for him?"

For a moment, Max stared at the young man. He might be trying to get a few bucks out of him. Pretending to know something to get a little business, promising information he didn't have. Max had been around this block before.

"You met him?"

"Yes. An African."

Max hadn't told Wilson that Samuel was from Africa.

The busboy added, "I'm off at eleven. We could talk after."

"Here?"

"There's a Tim Hortons near the mission you went to before. I'll wait for you there."

An hour later Max was seated in a booth with a view of the Tim Hortons tables where a few souls were blowing on hot coffee. The busboy arrived shortly after, scanned the room for Max, then sat in front of him.

"He treated my father," he said. "My family lives fifty kilometres away from the reserve at Duncan Lake. My father's a fishing guide."

One day he'd injured his arm while cleaning the day's catch. The cut had become infected. They had to act quickly. The hospital in Burns Lake was too far. His mother sent a message on the short-range radio, asking for a doctor. But it was too late in the evening and no one came. At dawn they saw a Land Rover drive down the path to their camp. A black man walked out.

Max showed Musindo's picture to the busboy.

"Yes, that's him."

The nurse had cleaned the wound with makeshift equipment at the camp. Only after his father had fallen asleep and was beginning the healing process did the busboy start to wonder why this stranger had arrived at their doorstep with no first-aid gear. Usually, doctors didn't travel without at least a small bag with the essentials, especially in the woods. And here was this man, who clearly had some medical knowledge, arriving empty-handed.

Of course, the nurse didn't want to be paid.

"We asked him who he was, where he was from, and how he'd gotten our call. He said he'd gotten our message on the radio, driving to Prince George."

"He lives here?"

"He didn't say. Didn't even give his name. He was very secretive."

When the stranger left, the busboy noticed the name of the car dealer on the trunk of his car. The car had been purchased in Prince Rupert on the coast, seven hundred kilometres west of Prince George.

That was good news. Musindo lived farther away in British Columbia. His sudden appearance in the life of this family hadn't gone unnoticed. Years later the young man remembered it.

"He saved my father's life."

"How did you know he came from Africa?"

Two days later his father had driven with a customer to Burns Lake. At the hospital they inspected the injury and the treatment given by the stranger. Professional care, but done with limited means.

The doctor had shown his father how Samuel had stitched him up with fishing wire. Classic bush medicine, he declared. And in Africa especially. He'd worked in Mali for years before being hired at Burns Lake. He'd sewn up his share of injuries with fishing wire in times of need.

"Since that day," the busboy concluded, "we've called him the African. The man who came out of nowhere."

Stopping by the refuge to see a friend, and hearing Wilson speak with Max, the busboy had his suspicions they might be talking about the same person. Which was why he'd come up to Max at the hotel bar. Maybe Max knew where the man who saved his father's life lived. His family wanted to thank him in person.

Max remained discreet about the real reasons that prompted him to track Musindo, but he promised the busboy to put him in touch with the nurse as soon as he found him.

After the young man left, Max went back to the Ramada and knocked on Roselyn's door. No answer. Fearing the worst, he ran to reception to get another magnetic key card and returned. He knocked again, then opened up.

Her stuff was scattered across the room, but no trace of Roselyn. Max ran to the window and spotted the Subaru in the parking lot, a short distance from the other vehicles. He ran into the corridor. A first blow to his head made him stumble; a second, harder this time, sent him into unconsciousness.

Max opened his eyes tentatively. It was daylight. He was tied up in the back seat of the Subaru. His head hurt horribly. Blood had run down his face and dried there. Where was Roselyn? The driver was rushing down a road in the middle of a forest. His accomplice turned to Max and pointed a gun at him. It was Bruno Shembazi, Inspector Kilonzo's deputy.

Surprise was painted on Max's face, and in bright colours. Shembazi burst out laughing. A warm, booming laugh, as if enjoying a particularly good joke. His eyes, his attitude, the way he held himself, all of it had changed. In Tanzania he had played the role of the long-suffering subaltern to perfection. Here, there was no doubt: he dominated the situation and was obviously finding pleasure in his new self.

"Through his incompetence and excessive ambition, Kilonzo damaged the reputation of all Tanzanian police officers. Following your arrest, he was already imagining himself chief of police, sitting in some air-conditioned office in Arusha, his hometown, with his car and driver and expense account. But now, because you got away, he's making sure kids cross streets safely in Dar es Salaam. You owe me an eternal debt, do you know that? I saved your life."

"What are you talking about?"

"Do you really think you could have gotten away from Kilonzo by yourself if I hadn't helped?"

Max remained silent.

"Some of my men were in the van. The motor-cycle belonged to the ministry. And do you really think Roosevelt Okambo was flying at that exact moment at that exact place just for fun? Come now."

Max now understood why Okambo hadn't believed him when he claimed he was acting alone. Max should have guessed that others were involved.

"Your life belongs to me now," Shembazi continued. "I can do whatever I want to you."

The exact words Kilonzo had spoken on his arrest. The two men had trained in the same school — with the Ugandan rebels.

"Why didn't you leave me in Kilonzo's hands then?"

"I had to stop the idiot from ruining my plans to find Samuel Musindo. All he wanted was for you to die so he could get a promotion."

"Because you've got other ambitions."

"I don't have ambitions. Only a keen sense of duty."

"Where's Roselyn Kerensky?" Max asked. "What have you done with her?"

Shembazi didn't answer.

"And what do you want with Musindo?"

"Only to lighten a father's pain," Shembazi answered after a short silence.

"You're working directly for Lugembe?"

"His daughter's killer is walking freely on the other side of the world, and you expect him not to intervene?"

"You killed Valéria? Sophie?"

"If only they'd collaborated, admitted their mistake, they would've survived. Lugembe isn't a monster. He just wants to find the man who killed his daughter."

"How did he come to know?"

"That Musindo was alive? The president's always been suspicious of the lawyer. He made sure she was being watched by a few key people in her life. They told him all sorts of interesting details."

"I thought they were allies, Lugembe and Valéria."

"That doesn't mean he should trust her blindly! History is full of lessons about how today's allies are tomorrow's enemies. Lugembe isn't in power only because of his beautiful speeches. Shaking Obama's hand, telling him what he wants to hear ... it isn't enough."

Adding to his history lesson, Shembazi told Max, "In Africa, democracy is a fragile thing, at the mercy of some hysterical general or another. Sooner or later vicious clowns like Idi Amin will come out of the barracks and try to impose their law. Lugembe won't make the mistakes of the past. He believes in democracy, but he isn't naive."

"So everyone's being watched."

"You could put it that way."

Lugembe had been informed of Valéria's panicked visit to the elder Musindo. He understood that the latter had put up his golf course for sale a minute after she left. He knew something was off. He'd sent Shembazi to pay a visit to the lawyer and her daughter. And he'd tried to get them to talk. Under torture, Valéria or Sophie had admitted that Samuel was still alive but hadn't told him where he was hiding, or his new identity.

Learning that his daughter's killer was on the lam, Lugembe, skeptical at first, carried out his own little investigation. It had convinced him that he'd been hoodwinked years before, and that sent him into an absolute rage. The rage of a head of state realizing that the laws he was supposed to defend were being broken. And the rage of a father who couldn't tolerate that his daughter's killer was still unpunished.

Lugembe sent Shembazi after Samuel Musindo, forcing Kilonzo to take the man into his confidence. Kilonzo never realized Shembazi's real role. But Lugembe needed a personal snoop, someone he trusted absolutely and who could pursue the investigation to the ends of the earth.

Either the lawyer or her daughter had mentioned Albert Kerensky's name under torture. Lugembe sent someone to Texas to interrogate him, but Kerensky had disappeared without leaving a trace. Meanwhile, Max had made an appearance on the scene, devastated by the death of Valéria and her daughter. When Shembazi realized the extent to which this old lover was taking his personal investigation seriously, he decided to use him. Until the day Kilonzo chose to blame him for Zuberi's murder.

"Another one of your victims."

"No. That was Kilonzo. He was looking for a way to get you. When he learned the witch doctor had agreed to meet with you, Kilonzo prepared a little welcome party. A setup. He was hoping to pin the murder on you, as well as the con you'd run on Harris. He was sure he'd be noticed by his superiors for that."

Kilonzo had been ready to do anything for a promotion.

"Zuberi was in the dark. He'd been a small cog in the conspiracy, but a blind one. A screen to disguise Michieka's deception."

"Kilonzo must have thought he was the perfect patsy."

"But he couldn't prove his guilt," Shembazi said. "And Zuberi had contacts in the government, allies, secret friends. In an interrogation, a legal one, Kilonzo could've never held his own against the witch doctor, who could have used his associations. On the other hand, you ..."

"Easy prey."

"At first I thought you knew more than we did. But I quickly understood you were as much in the dark as we were. I let you go on your way, to continue your search. And I kept an eye on you. I let you go free so you could do the work for me. To find that goddamn nurse. Ingenious, no?"

"I have no idea where Musindo is."

"And that's why you came all the way to Prince George? Because you have no idea?" Shembazi burst out laughing.

The Subaru turned on a gravel road just outside Vanderhoof and continued for several long minutes before stopping in a rudimentary, improvised parking lot. A muddy field in the middle of an abandoned nursery. The sort of place that was now used only by truckers to make a U-turn. On the ground, thick tire tracks in half-moons and zigzags. Shembazi looked around as he got out of the car, giving Max the impression he was discovering this place for the first time. His kidnappers had waited for Max to regain consciousness before leaving the road and finding this isolated place.

"You're wasting your time, Shembazi. You got to me too early. If only you had waited —"

"Shut up."

With a gesture of his hand — the one holding the revolver — Shembazi ordered Max to get out of the Subaru. He exited slowly, carefully, pain ripping through his skull.

Shembazi's colleague, his face inscrutable, also got out. He pushed Max in front of him, away from the car. Had they decided to kill him here in the middle of nowhere? Max couldn't believe they'd do it, even if they must have been sorely tempted.

He'd likely be tortured, as they'd done with Valéria, Sophie, and the others. But he had nothing to reveal, which foretold long hours of suffering.

"Samuel Musindo's not hurting anyone anymore. It's ancient history, all of it. Why keep going after him?"

"He killed the president's daughter," Shembazi replied. "He has to pay."

"Just tell Lugembe you found him and killed him. He won't know the difference."

"You want me to betray the man who feeds and clothes me for a pathetic fraud artist? I should lie to the man I fought for in Uganda? The man I walked side by side with into Kampala to throw Idi Amin out? Is that what you're saying?"

"I can pay you. I've got a lot of money."

Shembazi leaned against the Subaru's hood, a smile on his face. He was enjoying himself and wanted the pleasure to last, as if he'd been waiting for this moment for a long time.

"That's the difference between you and me. You're alone and I'm supported by an entire country, by a government. I'm not motivated by money like you. I don't give a shit about your money."

"I have no idea where Musindo is hiding. I don't even know if he's still alive."

"Valéria Michieka wouldn't have been so anxious when she learned her secret had been discovered if he was dead and buried."

"Forget Musindo."

"Shut up!"

Before Max could answer, Shembazi's phone rang.

"Someone wants to speak with you," he told Max.

He held out the phone. Max had a feeling, a bad one, that was confirmed when Shembazi's toady pushed him toward his boss.

The phone was a Stellar.

Nervous, guessing what was on the other end of the line, Max took the smartphone.

On the screen, Roselyn Kerensky, tied to a chair. Behind her, crouching, a mountain of muscle: Ferguson, Jonathan Harris's right-hand man.

"Max?" murmured Roselyn, her voice weak. "Are you there, Max?"

The old woman seemed terrified.

"Yes, yes, it's me. Are you okay? Have they hurt you?"

Peas in a pod, the lot of them, forged from the same mould in the war against Uganda. Lugembe, Ferguson, Shembazi. The latter told him as much: Lugembe had hired them all for his protection and his secret service when he gained power.

"When Harris wanted to negotiate the terms for the implementation of his phone service on Tanzanian territory with the government," Shembazi explained, "Ferguson's presence on Harris's yacht gave Lugembe's negotiators an insight into the billionaire's strategy."

In Tanzania, thanks to the president's shrewdness, consumers would have access to leading-edge technology at a modest price.

When Max arrived on Harris's yacht, Ferguson had played along, though he knew who Max was. He'd seen him hanging around Valéria when he was on her surveillance team alongside other members of Tanzania's secret service. They hadn't known Max was a con man, and his cover had held. Until he went after Jonathan Harris. On the yacht, Ferguson had kept quiet for fear of compromising himself.

However, Max's performance had come to Lugembe's attention. At first the president found the situation rather funny. Harris was furious that the government wanted to tax his revenue at such a high rate. He demanded special favours. Seeing Max take a part of the man's fortune pleased Lugembe, even if he hadn't profited from it directly. Harris was humiliated, so much the better for that pretentious braggart who was always giving lessons in civility to everyone.

"You were right … on the *Sunflower*," Ferguson said over the phone. "Technology is a wonderful thing."

"Roselyn has nothing to do with this. Leave her be."

"Tell us where Musindo is hiding," Shembazi said flatly.

"Free Roselyn and I'll tell you."

"You're not in a position to negotiate."

"I have no idea where Musindo is. Roselyn doesn't, either."

"I'll give you one last chance."

"All I know is he landed in Vancouver. The rest of it is just conjecture. I'm travelling as blind as you are."

"Bullshit."

"Please, let Roselyn go."

"He doesn't know anything," Roselyn said on the other end of the Stellar.

"Make a little effort, won't you?" Shembazi coaxed.

Ferguson pointed his revolver at Roselyn's temple.

"Free her."

A long moment of silence, then a gunshot. On the Stellar's screen, Max saw Roselyn trying to catch her breath, her eyes closed. Ferguson, stoic, hadn't moved, the still-smoking revolver in his hand.

"Do you really want the murder of an old woman on your conscience?" Shembazi asked him. "And what about when her husband learns you're responsible for her death? When he finds out that killing Musindo also caused his wife's death … well, I wouldn't want to be in your shoes."

Before Max could react, another gunshot. Once again, Roselyn was unharmed, though how long would Ferguson keep missing?

"He lives in Prince Rupert," Max spat out, desperate. "A young Indigenous man met him. Musindo saved his father's life. All the kid knew was that he came from the coast."

"You see? All you needed was a little help to remember."

"Let her go now, please."

"Where in Prince Rupert?"

"I'll lead you there if you free Roselyn."

Shembazi was silent, as if evaluating the offer. Max knew he needed an argument that would convince him, something that could save Roselyn's life, and his own.

"He doesn't know you're after him."

"You spoke with him?"

"Yes. He expects to see me. If he figures out I'm not coming, he'll suspect something. You'll never find him then. He'll disappear without a trace."

Max was improvising, but he was having some effect. Shembazi was listening, not talking.

"Free Roselyn now. She hasn't done you wrong in any way, and she —"

A third gunshot. The Stellar's screen spattered with red.

"Roselyn!" Max shouted.

Shembazi ripped the phone out of his hand and threw it on the ground where he stomped on it for good measure. "Let's go."

Disgusted, broken, Max let himself be dragged to the Subaru's back seat. The door slammed behind him like one last gunshot.

32

Roselyn's death broke something in Max. He felt as if he'd woken up in the middle of a boxing ring, had been used as a punching bag by the heavyweight champion of the world. Pain in the pit of his stomach. It didn't fade. He felt responsible for what had happened. Roselyn had wanted only one thing: to find her husband. He'd brought her to this isolated part of the world without a care for her fate. Sure, he'd paid lip service to safety, asking whether she wouldn't be better off staying in Chicago or returning to Houston, but he hadn't spoken very loudly, or very long. He knew she'd be useful to him if they met Albert. Knew that if there was someone to talk some sense into him — if that was possible — it would be his wife. When she insisted and decided to come with Max, he'd felt relieved. Now he regretted that.

That was his life — a race to fix the latest failure, the latest mistake. An illusory life of constant repentance. Ironically, living on the wrong side of the law had sharpened his moral core. Roselyn's death was a wound as deep as Valéria's or Sophie's, though he'd known the old woman a few days at most. His guilt was untenable.

With Roselyn's death, Max's situation had only worsened. He'd created this story about Musindo — completely made up, of course, but a story that comforted Shembazi in his conviction that Max knew where to find the nurse. His pathetic attempt to save Roselyn had failed. And now, as Shembazi had predicted, if Max ever got away from these two goons, he'd have Kerensky on his tail, seeking vengeance for his wife's death.

But as soon as Shembazi and his muscle figured out he'd lied, he would have his brains splattered live and in colour on a Stellar screen.

All Max could do now was play it by ear and hope for the best. He was out of options.

First, to find Samuel Musindo.

Studying the forest zipping by through the car window, dark coniferous trees growing in tight rows, Max once again wondered why the fugitive had chosen this part of the world when he could have found anonymity in the crowds of Toronto or Montreal. If he could figure out what had motivated his choice, Max would have a chance at discovering where the nurse might be. But no matter how he turned the puzzle over in his head, nothing came to him. Musindo's motivations remained hazy.

Max knew little about the man, something he regretted now. How had Valéria come to abandon this child, and why had Thomas Musindo ended up with his guardianship? Was he Samuel's true father, or had he only acted as such to help out Valéria? Abortion was illegal in Tanzania, except in cases where the mother's life was in danger. Which clearly hadn't been the case.

A child who, when he grew up, became a trafficker and killer of albinos. Valéria had done everything she could to protect him, though she'd very publicly advocated for capital punishment. There was something off about the whole situation. Both in terms of the trafficking Samuel participated in and the means Valéria had employed to save his life.

Except, of course, if the young man was, despite appearances, innocent. But Max recalled that the nurse had confessed to the murder.

Perhaps that was what felt so strange. He'd spontaneously admitted to his guilt, even if the case was far from solid. There had been no direct witnesses to the murder. His lawyer, Jason Chagula, wouldn't have found it too difficult to sow doubt in the jury's minds. His admission of guilt was as strange as his decision not to incriminate the witch doctor Zuberi, who'd gotten off with what amounted to a slap on the wrist.

As they neared Prince Rupert, rain fell, a grey, monotonous mass, more mist than rain that soaked the landscape without flooding it. A scent of wet earth rose, mixed with that of the sea. They crossed the downtown core — a large, uninspired street with rundown hotels and boarding houses — and the port appeared. An industrial port. Busy, full of action and goings-on, flanked by canneries on each side. That explained the giant billboard they'd spotted stating, with obvious pride, PRINCE RUPERT, THE HALIBUT CAPITAL OF THE WORLD.

Near the wharf, with a backdrop of the same pine trees, fishermen were off-loading their catch to cannery employees, most of them Indigenous. Despite the industrial activity, the place felt like the edge of the world, far from everything. Farther still than Bukoba.

Shembazi's accomplice parked the Subaru in front of a sorry-looking McDonald's where, behind a storefront running with rivulets of rain, a few retirees sat mournfully, baseball caps screwed tightly on their heads. Facing the parking lot, they watched the newcomers. Their arrival hadn't gone unnoticed.

"So?" Shembazi asked, turning the engine off.

"I don't know where he lives."

"Enough, O'Brien."

"We made an appointment."

"Where?"

"Smile's Seafood Café. Tomorrow. Noon."

As they'd driven into the city, Max had noticed a billboard advertising the place, with its daily special, including the best halibut in British Columbia, simple, delicious meals for the whole family. Likely a rather popular diner-style restaurant, busy at noon with workers stopping in for a quick bite. A crowd that might be to Max's advantage.

Before Shembazi could say anything, Max added, "If Musindo sees I'm not alone, he'll disappear."

Shembazi hesitated, no doubt wondering if Max was bluffing. Finally, he told his colleague to start the car, and they drove to the outskirts of the city.

They found a motel there, a little off the main road, though its marquee could be seen in the distance, perched on a tall pole. A gas station abutted the motel. Hardly any cars in the parking lot. A lit sign on a truck proclaimed cheap rooms. Certainly, this place had known better days. It needed a coat of paint to start with.

Shembazi's accomplice walked into the reception to rent the room. Shembazi pushed Max out of the car into the now-pouring rain. Completely drenched, he was marched into a large humid room that smelled of cleaning products. Two queen-sized beds, a worn-out chest of drawers over which a large plasma screen had been installed. The only modern touch in an otherwise faded decor.

The two men handcuffed Max to the bathroom radiator and closed the door on their prisoner. Shortly after, Shembazi left the room in search of something to eat. Max could hear the television, which Shembazi's colleague had turned on. He inspected the radiator, solidly bolted to the floor. No way he could break free. In any case, even if he did somehow manage to get the handcuffs off, the bathroom window was too narrow to slip though. And he couldn't expect to fight his way out against an armed veteran of an African civil war.

Not much hope of escape.

Max had won a few hours, but all he'd really managed to do was prolong his ordeal. When he realized Max had led them astray, Shembazi would put a bullet in his head. If he didn't decide to first give him a little taste of the *kandoya*.

A few moments later Max heard Shembazi returning. The bathroom door opened. He tossed a sandwich and a soda at him the way he might have thrown a bone to a famished dog, then shut the door. Max kicked the sandwich away. He should have eaten, should have regained his strength, but he'd lost all appetite. The door opened again two hours later, and Shembazi threw a sheet at him.

That night Max slept fitfully, awakened over and over by the sound of his handcuffs rubbing against the radiator. Stiff, exhausted, he finally saw grey light appear at the small window above his head. His captors had taken his watch, so he had no idea what time it was. Very early in the morning, no doubt. On the other side of the door, not a peep. His two jailers were sleeping.

If he had the means to flee, now would have been the time. But despite his sleepless night, no great ideas had come to him.

Eventually, Shembazi woke up and walked into the bathroom to relieve himself. He leaned over Max. "I hope you're being honest with us. You know what we do to traitors in Uganda?"

Max had no desire to find out.

Shembazi smiled and uncuffed Max. "Come on now, up. I wouldn't want to miss our date."

Max was seated in a window booth at Smile's where a few people sat having a late breakfast. He wasn't much hungrier than the night before. The smell of bacon and eggs nauseated him. On the table, an abandoned plate, coffee gone cold. Maybe Smile's had the best halibut in the world, but it had given up on the coffee a long time ago.

Farther off, a server was preparing tables for the employees of the nearby McMillan Fisheries who usually came for lunch here. Near the back exit that led to the parking lot was Shembazi's accomplice. Shembazi himself was seated at the entrance. They controlled both doors. Perfectly positioned, Shembazi could see the kitchen from where he was.

What next?

As they'd made their way to the restaurant from the motel, Max had tried to come up with a plan, a way to get out of the trap he'd set for himself. He hadn't been able to think of anything. And so there he was, hopeless, convinced that Shembazi was already beginning to doubt the story about his meeting with Musindo.

Behind the counter, the server was pulling cutlery out of the dishwasher, moving quickly, as she probably did this time every day. Over her head, the clock showed eleven. Beyond the kitchen's swinging doors, the cook and his assistant were finishing their prep for lunch.

There was no way out of this one. No solution.

Worse still, Max was convinced that if he tried to run now, Shembazi and his man wouldn't hesitate to shoot at him in the middle of the restaurant. The war between Uganda and Tanzania, like all wars, had made them unconcerned about collateral damage.

Max had Roselyn's murder on his conscience. He wasn't about to become responsible for the mass killing of Smile's patrons.

"You haven't touched your plate," the waitress chastised him.

"It's delicious, I'm sure. Sorry."

"Do you want anything else?"

"No thanks."

The minutes passed as his coffee was warmed up and cooled down until little by little the employees of the canning factories began to fill every empty table, jostling one another like schoolchildren. The waitress quickened the pace. Soon it was eleven thirty, then noon. Then five past twelve and a quarter past. As time went by, Shembazi's face grew sharper, meaner. At twelve thirty he walked toward Max through the jam-packed restaurant, stopped in front of his table, and motioned for him to follow.

It was over.

Max got up, giving his seat to the people who were waiting in line. He felt like a lamb being led to the slaughter.

"Max O'Brien?"

A loud voice practically shouted over the hubbub from the back of the restaurant. At the end of the counter the waitress was holding the phone as if it were a tennis racket.

"Is there a Max O'Brien here?" the waitress repeated, clearly impatient. She didn't have a second to waste as plates piled up on the hatch that opened into the kitchen.

Max glanced at Shembazi, who nodded in silence.

"That's me!" Max cried as he rushed to the counter.

He took the phone out of the waitress's hands as she disappeared with four daily specials balanced on her arms. Shembazi stood right behind Max, scanning the restaurant for a black man with a cellphone. No one.

"O'Brien here."

A long silence.

"Rainbow Pier is what you're looking for. The old drop-off point for ferries going to Port Simpson. Ask the waitress. She'll know where it is."

A young man's voice. Nervous. Max could hear the Tanzanian accent. Samuel Musindo?

Max quickly answered, "Listen, Samuel, you absolutely —"

Shembazi cut the line and motioned to his partner to follow. Time to go.

33

In the Subaru, a few moments later, Shembazi couldn't contain his satisfaction. If he'd doubted Max's revelations at first, those doubts were gone. Soon he'd get his hands on Musindo and finally put an end to him, though he was, of course, officially dead. Afterward, he'd get rid of another thorn in his side: Max himself.

Meanwhile, Max wondered who had actually made the call. They must have been followed, the three of them. Shembazi and his accomplice were running head-first into a trap, with Max and Musindo getting first billing as the bait. Though his situation looked margin-ally better now — more players joining the mix could only help Max at this point — he still had no idea who might be waiting at Rainbow Pier.

As they drove, Max wondered whether he'd been led down the garden path the entire time. He'd followed a series of fabricated revelations, leading Max and his two pursuers toward this specific spot that had nothing to do with Musindo's true whereabouts. The phone call at the restaurant confirmed his suspicions: the three of them were small fry in a conspiracy much larger than they imagined. Max's only advantage over Shembazi and his accomplice was that he was aware they were being manipulated.

There had been a time when ferries sailed from Rainbow Pier, connecting Prince Rupert not only to Port Simpson but also to Klemtu, Bella Bella, and the Queen Charlotte Islands. Mostly Indigenous Peoples lived along the coast from Port Hardy, north of Vancouver Island, to the border with Alaska, south of Ketchikan. They had traded with the Russians when they owned a piece of Alaska, and later with the Americans. Early in the twentieth century, the construction of the railway had made Prince Rupert into the last important port before the American border.

Over the years, an increase in tourism and maritime traffic meant building new installations. Rainbow Pier had been abandoned, its wooden structure left to rot by the combined action of salt and wind blowing in over the Pacific Ocean.

It was hard to reach the place. A metal fence barred entry to the wharf itself, which could be seen through the gate about two hundred metres away. A yellow placard announcing DANGER completed the picture. Waves broke noisily, almost angrily, against the seawall built to prevent erosion. A grey sky loomed over this sinister picture.

The area was isolated. A good place to get killed.

Shembazi got out of the car first and looked around, his face anxious, tense. For the first time, Max detected nerves. Shembazi wasn't leading this little expedition any longer; he was being led.

Shembazi turned to Max, impatiently waving at him to get out of the car. His accomplice was standing guard next to the Subaru, scanning the environment.

"Walk in front of us," Shembazi ordered.

"If he sees you, he'll run."

"He won't get very far. And neither will you. So don't try anything."

Max approached the fence. From close up, he saw it was open, with a rusted lock hanging uselessly from it. Obviously, the city didn't come here much to check on the wharf. Max imagined how this secluded site could become a hot spot for teenagers looking for unsupervised time on the weekends. Cars and motorbikes parked every which way, bonfires near the water, beer bottles thrown here and there, shattered against concrete blocks because there was nothing better to do.

But for now, the place was quiet. Max stepped onto the path that led to the pier. He couldn't see its far edge, shrouded in a mix of mist and fog that rose from the water. Shembazi, gun in hand, walked a few metres behind him, scanning the surroundings. His partner was concentrating on the boulders, perhaps fearing the appearance of Idi Amin and his Libyan mercenaries.

Max walked steadily but slowly, trying to calm his nerves. If Samuel Musindo had laid this trap for Shembazi, with Max's involuntary complicity, he wouldn't bide his time. That was what Max feared: to be caught in a firefight, an ambush.

Suddenly, Max saw a silhouette loom out of the fog.

Seated on the ground, back to him, leaning against one of the concrete blocks at the entrance to the pier, a black man contemplated the ocean. The sound of crashing waves kept him from hearing Max. He turned to Shembazi. The two Tanzanians had noticed the silhouette and moved into position.

Shembazi's accomplice hid behind a boulder. The two men had Musindo in a pincer. Shembazi waved Max forward.

How would the nurse escape? Max had no choice but to follow Shembazi's order. He was a few steps away from the nurse and still the man hadn't budged.

Max called, "Musindo?"

No reaction. Strange …

Max walked forward, then around the man to face him.

It wasn't Samuel Musindo, but Ferguson, Harris's bodyguard. Dead, and more, if that was possible. He'd been shot at close range with a large-calibre weapon. His body rested against a concrete block.

Seeing the repulsion on Max's face, Shembazi quickly joined him. Max made his move: he took advantage of his captor's moment of confusion and despair at Ferguson's death to push the police officer hard in the chest. Shembazi tumbled over the concrete block. That was when Max heard a gunshot. Instinctively, he threw himself onto the ground, pulling Ferguson's body over him while trying to grab Shembazi's gun. From the corner of one eye, he saw the Tanzanian's partner collapse, a bullet in the middle of his forehead. The second shot hit Shembazi in the shoulder, then a third burst his head open.

Max got to his feet. A stranger dressed in hunting gear marched out of the undergrowth, a rifle in hand. An elderly man sauntering slowly toward him with the determination of someone who knew where he was going and had all the time in the world to get there. He had just killed two men but didn't seem unnerved in the slightest.

Max recognized him from the picture Roselyn had shown him: Albert Kerensky.

Without taking a moment's pause to glance at his two victims — he was so sure he'd killed them that he didn't even stop to investigate — he halted his advance and raised the rifle. Max heard him breathe in hard and realized that what he'd mistaken for calm and exceptional mastery were the symptoms of physical weakness. The man was sick, very sick, and avoided any unnecessary movement.

If Kerensky wanted to kill him, as he had the other two men, why hadn't he shot already? To enjoy the kill? To force him to suffer Ferguson's fate? Shembazi's gun was a few steps from Max, but he'd never get there in time.

"That way." Kerensky's voice was strong, surprisingly so considering his condition, as if illness had wracked his body but not his mind.

Max walked in the direction indicated by Kerensky, through the bushes. They hiked one hundred metres or so, following the contour of the coast, until they reached a Mercury Grand Marquis parked at the end of a dirt road.

Kerensky forced him to lie on his stomach on the rear seat, hands behind his back. Max felt his wrists and ankles being bound by plastic tie wraps, the kind from a hardware store. Kerensky then passed a chain between the two sets of straps, transforming Max into a pig ready for roasting. He could barely move, let alone go after the former Texas executioner. The elderly man slowly settled behind the wheel and drove off.

Max had begun to feel a bit more confident during their stroll to the car, thinking the man intended to let him live. But now his anxiety was back with a vengeance. He'd let him live, sure, but for how long?

When they reached an intersection and turned off the dirt road, Kerensky, without slowing, threw a sheet — it smelled new — over Max's body, covering him completely. By twisting his body, Max managed to uncover his face. Despite his precarious position, he realized they were now driving on the Trans-Canada Highway. Kerensky had left Rainbow Pier without even bothering to dispose of the bodies of Shembazi, Ferguson, and the third accomplice. Plainly, he wasn't afraid of what the police would think about such carnage. He simply didn't care. That worried Max more.

Before Prudhomme Lake, the Mercury left the main road and returned to the forest. On the radio, Kerensky found a country music station. Johnny Cash crackled to life. He pulled a can of Canada Dry out of the glove compartment and opened it with one hand.

His stillness made Max's skin crawl. "Kerensky, listen, please. You got what you wanted. Vengeance for Roselyn."

Kerensky didn't react.

"You won't get away. The police will come after you as soon as they find the bodies of those three men."

Kerensky turned the sound up.

They drove for a few kilometres on a poorly maintained track cratered by rain, ice, and snow. Likely used only by hunters in the fall, or tourists accompanied by guides. Kerensky seemed to know the place. He drove with assurance, zigzagging among the potholes.

The area was uninhabited, as if it had been closed for the season and everyone sent back to wherever they'd come from. In front of the Mercury, around a curve, a handful of unoccupied shacks, humble dwellings falling into ruin, seemingly abandoned long ago. Kerensky followed the trail for another kilometre, then stopped in front of a cabin raised on stilts on a series of large boulders, its porch facing a small lake, back against the road.

An isolated retreat.

After freeing his ankles, Kerensky dragged Max out of the car. Holding his weapon on him, he motioned for him to open the trunk. A black man in his thirties was tied and gagged with gaffer tape, his eyes filled with fear, shaking from terror and cold.

Max recognized Samuel Musindo immediately.

Valéria's son. The young man gave Max a terrified look, as if begging for his help. Max was as powerless as he was.

Kerensky freed Musindo's ankles and forced him out of the trunk and toward the cabin, threatening both men with his rifle.

The voice he'd heard at Smile's? Likely Musindo. Kerensky had made him call the restaurant before tying him up and throwing him in the trunk.

"This is madness, Kerensky," Max said. "I know what you want to do. You'll never get away with this. You won't get away with the other killings, either."

MARIO BOLDUC

Kerensky stared at Max. "Without justice we turn into wild beasts. Whoever manages to avoid it is avoiding the will and the right of men to punish their fellow men."

"So bring Musindo in, make him face justice."

"I am justice."

Inside the cabin, keeping Max in his field of vision, Kerensky tied Musindo to the bed in the middle of the room. Then he secured Max to a chair close by.

The place had been prepared for just this purpose. A set piece. Kerensky had let Max live so he could witness the executioner at his job.

"A death sentence without a witness is murder plain and simple," Kerensky continued. "Capital punishment is a ceremony because it's legally sanctioned, yes. But also because citizens can see the mandate they've given their government carried out."

"I've given no permission, not to you or anybody else, Kerensky."

"Not you yourself, of course. But the people."

"You're mad."

"I've never been more sane."

"You're about to commit murder."

"An execution. That's entirely different. There's no anger in me. No impulsiveness. Only a clear mind and a desire to make sure the sanction given this criminal is applied. Six years ago I was given a mandate. I'm here to set things right."

Musindo listened to the exchange, struck by the man's madness. Max, as well. He was trying desperately to think of an escape route.

"And then?" Max asked. "When it's done, when you've made things right …"

"The future isn't important."

As he spoke, Kerensky opened a suitcase on the kitchen table and pulled out a handful of small vials. A few syringes, as well. From time to time, he glanced at Musindo, who continued fighting against his bonds, but he never ceased to be calm and professional. He looked like a surgeon preparing for an operation.

"Normally, I offer prisoners an opportunity to speak their last words," he told Max, ignoring Musindo completely. "As long as they're not obscenities or insults." He turned to the nurse. "He had his chance at his last execution. No need to repeat himself. And a priest would do him no good."

Kerensky moved to the prisoner and ripped his shirt open with a single, rapid movement, attaching tiny suction cups to his chest. Musindo was fighting his restraints, trying to scream, but the gag wouldn't allow it. His agitation didn't bother the executioner, who continued his meticulous work.

"Cardiac sensors," he told Max, who hadn't asked. "They'll inform me of the death of the subject without my needing to manually measure his vital functions."

"Enough, Kerensky."

"Generally, these preparations are made before the witnesses arrive. But today, of course, the situation is exceptional."

From his suitcase, Kerensky put other objects on the table, which Max couldn't identify. Finally, he pulled out a long plastic tube that had a needle at its end. He examined it carefully.

Kerensky returned to Musindo. Delicately, he stuck the needle in his arm. The man fought again in vain. From the same suitcase, a second tube, with a needle, as well, which Kerensky fitted into another vein. The procedure had the appearance of an ordinary blood donation.

"A simple precaution, a secondary solution in case the injection doesn't take place as intended. Normally, the two tubes should be behind a wall, first connected to a harmless saline solution, and later, to sodium thiopental, a preparation that puts the condemned man to sleep."

Kerensky spoke to Max as if giving a lecture. Behind him, Musindo had stopped thrashing. A veil had gone over his eyes. His struggle had subsided. Part of him had already died.

The old man glanced at his watch. "We'll be able to start in nine minutes."

"Kerensky, please listen to me —"

"One more word out of you and I'll put you to sleep. And you'll miss the execution. Which would be a shame. For me, I mean. I'd need to find a new witness."

Kerensky returned to the table, his attention on Musindo as if observing an alien object, with no particular emotion but obvious interest. "The doctor isn't here," he muttered. "He won't come. But we'll still be able to record the time of death …"

At the appointed moment Kerensky made his way to one of the plastic tubes. He depressed a syringe. Musindo wanted to scream one last time, but that, too, was in vain. His face was deformed, prey to inhuman distress. Then he closed his eyes.

"This is the part I love most," Kerensky murmured. "Seeing anger become peace." With his eyes on his victim, he added, "He's sleeping. That way he won't feel pain."

Kerensky pulled scissors out of his shirt pocket and moved to cut off a lock of Musindo's hair. He returned to the table and slipped the hair into a small plastic bag.

"Pancuronium bromide will paralyze his muscles, including his lungs. It should be enough, normally. But I'll also inject potassium chloride to stop his heart in its tracks." He turned to Max. "Death will occur within seconds, but the tradition is to wait a few moments before declaring the execution a success."

Syringe in hand, Kerensky made his way to the second plastic tube. He was about the depress the plunger when —

"Albert, no!"

Without abandoning the syringe, Kerensky wheeled toward the bedroom door.

Roselyn propped herself against the door frame unsteadily.

"Go away!" he ordered.

"Don't do it, please!" Roselyn blurted out.

"Enough! Let me work."

"Stop!"

Ignoring her, he returned to his work, leaning over the plastic tube. A shot rang out. Kerensky's head exploded, sending pieces of cranium and brain flying across the room. Roselyn dropped the Beretta onto the floor, and soon joined it there, weeping.

34

Max had one concern: get out of the cabin before the cops arrived. Get Roselyn and Musindo out of this hell and hit the road quickly, as if speed could lessen the nightmare. The only car at their disposal was Kerensky's Mercury, which they would need to get rid of quickly. Back in Prince George, maybe, where he could rent another car. But for now, all that mattered was to put some distance between them and this terrible place.

After shooting Kerensky, Roselyn freed Max, and he immediately tried to wake Musindo but had no success. Instead, he carried him to the Mercury, and soon they were flying down Route 16. Next to him, Roselyn was lost in thought, still stunned by what she'd done: killed her husband. Max knew that while she suffered now, it would only be worse tomorrow, and the day after, for a long time to come. Her grief would be a horrible ordeal that she might never come out of.

They'd been driving for half an hour when Roselyn broke the silence. "Albert saw us arrive in Prince George. He followed us from Vancouver. When I was kidnapped by Shembazi and handed over to his accomplice, he saw the whole thing."

Kerensky had intervened and saved his wife's life; he'd shown up at the motel room Ferguson had rented. The Tanzanian hadn't been suspicious of an old, fragile-looking man. Kerensky killed him with a single shot, Ferguson's blood spraying the Stellar's screen. The former rebel didn't have a chance.

The executioner had already figured out where Musindo was, but before carrying out another execution, he first had to take care of Shembazi and his accomplice. Since they were two, with Max to boot, he couldn't eliminate them in the same way as Ferguson. He would need to lure them into a trap where he could pick them off as if they were the deer or feral pigs Kerensky loved to hunt with Glenn Forrester back in Texas.

"Where were you all that time?" Max asked.

"In the cabin. He'd rented it for the week. After Ferguson died, I tried to reason with him. I told him to turn himself in to the police. We spoke all night through to morning. I thought I'd managed to convince him. We would go together to the RCMP in Prince Rupert and explain the situation."

They wouldn't mention the murders of Clements and Arceneaux. Kerensky would say that he'd acted out of anger in regard to Ferguson, who'd been holding his wife hostage. An argument that wouldn't have convinced Peter but might get him out of Canada and back to Texas to go on living the life of a retiree. At least that was what Roselyn had hoped.

What she didn't know was that Albert was only pretending to mollify her. That Ferguson's body was in the trunk of his car. That the body was already part of Kerensky's plan to get rid of the two other Tanzanians. Roselyn had fallen asleep, drugged by a pill Albert had slipped into her water glass. When she woke hours later, she heard noises in the neighbouring room. Max's voice. She discovered Musindo connected to familiar plastic tubes and decided to intervene, knowing she wouldn't be able to reason with her husband.

"I didn't have a choice." She added, her voice low, "He turned me into a killer."

A little before Terrace, Musindo began to stir in the back seat. Max got off at the next rest stop and parked as far as possible from the other vehicles. Musindo sat up, lost, confused. Max opened his door for him. The nurse leaned over and puked on the asphalt. Minutes passed. The retching became bile as his body emptied itself of the drug Kerensky had administered.

Roselyn returned from the nearby gas station with water and ice. Musindo was recovering his senses, though he remained bewildered. But this was the second execution he'd survived — he was getting the hang of it.

Max brought him up to speed. Roselyn's intervention had saved his life. The night before, Musindo told him, Kerensky had called out to him in a supermarket parking lot in Prince Rupert. He was out of breath, seemed in pain, asked for help getting his groceries into his trunk. Musindo hadn't suspected a thing. Moments later he was locked in the same trunk, terrified. When the trunk opened eventually, Musindo recognized the kidnapper. Fear turned to panic. The rickety old man was his executioner from Tanzania. His worst nightmare had become a reality.

"His madness killed Valéria and Sophie," Max informed him. "And Thomas, your adoptive father."

"My real father."

So Max's first intuition had been right: Valéria and Thomas had had a short affair while she was still a university student. They'd agreed he'd keep the child. She later married Richard Stroner and had another child with him — Sophie. Valéria hadn't attempted to reach out to Samuel. He made the first move as an adult when he tried to find his biological mother.

Musindo told Max how, just weeks before, Valéria had warned him that Kerensky was hunting for him. Wanted to kill him. She told him to be very careful and that she was looking into ways to keep him safe, to find him a new place to live. She'd be getting her hands on a small fortune soon and would make a plan. Until then he had to watch himself and keep a low profile.

When he learned of the tragic death of his mother, his father, and his half-sister, his first thought was that Kerensky was responsible for the killings, just as he would be for Zuberi's murder. He'd had no idea Shembazi was after him, as well, under direct orders from President Lugembe.

"What about Jonathan Harris's ransom?" Max asked.

"I took it out of Valéria's account. I didn't know she'd just been killed. When I heard the news, I didn't dare touch a penny of it for fear someone would start following the money."

"I need to know," Max said. "Did you kill Lugembe's daughter?"

"I didn't kill anyone. I'm not guilty. I never was. I only wanted to help Clara."

"You knew each other?"

"We worked together. She was helping Valéria's organization."

When albinos were born at the clinic, Musindo made sure they ended up in the hands of adoptive families on Ukerewe. Their biological parents knew about this, and some chose to move to the island along with the child. For most parents, it was enough to know their children would live in safety. The nurse had been not only wrongly accused of Clara's murder but wrongly accused of trafficking in albinos with Zuberi and others of his ilk. Valéria hadn't been able to help him prove his innocence.

"What happened to Clara?"

Musindo took a deep breath. He closed his eyes, trying to put some order in his head. "We were in love. Completely devoted to each other. No one knew. Especially not her father. And one day she told me she'd learned something about his dealings in the past."

Musindo told Max and Roselyn the story of this young, ambitious politician, an excellent orator, a respected economist, but without a penny to his name.

Lugembe had fallen for Myriam Ikingura, who came from a well-heeled family in Dar es Salaam, her father an activist who'd worked alongside Julius Nyerere for independence. She had twins. Two little albino children from a previous marriage: Faith and Clara. But Lugembe had been attracted to Myriam more out of a desire to advance his career than out of true love. Especially since Myriam displayed erratic behaviour. She'd broken off ties with her family, gone against everyone, Lugembe first. Their marriage quickly became a convention, a partnership. At conferences, parties, receptions, she could be seen on the arm of her husband. The rest of the time they lived separate lives. Faith and Clara's mother drank like a fish in Dar es Salaam's ritzy hotels. She was seen wandering the streets after her legendary drinking sessions. Behaviour that was compromising, politically dangerous. Lugembe had felt forced to have her sent to the Mirembe Psychiatric Hospital in Dodoma. She lost custody of the twins, and Lugembe hired a nanny to take care of them.

And then one day Faith was kidnapped. The culprits took advantage of the nanny looking the other way. The next morning all that was left of the child, her clothes, in fact, was discovered in an abandoned house. Another victim of the witch doctors.

A terrible tragedy.

And Lugembe had been responsible for the kidnapping. He needed money for his political campaign. The one that got him elected to the national assembly and launched his political career.

Clara's twin sister was worth more than other albino children, it was said, because she was the daughter of a madwoman. Purity was guaranteed in the children of insane women, according to the outlandish beliefs, meaning that the charms and trinkets would be worth that much more. Faith represented a fortune. Financially stuck, Lugembe, ambitious and impatient, hadn't been able to resist the gold mine.

"Devastated by Faith's death, unaware of the role her husband had played, Myriam threw herself off the hospital roof. Maybe she was pushed because she had her suspicions about her husband. In any case, the suicide didn't harm Lugembe's career."

While working with Musindo and Valéria, Clara had come to better understand the complexities of the human trafficking in albinos. She became more interested in the investigation into her twin sister's kidnapping and death. She discovered that soon after the disappearance, the nanny's family had managed to regain their ancestral land that had been confiscated during the Nyerere government's agrarian reform. In other words, the nanny's oversight had benefited her family. There was no direct proof or out-and-out accusations, but Clara asked her adoptive father a few questions. He flew into a rage. With that, she sentenced herself to death, though she didn't know it.

Max now understood why Lugembe was so desperate to track down Musindo and kill him. Samuel knew the president was guilty, knew he was responsible for the death of his two adoptive daughters. If it became public knowledge that he'd sold Faith to fund his electoral campaign and killed Clara to cover his tracks, he could kiss the presidency goodbye. He would be completely and definitively ruined. There would be no more handshakes and hugs with Barack Obama. And so Lugembe had sent Shembazi to find and kill Musindo before his career was destroyed.

Devastated by her son's arrest and the accusation levelled against him, Valéria played both sides. As she urged President Komba to bring back capital punishment, she worked to avoid her son's death and find him a safe place on the other side of the world. A remote area where he could rebuild his life.

"And Valéria managed it by putting pressure on Albert Kerensky through his grandson," Samuel said.

Valéria had discreetly met the executioner at his hotel in Dar es Salaam. She explained that Adrian would live if he obeyed. Kerensky didn't have a choice. And she'd assured him that no one would ever know what had actually happened, not Lugembe or Komba or anyone else. Something that wouldn't be too hard to promise, since Kerensky was in Tanzania secretly. Legally, he didn't exist. But if he spoke up one day, he, too, would be caught up in Lugembe's wrath.

Kerensky had gotten the message. He faked the execution. Musindo stayed in hiding for a few weeks while arrangements were made for his escape with Sophie. They drove to the border with Burundi, the most porous crossing in the country. From Bujumbura they'd taken a flight to Amsterdam through Kigali. Samuel was travelling under his new identity. He played the role of an African businessman flying to Europe to meet with investors. They spent two days holed up in a hotel in Haarlem before heading to Canada, their final destination. To Lake McFearn, to be exact. Sophie returned to Tanzania the next week, once she knew Samuel was safe.

"Valéria had kept in touch with a good friend of her husband who worked at the Alcan plant in Kitimat," Samuel said. "Thanks to him, I eased into the community without attracting too much attention."

Each year on his birthday, Valéria went to see her son. They met in Prince Rupert or Prince George. Once they even got together in Vancouver.

Musindo was careful. He always drove with his shortwave radio tuned to the police channel. That was how he'd heard the call for help from the First Nations busboy and managed to save his father's life.

In short, he, Sophie, and Valéria had carefully planned and carried out his disappearance. All would have gone smoothly if it wasn't for Albert Kerensky going completely mad years later and deciding to hunt down Musindo to finish what he'd started. It would be his last execution. In his retirement home, he sat for months, bored, obsessively reviewing the details of his long career with the tie-down team. His thoughts turned to Samuel Musindo time and again. He couldn't forget the execution that never happened. To quell his demons, the former executioner went hunting.

Just like President Lugembe.

"Where are we?" Musindo asked when he finished his story.

"Near Terrace," Max told him, then explained his plan.

First, they'd abandon and destroy the car, then find another. Leave the area for good. After that he wasn't sure. Improvise again maybe. At this point it had become his speciality.

Musindo didn't agree. Kerensky's murder had probably been discovered, or the bodies of the three Tanzanians. They had to get off the road as quickly as possible. Disappear for a bit until things died down. "I know the area well. Trust me."

Max nodded.

They continued on the highway for a while, then Musindo told Max to turn right on a secondary road through the forest. After twenty kilometres or so, they reached a crossing. Musindo told him to go left, the track that looked in poorer shape. Two hours later, down a potholed path, they came to a crystalline lake.

Musindo indicated a cabin hidden by cedars.

"Where are we?" Max asked.

"Home."

Musindo got out of the car without waiting for the others. He ran to the entrance. A young woman burst out of the door and threw herself into his arms. They were quickly joined by a young boy. When they separated, Max was startled. The woman was albino. Musindo turned to Max and Roselyn. "This is Clara. And Daniel, our son."

At first, suspecting her father of having killed her twin sister, Clara wanted to denounce him publicly and try to drag him before the courts. Soon enough, she real- ized that would be a mistake. First, she had no concrete proof, though she was convinced Lugembe was guilty. But in Tanzania, you couldn't accuse the president of a terrible crime without compromising the entire government. Especially if the accusation came from Lugembe's daughter herself. If Clara went public with what she knew, the entire political class would get behind Lugembe, not only to protect him but to protect themselves. How many supposedly clean politicians had been involved with albino trafficking? How many of them still turned to witch doctors and bush healers in time of need?

Lugembe would simply retort that his daughter was as a mad as her mother, and Clara's accusation would be reduced to background noise.

The affair would quickly be put under wraps, leaving Clara defenceless and vulnerable, at the mercy of her adoptive father. And she knew he wouldn't think twice about eliminating her. An accident. Suicide, like her mother. A mysterious disappearance. The question wasn't if but how.

Clara had managed to escape a first attempted kidnapping outside the university gates, forcing the institution to hire more security guards. But the young woman knew she wouldn't be lucky twice. Her adoptive father had ordered a hit on her. According to Valéria, they needed to outsmart the man. He wanted his daughter's death? Fine, Valéria would give it to him. A masquerade that would make him believe she was dead and gone. Samuel would replace her body with that of a patient who had died a few days earlier.

"But things didn't go as planned," Musindo explained.

He was arrested for murder.

After the fake execution, he joined Clara at Lake McFearn.

"Why here?" Max asked. "Why choose this place?"

Musindo glanced at the rain splashing on the rocks. "It's one of the least sunny regions in North America. It's always wet and cloudy in Prince Rupert. What better place for an albino who can't stand the sunlight ..."

35

In Huntsville the streets were congested with cars parked every which way, including in the schoolyard and behind the church, where an improvised paid lot had been set up. Max left his Grand Cherokee there after depositing a few dollars in the hand of a polite young man who suggested he use the side door to enter the church, what with all the congregants on the front steps. Max slipped among the cars, hurried, regretting his tardiness. He wanted to arrive after the beginning so he could blend in with the crowd, but this was too late indeed.

So far his presence in the United States hadn't been noticed by the police. In Tanzania he was still being hunted for Zuberi's murder, but Kilonzo would eventually be implicated in that killing, if ever someone decided to investigate it further. Max doubted that would happen. The authorities would find exactly what they needed in the official version: Valéria and her daughter had been killed by Zuberi, who'd been murdered in turn by Cheskin out of revenge. Cheskin, who'd now disappeared, had done a favour for the Tanzanians. He wouldn't be missed much.

For Bruno Shembazi, Ferguson, and their strong-arm accomplice, it would be a bit more complicated. But it was unlikely that Thomas Musindo's murder would be tied to Valéria's. The bodies of the three men on that pier in northern Canada would surely raise a few eyebrows. But no one would find any answers. In short, Max wasn't overly worried about either Canadian or American authorities.

In Tanzania, however, especially in the president's inner circle, Shembazi's failure to complete his mission might cause renewed interest in a search for Samuel Musindo. Lugembe was probably having trouble sleeping. He had considered Musindo easy prey, and now three men were dead. Shembazi and Ferguson had inspired fear in most people, yet they'd failed miserably.

But Max figured Lugembe wouldn't cause too much trouble unless Samuel threatened or denounced him, which he had no intention of doing. Samuel wanted to protect Clara and would keep quiet.

Max entered the crowded church without attracting attention and stood behind the pews. A minister was speaking about Albert Kerensky with great emotion, explaining how they'd met years earlier. In a warm, powerful voice, he described a passionate, meticulous man who'd taken his difficult job seriously. Being responsible for another man's death was an unbearable burden, the minister declaimed. The Bible said, "Thou shalt not kill," but the state decided otherwise. And men like Albert Kerensky were needed to do this work day after day, year after year. It was easy to find reasons why Kerensky had overstepped, at the end of his life, the powers conferred on him. It was important to understand and forgive, to put oneself in the executioner's shoes before judging him.

All around, the churchgoers nodded. What the minister said was directly relevant to their own lives. Most people here, those attending Kerensky's ceremony, worked in similar fields: wardens, members of tie-down teams, prison doctors, and chaplains. The news of his death had sent a shock wave through the American penitentiary system. Unsurprisingly, executioners stood in solidarity with their former colleague. Many of them had come from far away to pay their respects. From Louisiana, Mississippi, Alabama, Kentucky, Arkansas, and more places still. Next to Max were dozens of killers, none of whom had to fear the long arm of the law. They worked for it.

As the minister continued his eulogy for Kerensky, Max observed the executioners. From his place in the back, he could see only the napes of their necks, their heads slightly bowed, contemplative, solemn. Max had expected the square-jawed, broad-shouldered appearance of a prison guard with a bulging stomach tucked into a too-tight shirt. There were some like that, but not the majority. Executioners came in all sorts of models. Some looked like brutes, others like professors or civil servants. One of them would have been at home in a dentist's office.

That one there, on the left, looked as if he played bridge every Saturday night. A small man, a bit farther off, was almost delicate, fervently holding on to his wife's arm.

Normal. All of them seeming like anyone else. And that was what made the atmosphere of the church so damn oppressing, at least to Max. Thousands of people, most of them criminals, the worst of the worst, had been sent to eternal sleep by the actions of these men who now gathered to pay homage to one of their own.

Max glanced at the front of the church. Kerensky's casket, draped with the American and Texan flags. The Stars and Stripes next to the Lone Star. Roselyn sat in the front row alone. From this distance, Max couldn't guess what she was thinking. Two days after they reached Samuel Musindo's place, Roselyn's son-in-law had called to tell her that the RCMP had found her husband's body in a cabin in British Columbia. Peter had no idea Roselyn was nearby. He thought she was still in Chicago. Following Max's advice, she had told him nothing about their meeting, or what they'd discovered on their way to Prince Rupert.

"What happened?" Roselyn had asked Peter.

"The police are investigating. They found three more bodies on a wharf a few miles away. The crimes could be connected."

Roselyn asked him whether Albert's body would be repatriated. According to Peter, that would be the case in the next few days, once the RCMP had concluded their inquest.

Before they left, Max had stopped at the Prince Rupert post office to pick up a general-delivery package

Teresa Mwandenga had sent him. In it was the small toy truck Valéria had wanted to give Daniel.

Max learned from Mwandenga that Harold Scofield had landed in Bukoba to continue the foundation's work.

On their last night in Prince Rupert, Max took Samuel aside. "Your mother was an incredible woman. Your sister, too."

"I know. I'm the only one left now. I lost my two families. And I don't even carry their names anymore, either one." He stared into the distance, thoughtful. "What they did for me, especially Valéria ... I'll never forget it."

"And now? What are you going to do?"

"Raise my son. Keep on living."

Back in Huntsville, Roselyn had emptied her husband's room at Stanford Hill with Peter's help. Albert owned little. A few hours and everything was stuffed into boxes and placed in Peter's pickup. That night, after dinner with Adrian, Peter took her aside and revealed that the Beretta that had killed Albert was registered in her name. He told the police that Albert had taken it out of a lockbox that his wife had in a storage facility in Houston.

"Your husband's killer is still out there," Peter added.

"Someone who was after Adrian. Because of his work."

Peter nodded. It was his theory, after all. "Do you hope they find who did it?"

"Whoever killed him?" She hesitated, then added, "I think Albert went down a strange and torturous road. I don't want to go down that same path."

Peter didn't answer. He was lost in thought, anxious. Roselyn felt he wanted to confess something but didn't know how. "One day your husband came to my office. It wasn't long after Norah had passed away. He seemed troubled. I wasn't in great shape, either, you can imagine."

Kerensky had launched into a speech about how much pain he was in, how powerless he felt. Peter endured the same thing. And then Albert told him how Norah's illness and death weren't a matter of bad luck but a consequence of what he'd done or hadn't done. Peter didn't understand and his father-in-law wouldn't elaborate.

"I felt as if he was debating with himself." For Albert, Norah's death was punishment for having contravened the most basic principles of his work. Death was a distinct entity, a being in itself, with its codes, laws, requirements. Those who worked with death, and collaborated with it, handed it to others — they couldn't let it down. Mistreating death was something you simply didn't do. Yet Albert had done just that. He'd cheated death, and in turn, furious at the betrayal, it had gone after his daughter, whom he loved more than anything. Norah's illness, her demise, that was his fault. His personal punishment.

"He felt responsible for what had happened," Peter said.

"You really think so?" Roselyn asked, surprised.

"I don't know. Your husband believed in God, even if he sometimes stood at a distance from religion. His faith was a little twisted, let's say. But he followed his own code and was guided by his own rules. Norah's death shook his world, the tidy little universe he thought he dominated."

"What are you trying to tell me, Peter?"

He cleared his throat. "Before he left my office, your husband told me, calmly, as if he was saying good morning or good night, that Norah's death had made him realize his life wasn't his own but was tied to every other life, including those lives he'd put an end to. All those men and women."

Roselyn looked away from Peter. Albert had used that same strange vocabulary with Glenn Forrester. Her husband had been sick in the head, she told herself. A stranger even to her. He'd admitted those bizarre feelings to her son-in-law, and to a friend, but not to his wife. That just demonstrated again the extent to which their marriage had been a failure, an illusion. Roselyn regretted not having been witness to his descent into madness. She could have done something, intervened before it was too late. *But*, she thought, *would I really have reacted better than Glenn or Peter? Perhaps not.*

"Peter," Roselyn finally said, "let's never talk about any of this again."

At the end of the ceremony, six men walked to the casket according to a ritual as old as death. *Prison guards*, thought Max. Kerensky's colleagues. The oldest man among them might be Glenn Forrester, whom Roselyn had mentioned. A tall fellow with a full head of grey hair. The six of them raised the casket and carried it out of the church, soon followed by Roselyn, Peter, Adrian, and the rest of the attendees, falling in behind the procession in silent disorder, heavy with emotion.

Max caught up with the group behind the cemetery. Kerensky would be buried next to his daughter.

While the prayers were being recited, Max's thoughts turned to Valéria, who had worked so hard to ease her conscience by defending the rights of albinos. He regretted that she'd kept him so distant from her secrets but couldn't begrudge her that. His own life was hardly a shining example of transparency. He had no lessons to give anyone.

Once all was said and done, Valéria herself had played a game with death. She had tried to speed past it, overtake it on the right, but death had caught up with her, just as it had Kerensky. By trying to save her son, she'd set off a chain reaction that had come back around and hit her square on when she was least expecting it.

Max was surprised when he realized he wasn't angry at Kerensky, whose madness had been the match that had set this hidden pyre aflame. He couldn't help seeing Kerensky as a victim of fate, of his ego and his pain. His life had dwelt in death. It had become his sole reference, his home and hearth, his miracle solution.

Once the casket was lowered, Max said his good-byes to Roselyn Kerensky, who introduced him to Peter and Adrian.

"I didn't think I'd see you again. You were there for the ceremony?"

"Yes."

"There were as many people as for Norah's funeral." Then she added, "I'm happy you came."

As he meandered through the streets of Huntsville, Max caught a glimpse of the Walls Unit. In this penitentiary, and others like it, thousands upon thousands of prisoners paid their debt to society. And yet, in the very streets he was walking, men and women lived their lives as if nothing at all was happening, stopping at red lights, waiting for the bus, reading a newspaper. Teenagers staring down at their phones. A child, his face covered in ice cream. A policeman writing a ticket. A normal life for normal people who'd made death on command an industry like any other, bereft of anger or emotion. Clean and painless, handed down coldly, without remorse or second thoughts.

Valéria came to mind, that time in Bukoba, during his first trip there.

"Come. You'll love it," she'd told him after they kissed. He had just stepped off the small plane that had taken him from Mwanza, the last of the puddle jumpers he'd taken to cross Africa.

"Let's go home," Max said. "I want you all to myself."

Falling into bed with her, somewhere, anywhere, was something he'd been dreaming of since he left the United States a century earlier.

Valéria burst out laughing and ran along in front of him down a narrow path. Max followed her like a zombie, his clothes smelling of stale airplane air, wondering where she was leading him and why it was so urgent when there were so many other things to do — and he could suggest one in particular.

Before seeing the fishermen, he could hear their song, their voices riding the wind blowing through the trees. And then they appeared, all of a sudden, in tight formation, standing in their boats, a breathy, chanted song rising from their throats all together as they paddled toward the pier in unison. It seemed like a well-orchestrated choreography. Twenty small boats or more, all coming back heaped with fish. They slid swiftly over the flat water. The sun was setting behind them, part of this idyllic picture of an Africa that existed only in the minds of tourists or photographers who specialized in the exotic.

"It's wonderful, isn't it?"

"What are they singing? Do you understand the words?"

Valéria smiled again. "No idea. But it's beautiful."

ACKNOWLEDGEMENTS

I want to thank the following people for their help in writing this novel.

Don Sawatzky, director of operations for Under the Same Sun, answered my questions and gave me access to documentation concerning the fate of people with albinism, in Tanzania in particular. More information on the work done by the organization can be found at www.underthesamesun.com.

Dr. Gilles Truffy reviewed many of the medical aspects of this story. Nicole Landry came up with the name of the series, while Francine Landry offered comments and suggestions throughout the writing and editing process.

Special thanks to the entire team at Libre Expression, especially Johanne Guay, Carole Boutin, Jean Baril, Lison Lescarbeau, and Pascale Jeanpierre. I'm grateful for having had the chance to work with my editor, Monique H. Messier, who offered invaluable advice and constant encouragement.

Thanks also to Jacob Homel for his translation, and to editor Michael Carroll and the team at Dundurn Press.

MYSTERY AND CRIME FICTION
FROM DUNDURN PRESS

Birder Murder Mysteries
by Steve Burrows
(BIRDING, BRITISH COASTAL TOWN
MYSTERIES)
A Siege of Bitterns
A Pitying of Doves
A Cast of Falcons
A Shimmer of Hummingbirds
A Tiding of Magpies

Amanda Doucette Mysteries
by Barbara Fradkin
(PTSD, CROSS-CANADA TOUR)
Fire in the Stars
The Trickster's Lullaby
Prisoners of Hope

B.C. Blues Crime Novels
by R.M. Greenaway
(BRITISH COLUMBIA, POLICE
PROCEDURAL)
Cold Girl
Undertow
Creep
Coming soon: *Flights and Falls*

Stonechild & Rouleau Mysteries
by Brenda Chapman
(FIRST NATIONS, KINGSTON,
POLICE PROCEDURAL)
Cold Mourning
Butterfly Kills
Tumbled Graves
Shallow End
Bleeding Darkness
Coming soon: *Turning Secrets*

Jack Palace Series
by A.G. Pasquella
(NOIR, TORONTO, MOB)
Yard Dog

Jenny Willson Mysteries
by Dave Butler
(NATIONAL PARKS, ANIMAL PROTECTTION)
Full Curl
No Place for Wolverines

Falls Mysteries
by Jayne Barnard
(RURAL ALBERTA, FEMALE SLEUTH)
When the Flood Falls

Foreign Affairs Mysteries
by Nick Wilkshire
(GLOBAL CRIME FICTION, HUMOUR)
Escape to Havana
The Moscow Code
Remember Tokyo

Dan Sharp Mysteries
by Jeffrey Round
(LGBTQ, TORONTO)
Lake on the Mountain
Pumpkin Eater
The Jade Butterfly
After the Horses
The God Game
Coming soon: *Shadow Puppet*

Max O'Brien Mysteries
by Mario Bolduc
(TRANSLATION, POLITICAL THRILLER,
CON MAN)
The Kashmir Trap
The Roma Plot
The Tanzania Conspiracy

Cullen and Cobb Mysteries
by David A. Poulsen
(CALGARY, PRIVATE INVESTIGATORS,
ORGANIZED CRIME)
Serpents Rising
Dead Air
Last Song Sung

Strange Things Done
by Elle Wild
(YUKON, DARK THRILLER)

Salvage
by Stephen Maher
(NOVA SCOTIA, FAST-PACED THRILLER)

Crang Mysteries
by Jack Batten
(HUMOUR, TORONTO)
Crang Plays the Ace
Straight No Chaser
Riviera Blues
Blood Count
Take Five
Keeper of the Flame
Booking In

Jack Taggart Mysteries
by Don Easton
(UNDERCOVER OPERATIONS)
Loose Ends
Above Ground
Angel in the Full Moon
Samurai Code
Dead Ends
Birds of a Feather
Corporate Asset
The Benefactor
Art and Murder
A Delicate Matter
Subverting Justice
An Element of Risk

Meg Harris Mysteries
by R.J. Harlick
(CANADIAN WILDERNESS FICTION,
FIRST NATIONS)
Death's Golden Whisper
Red Ice for a Shroud
The River Runs Orange
Arctic Blue Death
A Green Place for Dying
Silver Totem of Shame
A Cold White Fear
Purple Palette for Murder

Thaddeus Lewis Mysteries
by Janet Kellough
(PRE-CONFEDERATION CANADA)
On the Head of a Pin
Sowing Poison
47 Sorrows
The Burying Ground
Wishful Seeing

Cordi O'Callaghan Mysteries
by Suzanne F. Kingsmill
(ZOOLOGY, MENTAL ILLNESS)
Forever Dead
Innocent Murderer
Dying for Murder
Crazy Dead

Endgame
by Jeffrey Round
(MODERN RE-TELLING OF AGATHA
CHRISTIE, PUNK ROCK)

Inspector Green Mysteries
by Barbara Fradkin
(OTTAWA, POLICE PROCEDURAL)
Do or Die
Once Upon a Time
Mist Walker
Fifth Son
Honour Among Men
Dream Chasers
This Thing of Darkness
Beautiful Lie the Dead
The Whisper of Legends
None So Blind

Border City Blues
by Michael Januska
(PROHIBITION ERA WINDSOR)
Maiden Lane
Riverside Drive
Prospect Avenue

Cornwall and Redfern Mysteries
by Gloria Ferris
(DARKLY COMIC, RURAL ONTARIO)
Corpse Flower
Shroud of Roses

Book Credits

Acquiring Editor: Carrie Gleason
Project Editor: Jenny McWha
Editor: Michael Carroll
Proofreader: Shari Rutherford

Interior Designer: Jennifer Gallinger

Publicist: Michelle Melski

Dundurn

Publisher: J. Kirk Howard
Vice-President: Carl A. Brand
Editorial Director: Kathryn Lane
Artistic Director: Laura Boyle
Director of Sales and Marketing: Synora Van Drine
Publicity Manager: Michelle Melski

Editorial: Allison Hirst, Dominic Farrell, Jenny McWha, Rachel Spence, Elena Radic
Marketing and Publicity: Kendra Martin, Kathryn Bassett, Elham Ali